TOR BOOKS BY **DAVID D. LEVINE**

Arabella of Mars

Arabella and the Battle of Venus

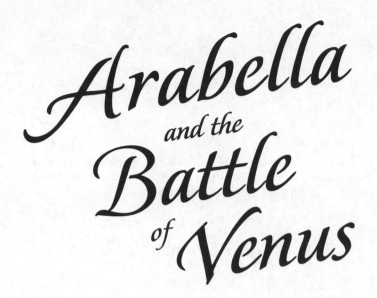

Arabella
and the
Battle
of Venus

THE **ADVENTURES**
OF **ARABELLA ASHBY**

BOOK **TWO**

DAVID D. LEVINE

TOR

A TOM DOHERTY ASSOCIATES BOOK
NEW YORK

ARABELLA AND THE BATTLE OF VENUS

Copyright © 2017 by David D. Levine

A Tor Book
Published by Tom Doherty Associates
175 Fifth Avenue
New York, NY 10010

www.tor-forge.com

Tor® is a registered trademark of Macmillan Publishing Group, LLC.

The Library of Congress Cataloging-in-Publication Data is available upon request.

ISBN 978-0-7653-8282-5 (hardcover)
ISBN 978-1-4668-8950-7 (ebook)

Our books may be purchased in bulk for promotional, educational, or business use. Please contact your local bookseller or the Macmillan Corporate and Premium Sales Department at 1-800-221-7945, extension 5442, or by email at MacmillanSpecialMarkets@macmillan.com.

First Edition: July 2017

Printed in the United States of America

0 9 8 7 6 5 4 3 2 1

This book is dedicated to Janna Silverstein, with love and gratitude.

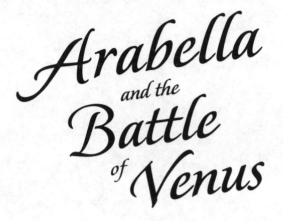

I

MARS, 1815

1

AN UNEXPECTED LETTER

Arabella Ashby sat at the writing-desk which had been her father's, and was now her brother's, staring out across the endless ranks of *khoresh*-trees which were her inheritance, her livelihood, and her legacy. And also, at the moment, her greatest vexation.

The wood of the *khoresh*-tree, known to the English as "Mars-wood," was at once the strongest and the lightest in weight of any in the solar system. It was this wood which composed the aerial ships of the Honorable Mars Company, of His Majesty's Royal Navy, and even of the defeated tyrant Napoleon's *Marine Aérienne*. Arabella's family had been tending and harvesting these trees for generations—nearly as long as the English presence on Mars itself—and from her earliest girlhood she had climbed them, sported among them, picnicked in their shade. Yet it was only in the past few months, ever since her tumultuous return to Mars from Earth, that she had learned just how tedious their up-keep could be.

At the moment it was *tokoleth*-grubs which required Arabella's

attention. The grubs had infested the southern acreage, and on
the desk before her lay two offers to eradicate them—one from a
Martian firm, whose tame predators were reliable but came at a
grotesquely high price, the other from Englishmen, whose novel
chemicals were cheaper but might damage the trees—but her
thoughts would not remain focused upon them. Instead, her eye
kept drifting to the *Fort Augusta Courier* nearby, which proclaimed
in large type: ASTONISHING EVENTS. ~ BONAPARTE
ESCAPES MOON. ~ GREAT OGRE FLEES TO VENUS. Though the
news was months old and tens of thousands of miles distant, it
occupied her mind exceedingly.

She was still attempting to redirect her concentration to the
tokoleth-grubs when Martha, her lady's maid, entered. "Letter for
you, ma'am," she said.

Arabella took the letter—exceedingly battered, with evidence
of the seal having been broken and replaced—and her heart leapt
as she recognized the hand in which it was written. It was that of
Captain Prakash Singh—the commander of the Honorable Mars
Company airship *Diana*, and Arabella's long-absent fiancé.

My dearest Arabella, it began, and as she read, it were as though
his voice, low and steady, tinged with the subtle accent of India,
and always supremely confident, breathed in her ear.

> *I regret exceedingly that I must inform you that, just as
> we were preparing to round Venus's horn after a reasonably
> profitable call at Fort Wellington,* Diana *was intercepted
> by* Résolution, *a French aerial man-of-war of sixteen
> guns, and were compelled by superior force of arms to return
> to the planet's surface. The ship and all her cargo and
> fittings, regrettably including Aadim, have been im-
> pounded, and her officers and company are being held as
> prisoners of war.*
>
> *I am told that no exchange of prisoners is currently an-*

ticipated, and we may be required to remain here until the war's end, which I devoutly hope will not be long. My officers and I have given our parole, as a matter of course, and are currently at liberty in the fortress town of Thuguguruk; the men are imprisoned in the ancient chateau above the town. I am doing what I can to make them as comfortable as possible.

Although some of the other prisoners have sent for their wives, I must insist that you remain on Mars. Conditions here are far from pleasant; the local food is atrocious, and the climate entirely inhospitable. At any rate, as we are not yet married, it would be both unseemly and contrary to my captors' regulations for you to join me here.

Letters are, unfortunately, not permitted prisoners. I am not without resources, however, and I have induced one of our Venusian gaolers to smuggle this missive to the nearest English settlement, from which I hope it will reach you without undue delay. I will attempt to write to you as often as I may.

Please know that you are ever in my thoughts.

Your most devoted
Captain Singh

Captain Singh was the most intelligent, the bravest, and the most honorable man Arabella had ever known. From the very moment she had met him—she had been in disguise as a boy at the time, and mere moments from signing on with the Royal Navy—he had treated her with the utmost decency and respect, and had saved her life on that occasion and many times since. She, in her turn, had lied to him—a necessary deception as to her sex, which had been the only way to obtain rapid passage from Earth to her birthplace on Mars—but had served faithfully as his captain's boy. In those tumultuous months she had worked diligently at her duties, fought a battle with a French corsair, nursed the captain when he was sick, and even helped to break a mutiny before her deception had been revealed. But despite her duplicity, he had shared with her his personal history and the secrets of Aadim, his automaton navigator, and they had grown close. So close, in fact, that when her brother Michael, grievously injured, insisted that she marry immediately in order to insure the continuity of the estate in case of his death, the captain had been her first and only thought. The captain—and Aadim—had agreed, in what must surely be the strangest proposal in the history of romance.

But before the wedding could be performed, he had been called away to Venus on urgent Company business. His eagerly anticipated return, and the nuptials which would follow, had been delayed by months—months of silence from the captain, accompanied by increasingly distressing news of the monster Bonaparte's resurgence. Her nineteenth birthday had come and gone without the slightest word from him. And now this letter had arrived.

The letter's flimsy, crumpled paper trembled in Arabella's hand as she read it over a second time and then a third, searching in vain for some particle of hope therein. Surely there must be some mistake! Surely he had already been released, and was even now making his way back to Mars! But no matter how hard she stared at her fiancé's firm, even handwriting, no matter how tightly her fingers gripped the paper, no succor could be found.

Her husband-to-be was a prisoner of war.

This matter could not be allowed to stand.

———

Arabella was just rising from her seat when the door opened, admitting her brother Michael. Still wearing the large floppy hat and fur-lined leather coat which were his habitual garments when riding the plantation's boundaries, he rushed to her as quickly as he could, his crutch thumping on the floor-boards. The wrappings on the stump of his leg, she noted automatically, were due for changing.

"I am informed," he gasped as he clumped across the floor, "that you have received a letter from Venus."

Wordlessly, she held out the letter, the expression on her face forestalling any further questions. He read quickly, then let his hand drop, the letter rattling against his thigh and his eyes filling with solicitude. "Oh, dear Arabella . . ."

"Do not be concerned for me," she said, though her voice trembled. "So long as my captain is alive and healthy, I will be well."

"You are very pale, Sister. Pray take a seat, and I will send for *lureth*-water."

She sank back into her chair—realizing as she struck the seat how weak her knees had become—and watched numbly as Michael moved to the bell-pull in the corner. *Lureth*-water would help, she supposed, though what she truly craved at the moment was a full ration of good Navy grog. "If only those fools on the Moon," she muttered, half to herself, "had managed to keep Bonaparte locked up."

At the end of the War of the Sixth Coalition, Napoleon had been completely defeated, forced to abdicate and sent into exile on the far side of the Moon. But after less than a year of exile he had somehow managed to escape, decamping to Venus with a substantial contingent of soldiers and airmen. No one seemed quite certain why he had chosen that planet rather than returning in triumph to Paris, from which King Louis had already fled with an army at his heels, but there Napoleon was—he had already taken the Venusian continent of Gomoluk, and seemed quite intent on taking the entire planet.

Martha returned, with a pitcher and two glasses on a tray. Arabella sipped at hers without tasting. "I do not understand," her brother said, "why the Company sent your fiancé to Venus at all, under these conditions!"

"Nor do I." She drummed her fingers on the table, then rose and paced to the window. "But he assured me, before he left, that his assignment was of the utmost importance." The *khoresh*-trees stretched to the horizon, rank on rank, like the tall masts of so many aerial clippers. They reminded her of the scene at the docks in London, where she had met her husband-to-be for the first time.

Arabella turned and strode toward the bell-pull. "I shall go into town, and importune the Company and the government to intercede on his behalf." But before she could reach it, Michael stayed her with a touch on her arm.

"Pray do not disquiet yourself, Sister," he said. "I am sure they are already doing all that they can."

She paused momentarily, then continued to the corner and gave the embroidered ribbon a firm tug. "Perhaps. But if there is any thing which can be done to encourage them to further action, I intend to discover it and do it."

His Excellency General the Honorable Sir Northcote Parkinson, Governor-General of the Presidency of Fort Augusta, proved to be a frail old man who affected an old-fashioned powdered wig. "My dear girl," he said after the preliminaries had been discharged, "I am afraid that the situation is far more complicated than you imagine."

Arabella sat rigidly on a stiff high-backed chair, wearing her best gown—finest Venusian silk, luminous white, trimmed in ribbons of pomona green—with gloved fingers knotted in her lap. Weeks of supplication, insistence, and pure unalloyed obstinacy . . . visit after visit to first Company House and then Government

House . . . had finally obtained her an audience with the Governor-General himself, one of the most powerful men in the entire Honorable Mars Company, and His Majesty's representative on Mars. She had not expected him to be so thin and stooped.

A drop of perspiration trickled down the back of Arabella's neck, and she shifted in her chair. A robust fire roared in every fire-place of Government House, for the comfort of the English, but for her part she found the heat oppressive.

Lord Parkinson adjusted his pince-nez upon his nose. "You are aware, of course, that a state of war does not at this time exist between the governments of England and France."

"Of course, Your Excellency. But as my fiancé *is* being held as a prisoner of war by the French . . ."

He silenced her with an upheld index finger. "Officially he, along with the other English subjects unfortunate enough to have been in Gomoluk when Napoleon captured the territory, are not prisoners of war but *détenus*, or hostages. Many of these are prominent landholders, Company factors, and other significant individuals. Even my own counterpart on Venus, Lord Castlemare the Governor-General of the Presidency of Gomoluk, is being held under house arrest. And their fortunes, their safety, indeed their very lives, are the subject of negotiations being held even now at the very highest level." He removed his pince-nez, closed his eyes, and shook his head with weary resignation. "For the Company to intervene at this delicate moment, even indirectly, would be considered an act of war."

"But Napoleon has already—!"

Again he silenced her, this time by patting the air between them. "I understand your perspective, but please do hear me out. It may appear to you that Napoleon has already initiated hostilities, by taking control of territory under Company jurisdiction. But it is important to understand the distinction between the Company and the government." He folded his hands primly upon the desk before him. "You were born and raised on Mars, I collect?"

Arabella seethed at the Governor-General's condescension, but fought to keep her temper in check. Displays of strong emotion had already set her back several times in her long struggle to reach this point. "I was, Your Excellency."

"Then all your life you have understood John Company to be the government, and the government to be the Company. We even wage war against the local satraps and principalities. But the Company rules Mars and Venus—portions of Venus, I should say—only as representative of His Majesty and His Majesty's government back home. And only the king himself may declare war upon another sovereign power."

"By which you mean France."

"By which I mean France."

"But Napoleon is *not* Emperor of France," Arabella insisted. "He was deposed by the Sénat after the capture of Paris! Is mere escape from captivity sufficient to transform a criminal into an emperor?"

"Perhaps not. But the loyalty of his marshals, generals, and admirals . . . may very well be." He spread his delicate white hands in a gesture of resignation. "As I have said, the situation is complicated."

Arabella bit her lip, to prevent an unseemly comment from escaping. "But surely some diplomatic solution . . ."

"Please do rest assured that the Company is already doing every thing in its power to bring *Diana* and her company safely home." His watery blue eyes above the pince-nez met hers levelly.

"Which you may not describe in more detail."

"Regrettably." But his face and voice betrayed no regret at all, only annoyance at her importunity.

At that moment an aide appeared and whispered rapidly into

the Governor-General's ear. Immediately the great man rose, saying, "Unfortunately, my presence is required elsewhere."

"I thank you, Your Excellency, for your kind attention." Her tone, she thought, was sufficiently civil for propriety; she took what pride she could in that small accomplishment.

"Your servant, miss," he replied mechanically, but his eyes and thoughts were already directed elsewhere. He cleared his desk of papers, stuffing them hurriedly in a drawer, and then he and the aide departed, conferring urgently between themselves.

She remained in her chair for some time, breathing hard through her nose, lips tightly pursed . . . for she had not failed to note that, though the Governor-General had removed his private papers from the desk, he had not taken the time to lock it. Perhaps it had been due to the haste of his departure, or perhaps he had not thought of a young woman as any kind of threat—or, indeed, worthy of any consideration at all.

For a moment she hesitated. Then, glancing all about, she stepped to the other side of the desk and pulled open the drawer.

Most of the papers therein were meaningless or pedestrian. But one—a brief note, hastily scrawled, dated the previous Tuesday—struck Arabella like a thunderbolt. *Talleyrand has recalled Savary to Paris,* it said, *for insufficient severity. His replacement, Fouché, departs Paris for Venus on* Indomptable, *sailing at the full moon.*

In recent weeks she had studied the gazettes assiduously for any news of the war. Talleyrand, she had learned, was Napoleon's chief diplomat, who had taken charge in Paris on Napoleon's behalf after the departure of King Louis, and Savary was Napoleon's minister of police—and, as such, the man responsible for the treatment of prisoners of war, including her husband-to-be. From all accounts he was a man of honor. But Fouché, known as "The Executioner of Lyon," was an entirely different matter. During the Terror he had dispatched hundreds; his methods were brutal even by the standards of that horrific time. It was said that at Nantes he would take the poor unfortunate Royalists out on the river, tie them in pairs, male and female, and drown them together, calling this *Le Mariage de Nantes*.

Arabella had to bite her knuckle to prevent herself from crying out. Even so, a gasp escaped from her.

"What's that?" came a voice from without, accompanied by the sound of footsteps.

Panicked, Arabella stuffed the paper back into the drawer and pushed it closed. Then she ran, half-blinded by tears, from the room and down the corridors, ignoring the concerns of those she passed. Once she achieved the cool air outside Government House she paused, gasping, hands on knees. The back of her fine dress was soaked with perspiration.

Fouché—"The Executioner of Lyon"—was to replace the honorable Savary as her captain's gaoler. And he would be sailing for Venus within the month . . . might already have departed.

What might such a monster do to a prisoner accused of espionage?

A solicitous older couple soon approached her, asking what was the matter. She quickly straightened, doing what she could to put her face and dress in order, and explained that she had received some bad news but was in no need of further assistance. She curtseyed, not meeting the strangers' eyes, then hurried down the steps, bound for the tea-house where Martha and Gowse awaited her.

But as she began to cross the street, the bells of the clock on the tower of Company House across the way drew her attention.

The Company House orrery clock was one of the greatest treasures of the town of Fort Augusta, and the clock tower had been among the first structures repaired following the end of the recent insurrection. The clock itself had only recently been put back into working order, and its precious metals and gemstones shone in the late-afternoon sun. The mechanism behind it, she knew from having once had the privilege of viewing it with her father, was still more impressive—the ingenuity of its brass and steel was far more valuable to her than any gold or platinum frippery.

As befitted Company House, the administrative headquarters of the Honorable Mars Company for the entire Martian territory of St. George's Land, the clock told not only the time but the positions of the Company's planets in their orbits, indicated by jeweled spheres which ran in tracks surrounding the clock face. From the center of the dial, a smiling Sun's polished golden rays spread to touch the planets which danced attendance about him. Venus, the innermost planet displayed, glowed green with emeralds; next came Earth, sparkling blue and white with sapphires and diamonds; and finally Mars, the outermost, gleamed with the red of rubies and garnets. Beyond the planets, the symbols of the constellations were set into the stone wall in burnished brass.

As the last notes of the hour echoed into silence, Arabella noticed that green Venus and red Mars were in conjunction in Leo—both near five o'clock on the clock dial—while blue-and-white Earth orbited in splendid isolation in Capricorn, near ten o'clock.

The jeweled planets, she knew, were grossly exaggerated in size, and their orbital tracks were not entirely to scale. But the positions of the planets within their orbits were as accurate as clockwork could make them, and from her work in maintaining and running Aadim, *Diana*'s automaton navigator, she knew that could be very accurate indeed. And as the clock had been so recently set in motion, she was certain those positions would be correct.

If she raised one hand, fingers spread, she could span the distance from Mars to Venus with ease. But from Earth to Venus—the distance that must be traversed by the French vessel *Indomptable* bearing the executioner Fouché—was many times farther, and the need for the ship to avoid the Sun's great heat made the voyage longer still.

She could beat him there. If she left immediately, she could arrive at Venus before Fouché.

What she would do when she arrived . . . she knew not. But she must make the attempt.

2

NO TIME TO LOSE

The *huresh*-coach rattled along, Gowse driving the scuttling creatures forward with more than usual haste. One look at Arabella's face had shown him her urgency, her need to leave town and return to Woodthrush Woods as quickly as possible.

Quite contrary to propriety, Arabella rode atop the coach next to her *huresh*-groom and former shipmate. The cool air whipping through her hair suited her desire for immediate action, and it served to revive her after the stifling warmth of Government House.

One of the team began to pull to the side—it was Nimrod, a scarlet-shelled buck with a strong will—but with a cluck of his tongue and a quick lash of the reins against Nimrod's carapace, Gowse brought the beast back into line. For a human, born and raised on Earth, Gowse had a remarkable facility with *huresh*. "They's no different from horses," he liked to say, "apart from the eight legs and the looking like giant beetles."

Gowse was a huge, burly airman with broad shoulders and the

enormous calves typical of those who strain at the pedals to pro-
pel their craft across the airy spaces between the planets. His unlovely face was marred by a badly broken nose—an injury which
Arabella herself had inflicted, in a fair fight, earning for herself
Gowse's respect and loyalty. So much so, in fact, that when *Diana*
had departed for Venus he had chosen to remain on Mars and
join the staff at Woodthrush Woods.

As they pulled through the plantation's gate—which still bore
the scars of the insurrectionists' forked spears—Gowse slowed the
team from its headlong pace so as not to startle any of the servants
or animals. With the rush of wind and the rattle of wheels somewhat stilled, and the storm of difficult sentiments that had been
clogging her throat somewhat abated, Arabella found herself able
to converse.

"I have had some news about the captain," she said after a long
hesitation. "Though I must confess it did not reach my ears
through any official channels."

Gowse gave her a sidelong glance. "Not good news, I'll warrant."

She shook her head, unsurprised by Gowse's comment—her
sullen silence and downcast expression on boarding the coach would
have made the character of her news quite clear—nor by his blunt-
ness. "It seems that Napoleon's chief gaoler on Venus is to be replaced, and his replacement is a man called Fouché."

"The Executioner of Lyon?" Gowse's expression darkened.

"You have heard of him?"

"Every airman's heard of him, Miss Ashby. Master gunners
frighten their powder-monkeys with tales of Fouché's cruelty.
When he was minister of police during the war, even cowards'd
fight to the death rather'n be taken as prisoners under *his* tender
mercies. Even Bonaparte's afraid of him."

Arabella felt her own mouth tightening to match Gowse's sour
expression. "Then there is no time to be lost."

He quirked an eyebrow at her.

She leaned in close. "Venus and Mars are in conjunction. To reach Venus, Fouché's ship will be forced to take the long route around the Sun, but the distance from Mars is much less. If I were to depart immediately, I could easily reach Venus before he does— as much as several months earlier. Time enough to devise some stratagem to free the captain from his imprisonment."

The carriage pulled up in front of the manor house then, and the stable-boys came running out to unhitch the *huresh*. "Won't be easy to find passage to Venus," Gowse said as he assisted Arabella down from the carriage, "what with Napoleon and all. But I'll ask around and see what's in port."

"Thank you, Gowse. I appreciate your assistance."

"Nothin' I wouldn't do for an old shipmate," he replied, and winked.

———

"Absolutely not!" Michael fumed, his eye fixed firmly on Arabella.

At this moment, she thought, her brother resembled their late father more strongly than ever before . . . but with an admixture of their mother's intransigence. Yet she knew what she must do, and she would not be stayed from her course.

They were alone in Michael's office. Father's collection of automata still adorned the high shelf behind the desk, all tidily dusted and polished, but hardly ever wound—a fact which caused Arabella some pain. Michael had never participated in the passion for automata which she had shared with her father, and now that the office was her brother's demesne those meticulously crafted devices stood motionless, nothing more than expensive knick-knacks. The automaton dancer, in particular, whose mainspring Arabella had broken in an excess of zeal as a young girl, seemed to look down in silent rebuke.

Arabella knew just how valuable a properly designed and

maintained automaton could be. If not for Aadim, *Diana*'s auto-maton navigator, she might not be alive to-day, and certainly would not be engaged to be married.

"I will not be dissuaded," she replied, returning his stare evenly. "In the first place, we are very nearly in a state of war with France. For all I know, war may already have been declared! For you to take ship at all under these circumstances, let alone to the disputed territory of Venus, is sheer folly!"

"The air is very large. On my last voyage, as you know, we were also at war, and *Diana* encountered only one French privateer, which we defeated." It had been a very near thing, to be sure, but she saw no need to mention that.

"In the second place, you are needed here." He gestured impa-tiently at the stub of his leg. "You know that I cannot survey the grounds and supervise the caretakers as I should."

"But you are improving every day! Dr. Fellowes assures me that you should be sufficiently recovered to ride *huresh*-back in a month or less. Until then, Markath can be your eyes and ears on the grounds. I know that you trust him implicitly."

"He is very good," Michael acknowledged. "But he is only a Martian, and your particular skills—your rapport with the ser-vants, your methodical care with the books, a thousand other things—are invaluable in the running of the estate."

"You flatter me, dear brother, but you and I both know that Khema is ten times as valuable as I." Khema had been Arabella and Michael's *itkhalya,* or Martian nanny, when they had been children, and had taught them the ways of the desert and all things Martian. She had been instrumental in quelling the rebel-lion, and now served as the plantation's majordomo. "Nothing whatsoever would be accomplished on this estate without her. In fact, during the rebellion, when she alone was responsible for the estate, every thing ran smoothly . . . despite the violence all around! I dare say that neither you nor I could have done as well."

Michael pursed his lips, neither conceding her point nor offering any thing to gainsay it. "In the third place," he said after a time, "even if I were so foolish as to allow you to travel to Venus, what could you possibly accomplish there? Surely the assistance of one young woman, even one so formidable as yourself, cannot make any difference against the massed might of Bonaparte's forces." He drew himself heavily from his chair and clumped across the floor with his crutch, then took her hand gently in his. "The captain is brave and very resourceful for a man of his race."

Arabella glared at her brother. Although he had acceded to her betrothal to Captain Singh, he had never been completely comfortable with the captain's color, accent, or religion. "For a man of *any* race."

He acknowledged her correction by ducking his head and raising his hands, palms spread. "All the more reason for us to be certain that if any thing can be done to effect his release, he will do it. Nothing can be gained by you risking your life in such a foolhardy manner."

Arabella straightened. "I have been reading the *Naval Chronicle*, in which are accounted the experiences of many English officers who escaped Napoleon's European prisons during the recent land wars. Though many brave men managed to depart the prison itself through their own resources, most were recaptured before they reached neutral territory. Most of the *successful* escapes—those in which the escapees actually returned to England—were made possible only through the instrumentality of paid agents in the neighboring villages, on terms arranged by the fugitive's friends at home."

"I fail to see how this is relevant."

"Let me put it to you plain: successful escape from Napoleon's prisons requires help from outside—local guides, accommodations, forged papers, and, if necessary, even bribery. During the European wars, locals opposed to Napoleon were well known to the English, and payment and instructions for their services had only to be conveyed over the short distance from England to France. But in this case, our knowledge of the situation on Venus is extremely limited and the distance is very much greater. To obtain the equivalent assistance would require months and months— months Captain Singh does not have—and the chance that payment and instructions would be intercepted en route is very great. To ensure success I must voyage to Venus myself, and as soon as possible, in order to arrange and fund his escape from close at hand."

"You have done your research," he acknowledged grudgingly. "But I still cannot countenance such an adventure."

"I am sorry," she said, and cupped Michael's hand in both her own, "my dearest brother, but this is a thing I must do."

Michael drew his hand from hers and turned to the window, where rank on rank of *khoresh*-trees marched to the horizon. He stood in that contemplative pose for a long time before turning back to her. "You are a most vexing young woman, you know." But his face bore a slight, whimsical smile.

"I know," she replied, feeling her own mouth curve into a matching expression.

He blew out a breath. "As your brother, I could forbid you to go. But you and I both know that, even if I did so, you would do whatever you wish regardless. I suppose I have no choice but to accede to your request."

She embraced him then, but her inward feelings bore no taste of triumph . . . rather, her sentiments combined concern for her captain, love for her brother, and anxious anticipation over events to come. "Thank you," she breathed in his ear.

They held each other a moment longer; then he straightened awkwardly, nearly dropping his crutch in the process, and stumped to the desk. "You will require funds," he said, seating himself and bringing out the ledger-book from its locked drawer. "I will instruct our banker to furnish you with a letter of note. Will five hundred pounds suffice, do you think?"

The astonishing figure made her breath catch in her throat, emphasizing as it did the gravity of the task before her. It was, she knew, a very substantial fraction of the plantation's income, and equivalent to a year's living—a very comfortable year's living—for many a smaller landholder. Yet she knew from her readings that passage, paraphernalia, and influence—bribery, to be blunt— were all necessary for a successful escape, and could be extremely expensive. "I should hope that it would be," she said at last. Then, considering, she added, "Be sure to instruct him to make certain that it is payable at Venus."

He paused, tapping the pen upon his chin. "What currency do they employ there?"

"I . . ." She swallowed. "I do not know."

They looked at each other for a long moment, both very much aware of how many unknown considerations stood between Arabella and her captain.

Then he took out a sheet of paper and began to write.

3

SEEKING PASSAGE

"I am terribly sorry, miss," the purser said, "but there's no passage to Venus to be had for love nor money. Not on this ship . . . nor on any other, I'd warrant."

They stood on the deck of *Calliope*, a fine four-masted packet ship recently arrived from Ceres, which rested on her sand-legs in Fort Augusta's harbor. That wide stretch of flat, soft sand—perfect for the mooring of ships of the air and sheltered from the prevailing winds by the rocky hills north of town—was the principal reason for the fort's presence in this location and for its prominence on Mars Company route maps. But at this moment the harbor was so crammed with ships that barely another could be squeezed in. Hundreds of masts stood barren of sail, and only two of the five massive furnace-houses sent smoke upward from their chimneys. With Earth so far away in her orbit, and Venus under embargo by the Coalition of nations united against Napoleon, the number of departing ships requiring the furnaces' hot air for their initial ascent had been reduced by more than half.

The few ships which were departing were bound for Ceres or one of the other asteroid colonies, and as soon as *Calliope* had landed Arabella had made her way on board in hopes the new ship carried news of a change in the war's fortunes, or perhaps that her crew had not yet heard of the embargo, or, failing that, that she might be able to entice them to risk violating the embargo for a sufficiently large fee. But none of these eventualities had come to pass. Now she stood disconsolate on *Calliope's* deck, her constant sense of unhappy separation from her fiancé only strengthened by the familiar scents of tar and hemp rope. Her discomfort was further heightened by the presence of Martha, who held herself so rigidly that she seemed to be attempting to levitate from the filthy deck through sheer force of propriety.

"I thank you for your time, sir," Arabella said, and gave the purser a curtsey before making her miserable way back to the coach.

"No luck?" Gowse said as she trudged into view.

"Alas, no."

Gowse grunted and shook his head, his eyes downcast. But after Martha had entered the coach, before Arabella could ascend he stayed her with a raised finger.

"What is the matter?" she asked.

"I have a friend," he murmured very low, "well, a colleague, who may be willing to take you to Venus. But you might find him . . . unsuitable."

Arabella studied Gowse's unlovely face. "Unsuitable in what way?" she whispered.

"He's a privateer. Sailing under the flag of one of the Martian satraps."

Arabella drew in a hissing breath at the word *privateer*. It brought to her mind the smells of gunpowder and shattered *khoresh*-wood, the crash of cannon and the screams of injured airmen. It had been corsairs—French privateers—who had attacked and disabled

Diana on her way to Mars, and Arabella bore no love for the species. But then she considered Gowse and what she knew of him. "Nonetheless, he must have some finer qualities, or you would never have thought to mention him."

"Aye," Gowse said, and nodded. "He's a fine airman, excellent navigator, sharp as a tack. Cheeky b—d, but I'd trust him with my life. But he . . . well, let us say that he made an enemy in the Admiralty on account of a gambling debt, and he lost his commission. Since then he's had to turn privateer to keep body and soul together."

A throat-clearing sound came from within the coach, and Arabella assured Martha that she would ascend in a moment. "And what might be the name of this paragon of virtue?" she whispered to Gowse.

"Fox. Daniel Fox, captain of the *Touchstone*."

"Fox." She rolled the name around on her tongue, finding the flavor uncertain, but very keenly aware that no other vintage was on offer. "Very well. Pray ask your friend Mr. Fox to call on us at his earliest convenience."

"Aye aye, Miss Ashby," he said, and touched a knuckle to his forehead.

———————

Two days later, Arabella stormed into the stables, where she found Gowse polishing Hector's carapace. "Why can Fox not call upon me here?" she demanded, waving a paper that Martha had just brought to her. *Fox cant come,* read the note in Gowse's scrawl. *You must go to him.*

"He's at Burke's Club," Gowse said, "and he's no interest in leaving . . . though he'd accept a call from you there."

"He would *accept*—?" Arabella huffed, appalled at Fox's impertinence.

"So he says." Gowse shrugged. "As I told you, he's a cheeky b—d."

Arabella paced the stall. Hector, sensing her mood, scuttled away to the corner. "And you have no other friends who might conceivably be persuaded to provide passage to Venus?"

Gowse shook his head. "I've put the word all around, but what with the embargo, there's no ships to be had. It's Fox or nothing." He spread his palms. "Course, some other ship could come along next week."

Arabella was keenly aware of how far a ship could travel in one week, once she had attained the trade winds which blew between the planets at rates approaching ten thousand knots. By now Fouché might have covered as much as a quarter of the distance to his destination; she could not afford to wait even a week more if she were to have a chance of freeing the captain before the Executioner of Lyon reached Venus.

She drew in a breath, then blew it out in a forceful sigh. "Very well," she said. "Make preparations for a call on Fox."

―――――――――

Burke's Club, an establishment of which she had never before even heard, lay in Gokhura Street not far from the docks. It proved to be a private dwelling of middling character, lacking any sign and indistinguishable from its neighbors save that the hall door stood ajar. "This is the place," Gowse said, glancing up and down the street. "But it's no place for a lady, miss. Perhaps I should go in and—"

"I must speak with this Fox myself," Arabella interrupted, pushing past him and striding through the half-open door.

The hall, once her eyes adjusted to the dimness within, proved to be interrupted in the middle by a second door, in which was constructed a small spy-hole. A single watery eye immediately came to the hole, blinking out at her in leery astonishment. "Is this Burke's Club?" she demanded of it.

"It is, miss."

"Pray let me in. I understand that Mr. Daniel Fox is in residence, and I desire to speak with him immediately."

Again the eye blinked, then retreated. Muttering came from within, and she heard the name Fox repeated several times. Gowse came up beside her, and they waited together in silence.

After some minutes the door creaked open, revealing an older man in a cheap yet fashionable coat. "Mr. Fox is here, miss, though he cannot come to the door."

"Then I must go to him."

The older man glanced to Gowse—who merely shrugged—then gave Arabella a slight bow and admitted them within. "Welcome to Burke's, miss. You'll find Mr. Fox in the hall upstairs."

At the top of the stairs they were met by yet another door, this one heavy and iron-bound, which swung open as they approached. Beyond it lay a single large room, well illuminated by substantial chandeliers, the daylight being completely excluded by heavy curtains. Several large oblong tables filled the space, each covered with green baize and surrounded by a boisterous crowd of men. Some were in shirt-sleeves; others wore coats in the latest colors and trimmed in gleaming Venusian silk. Martian and human waiters carried trays of food and drink, and the atmosphere was pungent with the smells of roast meat, strong wine, and snuff.

"Which one is Mr. Fox?" Arabella inquired of the doorman.

He gave her a peculiar little smile. "At the hazard table, miss," he replied, gesturing. "In the blue jacket."

The indicated gentleman was, at that moment, standing at the head of the table and shaking his cupped hands vigorously above his left shoulder. He was, in Arabella's opinion, quite attractive, with a strong chin and aquiline nose. His sandy brown hair was cut in a fashionable Brutus style, but his strong and sinewy hands showed that he was not the type of captain who forbore hauling on a line himself. And though he was not yet forty, the blue eyes in his wind-burnt face bore wrinkles in their corners from frequent smiling.

With a whoop, Fox brought his hands down, casting a pair of dice down the length of the table. The men around the table drew in a collective breath as the dice rolled to a stop, then erupted in a shout of mingled triumph and despair—depending, she supposed, upon how each man had wagered. Fox himself regarded the dice silently, with an expression that attempted to cover disappointment with a self-consciously cheerful determination.

For a moment she considered this man, this privateer captain. Could she truly bear to take passage from one who was little more than a legalized pirate, sailing rapaciously beneath the flag of a Martian satrap? Not too many months ago another privateer, albeit a Frenchman, had nearly killed her captain and herself. Yet Fox was her best hope—indeed, at the moment, her *only* hope— to rescue Captain Singh from Venus, and perhaps she could learn to respect his skills if not his occupation. She straightened her back and stepped forward.

As Arabella approached the table, the player to Fox's left, a lean gentleman with very prominent ears who wore a dark leather *thukhong*-jacket, took up the dice. Fox sat and gestured to a passing waiter, who filled his goblet to the brim with wine. The pile of coins in front of Fox, she noted, was considerably smaller than that of any of his neighbors.

"Mister Fox," Arabella said. "My name is Arabella Ashby. May I have a word with you?" To introduce oneself was an impropriety, she knew, yet for a young unmarried woman who had already invaded a gambling-hell without proper companionship it was a comparatively venial sin.

Fox looked up at her with bleary suspicion. His eyes were quite blood-shot and underlined with substantial dark circles, but as they swam into focus on her his expression changed to one of somewhat inebriated delight.

"Of course, my dear Miss Ashby. Always a pleasure. Where do I recall having heard the name before?"

"I approached you by means of my manservant Gowse, who I believe is a friend of yours."

He blinked. "Oh yes, the adventuresome heiress!" He looked over her shoulder at Gowse, who was just catching up to Arabella in her headlong advance. "You did not tell me she was such a beauty."

Fox's slightly slurred but apparently sincere compliment flattered, vexed, and embarrassed Arabella in equal measure. "Sir," she replied, firming her jaw, "I require passage to Venus, as soon and as speedily as possible, for which I am prepared to compensate you handsomely. Are you able to provide it, or must I look elsewhere?" The fact that she had nowhere else to look, she thought, was immaterial; the projection of confidence was all. This was one of the lessons she had learned from her Captain Singh.

Fox inclined his head and gestured to the tiny heap of coins before him. "I am not, alas, currently in a position to provide any such thing. I must confess that at the moment I am very slightly in arrears to the bank—"

At this point a lean, sharp-eyed, and decidedly sober gentleman in a dark frock coat, who had moved up very quietly as Arabella and Fox had been conversing, spoke up. "To the tune of three hundred twenty-nine pounds ten shillings, including interest."

"Yes . . ." Fox acknowledged, casting the dark-coated fellow a rather irritated glance. "I have been here for three days and two nights," he declared, returning his attention to Arabella and Gowse, "and I have no intention of departing until I have restored and indeed redoubled my initial stake."

The sharp-eyed gentleman's countenance, though guarded, could not help but reveal to Arabella's eye his low estimate of

Fox's chances of success in this endeavor . . . and the pleasure he felt at the prospect.

Three hundred twenty-nine pounds ten shillings, Arabella thought, was an appalling amount of money to squander at hazard. But it was not terribly much more than the three hundred pounds Michael had allowed her for passage, over and above the five hundred pounds allocated for expenses. "If I were to settle this debt for you, would you convey me to Venus in exchange? Immediately?"

"Miss!" gasped Gowse, appalled at her effrontery. The sharp-eyed gentleman looked daggers at her, no doubt furious at the prospect of being deprived of Fox's forthcoming additional losses.

But Fox, though well supplied with wine and overconfidence, was apparently not completely lacking in wits. He regarded Arabella for a moment with hooded eyes, lips pursed, then nodded slowly. "Could we say, perhaps, three hundred fifty?"

Arabella's eyes met Fox's. Part of her wanted to appease this man—this handsome, flattering captain who was her only known means of transport to Venus—but the shrewder, more cunning part sensed that he was a wild *huresh* who required a firm hand on the reins. "Three hundred twenty-nine," she stated succinctly, "and ten shillings."

Fox seemed about to balk. But then the player to his left nudged Fox's elbow. "I've seen how you play," he said. His accent suggested Mars's northern colonies. "I suggest you take the young lady up on her offer."

At that Fox bristled. The other player pointedly glanced down at Fox's very diminished stake, then back to Fox, and shrugged.

Fox's eyes, too, drifted down to the small pile of coins on the table before him. He contemplated it for a bit, then shook his head and looked up, smiling and raising his wine cup to Arabella. "Very well, Miss Ashby. We have a deal."

———————

She waited until after breakfast the next day to tell Michael, when he would be rested, well-fed, and happy in the view from the verandah. *Chakti* chittered in the shrubbery, and the *khoresh-trees* marched to the horizon in orderly rows. "I have engaged a ship to take me to Venus," she said as she passed the scones. "She is called *Touchstone,* out of Sor Khoresh, captained by a man named Fox."

"One of Tura's privateers?" he replied, shock and dismay clear from his tone.

Sor Khoresh, north of Fort Augusta, was one of the more powerful Martian satrapies, independent monarchical states which ruled the portions of Mars outside of the Honorable Mars Company's control. In the vast deserts beyond the borders of St. George's Land, the satraps of Mars were as powerful as any European king—only their lack of gunpowder and aerial ships prevented them from projecting that power beyond their own planet, and their treaties with the Company prevented them from acquiring those things for themselves. In exchange for this limitation and other considerations, they received considerable autonomy and substantial assistance from the English; and Tura, the satrap of Sor Khoresh, had taken every advantage of the situation.

Though the satraps were denied ships of their own, one of the powers permitted them by treaty was the granting of letters of marque—official documents authorizing, in effect, legalized piracy—to the ships of certain Earthly nations. Thus, many Russian, Dutch, American, and even English captains sailed the air as privateers under Martian flags, capturing the merchant ships of France and her allies, and sharing the spoils with their Martian sponsors. The arrangement profited the privateers and the satraps, and benefitted the English cause, so no one objected to it—save the French, of course, and their opinion was of no consequence.

"I intend to depart as soon as possible," she continued. "You know I will not be dissuaded."

"I do," Michael spat, throwing down his napkin and pushing himself to his feet. "And *you* know I can be every bit as stubborn as my sister." He fumbled his crutch under his arm and began stumping about in agitation. "Even on Mars, there are certain proprieties which must be maintained. If I cannot persuade you to set this dangerous project aside, then I must at least insist that you be properly chaperoned."

"I could not possibly be saddled with such an encumbrance!"

Michael continued, undaunted by Arabella's outburst. "For an unmarried young woman—and though you are engaged, this is indeed your state—to be seen unchaperoned in mixed company is very damaging to your reputation. Though I know you care little for your own reputation, poor behavior on your part reflects badly on the entire family." He took a breath, let it out. "I will ask Lady Corey to accompany you to Venus." He nodded to one of the servants. "Bring me paper, pen, and wax."

"Lady Corey?" Arabella gaped. "She is entirely inappropriate!"

"There is none more appropriate on this planet." The servant returned with the requested implements, and Michael immediately settled himself at the table and began scratching out an invitation.

Michael's statement was true, in some ways. With Arabella's mother on Earth, tens of thousands of miles away, and no living aunts or cousins any where on Mars, the widowed Lady Corey— a long-time friend of the family—was her most appropriate mentor and protector in the eyes of society.

But for the journey which Arabella anticipated, Lady Corey was the worst possible companion. After the horrific events of the insurrection, which had cost the lives of Lady Corey's husband and many members of her staff, Arabella was certain that if any thing even slightly untoward should happen to occur on the voyage, the elderly lady would be completely undone by distress.

"Please, Michael. I beg of you not to ask this of her. You know that I am entirely able to defend my own honor."

Michael folded and sealed the letter. "Take this to Lady Corey at Miranda House," he said to the servant, "and await her response." He returned his attention to Arabella. "It is not merely your honor that concerns me. You require guidance and a proper introduction to society. After all, you are soon to be a married woman."

"I shall never be married at all if my fiancé dies tortured to death in a prison on Venus!"

Michael's only response to this outburst was a small, disgusted sound. "Lady Corey is far stronger, and will be far more helpful, than you think. Merely meet with her—this is all I ask."

"Oh, very well." But Arabella's mind was already spinning with a stratagem to evade this unwanted imposition.

"Good morning, Lady Corey!" Michael cried, rising with as much grace as he could muster. "Thank you so very much for joining us on such short notice." The Sun shone brightly on the best silver tea-service, tidily arrayed on the sitting-room table. All the finest had been brought out for the great lady's visit.

Arabella curtseyed, fighting to keep a pleasant expression despite the tightness of her jaw. It was already a day later than she had hoped to depart for Venus, never mind the additional days which would likely be lost in preparations if Lady Corey were to accompany her.

Lady Corey accepted Michael's proffered hand and, with his help, seated herself upon the settee. "It is no trouble at all, Mr. Ashby. It is always a pleasure to visit with you."

Lady Corey had always reminded Arabella of a ship of the sea,

with her generous bosom and plump arms swelling like sails before the press of wind. Her age was something over forty—ancient
to Arabella—and her hands were soft and pale. She wore a round
robe of fine iron-gray cloth, trimmed with chenille fur and clasped
with lozenge clasps of jet. Her ear rings and necklace were also
of jet, emphasizing her continued state of mourning, her beloved
Lord Corey having been crushed by a Martian catapult-stone less
than a year earlier.

All in all, Arabella thought, Lady Corey was like a beautiful,
expensive, stifling cloak which Michael intended to throw over
her, when what she truly required was a *thukhong*—a rough, practical garment in which she could move, run, and fight.

They spoke for a time of the weather and other inconsequentialities—with Arabella fidgeting impatiently—before Michael
finally broached the topic of his invitation. "As you know," he
said, "Arabella lacks any female relatives on Mars."

"This may explain her questionable choice of fiancé." Her
expression, still pleasant, nonetheless betrayed her distaste at
Arabella's near-scandalous behavior.

Arabella opened her mouth to defend Captain Singh, but
Michael interrupted. "She plans a journey," he said quickly, "in
the very near future, and we were hoping that you might be willing to accompany her as chaperone."

At that Lady Corey's round, pink face brightened, and
Arabella's hopes declined correspondingly. "A journey? How delightful. My daughter has been encouraging me to get away from
town, with all its unpleasant memories. I would be delighted to
accompany dear Arabella . . . once my responsibilities here have
been discharged, of course." Arabella's spirits fell still further.
"Where might she like to go?"

Arabella cleared her throat, forcing Lady Corey to meet her
eye. "Venus is my destination," she enunciated clearly.

"Oh," the great lady replied, recoiling slightly. "Are you certain?

If you wish a holiday, I understand the sand-falls at Sor Khoresh"—
unlike many Englishmen, she managed the *kh* in Khoresh quite
creditably—"are lovely at this time of year."

"I have important business there."

Lady Corey's glance flicked from Arabella's face to Michael's
and back. "Really, I cannot imagine why any well-bred young
woman should want to visit such an . . . uncivilized place as Venus.
Surely it has nothing to offer in the way of entertainments."

"I have no idea," she replied honestly, then realized this question presented an opportunity. "Perhaps my old *itkhalya* Khema
can offer some suggestions." Immediately she rose and tugged the
bell-pull, ignoring Michael's puzzled expression.

Conversation continued, somewhat strained, until Khema arrived. Arabella hid her nervousness by buttering her crumpet.

"Ah, Lady Corey!" Khema said as she entered, ducking and
turning sideways to fit through the sitting-room door. "So delightful to see you again!"

Though her command of the English language was impeccable
and her manners unimpeachable, Khema was nonetheless quite
an intimidating sight. During the recent insurrection she had
transformed into an *akhmok*—a sort of natural general—and now
loomed nearly eight feet high and almost half that broad, with
spiny protrusions at every joint. Yet, despite her bulk, her movements were so fluid and graceful that her curtsey was neither
laughable nor intimidating.

At least, it was not intimidating to Arabella or any other member of the Ashby household. Yet Lady Corey, Arabella was certain,
would find Khema's appearance distressing; her reactions would
demonstrate to Michael how inappropriate it would be to encum-
ber Arabella with her as chaperone for the voyage.

"We were wondering," Arabella said brightly, "if you could
recommend any leisure activities on the planet Venus." She rose

and stood at Khema's shoulder, gesturing to Lady Corey. "Lady Corey will be accompanying me there as chaperone." She took a small step forward, deliberately approaching Khema slightly closer than Martian etiquette permitted.

Unconsciously Khema edged away from her, taking a step toward Lady Corey. The hard carapace of her foot thudded heavily on the carpet. "I have never visited that planet myself." Again Arabella eased forward, forcing Khema still closer to Lady Corey. "But my cousin Sutkheth has traveled there several times, and she speaks very highly of the water gardens of Munungulawala and the hot baths at Gonuwamanaga." Another step. "And, of course, Venusian cuisine is renowned throughout the solar system." By now Khema loomed directly above Lady Corey, the spines of her pectoral plates practically pricking the great lady's cheeks.

"Do tell us more of that cuisine," Arabella said.

Khema turned slightly toward Arabella, her eye-stalks rising in an expression of uncertainty. "It may be . . . a bit beyond the English palate."

Arabella returned Khema's expression with a significant lift of her eyebrows and a gesture in Lady Corey's direction. "Please do. I am certain it will make a *great* impression."

Khema considered this for a moment, then pulled her eye-stalks back slightly—a subtle Martian gesture of understanding and acknowledgement, which Arabella knew well—then leaned over Lady Corey and began to describe the finest delicacies of Venusian cookery with great enthusiasm and many details, smacking her mandibles with relish as she described its tentacular and blubbery delights.

But Lady Corey's reaction to this recitation was not at all what Arabella had anticipated. She seemed undeterred, in fact enthusiastic, and her expression, rather than showing disquiet at Khema's proximity, was one of interest and delight. The great lady and

Khema were soon comparing Venusian to Martian vintages and spices, even discussing famous Martian *chefs de cuisine* of their acquaintance.

"You must understand," Lady Corey explained to Arabella's astonished expression, "that I came to Mars as a very young girl, back in George the Second's day. In those days there was very little in the way of proper English cookery to be had; we all dined *à la Martien*, as we said, at nearly every meal. Not like to-day, when any family of any standing whatsoever employs an entire kitchen staff imported from London, and even the servants dine on beef and onions. However"—here she leaned in over her tea and scones and confided in a low voice—"I must confess that I still relish a nice *sukuresh gonash*. It reminds me of my younger days."

"How fascinating," Arabella replied, quite taken aback.

"This has been a delightful conversation," Michael put in then, "but I am certain that Khema has other duties to attend to." At this, Khema curtseyed and departed.

Once Khema had gone, Lady Corey turned to Michael. "If you will, my dear sir, I would like a private word with your sister." She favored him with a demure smile. "If I am to serve as her chaperone, we must be permitted a few . . . female confidences."

"By all means," Michael replied, and with as deep and respectful a bow as could be managed with a crutch, he too took his leave.

As soon as the door had closed behind him, Lady Corey's expression hardened. "Do not think," she said to Arabella in a low intense voice, "that I do not comprehend your precise intent in calling your *itkhalya* into this room."

"I am certain I do not—"

"Do not be coy with me," Lady Corey interrupted, straightening, and Arabella found her mouth shutting as though moved by clockwork. "Your intention was to intimidate me, and I must confess that for a time I was nearly intimidated." She closed her eyes. "Though it has been nearly a year, the memories of my dear Lord Corey's death are still painful." She seemed to draw herself together then, and when her eyes reopened they were hard and gray and sharp as best Martian steel. "But I have lived among Martians all my life, and seen many a rebellion and uprising before last year—they were quite common when Cornwallis, rest his soul, was Governor-General—and it will take more than an *akhmok* to bullyrag *me*."

"I . . . I beg your pardon, Lady Corey," Arabella stammered, completely nonplussed.

Lady Corey's mien softened then, and she patted the sofa beside herself. Almost against her will, Arabella shifted to the indicated spot. "I am well aware, my dear Miss Ashby, of your reputation for independence and temerity. It has served you in good stead so far, and you have achieved much. It could even be said that I, and many other members of our household, owe you our lives. But if you are indeed to marry—and I would counsel you to give the matter much greater consideration than you have as yet demonstrated—you must enter into society. This requires an entirely different set of capabilities from those you have hitherto displayed."

"I thank you for your counsel," Arabella replied, attempting to regain control of the conversation, "but my immediate concern is to attain my fiancé's release from Napoleon's custody, and for this task I am certain that independence and temerity are the very qualities which are required."

"Indeed," the great lady replied noncommittally, her eyes hooded. "However, a genteel lady never forgets the social graces, *no matter the circumstances*"—she flicked her fan sharply to emphasize each word—"and in this area I fear your deportment is sadly lacking."

"I fail to see how the 'social graces' can bring about my fiancé's freedom."

"Poor behavior reflects ill upon one's family and upon one's station in life. Without family and station, one lacks influence. And without influence, little of consequence can be accomplished." She leaned forward, her expression firm. "You lack judgment, and have been suffered to govern yourself by whim rather than by any rational consideration of right or consequence. This cannot be allowed to continue."

The two women's eyes locked for a long, contentious moment, which was broken by Lady Corey drawing a breath and reaching for her tea-cup. "In any case," she said, "propriety demands that you be chaperoned, and so a chaperone you must have. And in that capacity, as your brother has requested, I will happily serve. Though you sometimes strike me as incapable of improvement, I feel honor-bound to make the attempt."

A sharp retort rose to Arabella's lips, but she held it back. She would accept Lady Corey as chaperone, she decided, in order to mollify her brother. And she would escape her strictures as soon as she could, as she had done with her mother. This was a game she could win.

"I look forward to sharing your company," Arabella said mildly, and raised her own tea-cup in salute.

"As do I." Lady Corey sipped her tea. "You require looking after, my dear, and I believe I am just the one to do it . . . and give you a proper education in the womanly arts into the bargain."

Suddenly Arabella wondered if she herself had just been maneuvered into an unfavorable position.

4

TOUCHSTONE

Arabella leaned from the window of Lady Corey's coach, eager for a glimpse of Fox's ship *Touchstone*.

Lady Corey had, to Arabella's surprise, packed quickly, and had appeared with her coach at Woodthrush Woods promptly the next morning to take Arabella and her baggage to the ship. After a tearful and somewhat awkward farewell to Michael, they had collected Fox at his club and proceeded thence to the harbor.

"She is as sweet a flyer as any I have ever sailed," Fox was saying as the coach clattered along. "Clean of line, swift, and weatherly. You will surely love her as much as I."

The harbor came into view then, a vast expanse of flat red sand crowded with hulls, sails, envelopes, and masts. Most of them were stolid cargo vessels, but one was a lean and sturdy clipper with an aggressively raked mainmast. "Is that she?" Lady Corey inquired, pointing.

"Ah . . . no." Fox pointed. "*That* is she."

Arabella's first reaction was disappointment, for *Touchstone* seemed very small and rather shabby by comparison with her memories of *Diana*—a ship which was, she reminded herself, a Mars Company clipper of the first water, an "aristocrat of the air." This *Touchstone* was a fighting vessel, she thought, a bantam rooster of a ship, small and light and no doubt designed to out-maneuver and outgun her larger, heavier prey. She was built to fight and win, not to look good.

Still, despite these attempts to reassure herself, even from this distance she could not fail to notice the tarnish on her copper bottom, the worn and patched condition of her sails, the rather slovenly state of her standing rigging. When she was an airman aboard *Diana*, even though a lowly waister, she would have earned—nay, deserved!—her captain's scorn for such a sorry job of belaying.

"She seems a . . . sprightly ship," Arabella said to Fox. "How many guns has she?"

He gave her an appraising glance at that. "A very perceptive question, Miss Ashby. Eight eight-pounders on the gun deck, and a pair of three-pound stern-chasers on the quarterdeck."

Arabella nodded approvingly. "*Diana* has but three four-pounders, and to the best of my knowledge no stern-chasers at all."

"Of course she does," Fox replied with only a slight hint of condescension. "She is a mere cargo vessel, while *Touchstone* is a ship of war." Arabella bristled at this dismissal of *Diana*, but said nothing. "And the number of guns must, for reasons of aerial equilibrium, correspond with the number of masts. Your *Diana* is, I gather, a three-master?"

"She is." Arabella herself had seated the starboard and larboard masts in their keelson-plates on the lower hull during the swaying-out ceremony upon departing Earth's planetary atmosphere.

"Whereas my *Touchstone* has four masts, for speed and maneuverability, with a matched pair of guns for each." He pointed to the ship's bow, where eight gun-ports were indeed ranged evenly in pairs about the central bowsprit: above, below, starboard, and larboard, presumably corresponding with the roots of the mainmast and the three lower masts—not currently fitted, as the ship was grounded—within her hull. Her figurehead, Arabella noted, was a hunchbacked fool in diamond-patterned motley. "She throws a weight of metal equivalent to one of His Majesty's second-rates, and I'd match my crew's speed of fire against even a first-rate!"

This news caused Arabella to reconsider her opinion of Fox's ship. She had served as a powder-monkey aboard *Diana*, and the sound of her three four-pounders firing had been like the pounding of the knocker on the gates of Hades; she could not imagine the sound of eight guns each firing an eight-pound ball at the same time. Furthermore, *Diana* had very nearly been defeated by a four-masted privateer not unlike *Touchstone*, and that one had carried just four guns.

Even so, she still felt that *Touchstone* was inferior to *Diana* in every other way, and Fox's dismissal of her fiancé's command as a "mere cargo vessel" rankled.

Touchstone stood away from the other vessels on the sand of the harbor, and plainly had stood so for some time, as her crew had erected tents on the sand beside her hull. A thread of smoke rose from the nearest such. As they drew closer, Fox leaned out the carriage window and called "*Touchstone!* Ahoy, *Touchstone!*"

In response to Fox's call, several men came rushing out from the tents, hallooing and waving their arms. "Ahoy the coach!" came one cry, and "Captain! Captain Fox!" another. Fox grinned like a fiend and waved his hat.

Fox opened the door and leapt from the coach even before it stopped. His men immediately crowded around him, grinning and calling out "What news!" and "Where away?" and such.

But one man hung back from the crowd, grinning as widely as

any but quietly waiting his turn rather than pressing forward with the rest . . . and it was that patient, forbearing attitude as much as the darkness of his face and breadth of his shoulders that made Arabella recognize him. "Mills!" she called, ignoring the footman's proffered hand as she jumped down from the coach. "Mills, can that truly be you?"

Mills seemed puzzled at first, but as Arabella rushed toward him his face lit with recognition. "Ashby!" he cried, and upon meeting he crushed Arabella's hand in his, pumping it up and down in a manly greeting more suited to old messmates than a common airman greeting a gentle lady. For old messmates they were, or had been when she had posed as Arthur Ashby, and together they had endured storm, strife, battle, and mutiny.

"*Sir!*" came Lady Corey's voice from behind Arabella, as she stepped down from the coach. "Leave off this improper behavior at once!"

"Oh no, Lady Corey!" Arabella cried, stepping back from the abashed and quite concerned Mills. "The impropriety is entirely mine. Mil . . . *Mister* Mills and I served together aboard *Diana,* and I was overcome by the surprise of encountering him here." She cleared her throat and introduced Mills and Lady Corey to each other.

Mills, to his credit, made a very presentable leg. "I am very pleased to meet you, ma'am," he said, which was, she thought, about as many words as she had ever heard him string together in one sentence. Though she thought Mills quite intelligent, his native language was some West African one, and in English he was quite taciturn.

Lady Corey accepted his greeting with the slightest possible nod and an extremely dubious expression.

"How did you come to be here?" Arabella asked Mills. "I had thought you still aboard *Diana.* Which—have you heard?—was captured by the French at Venus."

"I heard," he said, his expression going grim. He shook his head, then continued. "Just before we sailed, Gowse"—he pointed to where Gowse was being introduced by Fox to *Touchstone*'s crew—"told me Fox was taking on crew. And look at me now!" He beamed and swept his hand down the long, muscular length of himself. "Captain of the mizzen-top!"

"I give you great joy of it!" cried Arabella, though she held herself back from shaking his hand. "I cannot fault you for accepting such a promotion." Aboard *Diana,* she and Mills had been waisters, lowest of the crew; to become a topman, never mind the captain of a top, was a considerable step, and such a rapid rise was indicative of considerable ability.

"Aye," Mills acknowledged, though again his face clouded. Clearly he was thinking of his shipmates aboard *Diana.*

"You would only have been captured with the rest," she assured him.

"Prior familiarity or no, Miss Ashby," Lady Corey sniffed, "this conversation has already gone on entirely too long for propriety. In any case, I believe Mr. Fox is requesting everyone's presence." She held out an imperious elbow. "Come along, child."

Arabella rankled at Lady Corey's none-too-polite request. But Mills, seeing her draw breath for a harsh retort, met her eyes and gave a very slight shake of his head.

For a moment Arabella glared back at him. Then, seeing the value of his silent counsel, she relented. "Very well. Let us see what Mr. Fox has to say."

The three of them walked over to where Fox, standing atop a barrel and surrounded by his men, was beckoning. "This is Miss Ashby," he said, indicating Arabella as she approached, "who rescued me from that mountebank Burke and his fraudulent, cogged games of so-called chance." At that the men all applauded Arabella, which she acknowledged modestly. "And it is to return that favor"—here his mien turned serious—"that we will be taking on a new commission."

The men all grew quiet, some glancing nervously at Arabella.

"Now, boys, we will not be leaving off privateering. That is a living far too profitable to give up so easily!" A few men chuckled at that; others grinned and poked each other in the shoulder. "But we will be fishing in new waters, where the fish run bigger . . . much bigger." He bent down upon his barrel, bringing his face almost to the level of his men's heads, and spoke low, just loud enough to be heard. The men leaned in attentively. "Aye, some are sharks indeed, whose bite is fierce. But I owe this young lady my fortune—indeed, my very life!—and for her I will risk shark-bite or worse. And the *bounty* on a shark," he said, raising his body and his voice a bit, "is much greater than on the minnows we have been catching here!"

The tension in the scene was palpable. "Where away, Cap'n?" cried one of the men.

Fox leapt to his feet atop the barrel, pointing to the sky. "To *Venus,* lads!"

Pandemonium ensued. Most of the men, caught up by Fox's enthusiasm, cheered and huzzahed. Others muttered darkly, looking skeptically at each other. Mills could be counted among the skeptics, but his level gaze was directed solely at Arabella.

"Isn't *Bonaparte* at Venus?" called one of the skeptics.

"Precisely!" Fox cried, pointing to the man. "And it is he who is the greatest shark of all! Who among you desires the Great Ogre's destruction?"

"Me!" they all chorused, save an educated few who called out "I!"

"As do I, lads! In this I take second place to no man! And so I intend to take the fight to Venus—to Bonaparte himself!—and destroy him personally, or at the very least as many Frenchmen as I may!"

Though this statement rallied the men, it raised consternation in Arabella's heart; she sought rapid transportation to Venus, not engagement with the French. But she could not fault Fox's enthusiasm, and his leadership abilities were plainly very impressive; not only would he be happy to carry her thence, but she was now confident that he and his crew could pick their way through the French defenses and deliver her to the planet's surface.

"Three cheers for the captain!" came a cry from the back of the crowd, and Arabella joined in with the rest of the men in a full-throated "Huzzah! Huzzah! Huzzah!"

———————————

Just after dawn the next morning, Arabella stood at *Touchstone*'s quarterdeck rail, looking up at the ship's single large balloon envelope. The balloon, which swelled like a great white *skurosh-melon*, strained at its shrouds as it filled with hot air from the port's mighty launch-furnaces.

"Prepare to cast off!" came a cry from close at hand. It was Liddon, the chief mate—a lean man with a long white scar on his cheek, whose fierce visage belied the kindliness with which he had welcomed the ladies aboard. The command was repeated down the deck; men moved into position.

Despite her experience as an airman, this was in fact only Arabella's third aerial ascent. The first time she had been confined to her cabin; the second, she had been entirely inexperienced. This time, at least, she understood the shouted commands and was in a position to form an opinion of the men's responses to them.

Although *Touchstone*'s crew had at first seemed a rather filthy and disheveled lot, matching the untidy state of their ship, as they worked to make the ship ready for ascent they struck her as experienced and attentive to their duty. As Fox bounded about the quarterdeck, calling out orders, occasionally changing his mind and countermanding them—a marked contrast to her own Captain Singh's calm, steady command—they were relayed by Liddon to the appropriate quarter of the ship with brisk despatch, and the men there leapt to comply with hardly a wasted motion. Where individual action was needed they performed their jobs with admirable efficiency; where co-operation was required the men worked wonderfully together. Watching the ship prepare for ascent reminded Arabella of the workings of a finely crafted and well-maintained automaton.

Which drew her thoughts to Aadim, *Diana*'s unique automaton navigator. What had become of him, with the ship in the hands of the French? Her own hands wrung together in concern and frustration; tens of thousands of miles separated her from Aadim, *Diana*, and Captain Singh—her captain, her fiancé, her maharajah.

Oh, how she wished she could be a part of those workings! To be laboring along with the crew, to be doing *something* to move the ship forward and closer to rescuing her fiancé. But though her fingers itched to haul on a line, on this voyage she would be nothing but a passenger. Even if Fox could somehow be convinced otherwise, Lady Corey would surely prevent it.

The calls and responses down the length of the ship crescendoed, then died away. "All hands report ready for ascent," Liddon told Fox.

Fox's eye gleamed, and he grinned at Arabella. "Now the fun begins," he said to her, then turned back to Liddon. "Well, then, what are we waiting for? Cast off!"

"Ballast away!" Liddon bellowed.

With a deep wooden *thunk*, ports in the hull below Arabella's view swung open, letting streams of sand hiss out onto the plain below. A rising cloud of red dust obscured the view of the other ships . . . but only for a moment, as *Touchstone* herself rose out of that dust cloud and into the pale blue cloudless sky above. The rapidity of her ascent made Arabella's stomach giddy, and even the staid Lady Corey let out a surprised whoop.

Touchstone ascended from the forest of masts around her like a toy lifted from a tub, giving Arabella a view of dozens of ships laid out like so many automata on a master craftsman's bench. In moments the full scope of the harbor became apparent, a vast expanse of red sand dotted with ships of every description. That lake of sand lapped at Fort Augusta's docks, beyond which lay a busy confusion of warehouses and chandleries serving the aerial trade, then crowded lanes of town-houses and shops, and finally the great bulk of the Fort itself, whose great red sandstone walls loomed apparently impregnable above the town. But the town was still pock-marked with burns and wreckage from the recent insurrection, and Arabella knew that even the fort might have fallen if the fighting had gone on much longer than it had.

Eventually, though, the entirety of Fort Augusta town dwindled to a mere stain upon the landscape, and Arabella turned her attention forward and upward.

There, glittering in the sky above the rising Sun, shone the planet Venus.

IN TRANSIT, 1815

5

NAVIGATION

Arabella floated at the quarterdeck rail, gazing up at the great globe of Mars which loomed overhead.

After departing Fort Augusta, *Touchstone* had risen from Mars's planetary atmosphere into the interplanetary atmosphere. Along the way the men had performed the traditional shipboard ceremony of the falling-line, followed by the swaying-out of the lower masts.

Arabella could not recall that day without considerable melancholy. The events of *Touchstone*'s falling-line ceremony were similar to those she had experienced upon her departure from London aboard *Diana*: the slow fall of a gold sovereign from the quarterdeck, demonstrating the diminution of gravity, and the scramble of the crew to catch it after it bounced. But as *Touchstone*'s crew were all experienced airmen, there were no "new fish" to be hazed by being thrown briefly overboard. It was with a mixture of anger, anguish, and nostalgia that she recalled her own such hazing; it had been terrifying, cruel, and unnecessary, but it had also marked her initiation into the fraternity of aerial sailors.

Also, of course, it had marked her entry into the service of the man who would eventually become her fiancé, the excellent Captain Singh.

Her first significant act as a freshly initiated airman had been to be lowered over the side to guide the larboard mast, which was stowed at the ship's side while in port, into its socket in the lower hull. That, too, had been terrifying at the time, but also deeply satisfying, for without her lower masts the ship could not maneuver in the atmosphere at all, and would surely be dashed to pieces by the winds of the Horn—the zone of perpetual storms where the planetary and interplanetary atmospheres ground together like mill-stones.

For the equivalent swaying-out aboard *Touchstone*, Arabella's role was only that of an observer, as she leaned out over the rail to watch a young, lithe airman perform the task with the calm, almost bored, assurance of one who had done so a thousand times before. And the most interesting part of the exercise to Arabella— the swaying-out of the mizzen, or bottom, mast, which *Diana* lacked—had been completely invisible to her beneath the curve of the hull.

The whole exercise had left her feeling small, weak, and useless, and made her miss her captain exceedingly. After the swaying-out she had retired to her cabin, a tiny triangular closet barely large enough to accommodate her hammock and Lady Corey's at night, and sobbed herself to sleep.

In any case, the masts had been properly fitted and *Touchstone* had passed safely through the Horn, using the tempestuous winds there to direct her path to the great interplanetary wind current in which she now found herself embedded. Though the wind in the ship's vicinity seemed very nearly still, *Touchstone* was now moving at a speed of some thousands of knots toward Venus.

Or so Arabella hoped. At this point she was no longer as certain of this as she would have expected, or liked.

"Oof!" she exclaimed suddenly, as a soft missile of bombazine and tulle collided with her from behind.

"Oh, dear," said Lady Corey, grasping the rail and pulling herself down to the deck. "I am so terribly sorry."

Automatically Arabella checked her safety line, which coiled lazily from her ankle to an anchor point at the base of the mainmast. It was intact and properly attached at both ends, which would prevent her from being swept overboard and lost for ever in case of another such accident. A similar safety line was—somewhat to Arabella's regret—properly attached to Lady Corey.

The two of them, along with every one and every thing else on the ship, were now in a state of free descent. According to the theories of natural philosophy, as Arabella understood them, they were all falling together toward the Sun, but also simultaneously speeding around it—somehow the two together combined to give the impression that gravity no longer existed in the vicinity of the ship. It all seemed terribly counterintuitive.

But despite her failure to comprehend the philosophical principle or the mathematics, Arabella well understood the practicalities: every thing floated as though under water, lacking the usual concepts of up and down; objects left untethered and unattended could easily drift away and be lost overboard; and her skirt tended to rise up above her hips in a most shocking fashion and must perforce be confined by a sort of large garter at the bottom.

Having been dressed as a boy when she had learned to maneuver, and indeed to fight, in a state of free descent, she missed her masculine clothing terribly. Trousers were ever so much more practical than skirts, and when dressed in them she was every bit as nimble in propelling herself through the air as any other airman, and in fact better than some. The basic principles were quite simple: you pushed off against something with a hand or foot, and traveled in a straight line until encountering something else—such as Gowse's nose.

Now, though, she must perforce spend the majority of her effort simply keeping her clothing under control. And Lady Corey, lacking Arabella's experience, was even worse at it. She floundered in the air like some enormous, ungainly jellyfish.

"Your garter has slipped up again, Lady Corey," Arabella said, helping the great lady to adjust it and to turn herself so that her feet were closer to the deck than her head was. Though there was no practical requirement to do such—indeed, some airmen spent more time upside-down than otherwise—it seemed to make Lady Corey more comfortable if she and those around her were all oriented in the conventional fashion.

"Thank you, my dear," Lady Corey said, brushing her dress down with one hand while clinging to the rail with the other. "I swear I shall never learn the knack of it."

"You will. You are already doing much better."

"So this is Mars," Lady Corey said, gazing up at the rust-colored sphere. "To think I have lived there nearly all of my life and never before beheld the whole of it, at least not since I was too young to remember."

"It is quite unlike the globe in your library, is it not?"

"Indeed. Where are the canals, and the cities?"

Marked clearly on any map or globe of Mars—in addition to the borders of the English territory of St. George's Land and the various Martian satrapies and princessipalities, which even Lady Corey understood could not be seen in reality—were the sites of the major cities and the razor-straight lines of canals between them. Yet these products of English and Martian industry were invisible from this distance, or nearly so.

"I think I may be able to point out Fort Augusta. You see the terminator—the edge of the illuminated area? Along that line it is sunset for those who live there. It is late afternoon at home, and so it must be somewhere on the illuminated side of that line, at a latitude of thirty-one degrees north—two-thirds of the way from the white polar cap at the top to the equator." She peered up. "That lighter-colored patch must be the Sukush Desert, and Fort Augusta is on the northern edge of that. Perhaps that small dark spot. Do you see it? If we had a telescope, we might even be able to pick out the glint of sunlight on the canals around it."

Lady Corey shaded her eyes, but after a while gave up. "Your young eyes may be able to pick it out, but not mine." She shook her head. "You say it is late afternoon 'at home.' Why?"

"Well, at this point in the voyage, the ship keeps the same time as our departure point. It is late afternoon here, so it must also be late afternoon there. We could ask Mr. Fox to consult the ship's chronometer for the exact time."

"But . . . surely late afternoon is late afternoon every where? The time is the time, is it not?"

"Oh no, not at all." She pointed up at the globe. "The time of day depends on where you live. To those living along the terminator, there, it is sunset. Over there, in the center of the illuminated area, it is noon. Around back, just past the planet's limb, or horizon, it is sunrise. And on board ship, we keep the time of our departure city until we come within telescopic sight of our destination, at which point we gradually adjust our time to match. Otherwise, when we land, we might find ourselves eating breakfast at midnight!"

Lady Corey's face showed nothing but incomprehension. "Breakfast at midnight?"

"It *is* complicated," Arabella said, not unkindly. "I will attempt to explain it again some other time."

There would be plenty of time for that—the voyage would last months.

Later that day, Arabella came upon her old messmate Mills. He floated near the capstan, and was working with great concentration upon a cylindrical construction of wood and leather held in his lap. "What is that?" she asked.

"Drum!" he replied, smiling and handing it to her. "My people call it *tama*."

"*Tama*," she repeated, inspecting the object. It was about eight inches tall and bore a taut head, made from what appeared to be lizard-skin, at each end. The two heads were connected by a surprisingly complex net of leather cords, whose tension he had been carefully adjusting. "And what is the purpose of these cords?"

"Changes the tone," Mills explained. Taking the drum back, he tucked it under his arm and beat several notes upon it with a curved stick. As he played, he pressed the drum against his side with greater or lesser force; the changing tension upon the cords caused the drum's note to rise or fall accordingly.

"How fascinating!" Arabella cried delightedly.

"Miss Ashby!" came a shrill cry from behind. It was Lady Corey, of course, hauling her way hand-over-hand along the gunwale. "I thought I made it quite clear to you, even before we left the ground, that conversation with"—she glanced sidewise at Mills—"*common* airmen is entirely inappropriate for a young woman of quality."

"Mills is no common airman," Arabella replied with a mischievous grin. "He is the captain of the mizzen-top, and an accomplished drummer besides."

Lady Corey was not amused. "I care nothing for your mizzen-tops, nor your futtock-grommets nor block-knees." She had, by now, dragged herself along the rail to interpose herself physically between Arabella and Mills, who looked over Lady Corey's shoulder with an expression of apologetic chagrin. "This man is entirely beneath your station, and I absolutely forbid you to engage in any form of intercourse whatsoever with him or any of his sort."

Fury rose in Arabella's breast, but she determined that she would *not* lose her temper. "Very well," she replied with icy calm. "In that case, I shall depart to consult with the *captain* on a matter of navigation."

"Upon navigation only?" Lady Corey asked, suddenly suspicious.

"Upon no other thing."

Lady Corey's eyes were full of doubt, but nonetheless she waved Arabella along. "Very well," she said. "But do not go out of my sight."

Arabella curtseyed with elaborate grace to Mills, and said sweetly, "If you will excuse me, sir?" And then she departed, without the slightest gesture to Lady Corey, who remained at the rail huffing with indignation.

She found Captain Fox—now that the ship was in midair, she supposed she must address him, and even think of him, by that title—on the forecastle, peering ahead with a telescope. Lady Corey remained within sight, though at the furthest extremity of the ship, looking back at Mars.

Unlike Captain Singh, who inevitably either floated with his head uppermost or actually stood with feet on the deck, held down by leather straps affixed to his belt, Fox seemed to enjoy floating horizontally, hanging insouciantly in midair as though lounging in a hammock. At the moment he lay at head-height above the deck, head pointing generally forward and feet aft, with the glass held to his eye. He was not, she noted, wearing a safety line—although seemingly foolish, this was the practice for most experienced airmen once outside the turbulence of the Horn, and indeed on her previous voyage she had adopted it herself. Suddenly she, with her skirt held down by a garter and her ankle tethered to the ship, felt simple and girlish.

"Captain Fox," she said, "may I have a word?"

"Of course, Miss Ashby," he replied, collapsing the glass and tucking it into his coat pocket. He did not, however, adjust his position in the air to match hers, which she took as a slight.

"It has to do with our navigation. I have not consulted any charts, of course, but according to my recollection of the winds near Mars at this time of year we should be taking the Vanderveer Current for the most rapid transit to Venus. Yet it seems to me that we are currently in the Simpson Current. Am I, perhaps, mistaken in this?"

He considered her for a moment before replying. "You are not *completely* mistaken, Miss Ashby. We are, in fact, embedded in the Simpson Current at the moment, and, may I add, making excellent time. By my calculations, our sidereal velocity—that is, relative to the fixed stars—is in excess of eight thousand knots. In the Vanderveer Current, we would be making at best three thousand."

"I know what sidereal velocity is, sir, and I also know that the wind speed of the Simpson Current is greater. But the Vanderveer Current would deliver us directly to the northern solar trades, which blow in excess of *ten* thousand knots and would deliver us to Venus much sooner."

He blinked. "The transfer to the trades from Vanderveer is tricky. Too early, and you could be ripped to pieces by the crosswind. Too late, and you must pedal for weeks to reach the main breeze."

"No competent navigator would have any difficulty with that maneuver. I have calculated it myself, many times."

"I see." Now he shifted himself in the air, using his hat to maneuver, until he was floating vertically to match her. "Apparently I must bow to a girl of eighteen years, whose vast navigational experience exceeds my own." The tone of his voice showed he believed no such thing.

"I am nineteen years old, sir, and I was trained in navigation by Captain Prakash Singh of the Honorable Mars Company, designer of an automaton navigator which made his *Diana* the fastest ship in the fleet. His knowledge of the navigational arts is unparalleled."

"I note that you claimed to have *calculated* the transfer many times. How many times have you *performed* it?"

She knew she was on uncertain ground now, but she chose to plant her feet firmly upon it. "The navigator's role is not to execute the maneuver. That is the role of the sailing-master."

Fox's already-displeased expression soured still further. "I will thank you not to school me in the use of my own crew, Miss Ashby, and I believe from your choice of words that the answer to my question is 'none.'"

"To be precise, that is not a transfer I happen to have been called upon to perform. But I did help to guide the ship through a similar transfer, from the southern trades to the Muller Current, on approach to Mars."

He snorted. "Trades to Muller is child's play. It's the inbound transfer that's tricky. And I note that 'helped to.' Who did the real work?"

"*I* did the real work, using the automaton to perform some of the calculations." Here, too, she recognized that she had perhaps overrepresented her actual experience. "True, Captain Singh inspected my work before performing the maneuver. But he pronounced it acceptable, and did not make any modifications."

"Acceptable?" He arched one eyebrow in a display of skepticism.

"He is a man of great restraint." Unlike yourself, she did not say aloud. "From him this was high praise." She paused, held her breath a moment, and then looked Fox straight in the eye. "If you permit me to calculate our course to Venus, I guarantee that we will arrive three weeks earlier than we would otherwise. Perhaps even sooner."

Fox regarded Arabella for a long moment, tapping one long finger upon his chin. "If you were a member of my crew," he said at last, "I could have you flogged for insubordination. And, given your stubborn intractability, I might very well choose to do so. However, as you are a passenger, and as I like your pretty face"— Arabella bridled at that, but chose not to interrupt—"I shall not flog you. Instead, I shall accept your offer, but on my own terms." Again he maneuvered in the air, as tidily as she had ever seen, and suddenly he was so close she could feel the heat of his body upon her face. "I desire a rapid arrival at Venus as much as you do. If you can work out a course that you can convince me will get us there faster, by even a single day, I will follow it. And if it succeeds . . . I shall write you a fine certificate proclaiming to all and sundry that you, a girl of nineteen, have bested me in aerial navigation. But if you try and fail . . ." He pulled back a bit and stroked his chin. "If you fail, you must give me a kiss."

"A kiss?"

"That is all I ask, I assure you. Just one kiss."

Arabella felt heat rise in her cheeks. "A heavy price for failure," she said, realizing even as she did that she was playing the coquette, and furthermore that her chaperone was no longer on deck. She had no idea where Lady Corey had gone, but for the moment she was not inclined to enquire after her.

Fox shrugged, and she was suddenly aware just how muscular his shoulders were. "No bet is worthwhile unless the stakes are serious."

Arabella considered the captain's proposition seriously. If nothing else, the exercise would serve to pass some of the long hours of the voyage, and keep her wits and navigational skills sharp. "May I make use of your charts and tables?"

"By all means. I desire a fair challenge."

"And who will decide whether my course is, in fact, sufficiently superior to yours that you will follow it, and hold you to it as regards the execution? I shall suffer no prevarication nor procrastination."

Fox considered, tapping his chin with one long finger. "Will you accept the judgement of Liddon, my chief mate? Though I count him a friend, he is often employed by the crew as a fair judge for wagers such as this. You may make any enquiries you desire regarding his impartiality."

Arabella pursed her lips, still considering. "Pending the outcome of such enquiries, then . . . I accept your challenge." And then, so full was her head with navigational thoughts, she unthinkingly put out her hand like a man.

The captain took the proffered hand, with gentlemanly delicacy, and gave it a brief polite shake. His grip, though restrained, plainly held considerable strength in reserve. "I eagerly await the fruit of your labors. Your servant, miss." Then he bowed in the air and departed.

Arabella was left staring at her own hand and wondering just what she had gotten herself into.

Three weeks later, she was still wondering the same thing.

She was in the captain's cabin, scratching away at a sheet of foolscap tacked to a writing-board in her lap, with charts and books of navigational tables floating in the air all around her. Paper not being cheap, she had already crossed and recrossed her calculations on both sides of the sheet and was now attempting to work diagonally. But the letters and figures were now so obscure, due to the multiple layers of ink, that she was having increasing difficulty keeping track of them all. With a disgusted noise she thrust her pen into Fuller's Patent Free-Descent Inkwell and gripped her hair as though to tear it out by the roots.

"Is the work not going well, Miss Ashby?" Captain Fox enquired, trying and failing to keep the smirk out of his voice.

In response she favored him with a most unladylike glare.

Sharing the captain's cabin—it was called the "Great Cabin," though it was barely as large as Arabella's bedchamber at Woodthrush Woods and untidily crammed with Fox's possessions besides—with Fox was a continual exercise in annoyance. The man could not keep still . . . constantly shifting, clearing his throat, humming snatches of risqué tunes, even picking his nose. A greater contrast with the dignified Captain Singh could scarcely be imagined.

"Perhaps a turn around the deck will help to clear your head," offered Lady Corey. Having *her* in the cabin made an already barely tolerable situation even less so, with the constant clack-clack-clacking of her knitting needles adding to Fox's humming, and the ever-growing length of the shawl she was working drifting everywhere. But the cabin was where the charts and instruments were stored, and Arabella could not be permitted to work there in Fox's presence without her chaperone, so the three of them must perforce crowd themselves in all together. At least the absence of gravity made the usable space somewhat greater, as Fox tended to spread his log-books and bills of lading on the ceiling.

"It is the *tedium* of the calculations," Arabella said—to no one, to any one; her gaze was directed out the wide aft window, spanning the full width of the ship, and the tiny red circle of Mars just visible against the deep cloud-flecked blue of the sky beyond. "With every sheet of paper I deface I understand more thoroughly why Captain Singh spent so much of his time and fortune building an automaton to perform this work." And, though she did not say this aloud, how much she missed his brilliance, his steadfastness, and the warmth of his long brown fingers on hers.

"And there you see the risk of automata," Fox replied. "They are all well and good as amusements, I grant you. But when they are built to perform the work of men, surely this must result in the atrophy of the mental processes they replace."

Again she gave Fox a glare. This time Lady Corey spotted it, and admonished Arabella with a slight shake of the head. "I must disagree, sir," Arabella said. "Would you also have us give up the *huresh*, or the horse, on account of the atrophy of men's legs?" She shook her head. "Instead, sir, I believe that automata have the potential to lead to the perfection of the human species, by taking away all tedium and make-work, leaving men's minds free to contemplate the greater questions of life." She sighed. "Such as the simple question of how best to make our way from here to Venus."

Suddenly Fox's eyebrows lifted, then slowly lowered, his face acquiring a sly expression she found not at all attractive. "I have just recalled," he said, "an item in my hold which could make our wager still more interesting."

Arabella's eyes darted to Lady Corey, who was looking back at her with sharp interest. "What 'wager,' Captain Fox?"

Before Arabella could speak in her own defense, Fox immediately and correctly assessed the situation, which was that Arabella had not informed her chaperone of the bet. "It was more in the way of a challenge, Lady Corey," he said. "I used the term 'wager' only out of my own habit."

"Gambling is a wretched vice," Lady Corey replied with a sniff. "A snare for men of weak character."

"I acknowledge this," he said, hanging his head melodramatically. "And yet I do persist in it, for more times than not it is I who wind up holding the snare, and some other poor wretch who dangles from it." To this assertion Arabella replied with a pointedly skeptical look, to remind Fox that when they had first met he had been well and truly snared, and he at least had the grace to look abashed. But he continued: "In any case, my challenge to Miss Ashby, which I mistakenly termed a wager, was to use the navigational skills she learned from Captain Singh to help us find our way to Venus more quickly." Though Arabella was annoyed at Fox's claim that *he* had challenged *her,* she did appreciate his solicitude and quick thinking in defusing Lady Corey's anger. "The item I just recalled," he continued, "was a trunk of clockmaker's materials which we seized from a French merchantman last year."

This news piqued Arabella's interest exceedingly. "What kind of materials, sir?"

"I know not." He shrugged. "But it seemed to me something that might fetch more in London than in Sor Khoresh, so rather than sending the trunk to Mars in the captured vessel I retained it here. We have not called at London since, so here I assume it remains. I must confess I had entirely forgotten its existence until now."

The forgotten trunk was, she reflected, probably noted on one of the untidy papers which littered the cabin. Yet another way in which Fox differed from her own captain. "I may be able to make use of it," she said.

"Then let us see if it can be located." He called for his purser, a dour plump man by the name of Fitts, and requested that the trunk be brought up from the hold. "Take two men," he said, "for as I recall it is extremely heavy."

―――――――――――

Heavy it was, indeed—though no larger than a common seachest, it required the full strength of two burly airmen to maneuver it through the door and bring it to a halt before it crashed through the cabin's broad window. Even in a state of free descent, heavy objects retained their momentum; this was another reminder that *weight*, which the absence of gravity reduced to nothing, and *mass*, which made objects difficult to shift into motion, were separate quantities.

The trunk's key, alas, had gone missing, if indeed Fox had ever possessed it, but one blow of the carpenter's chisel made short work of the lock. "Open sesame!" Fox cried as he swung up the lid.

What was revealed within did indeed make Arabella feel as though she had stumbled into Ali Baba's cave. The trunk contained layers of trays, each divided into numerous compartments lined with maroon baize. The top tray held tools—pliers, files, drills, fine saws, and a profusion of screwdrivers, each neatly housed in a fitted recess—and the others were densely packed with all manner of gears, cogs, wheels, springs, and screws. The bottom half of the trunk, below the lowest tray, was given over to raw materials: blocks of dense wood, sheets and strips of copper and brass, and bundles of rods in various materials and cross-sections.

"This is marvelous," Arabella said, unable to keep the enthusiasm out of her voice. "I am certain that I shall be able to make use of it."

"I am pleased," said Fox. He dismissed Fitts and the two airmen and returned to his paperwork.

Later, as Arabella was engaged in sorting and cataloguing the contents of the trunk, Fox paused in his work to yawn and stretch elaborately, his hands reaching nearly all the way from his position on the ceiling to where Arabella scribbled below. She strove to ignore him, but then a small papery sound called her attention upward.

Fox held a folded bit of paper between his extended fingertips, which he was fluttering at her. She glanced up at him—his eyes had a conspiratorial cast—and then at Lady Corey, whose attention was fixed on a troublesome bit of knitting.

Quickly Arabella reached up and took the paper. A moment later, after making certain that Lady Corey was still distracted, she unfolded it.

I am glad that you like the trunk, she read. *However, it comes at a price. If you make use of its contents and succeed in our wager, in addition to the certificate I shall gift you with a prize* huresh *from my stables upon our return to Mars. But if you use them and fail, in addition to the kiss you must have dinner with me, alone. Alternatively, you may retain the terms of our original bet and I will return the trunk to the hold. Do you accept?—F.* Beneath this was written, much smaller, *P.S. I swear to you I will not press the acquaintance any further than dinner.*

Despite Fox's assurances—which, notwithstanding her annoyances with the man, somehow she felt she could rely upon—she knew that accepting his terms would put her far beyond the bounds of propriety. Yet her hunger for the contents of the trunk was very great.

If she could but work with clockworks again in the context of navigation, it might keep alive her connection with her fiancé, as the harpsichord player had with her father. Already her mind whirred with possibilities for the contents of the trunk.

She turned the paper over and wrote one word on the back: *YES.* Then she placed it on her writing-board—where Fox could see it but Lady Corey could not—cleared her throat, and looked upward.

Fox met her eye, nodded, and winked.

Somewhat disturbed by her own actions, Arabella tore the paper into bits and put them with the other scraps.

6

A NEW MECHANISM

Weeks passed. Arabella busied herself with the clockmaker's trunk, often working late into the dog watches, filing and sawing and occasionally pounding together recalcitrant parts. As she worked, she did feel a connection with her dear departed father, her greatly missed Captain Singh, and the remarkable Aadim . . . and even with the anonymous French clockmaker whose tools and materials were now hers. He had been a fastidious man, she knew, with every screwdriver and bit of metal well oiled, properly ranged, and neatly stowed, and she was sorry he had lost his trunk. But such, she reminded herself, were the fortunes of war; the trunk, along with every thing else on the merchantman *Trianon*, had been taken by Fox entirely legally. If any one were to blame for the trunk's loss, it would be Napoleon.

The one thing she regretted was that all of the tools and materials were calibrated in French units of measure. Which, however logical they might be in theory, as a matter of practical use she found completely unintuitive.

The complexity and size of her workings soon outgrew the captain's cabin, and with the captain's permission, she transferred herself to the officers' ward-room. The officers quickly became accustomed to stepping around, and sometimes even eating around, her gears and springs and scribbled notes, and the corners of the room grew cluttered with navigational charts and tables of logarithms.

The officers were not unkind to her. She felt herself treated as a pet, or perhaps a curiosity, like a monkey that had been taught to crank a barrel-organ. But her project, though nowhere near as sophisticated as Aadim, was more complex than any barrel-organ or, in some ways, even her father's lifelike automaton harpsichord player.

The problem her mechanism was attempting to solve was easily enough stated: given the observed angles of declination and right ascension for certain well-known celestial bodies, such as Saturn and Polaris, what was the ship's position in space? This was only a small part of the function that Aadim performed, of course, but it was the foundation of all else—with repeated observations over time, and a sufficiently precise chronometer, this information could be used to determine her speed and direction of motion, which could be projected forward along the navigational charts to establish the exact time and angle for a future change of course.

The most difficult part was incorporating the motions of the planets, which were fiendishly complex but absolutely essential to the device's function, the fixed stars being too distant to establish the ship's position within the solar system. For each planet represented, she was forced to calculate and fabricate an entirely unique elliptical gear from sheet brass, a difficult and painstaking endeavor which, more often than not, resulted only in the waste of irreplaceable metal.

Gear after gear she spoiled; plate after plate of precious brass was eaten away. Soon all the two-millimeter plate was gone and she was reduced to riveting together two plates of the one-millimeter. She tried and failed to remake her earliest failures into better, smaller gears; she tried and failed to braze together half-ellipses which could be eked out from the remaining scraps.

Finally even the scraps of one-millimeter sheet brass were gone, and she was forced to confess that she had failed. The work simply required more precision than her tools and her skills could produce.

She supposed she would have to return to calculation with pen and paper. But after so many weeks of challenging, intriguing work with steel and brass the prospect seemed even more fatiguing than before.

Or, of course, there was the possibility of simply admitting defeat. A kiss and a dinner for two were not such a high price to pay. Might, in fact, be rather pleasant. Fox did have *some* good qualities. . . .

No! she thought, shaking her head sternly. She would not give in so easily. But what other option did she have?

She sat, despondent, listlessly rotating the small portion of one elliptical gear which had actually worked against one of the manufactured round gears with which it had been intended to mesh. Her best hand-filed gear teeth were simply too irregular for smooth continuous motion, but in this one small stretch she had managed to keep them regular, crisp, and even. If she had had more time and more materials, she might eventually have learned to do this for an entire gear.

Something nagged at her. She leaned in and peered minutely at the small section that meshed properly. It was perhaps one-quarter of the gear representing the orbit of Saturn. As she rolled it against the circular gear, back and forth, she imagined the great ringed planet himself, sweeping majestically through the chill outer reaches of the interplanetary atmosphere. Back and forth he sailed with the motion of the tiny gear, dashing at impossible speed, covering in seconds a distance of hundreds of thousands of miles, a distance which the real planet required many years to traverse.

Many years.

Arabella sat, stunned, as she suddenly comprehended her problem in an entirely different way.

She had been a fool.

She had wasted weeks and nearly all of her sheet brass.

But the game was not yet lost.

———————

Arabella scrapped nearly all of her completed work and began again on a new basis. She had been thinking at much, much too large a scale.

The elliptical gear for each planet was necessary to account for its motion throughout its orbit—an orbit which, for the outer planets, required decades. Aadim housed just such a set of elliptical gears within his massive base, but he had been designed to function for many years and had been built with the facilities of several specialized manufactories. Arabella's little mechanism need only work for this one voyage, of just a few months' duration.

And if one were considering the span of just a few months, the elliptical orbits of the planets were sufficiently close to a perfect circle that they could be approximated by a circular gear.

Her pen flew across the paper. Circular gears she had in plenty, but only in certain sizes. She would have to add smaller gears—ironically similar to the epicycles which the ancients had imagined, before they understood that it was the Earth that orbited the Sun rather than the other way around—to make up the difference between the available tooth counts and the actual motions of the natural planets. But even as she calculated the necessary ratios, she realized that she could turn this necessity to her advantage. By designing the mechanism so that the epicycle gears were easily replaceable, she could change them over time, compensating for the difference between a circular gear and the planet's actual elliptical orbit.

This simpler, more easily constructed, and more reliable mechanism could, with a little calculation, be made to serve for an indefinite period!

And if the primary gears were made larger . . . it would actually be more accurate over the short run than the elliptical gears she had at first envisioned. Even more accurate, perhaps, than Aadim himself!

Suddenly a hand touched Arabella's shoulder, giving her a start that sent gears and papers scattering all over the ward-room.

Enraged at the interruption, Arabella rounded on the intruder. After so many weeks, the officers should know better! But it was Lady Corey who was drifting away from her, hands clapped to her cheeks and face a knot of concern. "My dear Miss Ashby!" she said. "Please forgive me."

"I . . . I am sorry for my . . . intemperate reaction," Arabella said, trying to calm her racing heart even as she fought to remember the interrupted calculation.

"I apologize for the interruption," Lady Corey said, "but I have been concerned for you. We all have. You have barely moved from this spot in days. You have not slept except in snatches; you have hardly eaten a bite."

Even as Arabella began to protest that she had done no such thing, she realized with surprise that Lady Corey's words were nothing but the truth. She had, in fact, worked through meal after meal, snatching only the occasional biscuit or slice of ham from the officers' table, and she could not recall the last time she had returned to the tiny cabin she shared with Lady Corey for a full night's sleep.

Or a wash. Now that she considered her person, she was forced to confess that she had become as grimy—and, indeed, as noisome—as any common airman.

"Your concern is appreciated, and entirely appropriate," Arabella said, fastening her pen under its clip and, suddenly very aware of the disheveled state of her hair, trying to push it into something resembling order. "I have been, perhaps, too much engrossed in this mechanism of mine."

"Perhaps just a bit," Lady Corey said, with a small smile. "Might I perhaps entreat you to join Captain Fox and myself for a collation in his cabin?"

"I *am* famished," Arabella admitted. She looked around the ward-room, appalled at the papers, gears, and books scattered everywhere. "Pray let me collect my materials here, and freshen myself a bit, and I shall join you directly thereafter."

But despite her hunger, it was still exceedingly difficult to put away her notes without completing just one more calculation.

———

After that brusque awakening, Arabella strove to moderate her labors, take regular meals, sleep properly, and spend time with other people.

However, she still felt considerable pressure upon herself to complete her mechanism as rapidly as possible. For though she had grown to tolerate, and even occasionally to admire, Fox, she still found his navigation lacking—slipshod in places, in others overly cautious. The sooner she could work out a better plan and present it to him, the more quickly they would arrive at Venus, and the sooner she could set to work at releasing her fiancé from the clutches of the demon Fouché.

Thus it was that when Fox entered the ward-room, where Arabella was tightening the set-screw upon the epicycle gear for

Jupiter and Lady Corey was casting-on for a lightweight lace shawl—for as the ship drew nearer the Sun, the temperature was rising each day—Arabella set down her screwdriver and greeted him cordially rather than ignoring him as she would have before.

"I would like to invite you both to the quarterdeck," he said, "to observe a natural phenomenon rarely seen in these climes. Wind-whales!"

"Wind-whales!" exclaimed Lady Corey. "I had not thought to ever see one in my life."

Nor had Arabella. Wind-whales were rarely seen outside the orbit of Venus; the crews of whaling vessels were tough, hardy men accustomed to long stretches of stifling heat. And *Touchstone* had not yet even crossed Earth's orbit. "What can have brought them so far from the Sun?"

Fox shrugged. "I am no natural philosopher. Though I have noted that the temperature of the breeze, of late, has been far higher than any I have seen before in these currents; perhaps some new wind system has boiled up from Mercury and brought them with it."

Arabella glanced at her mechanism, which sat upon the ward-room table held in place by light clips. Several of the planetary gear systems were present and functioning, but Mercury—the smallest, fastest, and fussiest of the lot—was not yet among them. "Whatever the cause," she said, slightly distracted, "we would be remiss if we passed up this opportunity to observe them."

Arabella tidied away her work, making sure to fasten down her papers and workings lest they drift away in some passing breeze, and accompanied Fox and Lady Corey to the quarterdeck.

All the officers were there already, pointing and gesticulating and eagerly jostling each other for the use of the few available telescopes, and many of the men had paused in their work or interrupted their rest to perch in the rigging and stare sunward.

Arabella, shading her eyes and searching the sunward sky for a few faint specks, did not see the whales at first. But then, with a sudden gasp, she comprehended that the large, distant clouds which obscured her view were, in fact, the whales she sought. Vast curving shapes of sky-blue and white, mottled to blend in with the sky beyond, they would have been nearly invisible save for the shadows of their great fins, or wings, upon their bodies. "There they are!" she said, nudging Lady Corey and pointing.

Each whale had a long, narrow form: bluntly pointed at the head end, broad in the middle, then tapering to a broad vertical tail like a shark's. Two enormous sail-like wings spread from the center of each flank, rowing in concert to drive the creature forward. Smaller wings and fins dotted the whales' skin, gently sculling and angling themselves to control their path through the air.

They seemed to be dancing, swooping in lazy circles about each other, the shadow of one occasionally falling on another to create a pleasing play of light and dark in the sky. Delicate, graceful, majestic—despite their great size, they were not at all ponderous.

"How delightful," Arabella breathed.

"But also quite dangerous," Fox replied. "On the Venus circuit, many a ship—and not only whalers—is lost each year to those mighty jaws. A big male can swallow a ship like this whole."

Arabella peered at the whales. "I see no mouths at all."

"They use their teeth only when threatened," said Fitts, the dour purser, with dismissive reassurance, "and for combat between the males during *musth*, or mating season. For their nourishment they draw in great quantities of air through those openings at the front, straining it for the small creatures upon which they feed. I believe they are feeding now."

Now that Fitts had pointed them out, Arabella saw that each whale had two long narrow slits, resembling nostrils, at its pointed tip, and these repeatedly gaped open and shut with a rhythm like a giant's breath.

"Are they growing nearer?" asked Lady Corey. Indeed, in their ever-twining dance the whales had drawn gradually closer, looming larger in the sky.

"Perhaps," Fox replied. "Still, they are yet some considerable distance away, and show no signs of intending a closer approach. You need have no fear."

But something Fox had said earlier nagged at Arabella— nagged at her so severely that she was compelled to wrench herself from the fascinating sight of the whales' pavane. Neither Fox, nor Lady Corey, nor any of the officers seemed to note her departure; their attention remained fixed upon the whales as Arabella made her way belowdecks to the ward-room.

On the table there, her half-assembled mechanism lay gleaming and quiescent in its clips. Though its box-shaped outer frame enclosed as much air as clockwork, and only three of its intended seven sets of hands had been attached, the mainspring which powered the action was fully wound, and she had run all of the assembled portions through a test of their motion just that morning.

And three hands would be enough to fix the ship's position in space, if those three bodies—Polaris, Jupiter, and Saturn— happened to be in view. Which she thought they were.

With some trepidation she unfastened the clips. The device, especially in its current incomplete state, was rather fragile, and if she bumped it against any thing she might jar its gears out of alignment or even damage them. But though it was bulky and awkward, it weighed little, and she was easily able to guide it through the air out of the ward-room and into the captain's cabin, where the ship's chronometer and observational instruments were stored.

Although Fox's sextant was not so fine as Captain Singh's, nor connected with the navigational mechanism as Aadim's was, she was familiar with the use of the instrument. She quickly noted down the angles of Saturn, Jupiter, and Polaris, all of which were skyward of *Touchstone* and hence visible through the cabin's broad aft window, and set the corresponding specification hands on her mechanism appropriately. She then set her mechanism's clock dial to match the time shown on the ship's chronometer. Finally she held her breath, gave the key one final half-twist to tighten the spring to its full extent, and released the catch that put the action in motion.

The mechanism whirred and clicked, small gears spinning and large gears creeping. Indicator hands vibrated gently, moving slowly into position, as the wheels spun and the spring wound down. Then, with a definitive click, it stopped.

She bent down and inspected the positions of the three result hands.

She swallowed.

She inspected them again. Wrote down the values on a piece of paper. Checked the paper against the hands one more time, to be sure. Then, heart racing, she pushed herself across the cabin to where the current aerial chart was tacked to Fox's desk. With ruler and calipers she located the indicated position, marking it with a red-headed pin.

The pin was a good three inches on the chart from the ship's current position. Or, at least, the current position as determined by Fox's observations and calculations.

———

Fox held the pin between thumb and forefinger, waving it brusquely in Arabella's face. "I refuse to accept," he said with considerable heat, "that this . . . this *toy* of yours has fixed our position more accurately than I, with my years of experience."

Arabella plucked the pin from Fox's fingers and returned it to the hole from which Fox had pulled it. "Whether you accept it or no, it is correct. I have checked and rechecked its calculations. And the implications are devastating. We must begin pedaling immediately or we may be lost."

At that Fox gave a derisive snort. "If we obey your girlish whims, we will *certainly* be lost."

But Liddon, at least, was running his finger down Arabella's written calculations. Though he, too, had expressed skepticism of the mechanism's results, he was at least willing to inspect her written verification of them.

The cabin was crowded, with Arabella, Fox, Lady Corey, and Liddon all floating cheek-by-jowl above the chart, and the air was thick with tension. It had been a considerable struggle for Arabella even to get Fox and Liddon away from the whales and down to the cabin, and even more difficult for her to explain to them what her device seemed to indicate and why.

"What is this term here?" said Liddon, pointing to the paper.

"Compensation for the proper motion of Saturn. It is substantial at this time of the planet's year."

"Hmm." He ran his finger down his scarred cheek. "I must say that it is highly irregular to base a fix on Saturn at all."

Arabella set her jaw. "When the mechanism is fully operational it will take every visible planet into account. Saturn merely happens to be visible at the moment, and the corresponding dials on the device are functional. If I were able to incorporate more planets into the calculations, the result would be the same, only with even greater confidence."

"Piffle," said Fox. "Piffle and natural philosophy, I say. Dead reckoning and an accurate shot of the Sun have served aerial navigators for centuries, and I see no reason to suspect them now."

"You yourself said that the air was particularly warm!" Arabella protested. "And the whales—they are hardly ever seen in these climes! Can you not acknowledge that an unexpected breeze from sunward could have blown us far off course? In this circumstance, dead reckoning would be unreliable, as the air in which we are embedded would have moved along with us, and a solar observation confirms only our angular and not our radial position relative to that body. We could be a thousand miles nearer or farther the Sun, and your beloved Sun shot would be exactly the same!"

"She may have a point, sir," said Liddon, still inspecting the paper.

"You think you know a man," Fox fumed, glowering at his chief mate, then set his hands upon his hips. "Very well. Suppose I accept for the moment that this impossibility has occurred. What of it? If the air in which we fly has been moved as well as we, the currents are the same and our eventual destination unchanged."

Arabella shook her head. "Here, sir, I must confess I am less certain of myself. But from my reading, I believe that an upwelling of warm air will divert a major current such as the Simpson only slightly. If I am correct, and we continue on our present course for much longer, we will drift completely out of the current into the surrounding dead air. Even if we are not torn to bits by the difference in wind velocity, we will have no alternative but to attempt to pedal our way back into it . . . but to match speeds with such a strong current from a standstill, using pedals alone, may not be possible."

Liddon's scarred face showed that he was beginning to accept Arabella's position as a frightening possibility. "If what you say is so . . . what can we do?"

"Put all hands on the pedals at once, and pedal directly sunward with all our might. According to the charts, the Simpson Current is some fifty miles across in these parts; one good day's pedaling should put us back at its center if we are currently at its edge. Even if I am wrong, and we are in fact currently near the current's center as your calculations show, one day's pedaling will not put us outside it."

Liddon nodded slowly, then turned to Fox. "The girl's suggestion seems a prudent course, sir."

"Pedal directly sunward?" Fox's astonished face turned from Liddon to Arabella and back, then even, beseechingly, to Lady Corey. The great lady merely looked back at him blankly; she had plainly not understood a word in the past five minutes. "Have you all gone mad?" he gaped. "That would take us into the very midst of the *whales!*"

"Scylla and Charybdis," Arabella said. "We must choose one or the other, and the whales at least are visible—they can be avoided with careful navigation."

"Unless one of the males decides to charge!"

Arabella looked to Liddon, who shrugged. "This is very cold air for them. They may not be so aggressive."

Even Lady Corey put in a word, having recognized the classical reference. "The whales *are* visible," she said, "unlike the air currents. This much at least I understand."

Though outnumbered, Fox set his face in a determined scowl. "I care not what any of you say," he said. "I am the captain of this vessel, and I say—"

At that moment one of Fox's lieutenants—a Negro by the name of Johnson—burst into the cabin without knocking. "Begging the captain's pardon, sir," he stammered, "but we're losing the current!"

They all rushed out on deck, where a stiff breeze was whipping from larboard to starboard athwart the quarterdeck and the ship was showing a decided yaw. Amidships and forward, though, the air was still.

It was immediately clear to Arabella that *Touchstone*'s stern was beginning to emerge from the current—the cross-wind at the stern was, in fact, dead air, beginning to slow the ship's aft end even as her forward end continued to be propelled by the current. And the process was continuing; even as Arabella watched, the wind across the ship's stern strengthened and sails further forward were beginning to luff. It might be mere minutes before the ship fell from the current completely and became stranded in dead air.

Fox's eyes twitched rapidly from the whipping Sor Khoresh flag at the ship's stern to the whales which still danced ahead. "Scylla and Charybdis," he muttered, then raised his voice to a full-throated bellow of command. "To the pedals, boys!" he called. "Ply to sunward, with all your might!" Then, as the men dashed belowdecks, he commented to Liddon in a more conversational tone, "Do try to avoid the whales."

"Aye, sir," Liddon replied, bracing himself at the wheel.

In the ensuing pandemonium, as almost the entire crew hurried below and the shuddering, windswept ship yawed still further to larboard, Fox glared across the quarterdeck at Arabella. "Don't think that this cancels our wager," he said.

Arabella had no reply to that.

Moments later came a muffled grunt from belowdecks and the great, windmill-like pulsers—or propulsive sails—at the ship's stern creaked into motion. Within the ship's hull, Arabella knew, the men were straining at pedals, the effort of their muscular legs transmitted to the pulsers by a system of chains and pulleys. Pedaling was far slower than wind power, and the men's energy was not unlimited, but pedal power was the only method of propulsion under the full control of the ship herself.

And, at the moment, it was the only power that might save them from a slow death of hunger and thirst, marooned in dead air somewhere between Mars and Venus.

Even Fox ran below, whether to join in the pedaling himself or

merely to exhort the men she did not know. Only Liddon remained on the quarterdeck, clutching the wheel with a white-
knuckled grip.

Soon the pulsers were spinning like a top, creating a strong
man-made breeze that blew aft. Its strength was only a fraction
of the cross-wind that now tore across the entire aft half of the
ship, but it was persistent, and the men at the pedals were laboring as though their lives depended on it. Which, indeed,
they did.

The ship seemed to shudder on an invisible precipice, teetering
between the racing Simpson Current on her bow and the fatal
dead air astern. Arabella bit her lip and stared hard at a fluttering
studding-sail amidships. If the cross-current crept forward, the
sails forward of that one beginning to luff, she would know that
the battle was being lost. But if the spinning pulsers began to win
out, that one sail would cease to flutter and the cross-current
would move aft.

For an endless time nothing changed: the one sail continued to
ripple, the sails beyond it remaining still. "You are hurting me,
child!" Lady Corey said.

"Pardon." She tried to relax her grip.

And then . . . and then she saw a sail beyond her bellwether
give one lazy flap, and her heart sank.

Was this the end? Was this the moment that all was lost?

But . . . but no. That single flap was the sail's only movement.
And, a long minute later, her bellwether—that noble stuns'l—
slowed in its fluttering, then luffed gently, then ceased to move
at all.

Gradually, as the men below continued to grunt rhythmically
and the pulsers behind continued to spin, the cross-wind moved
aft, leaving one sail and then another to fall still.

Finally even the Sor Khoresh ensign at the ship's very stern ceased to billow in the cross-wind. Instead it waved directly aft, obeying only the man-made wind of the pulsers.

They had escaped the dead air.

But the whales still remained, swimming dead ahead.

"Why are we not stopping?" Lady Corey asked Arabella, her eyes fixed on the looming beasts. From this extremely reduced distance their forms showed far more detail, their flanks scarred and pocked, and even the clouds of tiny drifting aerial life upon which they fed had become visible.

Arabella glanced behind, seeking in vain the invisible wall of the Simpson Current. It might be a hundred feet behind, or just five. "We must put a good distance between ourselves and the edge of the current," she said, "lest some stray breeze push us right back out of it."

"But the whales!" Lady Corey cried, pointing.

The whales, indeed. They drew nearer and nearer, their huge swooping forms now looming above the ship and to both sides. The wind from each beat of their massive wings swept across the deck, making sails flutter and lines rattle against spars. The breath of their broad black nostrils could even be smelled—a warm, moist exhalation like a breeze off the sea.

One enormous eye swept past, regarding the tiny ship with wary caution. Ships not unlike *Touchstone,* Arabella knew, hunted wind-whales for their meat and the tough, resilient material of their air-bladders.

Arabella looked to Liddon, whose last command from Fox had been to avoid the whales. He was, indeed, doing his best, spinning the wheel hard a-larboard and calling commands to the topmen to set sails for a tight turn. But the whales, whether by unhappy chance or as a deliberate move to intercept the ship, were moving in the same direction.

They would never evade the whales this way. But else could they do?

Suddenly Arabella realized she could answer that question. She turned in the air, put one foot on the rail, and thrust herself away. Catching the ladder with one hand, she spun herself about and redirected her path downward.

"Where are you going, child?" Lady Corey called after her.

"The captain's cabin!" she replied.

7

CALCULATING A NEW COURSE

Arabella shot through the cabin door, checking herself on an overhead beam just before she crashed through the broad stern window.

Her half-assembled mechanism remained where she had left it, floating beside the chart table. It seemed a strange, fragile thing upon which to pin the ship's hopes of survival.

The device had been designed to be used in either direction: in theory, it could not only provide the ship's location from astronomical observations, but also provide a heading to reach a specified location. But the latter function was one she had not yet had any way to test. This would be its first trial, and any failure might prove fatal.

Fingers trembling, she set the mechanism's hands for a location to one side of the whale pod; a brief glance out the stern window at Saturn, now far to starboard from Arabella's last sighting, provided an approximation of *Touchstone*'s current heading.

Then she wound the key, moved the action lever from POSITION to HEADING, and released the catch.

The device's sound was different this time, some gears turning in the opposite direction, others now driving which had before been driven. It whirred and muttered to itself for what seemed like for ever.

And then it clicked, the hands coming to a definitive stop.

Quickly, using pen and paper, she translated the astronomical coordinates displayed on the specification hands to a course heading and sail plan . . . and stared appalled at the result.

The velocity result was a negative number.

She must have made some error, either in the design of her machine, or in setting the dials, or in her calculation. Negative velocity was an impossibility! Why, that would mean . . .

That would mean . . .

Suddenly understanding, she pushed off from the navigation desk with both feet, leaving papers and pins scattering in her wake.

———————

"Back pulsers! Back pulsers!" Arabella shouted as she emerged onto the deck. But Liddon only stared upward in stunned amazement, the wheel already jammed against its stop.

The pod of whales had grown so close that their great blue bodies now filled half the sky. And one—the biggest whale of all, the one directly ahead—was turning to charge the ship, the black lips pulling back to display two enormous rows of jagged teeth. Teeth large enough to tear *Touchstone* to flotsam.

Arabella pushed off the rail, shot across the quarterdeck, and caught herself on the wheel. "*Back pulsers!*" she shouted into Liddon's face.

The sudden, unexpected command roused Liddon from his

stupor. "Back pulsers!" he repeated automatically, calling down the scuttle to the lower deck. The command was repeated and re-echoed down the length of the ship, followed by a massive grunt as the men strove to cancel the great momentum they had spent the last half-hour fighting to build up.

The great spinning pulsers ground to a halt, then began to turn in the opposite direction—pushing air forward rather than aft. The man-made wind whipped Arabella's hair, growing until she and Liddon must cling to the wheel to avoid being blown along the deck. Lady Corey shrieked as she lost her grip on the taffrail, but was saved by her safety line.

The ship still swept toward the whale, whose jaws now gaped wide, displaying an enormous black tongue. But she was slowing, and turning as she slowed. "Brace main and mizzen topsails up on a larboard tack!" Liddon cried, and the topmen on the upper and lower masts—including faithful, clever Mills—sprang into action, shifting the sails to increase the turn.

The turning ship began to slip sideways in her path, the air sliding along the canted main and mizzen-sails joining the wind from her pulsers to nudge her further to larboard even as she continued to slow.

The whale's great jaws snapped shut on the very tip of the bowsprit, tearing loose a foot of *khoresh*-wood with a sickening crunch. But the rest of the ship slipped by unmolested, continuing to turn and slip sideways as she swept past one, then another of the whales in the pod.

In one terrifying minute they were through the pod, the whirring pulsers now pulling them stern-first through the air. Beyond the damaged bowsprit, the largest whale closed its mouth and turned away as though in dismissive disgust; the others continued their dance, never even noticing the smaller man-made creature that had coasted between them.

"Avast pedaling!" called Liddon through the scuttle, and with an exhausted groan from belowdecks the pulsers ground to a halt, leaving the ship drifting gently away from the still-gyrating whales. Arabella pushed herself across the deck to where Lady Corey floated, looking rather stunned. "Are you injured?"

"I do not think so," she said. "But Lord, child, what a ride."

Quivering with fury, Fox slammed his cabin door, shutting the protesting Lady Corey outside and Arabella in. "You may listen through the keyhole if you wish," he shouted through the door, "to satisfy the needs of propriety!"

When he turned back to Arabella, his face was black with anger. "I will have you flogged for this," he said, and she was utterly convinced of his sincerity. "Thirty lashes. For a passenger to issue a direct order to the helm in the midst of action is not mere insubordination, it is . . . it is mutiny! Sedition!" He held up a hand, forestalling her protest. "Liddon is far from blameless in this, I grant you; his punishment will follow yours."

"Flog me if you wish," she said, though her trembling hands belied her brave words. "It will not change the fact that you were wrong, and I was right!" Then, thinking quickly, she added, "And neither Liddon nor I have done any thing in the least improper."

To Fox's fierce, incredulous look Arabella explained, "Liddon had done all he could. He had put the wheel as hard a-larboard as it would go, but it was not sufficient, and he clearly had no other ideas. I happened to be in a position, with the help of my mechanism, to make a suggestion. I may have made it a bit forcefully, perhaps, but you must admit that, under the circumstances, a bit of shouting is understandable. In any case, Liddon agreed with my suggestion, and ordered the men accordingly. But it was Liddon's orders, properly given and duly executed by the men, which saved the ship!"

When she finished, both of them were breathing hard, their eyes locked above the captain's navigational table. Despite the disarray in which she had left the cabin, she noted that her pin was still in place on the chart.

"You are entirely too clever, Miss Ashby," he said at last through gritted teeth. "How long did it take you to concoct that?"

The fact was that the explanation had come to her just now, even as she spoke, but what she said was, "It is simply God's own truth. It was Liddon who avoided the whales, as you ordered him to; I merely reminded him of a possible action which had slipped his mind."

Fox shook his head, shut his eyes, and pinched the bridge of his nose. "Setting that aside for the moment . . . what was it that you said about 'you were wrong and I was right'?"

"That too," she replied, her confidence growing, "is simply God's own truth. Even you must admit that the events of the last hour show that my navigational calculations were correct: we were at the very outermost edge of the Simpson Current"—she tapped the pin—"and not in the middle of it, as *your* assessment showed."

Fox glowered at the pin. "And where are we now, then?"

"At this moment? I do not know precisely. But give me three minutes and I will have your answer, to within half a league."

"Three minutes?"

She swallowed, unnerved at his direct challenge to her casual assertion, and glanced out the window. "Approximately. Provided that Jupiter remains in view."

Fox turned his back on her to stare out the window, broad shoulders gently straining at the fabric of his jacket as his breathing gradually calmed. When he returned his attention to Arabella, his face was more decently composed. "Very well, Miss Ashby," he said. "I grant the *adequacy* of your"—he glanced at her mechanism with a skeptical eye—"device, though I do *not* accept that it makes you my equal in navigation."

Despite his protestations, Arabella understood that she had achieved a substantial victory. "Of course not." Then, with a small smile, she added, "Only my success in bringing us to Venus more swiftly than our current course will demonstrate that."

To that assertion Fox quirked an eyebrow. "We have already sunk the Vanderveer."

It was true that their last opportunity at that current had passed some weeks ago, but between bouts of construction on her mechanism Arabella had been studying the navigational charts. "There are other opportunities, for a bold navigator."

"Bold, are we now, as well as clever?" He ran a finger along his chin. "You are a woman of parts, Miss Ashby."

"More than you know, sir."

For a moment more he studied her, and she felt rather like a prize *huresh* being considered for purchase . . . though whether for racing or for breeding was an open question. "I could—I *should*—still have you flogged for insubordination," he said at last. "But in view of your explanation, and the favorable outcome of the event, I shall magnanimously forego your punishment." Then, suddenly, he put out his hand. "Our wager continues."

She took his hand . . . and then, to her surprise, he drew it to his lips and kissed it. "Sir!" she exclaimed in shock, pulling back her hand . . . though even as she did so, her lips curved into a treacherous smile.

"My apologies," he said, making as courtly a bow as was possible in the confined cabin. "I shall not presume again."

Arabella raised her chin slightly. "I trust you will not. And now, if you will excuse me, I must continue my navigational researches."

"By all means." And he bowed her out of the cabin.

"I do not understand why I do not simply strike him with a rope-end," Arabella said. "He vexes me so."

She and Lady Corey were in their tiny closet of a cabin, Arabella studying a book of navigational tables and Lady Corey knitting the decorative brim of a purse. Though there would have been more room if they positioned themselves head-to-toe, for the sake of Lady Corey's sensibilities Arabella remained in the same orientation as the other woman.

"When my children were small," Lady Corey said, "I noted that some of the boys would torment my girls by putting insects or sand-snakes down the backs of their dresses. And yet, somehow, it was those same boys who were the ones who later came courting." She tapped the side of her nose. "Men are forthright and competitive, Miss Ashby. Those things which they do which seem so vexatious to us may be, in fact, expressions of interest . . . though the men would fervently deny any such interest, and may indeed be unaware of it themselves." She paused to bind off her work, favoring Arabella with a serious look. "Such interest should, perhaps, be exploited."

Arabella closed her book. "I thought my chaperone was meant to shield me from such importune advances as his."

"My dear, you misunderstand the chaperone's full role. I am meant to guide you toward an advantageous match and away from disadvantageous entanglements."

"I do not consider my fiancé a 'disadvantageous entanglement,' and I will thank you to do the same."

Lady Corey sighed and set her knitting in her lap. "Miss Ashby, I know that your heart is set upon him, but I must encourage you in the strongest possible terms to reconsider this engagement. I do not merely consider myself your chaperone, but—after the many trials through which we have suffered together—something of a friend, and I hope that those feelings are reciprocated. And it is as a friend that I say to you that marriage to your Captain Singh would be a dreadful mistake."

Arabella felt her jaw tighten, but strove to keep her tone civil. "I do respect you, Lady Corey, and I do feel kindly toward you, to some extent even friendly. But I do not count your disparagement of the man I love as a friendly gesture." Even as Lady Corey drew breath to reply, Arabella continued to speak. "You spoke of the trials through which we have suffered together. Let me remind you that, apart from this recent episode with the wind-whales, Captain Singh was with both of us through every one of those trials, and with me for many more beforehand. Can you not understand the depths of my sentiments toward him?"

"Love," Lady Corey replied with a severe mien, "is a luxury that women of our station can ill afford. You must consider your family—not only your brother and the rest of your household, but your children!"

"I cannot imagine any better father for my children than Captain Singh. He is calm, caring, and exceedingly intelligent." Even as she spoke she felt her throat tighten; considering her captain's many fine qualities only reminded her how very much she missed him, and how she feared for his safety.

"I do not argue his intelligence and sincerity, but—my dear, besotted child—consider his *color*! Surely you have already noted society's disapproval of this match."

"I have not encountered any such," Arabella shot back defensively—though the captain himself had nearly declined her proposal for that very reason, being dissuaded from his refusal only by Aadim's intervention at the last moment.

"Then you are more blind than I had thought," Lady Corey sniffed. "Open your eyes, child, and your ears, and you will understand that by openly consorting with a person of his . . . kind, you are already bringing discredit to your family. Your brother has been entirely too forgiving of this. If you are so foolish as to carry through with this marriage the opprobrium will be inescapable. And your children—I beg of you, think of the children! They will be *black*!"

Throughout this harangue Arabella had only listened, teeth clenched and anger rising, but now she was forced to reply. "I would rather they be black as coal than that they be as small and petty as *you*." She gathered up her books and papers and prepared to depart the cabin. She had no idea where else she could go, or how she would endure the remaining months of the voyage in this woman's inescapable company, but for now she could no longer remain here.

But Lady Corey put out a hand and grasped Arabella's sleeve. "Consider the children!" she repeated. "Can you imagine the suffering they will be forced to endure? They will never fit in any where, and will certainly never be accepted into polite society."

"A society which rejects children with a father as fine as Captain Prakash Singh cannot be described as polite, or even civil!" She paused in her preparations, a large chart-book stuffed with scraps of notes clutched to her bosom; her heart thudded against the leather cover. "My *dear* Lady Corey," she said with icy politesse, "I may be a wild child—a provincial, unsophisticated colonial, raised in the desert and unsuitable for proper society—but my upbringing has given me a unique perspective." With a slight tap of her toes upon the deck she propelled herself gently upward, until she seemed to be looking down upon the older woman from a considerable height. "I have lived among Martians, among airmen, and among the gentry, and of the three the gentry are those whose company, and whose favor, I crave the least. They have no sense of *okhaya*. They have no respect for hard work and skill. And those qualities they *do* respect amount to nothing more than inconsequential differences of breeding, manner, speech, and, yes, *color,* which in the larger world amount to nothing more than decorative frippery." She bent at the waist, bringing her face to within inches of Lady Corey's. "The solar system includes not just the several races of man, but many distinct tribes of Martians, a whole planet of Venusians, and the dear Lord knows how many other races in the chill regions beyond the asteroids. In a world of such grand variety, the tiny difference between a human man of one color and a human man of another is as *nothing!*" She straightened and opened the door, preparing to depart.

But it was Lady Corey who had the last word. "Your 'perspective,' as you put it, is indeed . . . unique. But you will find, as you make your way in the world, that the favor and influence of society can either smooth or hinder your path. If you close that door"—she indicated the door upon whose handle Arabella's hand rested—"you will be closing yourself off from opportunities you can ill afford to forego."

Arabella did not trust herself to frame a civil reply. She closed the door without a word.

Still clutching the chart-book, eyes blinded by tears, Arabella drifted up the companion ladder to the ward-room. There she was forced to confront the confusion she had left in her wake, with tools and papers and bits of clockwork scattered everywhere. She was amazed that the officers had never reproved her upon the disorder in which she had left their eating-area.

But the disorder here was nothing compared to the horrific shambles she had just made of her life. Through willful obstinacy she had alienated her chaperone—the only other woman on the ship, and the one person here who was meant to be her ally and protector—and was now left without even a place to sleep.

Where could she go now? Some instinct remaining from her

days aboard *Diana* impelled her toward the captain's cabin; but Fox was not Captain Singh, and if she were to go to him with her troubles, she would find in the end, she was sure, nothing but ruin. And though she cared little for the opinions of polite society—as she had just told Lady Corey in no uncertain terms—in this case she knew that ruin would cost her own self-respect as well.

The other officers were, even after weeks in the air, an unknown quantity to her. She and Lady Corey had taken their meals in their cabin at first; later, though she had spent most of each day in the ward-room, she had been so thoroughly preoccupied by the work on her navigational mechanism that she had barely noticed the men who dined at the other end of the table. Liddon she knew slightly, but she considered him little more than an extension of his captain.

That left the men, whom she knew even less well than the officers, but who counted among their number Gowse and Mills.

At that thought she clutched the chart-book and cried still harder, for she felt she was in no position to call upon her former shipmates. After the incident with Mills and the drum she had held herself aloof from the crew, giving them only a polite nod when encountering them on deck. Lady Corey's omnipresence had given her little choice in the matter, but after so long a time of enforced formality she had surely lost whatever fellow-feeling might once have existed between herself and the ship's ordinary people.

She had truly fallen between two stools—too lowly for her chaperone and too lofty for her shipmates.

How she missed her captain!

———————

Eventually a polite knock upon the door roused her from her self-absorbed misery. It was Brindle, the captain's Negro steward. "Excuse me, miss," he said, twisting his cap in his hands. "It's past time for me to be settin' up for the officers' supper. I don't mean to disturb you and all, but . . ."

"No, no, that is quite all right," Arabella said, sniffing and wiping her eyes with a handkerchief. "I will . . . I will move elsewhere."

She left the chart-book with her other papers. The officers had been stepping around them for weeks, and one more book, however large, would not make that situation any worse.

Bereft of any plan, she drifted out on deck. The air was still, the ship being again well embedded in the Simpson Current, and already carried an oppressive warm dampness which would only grow worse as they drew nearer Venus. The sky in all directions was hazy and spotted with ill-defined clouds, with nary a bird, never mind a wind-whale, to distract the eye. Airmen drifted here and there in the rigging, no doubt inspecting and mending the sails and sheets.

Arabella pushed off from the mainmast and caught herself on the larboard rail, looking over it and along the length of the larboard mast. Unlike three-masted *Diana,* whose starboard and larboard masts extended downward from her hull at an angle, four-masted *Touchstone*'s starboard and larboard masts extended directly out to either side, parallel with the deck. Here, too, airmen picked their way like spiders along the delicate tracery of the rigging.

Somewhere below, obscured from Arabella by the bulk of the ship, lay the mizzen-mast, pointing straight down. This mast, which *Diana* lacked, was a mystery to Arabella—in all her weeks aboard, she had never even seen it.

Arabella glanced to either side, finding no one paying any attention to her, then swung herself over the rail and pushed downward.

Sailing down the ship's side, scarred *khoresh*-wood drifting past her nose and nothing but air beside and behind her, felt familiar and yet strange—familiar from her time aboard *Diana,* and strange because of the many months that had passed since then, the skirts that ballooned about her lower half, and the knowledge that she was disobeying convention if not direct orders.

She was taking a risk, she supposed, but it was one she had taken hundreds of times during her service aboard *Diana,* and neither she nor any of her shipmates had suffered any harm. While embedded in a major current such as the Simpson, cross-currents were very rare, and for an airman to drift beyond the length of a thrown line before coming to the attention of the watch on deck was practically unheard-of.

After a brief delicious free flight, she fetched up against the base of the larboard mast. Guiding herself along with brief touches on the mast and rigging, she made her way along the length of the mast to the larboard top-yard, or second horizontal spar—though, of course, relative to the ship, the larboard mast's yards ran vertically. From here she could see Venus and Jupiter, lost below the ship's hull from the deck, but more importantly she had a different view of the ship. Seen in profile, *Touchstone* seemed more handsome than she did from the deck, where her worn and much-varnished wood showed her age and the wooden pegs she used as cleats—by contrast with *Diana*'s polished brass—demonstrated her lack of quality. But as viewed from the larboard mast, with her mainmast standing proud and harlequin figurehead shining in the sun, she looked a noble vessel, a fighting ship well braced for any eventuality.

Arabella turned her attention downward, where the furled mizzen-t'gallant had just come into view and a blue pennant swirled languidly from the mast-head. Tempting though it was to leap directly toward it, the swish of her dress about her lower limbs reminded her that her skills might have withered from months of disuse.

Making her way cautiously from yard to mast to shroud to spar to halyard by short, yet exhilarating jumps, with one long brave spring from the lower larboard-shroud to the larboard mizzen-shroud, she soon attained the mizzen-top. There she paused to catch her breath, as her lungs were heaving from the unaccustomed exertion.

The world seemed to have inverted itself. From this vantage the Southern Cross seemed overhead, and Polaris below her feet. This sense of inversion persisted despite her positioning; when she turned herself about so that her head was closer to the hull, she felt as though she were hanging by her heels with the body of the ship below her. A peculiar sensation, despite her experience with free descent. Perhaps the ship's bulk exerted some influence upon the planet-bound experience of her mind.

Looking upward, or perhaps downward, from the top, she saw the ship as a long smooth form, her copper bottom gleaming in the sun. From this viewpoint—lacking the complications of hatches, binnacles, cleats, and rails—the ship seemed almost a living thing, a creature born to the air, her sleek hull somewhat resembling the wind-whales' muscular bodies.

"Ashby!" came a call, and she glanced down, or perhaps up, toward the pennant at the mizzen-peak. It was a familiar form that flew toward her—a dark muscular body and smooth bald head, the face split with a shining white smile. Mills!

Mills shot to her side with remarkable speed, bringing himself to an expert halt with one assured hand. She envied his ability—she had never been as accomplished even in her prime, and much of what skill she had once owned had evaporated from months of disuse—and also his shirtlessness, the sweat gleaming on the curves of his shoulders. Her own shoulders were already uncomfortable beneath clinging fabric, and she knew from her experience of an English summer that the discomfort would only grow worse as the heat increased.

She had to check herself from gripping his hand as an old

shipmate would. "Mills," she said instead with a proper midair curtsey. "How delightful to see you again."

"The same," he replied with an unpracticed but clearly sincerely-meant bow. "Would have hailed you on deck, but . . ." He shrugged and gestured downward meaningfully.

"I know," she said. "The deck is a different world from the tops, or even the waist." She sighed. "My chaperone thought it improper for me to be seen conversing with ordinary airmen, even my own former shipmates."

He frowned. "Should not be here, miss."

Arabella felt her own face falling into a matching expression. "I should not be any where, it seems. I cannot be seen with the men, the ward-room is engaged, I will not consort with the captain, and I have argued with my chaperone."

"What about?"

She sighed. "She thinks your Captain Fox would be a better match for me than Captain Singh."

At that Mills laughed aloud, a great booming "Ha ha ha!" that forced her to smile herself despite the gravity of her situation. "Oh, miss!" He wiped his eyes, then forced himself to serious-ness. "Captain Fox . . . a good man. Fine pilot, strong fighter. But no Captain Singh."

"I am glad you agree." But her pleasure at Mills's reassurance was short-lived. "However, Lady Corey raises a point I fear may be correct. She says that society will never truly accept him, or any children we may have, on account of their color." Even as she spoke the words she realized their impropriety. "Oh! I beg your pardon."

Mills waved her pardon aside. "It *is* hard, to be a black man." He turned his shoulder to her, pointing to his back, and for the first time she saw the scars that crisscrossed it. Aboard *Diana*, Mills had always kept his shirt on, and now she knew why.

"However can you serve with white crewmates?" she cried, shocked and appalled. "After white men did this to—"

He held up one broad pink palm to stop her words. "Not *only* whites, miss." The expression that came upon his face as he spoke those words was complex—troubled and regretful and bitter all at once—and though she longed to know more, the look in his eyes did not invite questions. "No race—no *man*—all good *or* all bad. A bad man . . . can be a good man." At her confused expression he closed his eyes, shook his head, held up a hand again. "Sorry, sorry." When his eyes reopened—dark, dark brown eyes with pale yellow whites—they fixed themselves on hers with deep sincerity. "What I mean . . . people is people. White, black—all *people*, with good and bad mixed in. Have to look for the good in every one."

"I . . . I see." She looked past Mills toward the Sun—Venus, their destination, was lost in the glare—and considered his words. "You have given me much to think about. I thank you for your counsel, Mr. Mills."

"Just Mills," he replied, deferring the title. Then he grinned. "Ashby."

Arabella returned the grin. "Mills."

They hung there in the air for a little while, admiring the view.

8

CROSSING THE LINE

Thirteen days later, Arabella presented her course to Fox.

Fox floated before the navigational desk in the great cabin, brow wrinkled in stern concentration as he read through the many sheets of Arabella's sailing-plan, handing each page to Liddon after he had perused it. Heading, speed, timing, currents, pedaling, even the set of the sails—all were laid out in exquisite detail. She did not wish to permit him any leeway to either dismiss her course as insufficiently considered or to spoil its advantages through careless execution.

Lady Corey was there as well, fulfilling the demands of propriety. The two of them had barely spoken since their argument, dining separately and sharing their tiny sleeping cabin in tense silence.

Also occupying the cabin was Arabella's mechanism, now complete, housed in a handsome case constructed from Venusian greenwood by the ship's carpenter. The case's four vertical corners were carved in imitation of Corinthian columns, with a decorative egg-and-dart border along the upper edge; all was carefully varnished, and embellished with tasteful touches of gold leaf. The overall effect was slightly spoiled by the several mismatched clock faces and hands, the best Arabella had been able to find among the French clockmaker's stock, which dotted the sides and top at irregular spacing dictated by the underlying gears and cams. But each clock face and lever bore a tidily-lettered paper label, and—apart from an unfortunate tendency to jam—the device now functioned almost exactly as Arabella had hoped.

"Well," said Fox, breaking Arabella's train of thought, "it certainly is . . . unusual."

"I acknowledge this," Arabella replied with a modest declination of her head. "But I am prepared to stake not merely my reputation as a navigator but my fiancé's life upon it."

By the time Arabella's device had been sufficiently complete to assist in the calculations, the Vanderveer Current was entirely beyond reach, and indeed it had seemed for some days that their current course in the Simpson could not be bettered. But a sudden insight late in the second dog watch one evening had been confirmed by the device: the parallel Edmonds Current, though slower than the Simpson, would carry them to a point where, with careful timing and determined pedaling, they could transfer to a particularly rapid stream of the northern solar trade winds. Even with not one but two time-consuming transfers between currents, this course would bring them to Venus a full eleven days earlier than their current one.

If all went well.

"This course calls for . . . a *considerable* amount of pedaling," Fox said. "The men won't like that."

"I acknowledge this as well. To show my sincere dedication to the course, and my appreciation for their efforts, I intend to take full part in that pedaling myself. I hope that will help them to accept it."

"Rather than be out-pedaled by a mere female?" Fox remarked. Then he shook his head. "I absolutely forbid it. It would be unseemly."

"Are you concerned for propriety? On my previous voyage, Captain Singh rigged up a screen, to shield the men's eyes from any . . . indelicate exposure." Wordlessly she gestured downward, to the hidden lower limbs which seemed to hold some unearthly power over men's minds.

Fox's eyebrows shot up. "Captain Singh allowed you to pedal?"

"He *required* it. It is his opinion, which I share, that the exertion of pedaling prevents the weakness of the limbs which affects so many passengers—and *officers*, if I may add—after a long aerial voyage."

"This supposed 'weakness of the limbs,'" Fox harrumphed, "is nothing more than a demonstration of the heightened sensibilities of the more elevated classes."

"After my first voyage from Mars to Earth," Arabella persisted, "I was required to be carried from the ship, and could not even walk for days thereafter. After my return voyage, during which I pedaled along with the men, I was able not merely to walk but . . . but to engage in quite strenuous activity." A full account of the excitement during the Martian rebellion would have to wait for another time.

"It is well known that Mars's gravity is less burdensome than that of Earth," Fox countered.

"Reflect upon your own experiences, Captain," Arabella said. "Would you not rather, upon arrival in port, be able to disport yourself as you please, rather than take to your bed?" That argument clearly had influence, and she pressed it. "And upon arrival at Venus, immediate action may be required to free Captain Singh from prison . . . *and* wreak the desired havoc upon Napoleon. Would you not rather retain your full physical powers for that eventuality?"

As Arabella spoke, Fox's face showed that he was giving her point some consideration. But when she finished, he paused, firmed his jaw, and took a breath to deliver a stern and final rebuke.

At that moment, to Arabella's astonishment, Lady Corey spoke up. "I should like to take a turn at the pedals myself."

"My *lady*?" Fox sputtered.

"I insist upon it," she said, raising her chin. "Although it has been many years since I have undertaken an aerial journey myself, I have frequently observed the debilitation wreaked upon the limbs of recent arrivals by the long voyage from Earth to Mars. Indeed, some . . . some women of a certain age find that they never completely recover their powers." Her gaze upon Fox's face was firm and unyielding. "If I am to serve as a proper chaperone to this . . . headstrong young woman, I must take any step, however distasteful, to retain my capacities."

Fox, nonplussed, glanced from Lady Corey to Arabella to Liddon. "Miss Ashby may have a point, sir," Liddon said. "I wouldn't mind being able to, ah, *disport* myself in port, the way I did when I was a foremast jack." He shook off an apparently pleasant memory and shrugged his shoulders. "It's worth a try, sir."

Fox gritted his teeth and blew out a breath through his nose. "I suppose I must defer to my betters in this," he growled, nodding to Lady Corey, who returned the acknowledgement with more grace than it deserved. "But the *course*, Liddon. What think you of the *course*?"

Liddon paged through the sailing-plan. "It is unusual, as you said, sir. I've never seen the like. And these transfers could be tricky." He tapped the page. "But with every man, and woman I suppose, pedaling, and the help of the greenwood box"—he gestured to Arabella's device—"I don't see that we can't do it."

"And would it save as much time as she theorizes?"

Again Liddon shrugged. "Hard to say, sir, but it might. It's certainly no worse than our current course." To Fox's hurt expression he added, "The box did get us past the whales, sir."

Fox rolled his eyes upward, spread his hands, and said, "Very well. Bound as I am by my own sense of honor, I assent to this course, and to the use of the"—he cast a disparaging glance at Arabella's mechanism—"greenwood box, in its execution." Arabella suppressed a smile of triumph. "But I must state my skepticism as to its success."

Arabella gave Fox a properly deferential and appreciative curtsey. "You have my thanks, Captain," she said, "and Mr. Liddon. I assure you that you will not regret this decision."

There followed some discussion of the details of the course, at the conclusion of which they all took their leave of each other. But as Arabella approached the door, Fox murmured to her, "I shall enjoy our dinner."

She gave him a predatory grin. "You had best begin preparing that certificate now, sir."

As they prepared for bed that night, Arabella cleared her throat. "I . . . I would like to thank you for your support this afternoon," she managed at last. "I am certain that it made all the difference in Mr. Fox's decision."

In response, Lady Corey fixed her with a cold gray eye. "It was only that I could not bear the thought of that man's smug face if he bested you in that argument." Then she sighed, and for a time she seemed to be studying the gently whirring clockwork mechanism that kept the lamp alight in free descent. "I will grant you this, child," she said at last. "Though your judgement, perhaps, leaves something to be desired, your strength of will is admirable. It will serve you well in later life . . . especially if you learn to *moderate* it when the dictates of propriety demand."

Arabella chose to accept this statement as a grudging compliment. "Thank you, my lady," she said. "Good night."

"Good night, dear," Lady Corey replied, and extinguished the lamp.

Grimly, Arabella pedaled on.

Her view this day, as it had been nearly every waking hour for the last five days, was limited: a rather shabby dressing-screen, the wooden handle before her, and the drawers straining across Lady Corey's substantial fundament. The smell, too, was the same—the still, stale funk of sixty perspiring privateersmen, overlaid with that of *Touchstone*'s aged timbers, generations of boiled salt beef, and the sting of gunpowder and slow-match. And the sound: the unceasing beat of the drum, the grunt and wheeze of the airmen as they labored, and the creak and slap of the wooden chain that transmitted their efforts to the whirling pulsers abaft. She ached every where, from her callused hands to the bruised arches of her feet.

At the moment, when she thought back on that meeting with Captain Fox, it was with more regret than triumph. But with every painful stroke of her legs she helped to drive the ship more rapidly toward Venus, and toward her beloved captain. Even a single day, she reminded herself, might make a difference.

And so she pedaled, and pedaled, and strove to ignore the perspiration that, in this blighted state of free descent, clung tenaciously to every part of her skin rather than running down as God intended.

Suddenly there came a snap and a clatter, and Arabella's legs whirled against an unexpected lack of resistance, sending her upper body lurching forward so that she nearly struck her nose against the handle. Shouts and curses accompanied the event, along with a low grinding and scraping that echoed through the old ship's timbers.

The chain had broken, again.

Arabella's feelings at the event were mixed. Annoyance was uppermost—annoyance at *Touchstone*'s poor state of repair, at the repeated failures and delays, and most especially at anticipation of Fox's smug grin. For it seemed that in Fox's mind every problem, difficulty, or unanticipated occurrence in their voyage could now be laid at Arabella's feet. *We would not be facing the necessity of repairing the chain so frequently,* he would surely say, *did this course not call for such extravagant quantities of pedaling.* But beneath the annoyance lay a strong undertone of worry, that he might in fact be correct—that she should have tempered her sailing-plan with greater consideration to the ship's and the men's capabilities, and that her lack of consideration might in fact cause the trip to take more time rather than less. And beneath *that*, undeniably, lay a feeling of relief, at the respite she would have while the chain was repaired.

"Oh, dear," gasped Lady Corey. "My . . . my drawers, they seem to be caught again."

Arabella drew one last sip from her leather water-bag, then left the empty bag rotating in the air as she drifted over to help the older woman. One Venusian silk flounce was, indeed, caught in the pedal mechanism. "If you would, please, pedal backward a bit," she said.

After they had freed the garment from the gears, Lady Corey bent one leg to inspect the grimy and tattered flounce. "Oh dear, oh dear," she repeated. "Ruined, simply ruined. And this was my last good pair." Her traveling cases, though enormous and filled to capacity, had included only three pair of underdrawers, and those only at Arabella's very stern insistence. Arabella herself had brought fourteen pantalettes of sturdy Egyptian cotton.

"Perhaps the sailmaker can repair them," Arabella offered. Aboard *Diana* the sailmaker's stores had included quantities of fine Venusian silk, in case repairs were required to the ship's balloon envelope.

"Oh no, I *could* not!" Lady Corey replied, pressing her hands to her cheeks in shock at the very suggestion. "I would absolutely *die* of embarrassment."

From the other side of the screen—it had been looted from a French merchantman, but, being too worn for resale, had served various purposes aboard *Touchstone* before being pressed into this service—came a decorous clearing of a throat. "Begging the ladies' pardon," came Liddon's voice, "but the carpenter says the chain is jammed in the channel and it may be some hours."

Arabella's mixed feelings of annoyance, worry, and relief all rose higher, but she strove to keep her voice level and polite. "Thank you, sir. We shall make ourselves presentable and be out shortly."

Dressing in the close confines of the screened enclosure was even more difficult than in the cabin, especially as they were both attempting to do so at the same time, and was complicated by Lady Corey's vain attempt to hide the damage to her drawers. The short length of her shift and the near-transparency of her dress made that task nearly impossible. "I suppose I must cut the flounce off," she muttered.

"The men will take no notice!" Arabella protested. "Leave it as it is. The stain may wash out, and I can take a needle to the tears."

Lady Corey seemed to be about to protest, but then caught herself. "Thank you, child. It is just so difficult to survive without proper servants."

Eventually they clothed themselves and the screens were taken away, revealing a hold already nearly empty of men. "You see?" Arabella said. "There was in any case nothing to fear."

But Lady Corey, still clutching at the fabric of her dress in an attempt to obscure the damage, was not comforted. "A lady must always comport herself properly, even in private."

"I must confess myself amazed," Arabella said as they floated up the ladder toward their cabin, "that you persist in pedaling despite the hardships it engenders. And I thank you once again for your support in this area."

"You are most welcome," Lady Corey said. "A chaperone's task is to defend her charge as well as advise her. And, though I am ignorant as regards the art of aerial navigation, it seemed to me that you had the right of it and the captain's objections should not go unchallenged. Also, as I said, it seems that my own well-being may depend upon this . . . exertion." She fanned herself fruitlessly with one hand. "Though I often question my own judgement in this."

"You will be thankful when we arrive at Venus and you are able to walk from the ship, rather than being carried in a sedan chair."

Lady Corey smiled ruefully. "I suppose. Though a sedan chair does sound wonderful just now."

The long days of pedaling to reach the Edmonds Current were followed by many weeks of serene sailing therein, then another stretch of pedaling to achieve the northern trades. The transfer to the trade wind was an occasion of some excitement, and certainly trepidation upon Arabella's part, but with the help of the greenwood box and the skill of Fox and his men the tricky insertion into the faster current was achieved with little more than a shudder and rattle of the sails. After that Arabella's days consisted of little more than reading, conversation, and increasing discomfort as they drew ever nearer the Sun. The stars and planets continued in their eternal courses, each day's observations confirming the ship's rapid progress, and the endless round of meals emphasized the sameness of the days.

In the middle of one such day Arabella was relaxing—as best she could in the sodden heat—on the poop-deck, when a sudden commotion of happy voices drew her attention. She closed her book, stowed it in her reticule, and drifted aft to discover the source of the sound.

She found a scene of hilarious gaiety, a stream of airmen emerging from belowdecks with broad smiles, clapping of hands, and rowdy cheers. Many of them wore colorful ribbons in their hair—the effect reminded her of the ribbons with which the warriors of Sor Khoresh adorned their helmets—and some played upon tambourines, bells, and even a concertina, adding up to a great profusion of happy noise. As they emerged from the companionway, they formed up in two ragged lines along the deck, continuing to clap and shout as their fellows paraded out to join them. Even those on duty in the rigging above participated in the hilarity, waving and hooting and turning somersaults in the air.

Of Captain Fox there was no sign, which struck Arabella as odd.

Soon nearly the entire watch below had paraded up the companion ladder and assembled themselves in line, continuing to applaud and to jest with one another as they gazed toward the hatch with apparent rapt anticipation. Several of them, she noted, also cast frequent glances toward herself, and toward Lady Corey, who had also been drawn out on deck by the clamor—but the meaning of these glances she could not discern.

After some moments of comparative quiet, the tumult rose up again, first with happy shouts from belowdecks, then with laughter and applause from those closest to the hatch. Then the cause of this laughter appeared: it was Gowse, captain of the afterguard, yet costumed and caparisoned as she had never seen him before.

Gowse was bare-chested, but the sun-darkened skin of his

chest and arms was painted with some green substance so that he appeared as some ancient statue encrusted in verdigris. His trousers, too, were dyed green. His face was obscured by a great spade-like artificial beard, crafted of oakum and likewise stained green, and his head and waist were festooned with plaited vines of brown cordage with green paper leaves. In one hand he carried a baton of *khoresh*-wood, crudely carved into the shape of a lightning bolt.

"I am Uranus!" Gowse called, waving his lightning bolt. The crew laughed heartily at this, but Arabella merely rolled her eyes at the tired, vulgar joke of pronouncing the god's name as "your a—s" rather than the correct "*yoor*-a-noos." When the laughter subsided, he continued. "I am Uranus," he repeated, "god of the sky! Bow unto me!" The men all did so, though with much laughter and no real respect. "But more important, this day, is that I am husband to Gaia, goddess of the Earth!" Applause at this. "And why is this day so important?" To this men shouted back "Why? Why?" and "Tell us, Your A—s!" and such like. Gowse smiled widely, clearly relishing the occasion and his role in it, and replied, "This is the day our ship—I mean, *your* ship, crosses the orbit of the planet Earth! This line in the sky, invisible though it may be, is sacred to Gaia, and here we, the gods, have installed a sort of turn-pike gate, which none may cross without paying a toll!" Somewhat to Arabella's surprise, vigorous applause greeted this announcement.

"Each of you," Gowse-as-Uranus continued, pointing around at the gathered men, "must pay according to your station. From the airmen, a penny. From the officers and idlers, a shilling. And from the passengers, half a crown!" At this announcement many men turned with broad grins to Arabella and Lady Corey, the only passengers, who looked at each other with some concern. "Failure to pay the toll risks incurring . . . *the wrath of the gods!*" This last he bellowed with considerable enthusiasm, brandishing his lightning bolt and shaking his head so that the oakum beard and paper leaves rattled—so vigorously, indeed, that he nearly lost both beard and garland, engendering still more laughter.

The whole situation was so ludicrous that, despite the unanticipated demand for payment, Arabella was quite caught up in the gaiety and laughed and applauded along with the men.

As the laughter died down, some of the men began to call "Gaia!" Others took up the call, and it soon became a rhythmic chant: "Gai-a! Gai-a! Gai-a!" They clapped their hands and rattled their tambourines, and such was their enthusiasm and clear anticipation that even Lady Corey smiled and clapped in genteel fashion.

"Very well!" Gowse cried out, raising both hands to silence the chant. "Because of your fond entreaties, the lady Gaia—our own Mother Earth—will deign to board your puny ship and accept the toll herself!" The men clapped and cheered, with many hoots and still more vigorous rattling of tambourines. "Lady Gaia!" Gowse called down the companion hatch. "Come aboard!"

The figure that sailed up from the hatch, to a mighty roar of laughter and applause, was just as green as Gowse and even more fantastical. A long, flowing dress of green-stained Venusian silk . . . even more plaits and garlands of artificial vines and laurels than Gowse bore . . . an enormous frizzled wig of green-dyed oakum . . . two enormous breadfruits stuffed into the front of the dress, bobbing and wobbling in free descent . . .

. . . and atop it all, green-painted and split with a broad white grin, the face of Captain Fox!

"*Gaia! Gaia!*" cried the men, laughing hysterically and casting themselves down in mock supplication.

"Gentle mortals!" Fox cried in a broad falsetto. "I welcome you to My domain! All are welcome within the orbit of Earth . . . yet the toll must be paid to ensure My favor!" From between his breadfruits, with a great grunting effort that caused much hilarity, he drew a burlap sack. "Pay now, or endure My wrath!"

Fox went from man to man to man, holding forth his rattling sack like a mendicant on Guy Fawkes Night, and each man put in his penny or shilling, with which they had plainly equipped themselves in anticipation of this moment. A few men, with downcast eyes, merely pantomimed payment, drawing an empty hand from a pocket and gesturing at the sack's mouth, and with these Fox dropped the Gaia pretense, making clear with his eyes that he understood their situation and bore them no ill will.

At last Fox-as-Gaia came to Arabella, smelling of sweat and tarry oakum and the coppery scent of the green paint, and his wide grin relaxed into a more serious expression. "It is a long-standing custom," he murmured low, in his own voice. "The money goes to buy drinks for the men."

"I quite understand," said Arabella, and from her reticule she drew a half crown and put it in the sack. Lady Corey paid as well, though not quite so happily.

Fox nodded and winked at the ladies and, with a gentle push of one foot against the deck, propelled himself into the air above them, catching himself upon a backstay. There he pulled shut the sack's drawstring, and with even greater effort—engendering still more laughter—crammed the now-full sack between his bread-fruits. "We thank you, gentle mortals!" he called, the falsetto now rather ragged. "Now we, the gods, must return to our demesne! Be ye welcome within the orbit of Earth, and good fortune to you!" With that he reversed himself in the air and, propelling himself off the backstay with a low twang, shot belowdecks to grand applause and a renewed chant of "Gai-a! Gai-a! Gai-a!" Gowse, too, bowed and took his leave, though not so ostentatiously.

Liddon now leapt to the quarterdeck rail and addressed the men. "All right, lads," he called, "you've had your fun, now back to work." But there was no rancor in it, and the men smiled and called "Aye aye!" Then Liddon winked. "Whiskey at eight bells!" he cried, and the men applauded, then dispersed to their stations with amiable chatter. Some of them glanced toward Arabella with slight apprehension as they passed; she smiled and nodded in reassurance.

"That was . . . quite a spectacle," Lady Corey said to Arabella.

"One of the more entertaining performances I have had the good fortune to experience," Arabella replied. "Well worth the price of admission."

"I am not certain I would go so far. But it did no harm, I suppose."

At that moment Fox returned to the deck, receiving a smattering of applause to which he bowed in acknowledgement. He had resumed his habitual clothing, though his face still bore traces of green paint. After consulting with Liddon and the officer of the watch on the state of the ship, he came over to the two women. "I am told," he said with a small self-satisfied grin, "that while I was . . . asleep in my cabin, we received a visitation from the gods of Sky and Earth. May I trust that you ladies were appropriately deferent?"

"We gave the gods every obeisance they deserved," Arabella replied with a matching small smile, which drew a smirk from Lady Corey. "May we expect that, now that the gods have been suitably appeased, the rest of the voyage will be without untoward incident?"

"I certainly hope so," Fox said. His smile did not vanish completely, but it became more contemplative. "I certainly hope so."

9

FLEUR DE LYS

After they passed within the orbit of the Earth, the tedium of the previous days resumed, to which was added the discomfort of still greater heat. Though *Touchstone* was now embedded in a mighty current, rushing toward Venus at just over eleven thousand knots, relative to the ship the air did not move, lying upon Arabella like a steaming towel hot from the wash-tub. The heat was already worse than any English summer day she had experienced, and as they drew still nearer the Sun she knew it would grow even hotter. And the days ran on and on, endlessly unchanging.

And then, one Wednesday, the lookout at the bowsprit called "Sail ho! On deck there, sail ho!"

Every one rushed to the bow for a better view—including Lady Corey, eager for any distraction from the tedium of endless travel, and Arabella with her. Fox sprang directly from the quarterdeck, shouting "Clear the way, there!" as he sailed the length of the ship, neatly dodging the mainmast and all its lines, before catching himself on the poop-rail. Even before he had properly come to a halt, he had drawn a spyglass from his pocket and brought it to his eye.

Arabella, for her part, squinted into the Sun, shading her eyes with a hand. The distant sail lay very near the Sun, and she feared for the captain's eyesight.

"Oh ho," muttered Fox, a low satisfied chuckle. "Oh ho ho *ho!*" He clapped the spyglass shut, turned aft, and called, "Mr. Liddon! Set a course to close, and pipe the watch below to the pedals!"

"Aye aye, sir!" came the immediate, and obviously quite pleased, reply. This was followed by a rapid stream of commands and piping which roused the crew to eager action.

"What have we, Captain?" asked Lady Corey, speaking before Arabella could ask the same question.

"French merchantman, I do believe. And on this course, at this season, she'll be heavy with Parisian luxuries bound for Bonaparte's Venusian colonies." He nodded to Arabella. "We have *you* to thank for this opportunity, Miss Ashby. We would most likely never have found such a rich prize on our original course."

But Fox's acknowledgement only made Arabella's heart fall. "My course was meant only to bring us to Venus more quickly, sir. I did not intend . . . rapine!"

Fox spread his hands. "*Touchstone* is a privateer, miss. Our letters of marque and reprisal not only permit but *command* us to subdue, seize, and take any French vessel we may encounter."

His words brought to mind a previous encounter between a privateer and a merchantman—one in which a French corsair had disabled *Diana* and nearly killed her captain—and brought the smell of gunpowder and blood strongly to memory. "I wish you would not, sir. You know that my need to reach Venus is exceptionally pressing."

Fox nodded. "I understand your reluctance. But I must give

chase. If I did not, the men would be sorely disappointed to be deprived of such an opportunity to enrich themselves at the expense of the Ogre of Paris. *Sorely* disappointed." He pointed to himself, then drew a finger across his throat. "If you catch my meaning. And, though I am loath to confess it"—his eyes and his mouth turned downward with reluctance—"I would welcome the assistance of yourself and your greenwood box in the enterprise."

Despite Fox's tacit acknowledgement of her navigational superiority—the first such she had received from him—Arabella was appalled. "I will *not* participate in such a barbarous action!"

"Your delicate sensibilities do you credit." He inclined his head to her. "I ask only because I suspect your navigation would increase our chances of success and reduce the time required for the chase and capture. However, I am entirely prepared to proceed without you; I have, as I am sure you are aware, carried out many such actions with nothing more than compass and sextant and my own crude methods."

Arabella's heart thudded in her chest. "How much time do you anticipate this action will require?"

Fox returned the spyglass to his eye and contemplated the distant ship. "Some days, I should imagine. Less, if she proves unworthy of our attentions. More, if she proves too stout a fish for our line." He lowered the glass. "Some merchantmen put up more of a fight than others."

"Indeed," she said, recalling the smell of blood and gunpowder, and a storm of deadly splinters. "I beg of you, sir, leave off this chase, for your own sake as well as that of human decency."

"I *am* sorry, Miss Ashby, but I may not. Now, if the two of you will excuse me, I have an attack to plan. May I assume you will not be pedaling?"

"I will *not*," Arabella snapped. Lady Corey's reply was only a cold stare.

"Very well." He bowed to both of them and departed.

The octuple crash of the great guns assaulted Arabella's hearing yet again, and she pushed the wax balls into her ears more firmly. Even so, she could not fail to hear the cheers that followed—the cannonballs must have successfully demolished the floating target.

Touchstone's crew, those not laboring at the pedals, had been drilling and drilling for days. The exercise, she knew, was intended to intimidate the French merchantman—growing nearer hour by hour, and already plainly visible to the naked eye—as well as to sharpen the men's speed and accuracy with the great guns. The prey, for her part, was doing the same, the triple pops of her cannon clearly audible in the intervals between Fox's drills. Her pulsers, too, whirled day and night, but *Touchstone* was a predator, built for speed and manned with a large and enthusiastic crew; that she would intercept the merchantman seemed a foregone conclusion.

Another horrific *bang* interrupted Arabella's concentration— they were coming more frequently now, indicating that the men were indeed improving—and again the impulse of the shot made every unsecured thing in the cabin lurch toward the forward bulkhead, including the book she was reading. She grasped the book as it tried to float away, and repositioned it in the air before her tired eyes.

It was a book of aerial navigation, open to the chapter on ship-to-ship combat.

She hated herself for studying it. The mere thought of partici-pating in any way in a vicious, unprovoked attack upon an innocent merchantman—the very type of attack which had nearly cost her captain's life—was abhorrent to her. Yet study it she did, for the thought of losing her life or liberty in an unsuccessful attack, and as a result being separated from her fiancé for years or even for ever, was still more abhorrent. If there were any way for her to ensure victory for *Touchstone,* she owed it to her captain to discover it.

It was a brutal, savage business, and only Fox's repeated assurances—and, obviously, survival to this point—gave her any reason at all to hope that such a battle could truly be won. "The key to successful privateering," he had said over supper the previous evening, "is for both captains to properly understand the balance of forces before the engagement begins. Only a foolish privateer, obviously, would even approach an obviously superior merchantman. And when approached by an obviously superior privateer, a merchant captain will generally strike his colors rather than suffer destruction. It is only when *both* captains believe themselves superior that a protracted battle occurs."

Fox seemed confident that the coming encounter would be resolved rapidly, bloodlessly, and in his favor.

Yet still both ships continued to drill.

Hours passed. Arabella's eyes grew bleary from relentless reading, and her ears rang from the endless practice of the great guns, yet still she pressed herself to comprehend the problem.

She had shifted her station to the captain's cabin, where the greenwood box rested, while Fox occupied himself on the quarterdeck, directing his men in their preparations for battle. Again and again she set the dials; turned the key; released the lever; endured the endless wait while the device performed its calculations; and transcribed the result into her commonplace-book. All the while she fanned herself against the cabin's stultifying heat.

Not infrequently did she wonder why she was even bothering. How could she, a novice navigator who had experienced only a single action, have the audacity to think that she might devise a stratagem that had eluded the minds of centuries of experienced airmen? Yet something—some nebulous concept, born of her reading and her direct experience—had taken hold of her mind and would not let go. It was as though there were a word on the tip of her tongue, or a memory just beyond recollection. And so she tried one idea after another, using the greenwood box to calculate the application of each, and discarded each as it proved impractical.

Again and again she returned to the incident with the windwhales, when the box had returned the impossible negative result which had saved them from the great bull whale. Some combination of forward and backward pulsers, some set of the sails, would—she was certain—provide a new and unanticipated tactic that . . .

The whirring of the gears halted with a definitive click, interrupting her thoughts, and she inspected the device's dials. This combination was different from any she had seen before, and at first she was distressed. Had she, in her distracted state, set the dials incorrectly? She reviewed her notes, examined the result again. No, all seemed in order, though unconventional in the extreme.

She translated the set of the mechanism's hands into a detailed sailing-plan. By now the calculations were second nature.

She inspected her own written result.

The whole maneuver lay as clear in her mind as though she were witnessing it spread out in the air before her. Drive forward at full speed, set main and mizzen sails hard a-larboard, pause, *then* back pulsers, while at the same time sheeting home starboard and larboard topsails. The imagined ship spun in the air, yawing and rolling simultaneously in a twisted corkscrew motion, and in a twinkling had reversed herself, swapping head for stern in less than three ship's lengths.

Properly applied, it would permit *Touchstone* to shoot past the prey, whirl about, and demolish her pulsers in the opening moments of the battle.

It was, she reflected, nearly insane to tumble in two dimensions simultaneously while driving forward at speed—certainly something no conventional navigator would ever have devised. Yet she, through dogged and perhaps naive persistence and with the help of the greenwood box, had stumbled upon it.

It would be dizzying in the extreme to perform, and would require the most particular coordination between pulsers, sails, and cannon. Yet *Touchstone* and her crew were, she was certain, capable of it.

But would it be moral for her to tell Fox about it?

A rapid victory would reduce or even eliminate the loss of life. But if she were wrong—if she had overlooked some flaw in her tactic—or if Fox and his crew failed in its execution, it might lead to disaster. Or, perhaps even worse, if it were successful . . . it might encourage Fox to seek out more opportunities for depredation, delaying their arrival at Venus still further.

Staring at the dials, she blew out a breath. She had succeeded in devising a unique stratagem. But what should she do with it?

"Ought we not go below?" Lady Corey said. Arabella could not recall ever having heard her so anxious.

"You may if you wish," Arabella replied, struggling to keep the tremor out of her own voice. "But I will remain here on deck." They were, she felt, in a reasonably protected location, in the ship's waist.

In the rigging above them airmen floated, one arm or leg hooked around a sheet or halyard, staring forward with grim concentration and ready to leap into action at a moment's notice. They were all properly dressed in shirts and trousers; whether this was for protection in the coming battle, or at the captain's orders for the women's propriety she did not know. Whatever the reason, she was glad of it, for it obviated Lady Corey's objections to her remaining abovedecks. How absurd, she thought, that the sight of a man's naked breast should be more objectionable than to see him possibly blown to bits.

From below came the rhythmic beat of the drum, with the accompanying grunts of the men and creaking of pedals, as the pulsers drove them toward their rendezvous with the prey. Abaft, Fox and the other officers prowled the quarterdeck, peering through spyglasses and muttering to each other. Ahead, the smoke and smell of slow-match drifted from the forward companion ladder.

Beyond the gun deck, of course, loomed the French merchantman, so close now that the open mouths of her three cannon were plainly visible—three dark circles like the pupils of some fierce aerial carnivore's eyes. Behind the guns lay a great spread of sail, ready for whatever maneuvers might be required, and far abaft of them the whirring pulsers that propelled the two ships ever nearer each other. Arabella wasn't certain, but she thought she heard the cries of the other ship's commander as he sought to rally his men for battle.

Fox's men needed no such encouragement. Fierce, disciplined, and highly motivated by their own thirst for plunder, they hung taut in the rigging and scattered about the deck—well trained, well armed, and entirely committed to the coming battle.

For her part, Arabella was torn. Again and again in the hours since her discovery she had begun to approach Fox or Liddon to tell them about her new maneuver, but each time she had held back. The idea would not be accepted, not at such a late moment before the battle. Or they would dismiss her completely, despite the success her navigation had brought them already. Or they would accept it, and disaster would result. And so she remained mute.

Yet she refused to quit the deck. She would observe the battle, with the maneuver tidily written out and neatly folded in her reticule, and present it to Fox when and if it seemed necessary.

She trembled with anticipation and consternation.

The French merchantman's sails now occupied a greater span of the heavens than Arabella's two hands spread out before her thumb-tip to thumb-tip. Airmen could be clearly seen bustling about the rigging, and the cries of their first mate plainly heard. Fox, on the quarterdeck above Arabella, gritted his teeth in a fierce grin, squinting through his spyglass.

The battle would begin within moments.

Fox collapsed the spyglass with a harsh metallic click. "Fire as she bears," he remarked to Liddon, "as we discussed."

"Fire as she bears!" Liddon called through the scuttle, and the order was repeated down the length of the ship to the gun deck beneath her prow.

A long moment passed in which the world seemed to gather its breath, Arabella along with it.

And then *Touchstone*'s eight guns spoke in perfect unison, a great blast of sound and fire that caused the ship to jerk backward in the air. Almost faster than the eye could follow, the eight balls emerged from the jet of flame and smoke and flew unerringly toward the target, diminishing to specks . . . and converged upon the pennant at the merchantman's mainmast peak, utterly obliterating it.

The rest of the prey's sails, her masts and rigging and crew and, most especially, her critical pulsers, stood completely undamaged.

Arabella stared in stunned incomprehension. The action had been flawlessly executed . . . and had completely failed to impair the merchantman in any significant way. How could Fox have thrown away his shot so thoughtlessly? Or was it the targeting that was at fault?

Whatever the reason the opening salvo had failed, it would take a minute and a half for the crew to prepare the next. *Touch-*

stone lay open to the French counterattack, which would surely follow within seconds. Yet Fox made no attempt to maneuver. Instead, the two ships continued to drive directly toward each other, pulsers whirling.

Silence lay over both ships, save for the fading echo of the opening volley.

And then a call from the merchantman's quarterdeck broke the silence. A single syllable of command, incomprehensible French sailing jargon.

Arabella grasped the rail and held tight, bracing to receive the impact of the French cannonballs.

A moment later the French colors—the proud blue, white, and red ensign that fluttered in the artificial wind from the merchant's pulsers—were drawn rapidly downward, pulled to the deck like water running down a drain.

A great triumphal shout arose from *Touchstone*'s crew.

Victory!

Mouth agape, Arabella looked from the defeated Frenchman to the smiling Fox and back.

———————————

To Arabella's continued astonishment, the French captain was all smiles when he came aboard, shaking Fox's outstretched hand most heartily as he stepped to the quarterdeck from the aerial boat that had brought him across.

Renaudin was his name, captain of the *Fleur de Lys* out of Marseille. "Good shooting, monsieur," he said in thickly-accented English after the initial round of introductions. "*Très bien fait.*"

Fox doffed his hat and bowed. "Your own men's bravery in the face of clearly superior fire is also to be commended," he replied. "I did not observe a single sign of trepidation through my glass."

Renaudin smiled blankly at Fox's elegant phrasing, clearly

grasping the sentiment though not the exact meaning. "*Vos hommes sont très courageux,*" Arabella translated.

After Renaudin's polite acknowledgement of the compliment, Fox continued, "I have taken the liberty of drawing up a standard plunder contract, in English and French, with only the description of the cargo to be filled in." From his coat pocket he produced a thick sheaf of papers. "And the amount of the ransom, of course."

"Plunder contract?" murmured Lady Corey to Arabella.

"I have no idea," Arabella replied, as indeed she had not.

Renaudin, obviously familiar with the concept, gave the document a cursory perusal. "*Trente mille livres,*" he said, which Arabella translated for Fox: thirty thousand French livres.

Fox and Liddon conferred, converting the amount into English pounds. "I had hoped for rather more," Fox said.

"That is all my owners permit me to offer," Renaudin replied, in French, with what seemed to Arabella a rather embarrassed expression. "It is the maximum the insurance will provide."

After Arabella had translated this for Fox, he said, "Surely your owners would rather expend a few thousand livres of their own money, over and above the insurance, rather than suffer the loss of such a fine ship? Perhaps a matching thirty thousand, to make sixty in total?"

The French captain frowned, but calculation showed in his eyes. Certainly he was considering the degree to which his owners would hold him personally responsible for such a substantial loss. But from her own time running the household at Woodthrush Woods, which involved considerable dealings with shipbuilders and ship owners, Arabella knew that even the larger amount under discussion was less than a tenth of the value of the ship, never mind her cargo. "If I decline to sign," he replied, "you would be compelled to take my ship by force, which neither of us would like, and risk her being re-taken before you could deliver her to Mars for condemnation."

Fox's face reflected conflicted feelings as Arabella translated Renaudin's words, but she herself felt that the French captain's point was well taken. "We are," she reminded Fox, "deep in French skies."

"With that consideration," Renaudin continued, "may I offer ten thousand gold livres cash in advance, to make forty thousand in total?"

Fox's expression grew predatory, but he plainly saw yet further advantage to be drawn, as he immediately countered, "Perhaps twenty thousand cash, to make an even fifty?"

To Arabella's translation of the offer, Renaudin replied with an expressive Gallic shrug. "Tell him fifteen thousand, mademoiselle, for a total of forty-five. No more."

Arabella translated the offer for Fox, adding, "I believe we have found the bottom of his purse."

"Done," Fox replied, and put out his hand.

———

At supper that night, Fox was in an expansive mood. He had invited Arabella and Lady Corey to dine in his cabin, and the wine was of an elevated vintage. The men, too, were in very good cheer, even the usually solemn Fitts.

"I am surprised," Lady Corey said, "at the enthusiasm of the men after this . . . anticlimactic conclusion. I would have expected them to be disappointed by the lack of battle." She gestured out the broad stern window, beyond which the French merchantman's undamaged pulsers turned steadily as the two ships drew ever further apart. Though both were bound for Venus, for obvious reasons they did not choose to travel together. "And Miss Ashby informs me that the amount of the, um, the 'plunder contract' was only a fraction of what you might have gotten for the ship and its cargo if you had captured it?"

"That is true," Fox replied. "If—*if*—we should manage to return her to Sor Khoresh and see her condemned as lawful prize."

"But surely your letters of marque guarantee that any French ship you may take is a lawful prize?"

Fox shook his head. "There's many a slip, my lady. Disputes over the ownership of the captured ship or the location of the capture, the presence of other nations' cargo on board, mistreatment or *alleged* mistreatment of the prisoners, irregularities in the paperwork . . . any of these, and many more, can delay or even scuttle an apparently ironclad condemnation. Not to mention the fact that we would have to put sufficient men aboard the prize to fly her, defend her from recapture, and control the prisoners the whole way from here to Mars. That would be at least a quarter of our current crew—men we may need at Venus." He took a sip of his wine, pausing a moment to savor it before continuing. "Much better, and far more civilized, to accept a smaller guaranteed payment."

This raised a question in Arabella's mind. "I fail to see any guarantee, on either side. What assurance do you have that the Frenchman's owners will indeed pay, beyond the fifteen thousand? And what assurance does he have that, having paid ransom to us, some *other* privateer will not come along and capture him?"

"It is all spelled out in the contract." He patted his jacket pocket. "Which asserts, in legally binding language in both English and French, that the captain has his owners' authority to negotiate on their behalf, and declares to all and sundry that the ship has been granted free passage to Venus for the next one hundred and eighty days. If Monsieur Renaudin should be waylaid by any other privateer during that time, he need merely present the contract and they will be compelled to release him." To Arabella's dubious look he continued, "Any violation of this agreement is a breach of international law. If the owners fail to pay, the ship is forfeit, and subject to immediate impoundment by *any* English vessel in *any* English or allied port. And as for other privateers . . . a plunder contract of this type is an absolute, inviolable impediment to lawful prize. Only the most desperate privateer would bother to capture a vessel so encumbered—he would never see a penny of prize money, and would most likely find himself imprisoned in the bargain."

Arabella remained unimpressed. "Unless he destroys the contract."

Again Fox patted his pocket. "He would have to destroy *all* the copies. Not to mention killing the entire crew, who would otherwise falsify his story—an act of barbarity which, in and of itself, would be a barrier to legal condemnation." He gave Arabella an arch look. "One might get the impression that you consider privateers a dishonorable lot, even after all the time we have spent together. I am mortified."

Against her will Arabella found herself smiling; she dabbed at her mouth with her napkin to cover it. "I meant no insult, sir. I merely wished to . . . to discover the particulars of this contract, of which I have never before even heard."

Fox waved a hand in airy dismissal. "Few landsmen have. They think the privateer's life one of nothing but adventure, violence, evasion, and escape. But, between letters of marque, bills of lading, rosters, inventories, and plunder contracts, it involves, in fact, more paperwork than any thing else."

After supper drew to a close, Lady Corey permitted a brief perambulation on deck before retiring. It was the first dog watch, the men conversing quietly as they caulked the deck. The seams between the deck planks had begun to ooze pitch in the heat, and regular caulking with oakum was required to prevent the sticky black substance from going every where.

The Sun loomed dead ahead, huge and bright and blazing in a sky gone white with heat; Arabella's hand at arm's length was barely able to cover his searing face. But when she did cover it, another star became visible—a star that had been lost in the Sun's glare, and itself grew brighter and larger each day.

The planet Venus.

10

VENUS

After her one summer in England—which she had after its end come to consider a form of Purgatory—Arabella had been certain that she would never again know such a misery of heat. But now she knew that at that time she had been far more gently used than she had known, for the vicinity of Venus seemed as much hotter than an English summer as England had been relative to Mars.

The men went about nearly naked now, with only the barest scraps of cloth preserving a tiny shred of modesty. Even Fox, whose attention to couture was as meticulous as that of any man she had ever met, generally went stripped to the waist. Despite this gross indecency, the stifling conditions belowdecks were so intolerable that even Lady Corey spent most of her time on deck. She lived in her filmiest, most diaphanous gown, and fanned herself so vigorously that the breeze blew her from one rail to the other. And as for Arabella, she dedicated one cup of her allocation of fresh water each day to dousing her hair and wetting a cloth which she wore at the back of her neck.

Venus grew larger and closer each day, and Fox had posted look-outs at the top of each mast, the bowsprit's tip, and the pulsers' hub. "We must discern any French ships before they make us out," he said, "in order to avoid them and land without being questioned."

Captain Singh had said that he was at liberty in the fortress town of Thuguguruk. The port city of Wuknalugna lay nearby, and there they would land in the guise of Dutch privateers, allied to France. Once successfully landed, they would deliberately slow their victualing, watering, and other activities, buying time for Arabella and Fox to investigate the prison and formulate a plan to extricate the captain . . . while, Fox insisted, causing Napoleon as much distress as possible. But if they were intercepted midair, they would have a much harder time of it. As effective a fighter as *Touchstone* might be against French merchantmen, a contest with a French first-rate would surely prove a serious challenge.

"I wish I could make out the continents," Fox said, squinting through his spyglass at the approaching planet, which now loomed larger than Arabella's spread hands thumb to thumb. Venus lay perpetually shrouded in cloud—a good thing, Arabella thought, else she would be even hotter on the surface—and so presented to the eye only a hazy gray ball swirling with meaningless patterns of wind and weather. And, as they were approaching her from the skyward side, most of that gray ball was further obscured by darkness. "Based on the charts and our chronometer—and, I must admit, with the help of your greenwood box—I place Wuknalugna just there." He indicated a point somewhat sunward of the terminator. "I intend to time our landing so that we arrive after midnight local time, but early in our morning so that we are fresh for skullduggery." He collapsed the spyglass. "But we must evade the French, brave the Horn, and fly below the cloud layer before we can be certain where on the planet we find ourselves."

"At least we will be able to walk when we arrive," Arabella said with a sly grin.

To that jibe Fox replied with nothing but a glare. He then turned away and demanded a report from the lookout at the main-top.

Arabella had, without doubt, won their bet. Even with the delay incurred in the capture of the *Fleur de Lys*, they had arrived at Venus a full nine days earlier than Fox's course would have achieved. But Fox had not yet conceded defeat—"We are not yet landed, Miss Ashby"—and, furthermore, refused to openly acknowledge the benefits that accrued to the officers and passengers from the pedaling they had done. Yet his sullen behavior when pressed on either topic showed plainly that he did understand that he had been bested, and by now she knew him to be enough of a gentleman that, though he might grumble about it, he would not default on his wager.

Suddenly Arabella's thoughts were interrupted by a cry from the larboard top: "Sail ho!" This was immediately followed by another from the bowsprit: "Sail ho! Five . . . no, *six* sail of ship!"

The air of the quarterdeck immediately became electric, Fox and the other officers surging forward, peering sunward through telescopes or spyglasses, or shading their eyes if they lacked instruments. "D—n me," muttered Fox, followed by an apology to Arabella and Lady Corey.

"What is it, sir?" asked Lady Corey.

Fox's expression as he focused his spyglass was troubled. "Unwelcome news, my lady. French ships of the line, or I'll eat my hat."

Arabella's heart pounded, but she strove to keep her voice level. "May I see, sir?"

Without a word, Fox handed over the spyglass. It took a moment for her to find the ships—to the naked eye they appeared merely white specks against the planet's dark face—but with the device's help she was able to make out six tiny forms, each looking like a six-petaled white flower. From this distance they appeared harmless enough, but she knew appearances could be deceiving. "Can we slip past them?"

Fox considered the sun, the planet, and the sky behind them before replying. "With the clouds as they are, there's a chance they might not have seen us yet." He returned the spyglass to his eye, peering at the French ships. "We could turn about and pedal for all we're worth, and return another—D—n! Excuse me, ladies."

A moment later Arabella heard a faint, distant pop. "Are they *firing* at us?" Even as she spoke, one of the distant specks seemed to flicker, followed shortly by the sound of another pop.

"Signaling," Fox replied, still squinting through the spyglass. "They've seen us, for sure." He turned to Liddon, who floated at his shoulder in an attitude of grim expectation. "The Dutch letters of marque . . . are they ready?"

"Aye, sir," Liddon said, "but I can't promise they'll stand up to a French captain's inspection. And with a squadron of that size they'll have a commander—and all his staff." He shook his head. "I doubt we can brazen it out, sir."

Fox clapped the spyglass shut. "Then we run for it."

"Aye aye, sir," Liddon replied, then turned away and called, "All hands to the pedals!"

As the command was repeated down the length of the ship, reinforced by the bosun's pipe, Arabella and Lady Corey found themselves being gently shepherded toward their cabin. "*Must* we run, sir?" asked Arabella of Fox, brushing an airman's hand from her elbow. "After coming all this way?"

Fox, though his attention was clearly elsewhere, did at least give her a considered reply. "We must, miss. Against six ships of the line we have no chance. But *Touchstone* was built for speed, and the men are in crack shape. We can certainly outrun six fat Frenchmen." But an edge in his voice betrayed his uncertainty.

The airman was growing insistent, and again Arabella removed his hand from her arm. "Then I will pedal with the rest."

Immediately Fox replied, "We can use every hand." He nodded to the airman, who released Arabella's arm, and turned to Lady Corey. "Will you be joining us as well, my lady?"

It was at that moment that Arabella began to be afraid.

———————

This time the screen, which had before been placed with gentle precision, was thrown up in perfunctory fashion, and the faces of the men performing the task were grim and fearful. Before, during the long days of pedaling to reach the Edmonds Current and again the northern trades, they had grumbled amicably; during the pursuit of *Fleur de Lys* they had been full of gleeful anticipation; but now they pedaled as though Satan himself were right behind them. And, indeed, he might very well be, in the person of Napoleon—or at least a squadron of his aerial navy.

"Oh my stars!" Lady Corey exclaimed behind her. Arabella turned around to see her, and saw that her foot had slipped from the pedal again. It was at least the third time this had happened, no doubt precipitated by her considerable nervousness. Her face, Arabella noted, appeared pale and clammy despite the hold's sweltering heat. Arabella withdrew her own feet from the pedals, which continued to turn, and went to help the older woman.

"What will they do to us?" Lady Corey whispered, trembling. "If they catch us?"

Arabella had no idea, but she firmed up her jaw. "We are civilians," she said with as much confidence as she could muster. "Under the laws of war, even the French must consider us inviolate." This seemed to reassure Lady Corey a bit, but even as Arabella gave her a sip of water her own mind remained troubled.

For many hours they pedaled, anxiety slowly draining away and being replaced with exhaustion. From time to time men came down from deck with food and water, but they brought no good news. The French were still in pursuit, were in fact gaining, and there was no sign of cloud or any other means by which they might be evaded.

Lady Corey labored until she fell unconscious, collapsing with a low sigh and floating gently away from the still-turning pedals. Arabella assisted the surgeon and his loblolly-boy in getting her safely settled in their cabin, then returned to her station.

On and on they pedaled, the men's grim silence relieved only by the endless creak and clatter of the gears and belts.

Finally Arabella too was defeated by exhaustion—so tired, she realized, that for some bewildered time it had been the ever-turning pedals that drove her legs rather than the reverse. It was only because of the screen that shielded her modesty that no one had noticed her state of complete stupefaction. Somehow she managed to extract herself from the pedals without injury, and to rearrange her clothing to a minimum of decency before coming out from behind the screen. She barely noticed the dispirited airman who took her place as soon as it had been vacated.

Weary though she was, she did not retire immediately to her cabin, but instead floated up to the deck to see for herself the progress of the chase.

The situation, grim though it was, seemed nearly ordinary. Though the pursuing French squadron had grown to six clearly visible ships, the officers and men on deck went about their business as they had done every day for the entirety of the voyage. There was, she supposed, little else to do. Cannon practice would not help—the French warships would not be intimidated by *Touchstone*'s eight little guns, and no amount of drill could raise the men's level of expertise sufficiently to defeat an enemy so numerous and so heavily armed. Each of the six French men-of-war plainly showed twelve gun-ports, and additional brass swivel-guns gleamed from their decks.

For a moment Arabella contemplated the French squadron,

which seemed to fill half the sky, and tried to imagine some maneuver or stratagem which might evade them. But she did not need her greenwood box to tell her that no such escape was possible.

It was with neither fear nor anger, only a sense of numb resignation, that she returned to the cabin—the cabin where Lady Corey still slept—and closed her eyes.

———————

The thunder of cannon awoke her.

It was not, in truth, all that loud. . . . It was a distant thunder, as she had heard from her bed in England one morning as a rain storm approached. But that sound had terrified her, portending as it did a pounding deluge of water from the sky—a thing which she, born on Mars, had never before experienced. The rain itself, when it finally arrived, had proved harmless enough . . . but this time, she was certain, the storm would not pass so uneventfully.

Another boom of cannon sounded. This time it was followed by a low keening, one which dropped in pitch as it peaked in loudness—a sound she had heard on only one previous occasion in her life, yet one which raised chills at the back of her perspiring, overheated neck.

It was the sound of cannonballs passing close by.

A short while later the ever-present creaking of the pedals clattered to a halt, together with the slight rocking motion the turning pulsers imparted to the ship. In the unaccustomed still silence, Arabella heard voices—some far off, others quite near—calling commands she could not make out. There were no further cannon shots.

With a heavy heart, Arabella drifted to Lady Corey's hammock and shook her shoulder until she woke. "I am sorry to disturb you," she said, "but I believe we may just have been captured."

The mood on deck, once Arabella and Lady Corey had made themselves presentable, was somber but not completely despondent. "It could be worse," Fox remarked as he watched the boat approaching from the French flagship, its air-sweeps sculling like a gull's wings. "If we were a Navy vessel, Liddon and I would now be frantically destroying our code-books and other secret documents. But as a privateer, I know no more of the Navy's plans than Napoleon himself!"

Arabella drew him aside, out of Lady Corey's hearing, and in a low voice asked him, "What is to become of us?"

Fox sighed and stared off skyward—toward Mars—for a while before replying. "*Touchstone . . . Touchstone* is lost." His voice faltered on that last word, and he blinked rapidly and turned away. Arabella, too, turned to the rail; she felt she should give him some privacy in his moment of distress. Then Fox cleared his throat, and she returned her gaze to his face. His eyes were bright, but steady. "As for our prize . . . frankly, I am uncertain. The plunder contract Renaudin signed is technically between his owners, as represented by him, and my owners, as represented by myself. It may be that, the agreement having already been sealed, the money will eventually be paid despite our capture." He sighed again. "The officers and I will give our parole, of course, and become gentlemen of leisure—of *enforced* leisure—likely in some town on Venus. The men will become prisoners of war, but I and the other officers will do what we can to make their lives easier." He reached and took Arabella's hand, and she did not object. "You and Lady Corey, as non-combatants, will become what the French call *détenus*. In essence, you will be held for ransom, to ensure good treatment of French prisoners by the English. I am certain that you will be treated humanely. At some point you may even be ransomed, and return home. But for the rest of us . . . I am afraid it is the end of the war."

Arabella felt her own eyes sting. "I am so, *so* sorry, sir. Were it not for my foolish desire to rescue Captain Singh, we would none of us be here."

Fox squeezed her hand—she had not even noticed that he was still holding it—and peered with great sincerity into her eyes. "My *dear* Miss Ashby, you have nothing to apologize for. Were it not for you and your entirely commendable desire to rescue him, I would be at this moment stranded in Fort Augusta, shackled to an immovable mountain of debt by that charlatan Burke." He straightened. "We may be made prisoner, we may suffer, but we yet live, and where there is life, there is hope." He leaned in, conspiratorially, and whispered, "And, besides, I believe we count among our number one who has given some consideration to the question of escape." To her puzzled expression he clarified, "By which I mean yourself."

But that comment, no doubt meant to reassure, only made Arabella still more miserable. "I . . . I thank you for your confidence, sir, but my plans—to the extent I had them—depended upon being *outside* of the prison, and equipped with money, friends, and a ship with which to depart the planet." She shook her head. "I must confess I had intended to assess the situation upon arrival and . . . and extemporize."

At that Fox actually smiled. "Well, then, we are in good hands. For I have seen how you 'extemporize,' and there are few whose considered plans I would prefer to your improvisations."

The conversation was interrupted by a cry of "*Ohé du navire!*" from the boat, followed by a heavily accented request for "permission to come aboard."

"Alas, I must go and treat with the French," said Fox, bowing over her hand.

"They seem polite enough, at least."

"That they do." He released her hand with great reluctance. "All will be well, miss. I have every confidence."

"I am sure that it will," she said, though her actual feelings were otherwise. "Thank you for your efforts on our behalf."

Fox bowed, turned from her, straightened his coat, and with a tap of his toe on the deck propelled himself to the rail, where the French officers were just descending from their boat.

The French were, indeed, polite enough, though rather brusque. Two French officers, their uniforms all brass and braid though they themselves were ill-shaven and rather malodorous, escorted Arabella and Lady Corey to their sweltering cabin and shut them up there. After that, the two women were reduced to speculation as to what transpired, based on what they could hear and the motions of the ship.

Arabella pressed her ear to the door, glad for the first time that it was so thin and permeable to sound. There was a great deal of shouting, in French and in accented English. "The French have taken command of the ship, I think," she told Lady Corey. "I believe our officers have been confined to their quarters." At that moment the drum began to beat—rather faster than before—and the slap and clatter of the pedals soon followed.

"What is happening now?" Lady Corey said, clearly struggling to keep the anxiety out of her voice as the ship's motion made her drift toward the cabin's aft bulkhead.

"We are under way, obviously." Arabella paused to think. "The French sent only one boat, so the men at the pedals must be ours, presumably under armed guard." She drifted to the hull and peered through the scuttle, though it afforded little view at the best of times. Through it she could see only blue sky—but then a French man-of-war appeared, her pulsers spinning as she pulled away from *Touchstone*, followed by a second. "At least some of the French are leaving us."

"Where are we bound?"

"To a prison-camp on Venus, I suppose." Tears welled in her eyes, blinding her, and this time she let them come. "After all this time . . . will I ever see him again?"

Lady Corey patted Arabella's hand. "Courage, my dear," she said, though her voice quavered.

VENUS, 1815

11

PRISONERS

After the ship's plunging, pitching, rattling passage through Venus's Horn—the area of tempestuous winds where the planetary atmosphere churned against the interplanetary atmosphere—Arabella and Lady Corey were permitted to come out on deck.

"At least the passage was not too bad," Lady Corey remarked as Arabella helped her to tighten her stays. The force of gravity had returned, which made the tiny cabin seem still more cramped and necessitated the use of stays to support Lady Corey's substantial feminine characteristics. "I have heard tales of passengers being thrown about the cabin like dice in a cup."

"I suppose that is to be expected," Arabella said. "The planet being smaller than Earth. Though her proximity to the Sun does add strength to the winds." She tied off the laces with a neat bow, reflecting that for all her reading on navigation and tactics, she knew very little of the planet upon which they were about to land. "There." She wiped her brow and returned her already-sodden handkerchief to her reticule. "I suppose we are presentable enough for the French."

"Better than they deserve." Lady Corey sniffed, and adjusted her bonnet. "Come, let us look upon Venus." She sighed. "Which I suppose is to be our home for the rest of the war."

"Unless we can escape," Arabella replied in a low mutter, to prevent the French guard outside their door from hearing.

As they exited the cabin—the guard gave them no courtesy, only acknowledging their appearance with a grunt—Arabella felt unaccountably as though she were entering a place she had never visited before. And as they passed through the ward-room and went up the companion ladder, this feeling only strengthened. Was it simply the knowledge that the dear *Touchstone* was now a French possession, reinforced by the presence of uniformed and unshaven French airmen on every deck? Or was it the reappearance of gravity? Though Venus's attraction was not as great as Earth's, for which Arabella was very grateful, it was greater than that of Mars, and the downward force certainly lent to the familiar surroundings a peculiar impression. Every step felt as though she were slogging through soft sand.

The feeling of strangeness grew still stronger as they emerged on deck. Where for the last several months the Sun had shone down upon the deck through every bell of every watch, excepting the occasional storm, they now found themselves embedded in the unending clouds which shrouded Venus's face. In every direction Arabella could see nothing but dim and dismal gray, and the warm dampness of the air lay upon her skin like a heavy, sodden blanket. Furthermore, the starboard, larboard, and mizzen masts had been unshipped and now lay stowed against the gunwales, leaving the hull clear for landing.

A French officer, his breast and shoulders bedecked with great quantities of gold braid, met them as they were escorted onto the quarterdeck. "I welcome you to Venus, *mesdames*," he said in strongly accented English. "I am Lieutenant Desjardins, in command of this vessel. I apologize for the view, but we shall emerge from the clouds shortly." And, indeed, even as he spoke the enveloping fog began to thin and shred, gradually parting to reveal the land below.

The sight, as it emerged, was not an encouraging one. Spread out below the ship lay an endless forest, or jungle, with nodding clumps of strange vegetation marching to the limits of view in every direction. The colors were predominantly dark greens, ranging from a dark bottle green to nearly black, with only occasional patches of tan and yellow to break the monotony. Here and there a glint of reflected light showed that water pooled at ground level. The whole presented an effect that was half jungle and half swamp, and Arabella could discern no buildings, canals, nor roads—no sign of civilization whatsoever.

"How dreadful," Lady Corey murmured, though for the benefit of the French her face was fixed in an expression of half-cheerful determination. Arabella could not but agree.

As the ship continued her descent below the clouds, drifting along beneath her inflated envelope, Arabella began to make out individual plants—a mix of ferns and broad-leafed trees like gigantic aspidistra, rising above low swampy undergrowth. Suddenly a flash of movement caught her eye.

It was a native—a Venusian aboriginal—looking very much like the illustration she had seen in the one book in her father's library that treated upon Venus. He stood upon a rock in the midst of a pond, staring upward at the ship with distended and expressionless eyes. His skin was a pale green, his mouth a wide slash beneath which an inflated throat-sac worked, his limbs long and muscular; the whole effect was rather that of a man-sized frog, dressed in loose and flowing shirt and trousers which clung damply to his skin. His fingers and toes were broadly webbed, and a satchel made of some dark, rubbery-looking stuff hung at his hip.

The two of them regarded each other for a moment—though Arabella was sure the native was only gazing at the ship floating above him, not herself in particular—before he suddenly doubled over and slipped into the water without a splash.

"Did you see that?" Arabella said, tugging Lady Corey's sleeve and pointing. "It was a Venusian!"

"I did," Lady Corey replied with cold indifference. "Disgusting."

Arabella peered into the murky pond's depths, hoping to catch a glimpse of the native swimming—were their habitations beneath the water's surface?—but the pond fell away behind the ship without any further signs of life appearing.

The ship drifted still lower, offering a more detailed view of swamps, pools, trees, and lower vegetation. Once a large flying creature, with leathery wings and a long tail that ended in a spade-shaped fin, flapped lazily across a slowly flowing stream . . . and then something black and shining, all scales and teeth, leapt from the stream, returning to the water with a violent thrashing splash and leaving nothing where the flying thing had been.

Shouts and commands from the quarterdeck. The rhythmic grunts from the men shoveling coal in the furnace-room belowdecks increased their tempo. Their labor brought a rush of heat which Arabella could feel on her already-flushed face, the balloon bulged, and the ship rose sluggishly, carried along by the fetid breeze over a small rocky hill. And on the other side of that hill spread a broad lake, whose dark, still waters reflected the gray bellies of the clouds above . . . and the buildings of a town on the far side!

The town—no, on closer inspection it could perhaps be termed a city, for many of its buildings blended in with the trees around it and it was larger than it at first appeared—was plainly a port, for many masts swayed above vessels moored in the lake's water. But though most, perhaps even all, of the ships were plainly aerial vessels, Arabella sought in vain for the massive smokestacks of the furnaces which every aerial port must have in order to effect the launch of an interplanetary ship. "Do you see any furnaces?" she asked Lady Corey.

"Your eyes are better than mine, child."

Arabella's lips tightened in concern. "I fear that this port may not be equipped for launch. Even if we should escape, we will be unable to depart the planet from here." She peered at the ships more closely, trying to determine if they had all been landed here and abandoned, but, curiously, they all seemed to be in good running order, with fresh paint, clean white sails, and taut rigging.

Another set of commands in French rang out, repeated and translated into English for the benefit of *Touchstone*'s crew, and a moment later came the rattle of great cables as the ship's anchors, fore and aft, plummeted to the dark water below, each vanishing with a splash. The ship's forward motion halted, and she hung swaying for a time until a gang of sweating Touchstones came out on deck—carefully overseen by four French airmen, each armed with a sword and a brace of pistols. The men, glowering at their French captors all the while, shipped the bars to the anchor-capstan, then began to haul the ship downward against the diminishing force of her rapidly cooling balloon. As they pushed against the bars, walking in a circle around the capstan, they sang an air-shanty Arabella had never before heard, one whose lyrics were particularly rude and directed against the French. The guards seemed to take no notice, but whether it was pride or ignorance of English Arabella could not say.

After many verses of insult to the virtue of French women, *Touchstone* reached the water. With a final command, the hot air was spilled from her balloon envelope, and with a *whoosh*, a smoky smell, and a splash, she settled into the lake's black and swampy water.

"Welcome to Venus," Lady Corey muttered.

———————————

Now that *Touchstone* was truly landed, her envelope emptied and struck down on deck, there was no longer any possibility of escape from the planet and the officers were released from their cabins. "So this is Venus," Fox said as he came out on deck, fanning himself with his hat. "I trust you ladies were well treated?"

"We have no complaints," Arabella admitted.

"That was a terrible landing," he tutted, casting a critical eye on the state of the rigging. "The French may have invented the balloon, but it is the English who have perfected its usage."

"*Silence!*" cried the French commander, and with pistol and bayonet his men herded the Touchstones into groups of twenty on the deck, paying no respect to divisions or rank. The officers and passengers were spared this indignity, being allowed to remain at liberty on the quarterdeck. But two French airmen stood at the heads of the ladders, pistols drawn and keeping a gimlet eye on them.

Soon boats appeared, wide flat squarish things poled across the shallow lake by Venusian natives, each under the command of a French army officer whose red-and-blue uniform bore more brass buttons than Arabella had ever before seen in one place, including a row down each trouser leg. Each group of Touchstones was driven onto a boat, accompanied by an armed French airman, and poled away to the shore. The loaded boats floated very low in the water, and the men could easily swamp one simply by rushing to one side, but Arabella supposed that, even if the armed guard were not sufficient disincentive to do so, the fetid black water might be.

Another boat, this one of more conventional design but even so propelled by natives at the oars, pulled up to the starboard rail. "*Mesdames, messieurs,*" said the French commander with a bow, "if you will be so kind as to accompany me?" But despite his politesse, the two French airmen glowering beside him made it clear that refusing the invitation would not be permitted. Arabella declined the commander's proffered hand and stepped down into the boat without assistance.

As they rowed away from *Touchstone,* Fox looked backward with an expression of undisguised despair, and Arabella very nearly reached out to place a comforting hand on his shoulder. But then he pressed his eyes tight shut and shook his head, and when he reopened them his jaw was firm and his gaze was directed forward.

Arabella too looked forward, where the boats containing *Touchstone*'s crew were already beginning to unload, the men being mustered into lines on the dock. It might not be a pleasant prospect, but it was her future and it must be considered.

Once *Touchstone*'s crew had all been unloaded from the boats, they were marched through the city to a large open square, where again they were mustered into groups. The officers and passengers, as before, were treated more gently than the men, but even so it was made plain that they had no choice but to obey.

Most of the buildings they passed were one or two storeys, wider at the bottom than at the top; they were constructed of wide, flat green bricks, with black stone foundations and lintels and dark green tile roofs. But at one end of the square stood a large building looking very like an English town hall, though built of the same green brick and dark stone as the native structures. Above its broad wooden door a large French flag hung unmoving in the still and soggy air. The flag was new—crisp and pristine despite the humidity—and as the door opened and three French Army officers emerged from it Arabella speculated that this city had not been French territory for long.

"*Qu'avons-nous ici?*"—What do we have here?—called the officer with the largest hat and the most gold braid on his uniform, looking down upon the assembled Touchstones from the terrace at the top of the steps. Lieutenant Desjardins stepped smartly up, saluted, and began a lengthy disquisition in rapid French.

"What *is* he on about?" Lady Corey muttered.

"I cannot quite make it all out," Arabella replied in a similar undertone, "but he is describing the circumstances under which we were captured. Something about '*zone interdite*'—a prohibited zone?" She continued to listen, then snorted. "To hear him tell it, we put up rather a fight."

"By French standards," Fox murmured, "we did."

"*Silence*," snapped one of the guards—the meaning of the French word being clear even to Fox—and they obeyed.

At the end of Desjardins's report, the Army officer turned away and conferred with his two compatriots. But the discussion soon turned argumentative, and voices were raised—to such an extent that Arabella was able to discern the point of contention. "There seems to be some dispute over where to send us," she whispered to Fox and Lady Corey. "The one on the left is saying, I think, that more men are required to work in the ship-yard. But the one on the right says we should instead be sent to, to . . ." Then she heard a word which made her breath catch in her throat. ". . . to Thuguguruk!"

"That name seems familiar," muttered Fox.

"It is where Captain Singh is being held!" Then she shushed him, so as to pay closer attention to the argument as it progressed.

The discussion, though heated, did not last much longer; the commander snapped an order and both of his lieutenants straightened, saluted, and shut their mouths. He then paced for a moment on the terrace, stroking his chin, and finally nodded to the officer on the left . . . the one who wished the prisoners to be sent to the ship-yard. As that officer smiled triumphantly and the other frowned, the commander turned to the assembled Touchstones and raised a finger, preparatory to making an announcement.

"*Excusez-moi!*" called Arabella, interrupting him before he could speak.

All eyes turned to her, and she was nearly as shocked as they by her outburst. The two French Navy officers closest to her raised their pistols, but at a glance and a gesture from the commander they relaxed their guard . . . though only slightly.

The commander waved her forward, and she stepped hesitantly to the foot of the steps—accompanied by one of the French officers. Even as she walked, a plan began to formulate itself in her mind.

"*Oui, mademoiselle?*" the commander said, his expression more amused than annoyed.

"*Madame,*" she corrected, lifting her chin.

From behind her came a choked sound of surprise—most likely from Lady Corey, but it might have been Fox. She strove to put it out of her mind.

The commander bowed. "*Veuillez m'excuser, madame. Qu'est-ce que vous avez à dire?*" What do you have to say?

She paused a moment, struggling to recall her verbs. "*Mon mari est prisonnier de vous, à Thuguguruk, et je veux rester avec lui.*" My husband is a prisoner of yours, at Thuguguruk, and I wish to stay with him. Or should that have been *de la vôtre?*

In either case, apparently she had gotten her point across. "*Et quel est le nom de votre mari?*"

Arabella straightened. "My husband is Captain Prakash Singh, of the Honorable Mars Company airship *Diana.*" She did not realize until the complete utterance had escaped her lips that she had spoken in English.

At that name the commander's lip quirked in wry amusement. "Ah, yes," he replied, also in English. "The *musulman.* I know him well. He has been a, how you say, a thorn in my commandant's side." He held up a finger. "A very polite thorn to be sure, but a thorn nonetheless. And because of his thorny nature, I am afraid he and his crew are no longer at Thuguguruk."

At that statement, and the expression of cruel satisfaction on the commander's face, Arabella's heart shrank to a cold hard cinder.

"They have been transferred to Marieville," the commander continued—the unfamiliar name being pronounced in the French fashion, *Ma-rhee-vee*—"to labor on the *plantation de fer!*"

Arabella must have misheard that last phrase; it made no sense. Surely, even on Venus, iron did not grow on a plantation like a *khoresh*-tree?

"And because I am disinclined to break up a happy family," the commander went on, "and as there is always need for more laborers there, it is to Marieville that I shall send you and your shipmates, to toil for the duration of your captivity with your thorny husband and his crew. You will depart immediately." He called out commands in French, and the officers began herding the Touchstones away.

"And what of our possessions?" Arabella asked, suddenly petrified. "Are we to return to our ship for them, or will they be sent after us?"

The commander arched an eyebrow. "You have no possessions, *madame*, and no ship. Your *former* vessel, and all her contents, is now the property of His Imperial Majesty Napoleon the First, By the Grace of God and the Constitutions of the Empire, Emperor of the French. You may retain your clothing and any belongings you happen to have on your person." He clicked his heels together and bowed in the Continental fashion. "Your servant, *madame*."

Plainly she had been dismissed, and with a brusque gesture her guard directed her to return to where the officers and Lady Corey stood. But before she turned to go, she could not fail to see that *both* of the commander's two lieutenants were looking at her with venomous expressions.

And when she did turn, she saw the same expressions on the faces of Fox, Liddon, and all the other Touchstones.

———————

Arabella trudged along, fanning herself with her hand, the mud squelching beneath her feet on every step. She was very glad of her sturdy Martian-made half-boots, but her fan and every thing else remained in the ship—now property of Napoleon.

She paused, wiped her dripping brow with her hand, and looked up. The Sun—merely the brightest spot in the bright and roiling clouds—stood directly overhead, and seemed to have done so for ever, even though they had been marching for what certainly must have been hours and hours already. She hurried her step to catch up to Fox and Lady Corey.

"May I inquire the time?" she said to Fox, who had retained his pocket-watch.

Fox drew the timepiece from his waistcoat pocket. "Half past nine in the evening." He wound the watch as he continued in his plodding pace. "That is, of course, ship's time; local time appears to be a bit before noon. We were not, sadly, offered the opportunity to co-ordinate our chronometers before landing. I shall add this offense to my litany of complaints to address with Napoleon when we meet."

Arabella considered this information. No wonder she felt so very weary. "Why then have you not changed your watch to match the Sun?"

Fox shrugged. "It would not remain so for long. It is of Martian make, built for a day of twenty-four hours and forty minutes. Venus's day is twenty-eight hours and ten minutes." He contemplated the timepiece for a bit, then slipped it back into his pocket. "I do not imagine I will have the opportunity to obtain a local watch any time soon."

Lady Corey spoke up. "As it is so late in the day for us, do you suppose our captors will permit us to stop and rest soon?"

In answer Fox only looked at the French guards, who strode resolutely forward like men entirely habituated to long marching. Even the Venusians in their number, looking absurdly like taxidermy frogs dressed up in French Army uniforms, stepped along at the same pace. Though their broad webbed feet and the odd construction of their knee joints made their stride rather ridiculous, their bayoneted rifles were held in firm readiness.

"I see," said Lady Corey.

They fell into exhausted silence then, and plodded along together for a time. The damp and cloying air was redolent with strange smells—some exotic as cinnamon, others common as manure, and many unfamiliar and disturbing. The same air carried the sounds of the Touchstones' squelching feet—the men were being marched along in lock-step by their guards, while the officers and passengers were permitted to walk at their own pace so long as they did not fall too far behind—and occasional wailing animal cries from the dripping ferns to either side of the path. The mud, Arabella noted with disgust, had soiled her dress to the knee despite her best efforts.

Lady Corey cleared her throat demurely, and indicated with her eyes that she wished private conversation with Arabella. The two of them moved away from Fox, who took no apparent notice of their departure.

"So," said Lady Corey, "*Mrs.* Singh . . . when, exactly, were you planning to share the happy news of your nuptials with me?"

Arabella had not known that it would be possible to become more miserable than she already was. Her announcement had, of course, been a lie—an impulsive, spur-of-the-moment creation driven by her burning desire to be reunited with her captain—yet she dared not admit this even to those closest to her, for fear that this intelligence might make its way to the French. "I must apologize for my . . . my dissimulation," she stammered. "I knew that you would not approve."

"Indeed I do not." She sighed. "But what is done is done, and despite my reservations I do wish you joy."

"I thank you for that," Arabella said, and in that she was entirely sincere.

"Tell me about the wedding."

"It was . . . it was a private affair, obviously." Arabella's mind whirled. She had attended but two weddings in her life, one in Fort Augusta and one in England, and she racked her brain for telling details. "Only the captain and myself, and the, the sheriff." She knew from reading novels that a justice of the peace could perform weddings, but as to her knowledge no such office existed on Mars she imagined that the local sheriff might perform a similar function.

Lady Corey blinked. "I had no idea a sheriff could perform weddings. Still, I suppose Parson Keene, being so close to your brother, was out of the question."

"Indeed," Arabella breathed with relief.

"But who were your witnesses?"

"Well, Michael, of course, and—"

"So your brother *was* in on the secret?"

Arabella clapped her hand across her mouth before it could emit any other contradictions, thinking as rapidly as she could. "Yes, er, I, yes, naturally he was. I could not keep such important news from the one closest to me. But, but, Parson Keene, he is such a gossip, you know . . . if we had involved him, every one would have known before next Sunday."

"To be sure," Lady Corey said, but her eyes showed she had noted the discrepancy. "I am certain it was a lovely ceremony."

"Well, it was very rushed, to be sure. We were forced to use the . . . the number two drying-shed, though the decorations, the, er, the flowers, they . . ."

"My *dear* Mrs. Singh," Lady Corey sighed, interrupting. "The first thing you must learn about prevarication is to reduce detail to an absolute minimum."

This advice brought Arabella to a standstill. "I . . . I *must* apologize, Lady Corey . . ."

Lady Corey took Arabella's hand. "Come along, dear girl," she said, tugging her forward. "Those horrible frogs are staring." Moving like a worn and creaking automaton, Arabella resumed her trudging progress. "Equivocation is, sadly, one of the womanly arts, and one in which I can see you require considerable instruction." She looked upward at the Sun, still hidden behind Venus's perpetual cloud and still nearly at the zenith. "Fortunately, or unfortunately as the case may be, it seems that we have many hours yet for me to provide appropriate tutelage. . . ."

In some ways Arabella was grateful. Lady Corey's advice—be brief, remain as close to the truth as possible, and be genuinely apologetic whenever it is advantageous—*was* useful, and she could see that it would help her to keep her secret safe from the other captives as well as the French. Furthermore, the lessons served to distract Arabella's mind from her increasing weariness and the growing pain in her blistering feet. She suspected they did the same for Lady Corey, who despite her greater age and weight seemed to be bearing up well under the burdens of the march.

But still, all in all, being lectured by a baroness on how to lie, while trudging through the mud beneath the sweltering sun of Venus, was not how she would have wished to spend her day if she had been given the choice.

———————

Eventually, though the Sun still stood high in the sky, so many of the weary Touchstones were unable to proceed that the French were forced to call a halt to the march. Arabella collapsed upon a low shrub and, despite the day's light and heat, immediately fell into a deep and dreamless sleep.

She was awoken, far too soon, by a prod in the shoulder by a French rifle-butt, accompanied by the brusque offer of a tin cup of water. She roused herself and gulped it desperately. The bright patch in the sky was still well above the horizon, and as the prisoners were chivvied into motion she realized that they would be walking directly toward it. The entire back and one side of her dress were ruined, caked with mud and filth.

Though dimmed by the ever-present clouds, the Sun's light hurt her aching eyes and his heat made her face, indeed her entire front, feel as though she were sitting too close to the fire. But that direction, she knew now, was west.

She would need to learn much in order to escape. She vowed to hold this information in her mind.

Grimly, she placed one foot in front of the other.

———————

In the late afternoon, as measured by the Sun, a thunderous storm of rain blew up, soaking every one and every thing to the skin. The guards, seemingly accustomed to this meteorological phenomenon, did not even slacken their stride, and the prisoners were forced to do likewise.

The rain brought with it no freshness, only an increase in the steamy wetness of the air, and rather than washing the mud from Arabella's dress it merely distributed it more widely, changing the white silk to a clinging gray. Miserably she marched forward, head down against the pounding rain and arms crossed to retain what little modesty the sodden, near-transparent silk allowed.

So disconsolate was she that she did not even notice that Fox had approached her until his jacket was gently placed on her shoulders. "Oh, please sir," she protested, "I cannot accept this."

"The loan of a jacket is little hardship," Fox replied mildly. "I retain my shirt, waistcoat, trousers, and much else besides. Truly, the vast difference in the quantity of fabric allocated to fashionable men and women is inexplicable."

At this Arabella, despite the dreadful situation, found a smile drifting onto her face. And the jacket, its collar turned up, did serve to protect her from the pummeling raindrops and the leering eyes of the French guards. "In that case, I thank you, sir."

"Please do take care not to let any thing fall from the pockets."

"I shall endeavor to comply."

They slogged along together through the downpour for a little while, until Fox said, "I have been meaning to speak with you for some time upon a certain matter."

Despite the miserable heat, Arabella felt a chill. "What matter might that be, sir?"

"The matter of our wager." At once Arabella looked to Lady Corey, but though she walked not very far away from them, the clattering of the rain upon the ground and leaves would certainly prevent her from overhearing the conversation. "It cannot have escaped your notice that we are, in fact, upon the planet Venus."

"This is indisputable."

"And the date"—he sighed theatrically—"is, alas, several days sooner than the arrival date projected by my original course."

"*Eight* days," Arabella teased. "Perhaps even nine, depending on the exact hour of our landing."

To that Fox only glared, beneath dripping eyebrows. "In any event, it is clear that I owe you a certificate attesting to your navigational ability, and a prize *huresh* from my stables. May I beg your indulgence, under the circumstances, to delay payment until we return to Mars?"

"Of course, sir." Again she smiled, though the uncertainty of that date was troublesome.

"Thank you, madam." He fell silent for a moment, and his

streaming face was contemplative. "I suppose it is best, after all, that you won our bet. For a gentleman to share a private dinner with a married woman, let alone a kiss, would be too unseemly for even a despicable privateer such as myself."

At that Arabella laughed aloud, though her feelings at that moment were, in fact, extremely mixed. "And to do so with a woman *engaged* to be married would be acceptable?"

"Marriage is a state of being, madam, but an engagement is merely a statement of intention . . . and intentions can change."

"La, sir, you are more of a rogue than I had thought." But Arabella had to admit that she found herself flattered . . . and the tension between her pretended status and the reality was suddenly very palpable.

Eventually the downpour ended, as suddenly as it had begun, and Fox took his saturated coat back. And though its sodden weight was quite uncomfortable in the steaming heat that followed the rain, for reasons she could not quite articulate Arabella found herself somewhat bereft at its loss.

———————————

The rain having ceased, Arabella looked around at the steaming landscape. The plant life had changed while she had been slogging though the downpour; giant ferns had been replaced by squat, thick-bellied trees, more like English oaks than the towering spars of Martian *khoresh*-trees. The land, too, had risen, and—as her weary legs informed her—continued to rise gently, the mud through which they had trudged for the first part of their journey giving way to stony soil. This was a relief, though the stones greatly pained Lady Corey's slipper-shod feet.

And then they came to a clearing, and the view changed dramatically.

Arabella paused, looking out over a valley shrouded in mist.

They had, apparently, reached the peak of a low rise, and the ground descended away from them to the west. Across the valley, a substantial manor house—white-painted wood with a green brick foundation—looked down over the thick forest that filled the valley floor. But where the mist drifted, it was clear that the forest was heavily scarred with areas of bare earth—long narrow rectangles devoid of trees or any other plant life—and from many of these rose threads of smoke. And at the far end, the lower end, of the valley, stood an enormous pyramidal structure of green brick, from the top of which four large smokestacks belched black smoke which rose to mingle with the lowering clouds above.

The smell of all that smoke was strong and pervasive; if not for the rain, they would certainly have been smelling it for the last several miles of walking. And, Arabella realized, it was familiar; it was the smell of charcoal, to which she had become inured during *Diana*'s stay on the asteroid Paeonia. Yet there was another note to it as well—a metallic tang which brought to mind the taste of blood after biting one's cheek.

Iron.

"*Madame*," said one of the French guards, breaking into her reverie with the minimum of politeness, "*il faut que vous avancez*." Indeed, all the other Touchstones, the officers and Lady Corey as well as the men, had continued their trudging progress down the path while she had stood staring at the prospect before her. Only she and this one guard remained in the clearing.

For a moment she considered an attempt at escape. But the guard held his rifle at the ready, and she . . . she had nothing but the trivial contents of her reticule, her blistered feet, and her weary brain against unknown miles of French-controlled Venusian territory. She had not even the slightest idea in which direction freedom might lie; indeed, whether the prospect of freedom existed any where on this entire planet.

With a sense of exhausted resignation she inclined her head and plodded forward. The guard fell into step behind her.

"*S'il vous plaît,*" she asked the guard as they walked, "*qu'est-ce que c'est là-bas?*" What is that down there?

"*C'est la plantation de fer,*" the guard replied.

12

MARIEVILLE

At the end of the path—the increasingly well-worn path, which became a rutted road of packed earth before it ended—they found a stockade, a high wall of split logs, with a gate wide enough to admit a heavily laden cart. This gate opened to the call of their guards, the leader of whom went inside, leaving the Touchstones sweltering in the clearing outside the wall.

"Oh, I do hope that we will be able to rest soon," Lady Corey said, hands pressed to the small of her back. "What time might it be? Ship's time, I mean? It must be horribly late." Arabella, rubbing her perspiring feet one at a time, shared that sentiment. For, though the bright patch of clouds that represented the Sun still stood well above the western horizon, her body was more bone-tired than even a long day's slog through heat, damp, mud, and rain could account for.

"Four in the morning," Fox replied, nearly dropping his watch before managing to return it to his waistcoat pocket. Arabella shook her head and wiped her brow; whatever the hour, the air was hotter than the most sultry English mid-day.

The officer of their guards returned from inside the wall, accompanied by another French officer with still more braid on his shoulders and a more resplendent hat. This other officer was followed by a phalanx of fresh troops, comprising more Venusians than Frenchmen, who surrounded *Touchstone*'s airmen with brisk efficiency and marched them away. Gowse, Mills, and all the rest trudged through the gate without the energy even to look back. Arabella could only hope that she would see them again.

The Touchstones were followed by their previous guards, who would presumably receive rest and food within. But a few of the new guards remained behind, and led by their commander, they came over to where Fox, Arabella, Lady Corey, and the officers were standing. "Permit me to introduce myself," the commander said to Fox in accented English. "Capitaine Lefevre, *commandant* of Marieville." With a grand gesture he indicated the stockade behind him.

"Captain Fox, master and commander of the privateer *Touchstone* out of Sor Khoresh. Where have you taken my people?"

"To the barracks, where they will be fed and allowed to rest before beginning work to-morrow morning. We are not monsters, *monsieur*. As for yourself and your officers, you will naturally be permitted the liberty of our little town . . . provided that you make no attempt to escape or to hinder our operations in any way."

"We are gentlemen, sir," huffed Fox, stiffening. "We gave our parole when captured, as a matter of course. A man's parole is his word, and for an English gentleman to break his word is unthinkable."

"Thank you," replied Lefevre with a nod, and instructed his men to convey the *Anglais* to their *logements*.

"Brave heart, madam," Fox muttered to Arabella as he was led away.

Lefevre then turned to Lady Corey. "As for you and your . . . ?" He tilted his head, indicating Arabella.

"I am the Right Honorable Lady Corey, and this is my companion Mi—Mrs. Singh." Suddenly Arabella realized that, as a supposedly married woman, she no longer required—nor, indeed, could she depend upon—the protection of a chaperone. Even after the many sorrows of this extremely distressing day, this loss struck her with an unexpectedly poignant sting.

"*Enchanté,*" Lefevre said with a bow. "The two of you will be housed in the *manoir* along with myself and my officers. Our accommodations are, necessarily, rather spare, but we will do what we can to make you comfortable."

"If you please, sir . . ." Arabella said, then paused, not quite certain how to continue. She pressed ahead regardless. "My, my husband is Captain Prakash Singh of the Mars Company airship *Diana*. I am given to understand that he is imprisoned here."

"Ah yes, *le capitaine* Singh." Lefevre sighed dramatically. "As he is an officer, he is not, of course, imprisoned. Though this may not always be the case. . . . His actions on behalf of his men have often skirted the very limits of his parole."

At this reminder of her captain's assiduous dedication to *Diana's* people, Arabella's heart swelled painfully with love and longing. "If I may, sir, I wish to be . . . to be housed with him."

"Of course, *madame*. I believe he has his lodgings at the Auberge Gugnawunna, along with some of the other officers of his ship, and I will have you conveyed thence." He turned to Lady Corey. "And yourself, my lady? You would be most welcome at the *manoir*. We have been deprived of feminine company for time beyond measure."

The prospect of being the only human woman in a house full

of Frenchmen and Venusians clearly distressed Lady Corey, but she smiled and nodded her assent. "It would be my pleasure."

Lefevre turned his attention to his men, and Arabella took the opportunity to whisper to Lady Corey, "I am certain you would be welcome in the officers' lodgings."

"It would be beneath my station, my dear. And the opportunity to observe these frog-eaters at close quarters must not, alas, be lightly dismissed."

The moment passed, and Lefevre bowed and clicked his heels. "Madame Singh, my officers will conduct you to your husband. Lady Corey, may I accompany you to the *manoir*?" He held out an elbow.

"I would be honored," Lady Corey replied. She kept her voice pleasant, but her expression of sheer loathing—invisible to Lefevre and the other Frenchmen behind her—nearly made Arabella laugh aloud. Lady Corey smirked at Arabella's reaction; then her mien turned serious. "I have done all I can to prepare you," she said, taking Arabella's hands. "But from now on you will be on your own. Keep your wits about you, trust your instincts, and above all be polite to every one you meet."

Arabella's eyes stung with tears. "Will we see each other again?"

"In Heaven, if not before." Unexpectedly she leaned in and embraced Arabella—her bosom warm and soft, her fleshy arms unexpectedly strong. "Do be careful, Miss Ashby," she whispered in Arabella's ear. Then, with one final squeeze, she released her, took the Frenchman's arm, and departed with as much grace as she could muster—which was, Arabella realized, considerable, especially under the circumstances.

Watching the great lady sweep through the gate, Arabella felt herself a deflating balloon, with Lady Corey taking the very last of her air with her. Suddenly the lateness of the hour—four in the morning, had Fox said?—and the full weight of an exceptionally

long day spent tramping through heat, mud, and rain in unaccustomed gravity came crashing down upon her shoulders. It was all
she could do to remain upright as two unsmiling French officers
ushered her through the gate.

Within the stockade Arabella found what appeared to be a bustling
small town. Buildings of one or two storeys, roughly and apparently hastily constructed of peeled logs, stood shoulder to shoulder,
and in the streets between them men, Venusians, and animals moved
with a brusque, industrious attitude. The animals—squealing things
smaller than horses, supported on rubbery tentacles rather than
legs and having a glistening hide like wet black leather—pulled
single-wheeled carts loaded with lumber or charcoal, goaded on by
Venusians with iron prods. The Venusians took no apparent notice
of Arabella, while many of the humans—ragged and filthy men,
supervised by a few uniformed French soldiers—stared openly. No
doubt she was the first human woman they had seen since arriving
in this desolate place.

The stench of the town was oppressive. The streets reeked of
mud, the swampy muck of the Venusian animals, and slops from
the workers' meals; the air, dark with smoke, carried the same metallic tang she had detected earlier, only far stronger. Arabella held
a handkerchief to her nose, but as the smells were so pervasive she
feared she would have no alternative but to become habituated to
them. However, as the heat and gravity were still as oppressive to
her now as they had been when she landed, that habituation seemed
unlikely.

Finally her guards brought her to a two-storey building which
bore a sign above the door in tadpole-like curves which she took
for Venusian writing; below this, in smaller letters: AUBERGE
GUGNAWUNNA. Her guards conveyed her within—the doorway

was covered by a rubbery leather flap rather than a proper door—and, with a curt salute, departed.

Weary to her bones, blinking in the sudden dimness, Arabella stood swaying on her feet. The room held nothing but a few chairs and tables; doorways led to other rooms. "Hello?" she called.

A Venusian, wearing a cutaway coat of Continental style, ludicrously ill-fitting to his inhuman form, emerged from one of the doorways. Upon seeing her, he bowed low. "*Bon après-midi, mademoiselle,*" he croaked. "*Permettez-moi de me présenter; je m'appelle Gugnawunna, l'humble hôte de cette auberge modeste.*" I am Gugnawunna, the humble host of this modest inn.

So exhausted was Arabella that the ridiculous sight of a man-sized frog speaking elevated French drove her nearly to tears of despair rather than laughter. "*S'il vous plaît, monsieur, parlez-vous anglais?*"

"*Certainement pas!*" he huffed, plainly offended by the very suggestion that he might speak English.

Arabella sighed and racked her weary brain for some usable scraps of French. "*Je cherche mon mari,*" she managed somehow, "*le capitaine Singh.*"

"*Bien sûr, madame,*" the Venusian replied, correcting her marital status without a blink of his large, shining eyes. "*Il réside certainement ici, mais il n'est pas présent au moment. Souhaitez-vous vous asseoir?*" She didn't understand all of that, but "not present at the moment" was clear, as were the words "seat yourself."

"*Merci, monsieur,*" she assented with unfeigned gratitude, and sank into one of the chairs. It was hard and low and rather crude and splintery, but still a great relief. "*Avez-vous . . .*" She could not for the life of her recall the French for "something cool to drink," so she mimed drinking.

"*Quelque chose à boire? Naturellement, madame! Nous avons une jolie kulawagagna. Très rafraîchissant.*"

She had no idea what a "jolly *kulawagagna*" might be, but if it was "very refreshing" she was more than willing to try it. "*Merci, monsieur.*"

The Venusian did not move. "*Ce sera cinq sous, s'il vous plaît.*" Five sous. A sou was a French coin, a small one, though she had no idea of its relative value.

"*Je n'ai pas . . . pas d'argent vénusienne, monsieur.*" She fumbled in her reticule. "*J'ai d'argent anglais . . .*" Though, in truth, she had very little in the way of English spending money either. What she did have was a letter of note for five hundred pounds sterling drawn on the Bank of Fort Augusta, but that would do her no good for small transactions, and she feared it might not be negotiable at all in the French-controlled areas of Venus.

The Venusian's wide mouth drew even wider, an inhuman expression but certainly not one of approval. "*Nous ne pourrions jamais accepter une telle chose ici!*" In addition to his harsh tone of voice, the words "never accept" were unmistakable.

"*Je m'excuse, monsieur . . .*"

"*Vous pouvez néanmoins attendre ici,*" he sniffed—the last two words meant "wait here"—then without another word he turned and withdrew to the back room from which he had emerged.

Hot, heavy, thirsty, weary, exhausted, alone, and desolate, Arabella put her head in her hands and cried.

———

An unknown time later Arabella's misery was interrupted by the sound of the door flap, along with footsteps and a momentary decrease in the dimness of the room. The footsteps stopped suddenly, accompanied by the sound of an indrawn breath.

"Miss . . . Miss *Ashby*?"

Even as she raised her tear-streaked face she knew what she would see, for that voice, even after so many months of separation, was as familiar and beloved to her as her own: it was that of her fiancé, her beloved, her captain.

But the man she beheld was not what she expected. Instead, she saw a distressing apparition, like a figure of Death from some medieval manuscript—little more than dark skin stretched over long bones. Deep hollows lay beneath his eyes, and she could count every rib. He had a long, ragged beard, streaked with gray though he was only thirty-two years of age; his hair was bound up in a cloth; and he was shockingly naked, except for a sort of diaper of white cloth bound about his loins. But his eyes . . . they were still dark and full of intelligence, and though clearly very weary and sad there was no mistaking them.

"My dear Captain Singh," she began, and then words fled and she rose, stumbling, to fling herself across the room and into his arms. "My dear, dear, Captain Singh," she repeated, holding him close—feeling his collar-bone sharp against her cheek, smelling the smoke and sweat of his unwashed skin, but not caring . . . for finally, after all these months, she was reunited with her captain.

Then the sound of a throat being cleared made her raise her head.

Captain Singh had not been alone when he had entered. Richardson, *Diana*'s first mate, and Stross, her sailing-master, stood behind him. They seemed as thin and haggard as their captain, though unlike him they wore proper breeches, waistcoats, and shirts—albeit ragged and filthy—and their faces reflected a mixture of pleased surprise at Arabella's presence and shock at her unseemly behavior.

"Pardon me," she managed, separating herself from the captain. She noted that he had not embraced her as she had embraced him, and for this she was simultaneously impressed—by his propriety, even under these circumstances—and, she must confess, disappointed. "It was merely that I . . . that I have not seen my husband in so long." As she spoke, putting a slight but significant stress on the word *husband,* she looked directly into Captain Singh's face, willing him to understand.

That face, turned away from the officers behind him, displayed a rapid sequence of emotions—puzzlement, surprise, and dawning comprehension—which reassured Arabella that her love for him and trust in his intelligence were not misplaced.

"I am sorry not to have included you in the secret of our nuptials," she continued, addressing Richardson and Stross, confident now that her captain would follow her lead in this. "And I apologize for breaking the news to your officers in such a precipitate manner," she said to the captain. "I was forced to reveal the truth to Capitaine Lefevre so that I could be housed with you."

"I quite understand, mi—my dear," the captain replied. He stepped up to her and, quite chastely, kissed her upon the cheek. Though she would have preferred a more demonstrative expression of affection, she reminded herself that it was entirely appropriate under the circumstances. "In fact, I am glad that the secret is finally out. May I inform the people?" He meant *Diana's* crew.

"Of course, my dear."

"Congratulations, sir!" said Richardson, putting out his hand for the captain. "I wish you great joy of it." Stross, a Scotsman, was naturally more reserved but likewise offered his congratulations, and both wished Arabella happiness.

"As for myself," the captain said to Arabella, "I must apologize for my appearance. The heat and dampness of Venus are, as you have no doubt discerned, quite at odds with proper English dress, and I have reverted to the clothing of my youth in India. However, now that you are here, we will all certainly resume the attire expected of an officer and a gentleman." He cast an eye to his first mate and sailing-master. They nodded their assent, looking rather shamefaced.

"No apologies are required, sir," she said, dropping a curtsey.

"I am very happy to see you, no matter how you are dressed." But the gauntness and ragged clothing of all three of them were worrisome, and reminded her of the sorry state of her own dress . . . and her own considerable weariness, which had retreated momentarily in the face of the emotions of reunion but now came flooding back in force.

"I have forgotten myself," Captain Singh said after a long moment, breaking the uncomfortable silence. "I should invite you in to dress for dinner." He turned to his officers. "We can divide the room with a cloth, for privacy."

"Of course, sir," said Richardson, touching his forehead. "I will have one of the men find one and bring it up. Failing that, I am certain that Gugnawunna will be more than happy to sell us something." From his tone of voice, he expected the cost to be exorbitant.

But rather than thanking the men for their kindness, Arabella merely stood trembling and distraught. For she had no other clothing in which to dress, and that realization drove home the very great distance between herself and every thing she owned, knew, or cared for. All except her beloved captain.

And yet he, too, was more distant than she would like.

───────────

Arabella awoke with a start. All was dark, but the sounds and smells, not to mention the rough pillow beneath her cheek, were terribly unfamiliar. Alarmed, she sat bolt upright.

She found herself in a small and rather rudely-built bedchamber, dimly illuminated by a lambent greenish light from a single window. The walls were of rough timber chinked with mud, the bed and close-stool similarly rustic in construction, and the room was divided in two by a cloth hung from the ceiling. From the other side of that cloth came the snores of at least two people. The air was still and damp and, despite the apparent lateness of the hour, terribly hot.

Another snore, this one from much closer, drew her attention to the shadows beneath the window.

There, in a hard wooden chair, slept Captain Singh.

The sight brought the events of the last days flooding back. The capture of *Touchstone*, the long march across country, the reunion with her fiancé—no, her *husband*, she reminded herself, she must never relax that pretense even within her own mind—and then the way she had, shamefully, allowed herself to fall into a near-stupor from exhaustion as her captain and his officers had found her something to eat and laid her in this hard, narrow bed. After that she remembered nothing.

Arabella took a breath, held it, released it with a silent sigh. She had reached Venus, she told herself; she was alive, she was with her captain, all would be well.

Yet he seemed so terribly wan and thin, and his warm brown skin in the greenish light seemed chalky, gray, and unhealthy. All her brave plans and expectations to aid in his escape had collapsed; her way forward from here was uncertain at best.

She shook her head, trying to drive all such unprofitable thoughts away into the chirping, creaking darkness, and lay herself back down to sleep. But sleep would not come; indeed, she seemed more awake than ever.

What time, she wondered, would show on Captain Fox's watch now? It had been four in the morning the last time she had checked, though the Sun of Venus had stood at mid-afternoon. Now, deep in Venus's night, the time to which her body was accustomed must be late morning or early afternoon. Small wonder that she could not sleep. She would eventually, she supposed, become reconciled to Venus time, but for now she found herself wide awake.

The thought of Fox's watch naturally brought to mind Fox himself. He might at this moment be as sleepless as she, in his own quarters, wherever those might be.

As quietly as she could she slipped from the bed. She was wearing her chemise, she found, and her stays had been loosened but not removed. She padded barefoot across the floor and peered out the window.

The wan, greenish light, she saw, came from a lantern on a pole which stood in the street. Yet that lantern with its strange illumination was fueled neither by oil nor gas, but rather—she peered intently at it—a living thing! She had seen glow-worms once in England, and this seemed similar . . . though much larger, as long as her forearm. Its glowing after-parts pulsed gently and regularly with its breathing, and its mouth-parts seemed fastened to a bottle at the top of the pole, like a Martian *tukurush* supping from a *kekhel*-blossom. This bottle, she theorized, kept the worm supplied with nourishment.

The street illuminated by this peculiar living lantern lay vacant except for a pair of Venusians in French uniform, who marched along in lock-step with fixed bayonets. All else was quiet, and no candle gleamed in any of the windows that overlooked the street. Behind one of those dark windows, perhaps, lay Fox, wakeful or not.

The man could be annoying, with his glib self-assurance, his untidiness, and his ever-present smirk. But he was intelligent, energetic, and certainly did not lack for bravery; of all the men she had met in her voyages, he seemed the one most likely to be able to effect an escape from a Venusian prison-camp.

Other than Captain Singh, of course, she reminded herself. Though this exhausted, emaciated man did not much resemble the proud captain to whom she had proposed marriage so many months and miles ago.

Arabella gazed upon his sleeping face, with its sunken eyes and drawn cheeks. She longed to kiss his forehead and wake him and have him tell her that all would be well, but he plainly needed his sleep.

She slipped back beneath the sheet—even a single sheet was nearly too much in this heat, but propriety seemed to demand it—and lay staring into the darkness for an unknown time before, finally, returning to her uneasy dreams.

———————

The next time she awoke the room was empty of people and filled with sunlight. The cloth had been taken down, and the other bed, as narrow as hers, had been made up with naval precision; from without came the clatter of knives and forks, and she realized she was famished.

Her dress had been draped gently over the footboard of her bed. She picked it up and saw that, though it had been cleaned somewhat, the mud of the last day's long march had permanently soiled the hem. But despite that, and despite the revulsion she felt at the thought of putting even one more layer of clothing upon her person in this dreadful heat and damp, it was now the only dress she owned, and so she put it on.

Following the sound of cutlery and conversation, she descended the rough-hewn and creaking stairs to a parlor where her captain sat at a small table with Stross and Richardson, taking breakfast. Several other tables, likewise occupied, crowded the small space; she recognized some of the men occupying them as officers from *Diana,* though others were unfamiliar to her. Gugnawunna and two other Venusians bustled about with steaming plates.

The captain, noting her presence, at once stood and bowed. He had put off his uncivilized clothing and now stood shaved and uniformed as a captain of the Honorable Mars Company should.

Though his uniform coat was plainly quite worn and patched, he cut quite a dashing figure, and her heart thrilled at the sight of him. Richardson and Stross had likewise tidied themselves up.

All the other men in the room stood and bowed as well, and she dropped a curtsey in response. The captain introduced her to the other diners—the shock of being referred to as "Mrs. Singh" was somewhat diminished, but still very much present—and she seated herself at an empty chair at his table.

"I am pleased you are able to join us for breakfast," he said. The table was laid *á la Français,* with all the courses set out at once: a pie which smelled of fish; a plate of peas or something similar; soft white bread in the French style; wine, of course; and coffee. She gratefully accepted a cup of coffee, hoping its stimulating qualities would overcome the haze which still overlaid her brain from her long wakeful night. "We thought it best to allow you to sleep."

"I blame the French," she replied, buttering her bread. The butter was off, she realized, but she was so famished she ate it anyway. "They were so impolite as to capture us before we had an opportunity to synchronize ship's time with our destination."

"They can be terribly inconsiderate," the captain said, and for a moment his eyes had the same eager brightness she had once known. But that spark faded quickly, replaced by an expression of weary care. "Unfortunately, we cannot dawdle over our breakfast. We must all report for *appel,* or roll-call, at eight o'clock, after which I have secured an appointment with Lefevre to discuss the officers' gambling debts."

"Gambling?" Of all the difficulties she had expected to confront in a Venusian prison-camp, that was not one.

"Sadly, yes. Unlike the rank and file, officers are not required to labor on the iron plantation, and find themselves with nothing but time on their hands. Many of them have taken up that vice, to their great detriment, and several have gone so far in arrears that the senior officers have had to get up a subscription for them, to prevent them being sent down to the plantation to work off their debts. I intend to ask Lefevre to close the gaming-house." He sighed. "Although I believe he is personally profiting from the proceedings, I hope that an appeal to his honor as a gentleman may bear fruit."

The expression on Stross's face showed how little hope he himself held out of that, but one of the other phrases in the captain's explanation had caught Arabella's ear. "You said 'iron plantation.' When the French commander told us where we were going"—she did not mention that it was her intercession that had caused the Touchstones to be sent here—"he said *plantation de fer*,' and I was certain I had misheard. Surely iron does not grow on trees, even on Venus?"

"Iron *ore* does not, Mrs. Singh," said Stross, "but *refining* iron—turning the raw ore from the mine into bars of pure iron, ready to be made into cannon-balls or nails or what have you—requires tons and tons of charcoal. And that *does* grow on trees."

The making of charcoal was a grueling process with which Arabella was far too familiar. On her voyage from Earth to Mars, *Diana* had lost her coal stores in an attack by a French corsair and had been forced to stop at an asteroid and make charcoal to replace it.

Richardson wiped his mouth with a napkin. "The plantation is an invention of a Mr. Fulton, from America. It requires an iron mine, a limestone quarry, a forest, and a river in close proximity to each other, which explains why the town of Marieville was built in this particular spot, so far from even what the froggies consider civilization."

"*Diana*'s people," the captain said with considerable vexation, "must spend fourteen hours each twenty-eight-hour day, six days a week, cutting down the forest and burning it to charcoal for the blast furnaces."

Arabella was stunned. "Surely the rules of war prohibit compelling prisoners of war to labor in aid of their captors?"

The captain's face, already choleric, grew still darker. "Lefevre claims that the laws of Venus—to be precise, the laws of *French-controlled* Venus—permit this barbaric behavior. My arguments to the contrary have fallen on deaf ears." Again he sighed. "But it could be worse. The people of other ships labor in the dark of the mines—the death toll is appalling—or in the infernal heat of the furnace-house. At least I have been able to keep them from that."

As the captain spoke, Arabella's outrage at the situation rose and rose. But before she could express it, a church-bell rang without, and all the diners immediately leapt to their feet. "Eight o'clock," commented Richardson, "seems to come earlier every day."

"We must all report to the square," the captain said, drawing out Arabella's chair, "for roll-call. Twice a day, at eight in the morning and four in the afternoon. And we must report back to our lodgings by ten each night."

"Keep in mind," Stross said as they proceeded to the door, "that on Venus, with her twenty-eight-hour day, noon and midnight are fourteen o'clock."

The officers yawned and chatted desultorily among themselves as they made their way through the muddy streets toward the square. And then, as they rounded a corner, Arabella saw Fox, Liddon, and several others of *Touchstone*'s officers in a small group ahead of them. She immediately hallooed, quite improperly, and waved them over.

"Captain Fox," she said, "may I present Captain Singh, of the Honorable Mars Company airship *Diana*. Captain Singh, this is Captain Fox of the privateer *Touchstone* out of Sor Khoresh."

The two men shook hands. "Very pleased to make your acquaintance, sir," said Fox with sincerity. "I have heard so much about you."

"I would wish the circumstances were better, sir," was all Captain Singh said in reply, and at this Arabella was taken aback. She had thought he might offer thanks to Fox for bearing Arabella safely across the airy wastes from Mars to Venus—exhausted though she had been the previous night, she had provided a brief summary of the voyage—or at least to express the fellow-feeling of one captured captain to another. The captain had always been a reserved man, but this response, though polite enough, struck her as very nearly cold.

Nonetheless, Fox did not seem to take it badly, and the two captains proceeded to introduce their officers to each other . . . a rather lengthy process, at the end of which they were compelled to make haste so as not to be late for roll-call.

Once there—Lefevre, from where he stood at the top of the square, plainly noticed the distinctive Captain Singh arriving at the last minute, and muttered something to a secretary standing behind him—they lined up in the third rank, even as those in the front were already calling out their names.

There were perhaps sixty men present, and though they were all officers they were a ragged and shabby lot; Fox and the other Touchstones, worn though they were from the previous day's march, were by far the most presentable. She hated to think what the ordinary airmen—working fourteen hours a day at the backbreaking, filthy tasks of cutting wood, making charcoal, and mining iron—must look like.

Arabella was distracted from her observations by Richardson, standing in line on the far side of the captain, calling out his name, followed by cries of "Stross" and then "Singh." Arabella, last in line, automatically called out "Ashby" before, rather embarrassed, correcting it to "Singh."

The roll-call having concluded, Lefevre stepped up and said, "Permit me to extend an official welcome to the men, and ladies"— he nodded to Arabella—"of *Touchstone* who have recently joined us.

Welcome to Marieville, and I trust you slept well. You will find that, so long as you obey all of our rules and regulations, your life here will actually be quite pleasant, with a broad range of entertainments available to occupy your time."

"All of which," the captain muttered to Arabella without moving his lips, "line Lefevre's pockets, either directly or indirectly."

"However," Lefevre continued, "if you do *not* choose to respect the laws and customs of our little municipality, we will have no alternative but to restrict your access to these entertainments, restrain your liberties, and—if absolutely necessary—even to punish you." He shook his head, eyes downcast, in a theatrical show of distress at even the contemplation of such an action. "But I am certain that, as officers and gentlemen, you will not compel us to do so." Here he fixed Captain Singh with a particular glare, in reply to which the captain returned only a steady gaze. "Are there any questions? None? Good." He had not given even the pretense of pausing. "You are dismissed."

As the men shuffled wearily out of the square, Captain Singh spoke with Richardson, Stross, and *Diana*'s other officers. Arabella cast a glance at Fox as he departed, but he was engaged with the men of *Touchstone* and did not return it.

"I must meet with Lefevre now," Captain Singh said, "to see if the gaming-house may be closed. Mr. Richardson, pray continue in your efforts to obtain fresh straw for the men's beds. Mr. Stross, the repairs to the leak in the roof of the north barracks have proven inadequate, and require further attention." He continued in this vein until each of his officers had been given their assignment for the day.

"And as for myself?" Arabella asked.

The captain seemed nonplussed at the request. "If you do not wish to remain at the *auberge* . . . I suppose you may accompany me to the *manoir*."

She was not entirely satisfied with this response, but with the officers looking on she chose to say only "Well then, I shall accompany you."

"Very well," was his only reply.

The officers saluted and departed, leaving Arabella and Captain Singh together in awkward silence. "Mrs. Singh?" he said, breaking the moment by offering his arm.

She took it, and together they proceeded in silence out of the square.

———————

As they proceeded arm in arm up the gently climbing wooded path toward the manor house, the silence continuing as the captain occasionally nodded to acquaintances, the pressure within Arabella to say *something* built and built until she finally burst out, "I would have hoped you would be happier to see me!"

He paused and looked around—there was no one nearby at the moment—before replying. "I must confess I am . . . disappointed in you, Mrs. Singh. In my every letter I emphasized that you should *not* attempt to join me here."

"I received only one letter," she replied, trying and failing not to let her tone become defensive.

"That is unfortunate. Which one?"

She briefly described its contents—it was not difficult to do so, as she had read and re-read it so many times its every phrase was burned upon her heart.

The captain sighed. "Then I suppose you may be forgiven, as that was the very first of them and our circumstances had not . . . decayed, to their current state. Still, even in that first letter I did request that you remain safely at home."

"But I could not! Once I learned that the dread Fouché had been appointed as Napoleon's Minister of Police, I knew that I must at least attempt to inform you of the danger before his arrival."

"Ah, yes, the famous Executioner of Lyon. We have been well aware for some time that he is on his way; in fact, I received word only last week that he has already arrived on Venus."

Arabella was astonished at how coolly the captain reported this intelligence. "How can you be so calm? Are plans for your escape so far advanced?"

Again the captain looked in every direction before replying, and his face when he turned it back to Arabella was terribly grave. "There *are* no plans for escape, and you must put the very idea out of your mind. We are surrounded on all sides by miles of impenetrable jungle, rife with wild beasts and populated only by Venusians loyal to Napoleon. The majority of those who attempt escape are returned within days, to face the fiercest punishment; of the rest, we have heard nothing at all. We must assume they have fallen to the many hazards of this unpleasant planet."

The sound of footsteps on the path ahead interrupted their conversation, and they resumed their upward progress until the other party—a group of three Venusians in native dress, carrying empty leathery panniers and presumably headed to the market in Marieville for provisions for the *manoir*—had passed. As they walked, Arabella could not fail to notice how rigid were the muscles of the captain's arm beneath its sleeve.

They walked together for a time in silence. "I did not come to Venus without resources, sir," she said when the Venusians had passed out of hearing range. "I have done considerable reading on the subject of escape by prisoners of war, and I am aware that a key factor in a successful escape is money—which may be used to bribe guards, hire transportation, procure documents, and the like. To this end I have brought with me a letter of note, in the amount of five hundred pounds, from the Bank of Fort Augusta." She patted her reticule, into whose lining the note was securely sewn. "Such an amount might perhaps be sufficient to secure the cooperation of even the butcher Fouché."

"A generous sum indeed," the captain replied, "but much will be lost in the conversion to French livres. Napoleon has absolutely prohibited the bankers of Venus to answer any English bills for more than a hundred pounds. There are means of evading this prohibition, to be sure, but their costs are dire. And Fouché, despite his barbarity, is far too loyal to Napoleon to be swayed by mere money." He shook his head. "No, that note cannot effect an escape. But it can be used to better the men's conditions, and could in fact have substantial consequence in that area." He glanced sidelong at Arabella. "A husband can compel his wife to turn such a note over to him, for whatever purpose he desires. I would not, of course, do any such thing, and under our . . . current circumstances, I *may* not. But I can *request* that you do so."

Just at that moment they rounded a copse of trees and came upon the *manoir,* a large square house of whitewashed clapboard bustling with people, both human and Venusian. An enormous French flag flapped languidly in the damp, oppressive breeze.

"I will take your request under advisement," Arabella murmured as their feet crunched onto the gravel path leading to the entrance portico.

13

SURGERY

They were ushered into the sitting-room by a Venusian in an old-fashioned coat and powdered wig, which sat oddly on the wide skull behind his protuberant eyes. *"Attendez ici, s'il vous plaît,"* he croaked, and left them to wait upon Lefevre along with several French officers and a Venusian in native dress.

Arabella chose to wait in silence, rather than pretend light conversation with a captain with whom she was, to be frank, rather cross. In the absence of conversation, she took the opportunity to observe the Venusian carefully. He—or was it indeed a he? She had seen few of the natives so far, and had noted no distinctions of sex in dress or form among them—squatted comfortably on the floor between the provided chairs, wearing a shirt and long trousers of sheer white fabric and a vest of some leathery material. The fabric, she realized, was Venusian silk of the very highest quality—the same first-rate stuff, light and strong and air-tight, that made up the balloon envelopes of airfaring ships. Such an ensemble would be beyond the means of all but the most wealthy aristocrats of Earth or Mars, and yet a Venusian who gave every appearance of being a common tradesman wore it as though it were nothing but cheap linen.

The buttons on his vest, too, were unusual—highly polished stone, from the look of them, or perhaps wood, with an intriguing pattern of black and pale red. Perhaps they were coral? As she attempted to discern whether they were attached with thread or sinew, the Venusian reached into the leather pouch at his hip and drew out a short pipe of black clay, which he proceeded to fill with something resembling tobacco and set alight with a flint and steel. The smoke was pungent but not entirely unpleasant, and as the Venusian rocked back on his heels and puffed contemplatively she realized that, despite his bare webbed feet, he was no mere savage but a civilized creature. What thoughts, she wondered, ran through the mind behind those shining eyes?

Just then a human aide-de-camp appeared at the sitting-room door and brusquely bid Captain Singh accompany him to Lefevre's office. "I do not know when I shall return," the captain told Arabella as he rose. "Perhaps half an hour, perhaps more."

"I shall endeavor to occupy myself until then," Arabella replied with chill formality.

"Until then, my dear," he said, pointedly ignoring her tone, and departed with a deep respectful bow.

In the wake of the captain's departure, Arabella found her sentiments in turmoil. She was, to be certain, quite disappointed with his secrecy, his aloofness, and his apparent lack of interest in escape. But the very sight of him—the strong brown hands with their long fingers, the full lips which carried a slight smile even in these unpleasant circumstances, the posture still erect and unbowed despite his captivity—gladdened her heart, and as long as he was with her she felt that, somehow, all would be well.

"Arabella Ashby," she chided herself, "you are a silly, silly girl."

"You are looking well, Mrs. Singh," came a voice, as if in response to her unvoiced thought. Startled, she looked up. It was Lady Corey!

"Lady Corey! I am delighted to see you." And, in truth, she was, though her feelings toward the older woman were still somewhat mixed.

"And I you." She seated herself upon the hard bench beside Arabella, pointedly choosing the side away from the Venusian and his pipe. "When I saw Captain Singh in the hall I suspected that you might be here." Her mien turned serious. "How do you fare, in the town?"

"Well enough, I suppose. I share a room with the captain and two of his officers, though they have hung a cloth between our side of the room and theirs. The food is acceptable, though I gather it is quite expensive. And we must report for roll-call twice a day."

"How many beds?"

"Two," Arabella replied with deliberate ambiguity. She had not, she realized, considered the question of to-night's sleeping arrangements—the prospect of compelling her dear captain to sleep in a hard chair again pained her, but the alternatives were equally untenable.

Lady Corey nodded, though Arabella thought from her expression that she had noted Arabella's equivocation and chosen to accept it at face value rather than raise uncomfortable questions. "As for myself, I have been treated well. I have a small room to myself, and I share a Venusian servant"—her nose wrinkled— "with an American called Fulton."

"Fulton is here? I had not understood that he was present in person. He is the inventor of the iron plantation . . . I suppose he must be very clever."

"He certainly thinks himself so." Again her nose wrinkled. "We had not been acquainted for more than five minutes before he began to boast to me of the canal-digging machines, steam-powered river boats, and submarine vessels he has invented. Fancies himself a painter into the bargain. He even had the cheek to invite me to sit for a portrait! 'After,' he says, 'the current work is completed.'"

"And what 'current work' might that be?"

"I have no idea. Something terribly clever, I am sure."

"Hm." Arabella pondered the question. Judging by the large swaths of forest which had already been cut down, the iron plantation had been running for some time—years, perhaps—and its operations in the town seemed to be well in hand. An American with so many inventions to his credit would surely not content himself with the simple operation, or even improvement, of a process so settled. "I wonder what such a talented man is doing *here*, so very far from civilization. Perhaps you could make discreet inquiries?"

Lady Corey, clearly understanding the thrust of Arabella's query, nodded. "I shall." But then she tilted her head back slightly and regarded Arabella with an appraising eye. "Something is troubling you."

The simple truth of Lady Corey's statement caused Arabella's earlier disordered sentiments to return with renewed force—so strong indeed that she was compelled to bite her lip and turn away rather than burst into tears. "It is nothing."

"You are still a terrible liar, my dear girl." She patted Arabella's hand and rose from the bench. "Let us walk in the garden, such as it is."

———————————

The "garden" proved to be a simple patch of open ground behind the house, filled with plants in orderly rows. Large gourd-like growths on some of them implied it was a source of vegetables for the manor.

"Now," Lady Corey said once they were well away from any one who might overhear, "what is the matter?"

Arabella had been considering her answer ever since they had left the sitting-room, but still she hesitated before replying. For her to confess her mixed feelings toward her captain seemed a betrayal—of her fiancé, and of her own previous self—yet she could not simply deny that any thing was wrong. "I do not know how to behave in such a situation," she said. "This . . . place is made for men; it has no room for a lady. Yet I feel I must do *something*."

Lady Corey's expression turned calculating. For a moment she seemed about to call Arabella to account on her prevarication, but what she said was this: "The main and inescapable duty of the upper classes, especially in time of crisis, is always to *support*, the *common*, *people*." She emphasized each word with a firm gesture of her closed fan in the air, and her determined face showed how important she felt this advice to be.

"Gentlemen," she continued, "are taught from the cradle to plan and strategize, to command decisively, to stand bravely in the face of the enemy. They lead from the front. We gentle ladies, in our turn, must support the cause from the rear, by providing aid and comfort. In time of war, we visit the sick and wounded, to raise their spirits with kind words and gentle touch. We console the bereft and bring food to the hungry. Even in the unlikely case of defeat, we hold our heads high as we walk through the rubble, to show that the English are never, ever beaten."

The prospect was daunting. "I . . . I am not certain I am equal to the task."

"You underestimate your own abilities, my dear. I have seen you keep your head in situations that would cause most women—even, I daresay, most men—to run mad with despair."

"But that was different! During the siege of Corey House, I had duties—actions, negotiations, plans to make—and I was familiar with Mars and the Martians. Here, I am idle and ignorant!"

"Nonetheless, your inner strength is the same." She patted Arabella's arm. "In all circumstances, no matter how difficult, a

gentle lady's role is simply to be present and calm—to visibly display unswerving fortitude, no matter our inward feelings—so as
to hearten and encourage those around us. And you are entirely
capable of that."

Arabella took a deep breath and let it out slowly. "I will endeavor to keep your advice in mind. But it will be difficult."

"Of course it will. If it were easy, any commoner could do it."

——————

They returned to the manor house, where they found Captain
Singh in the sitting-room, engaged in conversation with another
English officer. Though Arabella had not been able to discuss the
true source of her agitated emotions with Lady Corey, the conversation had nonetheless been of some help to her, and after taking
their leave of Lady Corey and the English officer she walked out
on the captain's arm with greater confidence than before.

But the captain's mind was clearly elsewhere, and once they
had departed the manor house he confided in her that his discussion with Lefevre had not been fruitful. "He insists that these
'entertainments,' as he puts it, are necessary for the officers' morale, and absolutely refuses to shut the gaming-house. He did hint
broadly that a substantial payment, presented to him personally,
might persuade him to change his mind, but I fear that such a
transaction would only lead to further and greater such requests."
He shook his head. "We have no alternative but to take up a collection to pay the debts of those men who have been most deeply
ensnared. Though I fear the wealthier officers are already tiring of
these requests."

"Perhaps you can approach the less wealthy men—they may
have less to give, but surely there are more of them. If nothing
else, the request may serve as a reminder of the dangers of gambling, and help to prevent others from falling into the same trap."

"An excellent suggestion."

They walked in companionable silence for a time. "Is this," Arabella asked, "one of the uses to which you are thinking my five hundred pounds might be put?"

"Not in the least," he replied with some heat. "The officers who have indebted themselves at the gaming-house have no one but themselves to blame; it is mere common courtesy to redeem them. But the men who have been captured by the ogre Napoleon and put to work—horrendous work—in defiance of the laws of war . . . their conditions are no fault of their own, and it is our duty as Englishmen—and women—to ameliorate them as much as possible."

Surely, Arabella thought to herself, the best amelioration would be to escape this town and this planet completely, but knowing this suggestion would fall on deaf ears, what she said was "Please help me to understand the men's conditions, so that I may put the money to the best possible use."

The captain looked to Arabella with an inspecting eye, then cast that eye upward at the brighter spot in the clouds which represented the Sun. "Some eight hours remain until they return to the barracks. We officers are not permitted to visit them at their work, but we may observe them from a distance, if you like. Though I warn you, their situation is horrific."

"I believe that I must," she said, thinking back to her conversation with Lady Corey. "And to visit them at the barracks when they return there. It is, as you point out, our duty as gentlemen and ladies."

"Very well."

At the next turning, the captain directed them to a different path than the one by which they had come. This one twisted back upon itself and rose precipitously. "Mind your step, here," the captain warned at one point.

"I noticed you consulting the Sun for the time," Arabella said after they had cleared the difficult patch. "What has become of your pocket-watch?" The captain, an aficionado of all things mechanical, had possessed a very fine pocket-watch, an instrument of unsurpassed accuracy which showed the orbital positions of the major planets and chimed on the hour.

"I sold it," he replied without emotion. "Watson required medicine."

Arabella remembered Watson, one of *Diana*'s midshipmen, with considerable fondness; during the mutiny, he had leapt to her defense when she had been threatened with the lash. "I see," she said, and her feelings toward the captain warmed still further.

Eventually they found themselves atop an outcropping of stone from which they could look down into the valley. "There," the captain said, pointing.

Following his finger, Arabella made out the tiny figures of men at one end of a long strip of bare ground in the midst of the forest. Two of them labored rhythmically, one on each end of a long saw, to bring down a massive tree; others used axes to hew a previously-felled tree into pieces of manageable size. Nearby stood a group of round structures, each some thirty feet in diameter, from several of which threads of smoke rose into the air.

"What are those? Are they huts?"

"Those are the charcoal mounds, where the wood smolders into charcoal over a period of weeks. That French officer is the collier, in charge of the work. He supervises the men as they stack the wood and cover it with mud and leaves; there is no opportunity to sabotage the process." Indeed, she saw that the officer—readily distinguished from the filthy prisoners by the bright white, red, and blue of his uniform—kept a close eye on the work and was accompanied by several Venusians, also in uniform and armed with swords and pistols.

"Why is that man jumping up and down atop the mound?"

Despite the absurdity of the man's actions, the captain's face turned grim. "He is packing down the air pockets. It is the most dangerous part of the job."

Even as the captain spoke, the jumping man's feet crashed through the top layer of mud, leaves, and sticks, releasing a gout of smoke and flame. The man's cries could be plainly heard even across the great distance from which Arabella observed him. "Oh my goodness! Who is it?"

The captain peered in the man's direction. "I cannot be certain. Parker, perhaps, or Bates."

At the man's screams the French officer and several of his Venusians had immediately come running. But after they had clambered to the top of the mound and pulled the injured man from the smoldering pit in which his legs had become trapped, she was shocked to see that they simply rolled him down the mound's side to the ground, concentrating their attention instead on repairing the damage to the mound itself. "We must help him!" Arabella cried.

"We cannot," the captain countered, holding her back with a firm hand. "I have given my parole and may not interfere."

"But he is injured!" The man was clutching his leg and howling piteously.

"He will be attended to, once the mound has been patched. The bribes I have paid to the guards should insure that much, at least." He turned away from the horrific sight. "In any case, if we were to approach, we would be shot."

But Arabella could not avert her gaze. She bit her lips, the smoky air coming hot and fast through her nose, as she gazed down at the unfortunate man. Several others had come running from the chopping and stacking operations nearby, but two of the Venusians warded them away from the damaged mound until the repairs at the top of it had been completed. After that, they permitted two of the men to carry their injured comrade away, accompanied by two armed guards. The other men were herded back to their work chopping and hauling wood. "Where are they taking him?"

The captain, she realized, had already moved some way down the path toward the town as she had stood frozen with outrage. "To the barracks," he replied over his shoulder. "We will meet them there. Come, we must alert the surgeon."

Diana's surgeon was a portly bespectacled man called Withers. They hastened back to the town where, after making inquiries, they found him playing piquet in the sitting-room of his rooming-house. Upon being informed of the situation, his expression turned grim and he hurried upstairs to fetch his medical bag. "Another burn," he muttered as he departed the table. "Always burns."

From there they proceeded across the square, out the gate in the palisade—they were required to present their papers to the Venusian guards there—and down a path to a separate stockade she had not visited before. This high wall of logs, each sharply pointed at the top, enclosed the enlisted men's barracks, and once admitted therein she found a scene of such dire squalor she let out a gasp.

The barracks themselves were a series of long buildings, windowless and even more roughly constructed than the rude structures in the town, and beyond them lay an open latrine reeking with filth. "They will bring him to the mess-hall," the surgeon said, hurrying toward a central square building from which rose a stream of greasy smoke and a most unappetizing smell.

Within the hall they found long tables, each composed of a single large plank of wood laid over trestles, with an unpeeled log on each side serving as a bench. Venusian cooks, laboring over cauldrons of some bubbling, fishy-smelling concoction at the hall's far end, looked up briefly at their appearance and then returned to their work. The surgeon, obviously far too experienced at this task, spread a waxed cloth on one of the tables and began laying out his instruments nearby. Among them, Arabella noted with horror, was a bone-saw.

A moaning at the door drew her attention then, which was followed shortly by the door-flap opening to admit the men and guards she had seen departing the charcoal mounds. The injured man was indeed Bates, a member of *Diana*'s crew she did not know well. He had been a topman, and one of the mutineers, but as he had not injured any one during the mutiny he had been permitted to remain with the crew. The two carrying him she did not know at all. "Lay him on the table," the surgeon instructed. The guards took places by the door, neither helping nor hindering, but keeping their wide and shining eyes upon the proceedings.

Bates's feet and legs were blackened and weeping blood from several long gashes. He had been barefoot and without hose, but the injuries extended above his knees, and his breeches were charred and shredded to the hip. As the surgeon began to cut them off he spared a glance for Arabella. "You should step outside," he told her. "This is no place for a woman."

She was about to comply—the sight alone was stomach-turning, the smell of half-cooked meat and burnt cloth even more so—when her eyes caught Bates's. His staring eyes held so much agony, so very fearful and alone, that she checked her motion immediately. "No," she said, "I will stay." And she took Bates's hand.

"Well, then, take that and put it in his mouth." The surgeon nodded to a leather strap, deeply scored with tooth-marks.

He spared no more time or attention for Arabella. "Steady, sir," he muttered to Bates, and began teasing the charred fabric free of the skin to which it had adhered. Bates groaned past the strap clenched in his teeth, and his hand seized Arabella's painfully.

She placed her other hand on his shoulder. "Brave heart, Bates," she said, and held his eyes with hers. "You are an able airman of the Honorable Mars Company. You have weathered storm, enemy fire, and Martian insurrection. You can withstand this."

Though the whites showed all the way around his pupils and his breath came hard and fast through his nose, Bates nodded, bit down harder on the leather strap, and clutched Arabella's hand as though it were his last lifeline.

"Just a little more," the surgeon said.

But it was more than just a little more—the process of cleaning and then stitching Bates's burns and lacerations seemed to go on for ever. Bates moaned and writhed; the surgeon muttered occasional curses; Arabella kept her eyes on Bates's and tried to ignore the comparatively minor pain of his hand crushing hers. The captain, she realized vaguely, was fully occupied in holding Bates's body and other leg to the table against his thrashing.

At last the work was done, and the surgeon washed the blood and char from his hands. Bates, trembling, had never lost consciousness but lay gasping, completely spent. "I have done what I can," the surgeon told him. "The rest is in the Lord's hands." He looked to the captain. "He must not walk or do any work until the wounds heal."

"I will make the necessary . . . *entreaties* of the guards," the captain said.

"Can you give me something for the pain?" Bates's voice was barely more than a whisper.

"A little rum is all," the surgeon replied with a shake of his head. "The laudanum is long gone."

"Can no more be obtained?" the captain asked him.

"There is nothing those rapacious frogs can't supply," the surgeon replied in a venomous tone, "for the right price."

Arabella's eyes met the captain's then, across Bates's trembling body, and she nodded.

They stayed with Bates for a while longer while the surgeon stowed his instruments and took his leave. Bates slept, or perhaps fainted; Arabella swabbed his chill and sweating brow with her handkerchief. The captain excused himself to negotiate with the guards for Bates's care, then returned.

Eventually the sound of conversation from without, and the stamp of many feet upon the dirt outside, roused her attention. Then the door-flap opened and admitted a crowd of blackened, weary airmen, many of whom were well known to Arabella. "Young!" she cried with a mixture of glee at the familiar faces and suppressed despair at their bleak condition. They were all sunken of cheek, with red eyes and drawn expressions. "Snowdell! Taylor!"

"Miss Ashby!" said Young—ironically, the eldest of her former messmates—his own delight at seeing her plainly warring with exhaustion. "What on Earth brings you to this stinking planet?"

Before she could reply, the captain cleared his throat and stated mildly, "It is Mrs. Singh, now."

This announcement brought the men's chatter, which had been composed equally of concern for the injured Bates and surprise at Arabella's appearance, to a sudden halt—immediately followed by a clamor of reaction. "Give you joy of it, sir!" and "Congratulations!" and "Well now!" the Dianas said, pressing in on the captain to shake his hand and extending their felicitations to her. But the prisoners from other ships only trudged wearily past toward the bubbling pots at the far end of the hall.

The whole performance left Arabella in a whirl of muddled feelings. She smiled and accepted the men's congratulations, and was in fact quite glad to see their unfeigned joy at her supposed good fortune. Any thing at all, she realized, that could bring a bit of happiness to their terrible existence here was a benefit. But these were men with whom she had dined on salt pork, and swabbed decks, and battled corsairs and mutineers—they were, in some ways, closer to her than family. To deceive them, no matter how necessarily, brought her pain. Though of course, she reminded herself, their whole friendship had begun with a deception, regarding her sex, and that had turned out all right.

She and the captain joined the men at their supper: a thin and fishy broth, full of bones and scales, which was eaten from wooden bowls with splintery wooden spoons. She told them of her voyage, the encounter with the wind-whales, and such, and shared what news she had of the state of the war since their capture. Their attitude toward her, in turn, was an uncomfortable amalgam of the easy camaraderie they had once shared with the respect due a captain's wife.

"But *why* did you come?" her messmate Snowdell insisted, after her third or fourth attempt to subtly evade the question.

She hesitated before replying. "Although my husband"—she took the captain's hand—"did request that I remain safely on Mars, I could not leave him alone here once I knew the demon Fouché was on his way."

"Aye, Fouché," Snowdell acknowledged with a grim nod. "We've heard much of him."

"We've lived through every thing they've done to us up to now," stated Young defiantly. "We'll survive him too."

"Fouché!" said Taylor, raising his wooden cup of small beer, and he made it more of a curse than a toast. "*Fouché!*" chorused the others, and downed their drinks. The Venusian guards stationed at each end of the hall regarded this performance with cold indifference.

Arabella, too, drank her beer, and though the stuff was sour and foul, the company of her former shipmates made it tolerable.

———————

After the conclusion of their skimpy supper, the men were mustered, counted, and marched off to their barracks like so many draft-*huresh* being herded to their stalls. Arabella, promising she would return at her next opportunity, took her leave and returned to the town on the captain's arm.

"What frightful conditions," she said as soon as they were well out of earshot.

The captain, holding a torch aloft in the deepening gloom, only grunted in acknowledgement. Clearly he was lost in thought.

"What is the *purpose* of all this dangerous toil?" she prompted, attempting to engage him in conversation. "Is it merely make-work, to increase their suffering?"

"Far from it," he replied after a pause. "The charcoal feeds the furnace, where iron ore is melted down and combined with limestone to remove impurities from the iron. The resulting pure iron is cast into bars, which are transported to the nearby ship-yard."

"What do they do with the iron there?"

His fingers tightened visibly on the torch, such that its flame trembled. "I only wish that I knew. The ship-yard is under the very tightest secrecy. No news emerges therefrom, nor any workers; men are occasionally transferred from the plantation to the ship-yard, but never back. We do know that the quantities of iron emerging from this plantation are prodigious—though I gather the quality is inferior to that produced on Mars." He sighed heavily. "The numbers of cannon and cannon-balls that could be produced from this iron imply a vast fleet of ships is under construction. But the size of the yard and the limited availability of suitable timber do not support this, and there is no sign of the large number of hot-air furnaces that would be needed to launch such a fleet . . . or, indeed, any such furnaces at all. It is a vexing mystery."

They passed through Marieville's gate—their papers again being inspected—and made their way in silence through the rough town's gloomy streets to their *auberge*. There the captain met with Stross, Richardson, and several other officers to discuss the happenings of the day, while Arabella excused herself to their bedchamber. There she threw off all her outer clothing and collapsed in her shift upon the hard and narrow bed.

Despite her exhaustion, the darkness, and the somewhat reduced heat of the evening, she lay unsleeping, her mind all a-whirl and perspiration trickling down her neck and flanks.

Clearly she must devote at least a portion of the five hundred pounds to procuring laudanum and other necessities to ameliorate the men's horrid circumstances. But the only true and lasting relief lay in escape, especially with Fouché on his way, and the captain seemed uninterested in pursuing that avenue.

What could she do without his participation?

The sound of the door-flap, on the other side of the cloth that divided the room, interrupted her racing thoughts. A moment later the captain, in stocking feet, silently pushed aside the cloth and tiptoed toward the chair in the corner.

"My dear captain," Arabella whispered. "I will not see you sleep in that chair again to-night."

"It is no hardship," he protested in a matching whisper. "And, whatever we may pretend to the rest of the world, you and I both know that we may not share the bed."

A wicked thrill ran through her at the thought, but her sense of propriety made her push it away. "The bed is not large enough for both of us, in any case. No, I insist that I take the chair to-night. We shall alternate, night by night, to spread the discomfort."

"Absolutely not. I am inured to discomfort; you are not, and besides you have just arrived." He shook his head. "You will take the bed." He removed his coat and spread it over the chair's hard back and seat.

"You must consider the men's welfare, sir, if not your own! They require a captain who is well rested!" To this he made no reply, merely settling himself down on the chair, folding his arms, and ostentatiously closing his eyes. "Very well . . . if you will not accept comfort, then neither will I." And with that she took the pillow and blanket—thin and inadequate though they both were—and lay down on the uneven and splintery floor-boards between the bed and the cloth that divided the room.

For a time they lay thus in stubborn silence. Arabella did not sleep, and from the sound of his breathing neither did the captain.

Then that sound changed . . . not to the slow rhythm of sleep, but to a shallow, gulping, muffled sound. She sat up and looked across the bed.

The captain's coat-sleeve was pressed against his mouth and nose, and his eyes were tightly closed. But his cheeks were wet with tears, glimmering in the wan greenish light from the window.

Her heart went out to him then, and her body immediately followed. The chair made their embrace terribly awkward, but still they clung together for a long moment, he sobbing silently on her shoulder and she on his.

"The men . . ." he whispered in her ear. "They need me. The officers too. I must be strong." A trembling inward breath. "No one has offered any comfort to me in so long . . ."

"Oh, my *dear* captain," she whispered back. "I will do for you whatever I am able." She pulled away and looked into his face, which still shone with tears. "And, just for to-night, that is to insist that you take that hard, narrow, shabby bed."

"Your generosity is unbounded," he replied with a small ironic smile, wiping his eyes.

She shrugged, dabbing at her own eyes with the hem of her sleeve. "It is the least I can do."

They extricated themselves from the chair, and he folded his length into the bed. It was barely large enough for him alone. She brought the blanket from the floor and covered him with it, then tucked the pillow beneath his head. "Good night, my maharaja," she said, and gently kissed his forehead.

"Good night, boy second class Ashby."

The chair, even with the addition of the captain's coat, was miserably uncomfortable. But still she found herself smiling as she slipped into sleep.

———————

The next day, after breakfast, roll-call, and the morning colloquy with his officers, the captain said to Arabella, "My financial contact—the man who will discount your letter of note into French livres—is a suspicious man, and I must meet with him alone before introducing you to him. May I leave you to yourself for the day?"

"Of course, sir," she replied. "I shall endeavor to make myself useful here."

She made her way to the men's barracks, intending to offer the men what comfort and assistance she could, but the only Englishman she found there was Bates, who wanted little more than to sleep; the rest were out performing their horrific labors.

Left to her own devices, she decided to stroll nonchalantly about the barracks area and discover for herself its strengths and weaknesses. But two French guards—human, and officers by the amount of braid on their uniforms—immediately accosted her and requested, with polite but inflexible insistence, that she return to her lodgings in Marieville. They accompanied her to the stockade gate, and kept her under keen observation until she was well down the path to town.

Returning to town, frustrated and feeling rather useless, she determined that she would not simply retire to the *auberge,* but would rather wander the streets and familiarize herself with the lay of the land.

Most of the town was given over to the business of making iron. A heavy pall of rusty-smelling smoke and dust overlay every thing, and the natives' carts rolled hither and yon, the great weight of their cargo driving the single wheel deep into the mud of the streets. Among that cargo she recognized iron ingots and the rough red rocks of iron ore; bags of white powder must be limestone from the quarry. Other carts bore foodstuffs, and stacks of limp weeds she assumed must be fodder for the animals.

After the production of iron, the second business of the town seemed to be housing, feeding, and entertaining the French and their English captives. She found streets of *auberges,* inns, and lodging-houses, all with signs in French as well as Venusian curves, but some also bearing names in English; among these were interspersed a variety of clubs, shops, and restaurants, almost all of them run by Venusians. In one of these she drank a glass of sherbet, to refresh herself after her long walk in the already-stifling heat of the morning, and found that this small indulgence consumed most of the local money the captain had given her. The prices, she began to realize, were indeed ruinously inflated.

She also found the gaming-house, which bore a large sign in French alone: CETTE BANQUE / EST MAINTENUE / POUR LES ANGLAIS / LES FRANÇAIS SONT INTERDITES / À JOUER ICI. This bank is maintained for the English; the French are forbidden to play here. At that she could only smile ruefully and shake her head. The town's French administrators were obviously well aware of the destructive power of gambling, and wished to direct that weapon only at their captives and not at their own men.

As she turned away from the gaming-house, she was surprised to hear a voice from behind her calling "Miss Ashby!" She turned back and was even further surprised that the source of the call was Captain Fox, just departing the establishment and tucking his wallet into his jacket pocket.

"It is Mrs. Singh now, sir," she reminded him, even as she approached him with a genuine smile.

"I beg your pardon, ma'am," he said, smiling equally broadly and bowing over her hand. "I am pleased to see you well."

"And I you." She cast a glance over his shoulder at the door from which he had just emerged. "I would have thought that, after Burke's Club, you would give up gambling for ever."

At that he had the grace to look abashed, but only for a moment. "Perhaps a wiser man than I would have done so. But"—he patted his pocket—"my luck so far has been exemplary."

"Do not depend upon that, sir. I have reason to believe that the games are not entirely legitimate. They may only be allowing you to win at first, in order to set the hook more deeply."

"I thank you for that advice." The expression on his face seemed to indicate he had no intention of following it. However, that expression quickly changed to one more earnest and circumspect, and he glanced up and down the street before continuing in a lower register. "May I have a word with you, in private?"

Her initial reaction was to refuse, for propriety's sake, but then she reflected that in every one's eyes she was now a married woman, and furthermore Fox's attitude was not at all salacious. "Certainly, sir. Let us walk without the palisade."

They made their way to the gate, and through it to the wooded paths beyond. As they walked they discussed mutual acquaintances—the Touchstones were employed in the dreadful heat of the furnace-house, hauling carts of ore to the top and removing bars of hot cast iron from the bottom, and were housed in a separate barracks from the Dianas—and commiserated upon the miseries of the Venusian climate, especially the torrential rains which drenched every thing each afternoon.

Once well away from the guards, shaded by the over-arching limbs of giant ferns and surrounded by the rustles and chitters of the local fauna, Fox paused and said, "I must apologize for being the cause of your incarceration in this awful place."

"No apology is necessary, sir. It was I who insisted on coming, and the French who captured us and brought us here."

"Nonetheless, as captain it was my responsibility to keep my ship, crew, and passengers from harm, and in that I have failed." He looked around before continuing. "I intend to make it up to you."

His tone and expression were so earnest that her heart raced a bit. "How so?"

"My officers and I have formed a plan of escape, and I would have you join with us."

This statement did nothing to calm her exhilaration, especially given the contrast with Captain Singh's reluctance to consider the possibility. However, she immediately realized, her captain's caution was not without a sound foundation, and she attempted to tamp her enthusiasm down. "I thank you for the invitation, sir, but the difficulties are enormous. We are surrounded by trackless jungle, hostile natives, and fierce beasts. What is your plan to evade them?"

"Once every eight days, a train of carriages comes from the port bearing supplies, departing nearly empty. We intend to secret ourselves aboard, then once we reach the port, purchase passage off-planet."

"How many is 'we'?"

"My entire crew, or at least as many as we can convince to take the risk."

"How can you possibly avoid detection?"

Again he patted his pocket. "This is why I have been engaged in multiplying my funds. With sufficient money, all things are possible."

At that moment, Arabella was very keenly aware of the letter of note that stiffened the lining of her reticule, but the thrilling possibility of escape warred in her breast with deep skepticism of the plan's chances for success. Bold and simple though it was—in fact, *because* of its boldness and simplicity—it seemed vulnerable. Even a single insufficiently-bribed official could bring the whole plan to a disastrous halt. "I . . . I thank you again, sir, and I will give your invitation serious consideration." She bit her lip. "However, I could not possibly consider attempting to escape without my husband, and indeed the rest of his crew."

"I cannot say I did not expect this response." Fox closed his eyes and shook his head. "I must apologize, but there is no possibility of expanding the scheme much beyond my own crew. As you were my passenger, I accept some responsibility for you, and of course I feel very tenderly toward you as a person. However, the supply-train is only so large, and my funds extend only so far." Arabella's hand tightened on her reticule, which crinkled; Fox looked deeply into her eyes. "Your husband is a brave and experienced captain, and I am certain he has escape plans of his own. He would, I am sure, prefer that you make your way to safety when you can, and he will follow as soon as he is able."

She dropped her eyes from his earnest gaze, too ashamed to admit Captain Singh's unwillingness to consider escape as a possibility. "I would have to consult with him first."

"I must ask that you do not. The more people who know of the plan, the greater the chance of detection."

She turned away from him, her arms crossed upon her breast with the reticule clutched tightly beneath them. Weak, hazy sunlight filtered down through the sweltering fronds, and alien creatures muttered in the undergrowth. It was a beastly place, and she desired nothing more than to depart it, the sooner the better . . . but to do so without her captain would fly in the face of her very reason for coming here.

Arabella sighed and turned back to Fox. "In that case I must decline. But I thank you most sincerely for your consideration, and I wish you the very best of fortune."

Fox inclined his head. "I do understand, ma'am, and if circumstances change you may always approach me."

"I hope that you will do the same for me."

"Of course." He offered his elbow. "May I accompany you back to your lodgings?"

They returned to Marieville in silence, each occupied by their own thoughts.

14

FOUCHÉ

Captain Singh's "financial contact" proved to be a small, oily Frenchman whose position in the *manoir*'s kitchen staff sent a substantial stream of funds passing through his greasy fingers. She distrusted him immediately—and the captain assured her that this distrust was not unreasonable—but he was, the captain assured her, both cowardly enough and shrewd enough to keep the transaction secret for his own safety.

In exchange for her five-hundred-pound note, Arabella received four hundred and eighty livres in twenty- and forty-livre gold coins, each stamped with Napoleon's head surmounted by a laurel wreath. The reverse bore another laurel, the words EMPIRE FRANÇAIS and VENUS, and an inscription in the worm-like Venusian script. Arabella retained one hundred livres for herself and gave the rest to the captain for the benefit of the crew.

"At the official exchange rate," the captain remarked as they departed the shed behind the *manoir*, "you would have received over twelve hundred livres. But exchanging such a large quantity through official channels would be illegal, and even in many smaller transactions would certainly have been noticed. This is, I believe, the best rate we could practicably have obtained."

"I am certain that it is." And, indeed, she did trust her captain, with her funds, her heart, and her very life—though she wished he would take her further into his confidences, and that he would at least entertain the possibility of escape.

Still, she reflected, even if she must spend the rest of the war in this sweltering jungle, at least she would have the company of her beloved.

———————

Days passed. The captain quickly put Arabella's money to good use, obtaining laudanum for the relief of Bates's pain and good red meat to supplement the meagre rations supplied by the French, as well as other long-needed necessities. Arabella was not made privy to the means by which these supplies were obtained, which vexed her somewhat; the captain apologized, but said that the men with whom he was dealing were secretive and wished to keep the number of people involved to a minimum.

The effect of these additional provisions on the men's morale was dramatic and immediate. Even as the men went off to their labors they seemed to do so with more spring in their steps, and in the evenings the barracks rang with ribald songs. The fact that Arabella was the source of this bounty was no secret, and the Dianas' already affectionate attitude toward her grew even warmer.

But Fouché was still on his way—according to rumor he would arrive and take charge within days—and she feared that once he did the small comforts her funds had obtained, and more, would be taken away, leaving the men even worse off than before she had arrived.

And so she fretted, and paced, and slept poorly even on those nights when she had the use of the bed.

One afternoon she found herself at a small cafe, sharing a table with Fox while her captain was off on some errand of his own. "Why," she demanded of Fox, "do the strictures of parole carry so much weight? It seems to me that if you and the other officers took it into your heads to walk away from Marieville this afternoon, you could do so and the guards would not stop you. Yet none of you have done so, and indeed it seems Captain Singh would not even consider the attempt."

Fox sipped his tea—it was weak, insipid stuff, the Venusians lacking the least conception of its proper preparation—and stared off into the distance for a contemplative moment before replying. "An English gentleman's parole," he said, "is his word of honor—stronger than any chain and more durable than any wall. When a man gives his parole as a prisoner of war, he promises not to take up arms against his captors, nor indeed to hinder them in any way, and that promise is as binding as any debt, or even a proposal of marriage. To renege on such a solemn promise would blight a man's honor and prevent him from being trusted by any one thereafter."

"Even a promise given under duress, to such villains as the French?"

"Even so; a man's word is his bond. Indeed, a promise of parole has the very force of law." He set down his cup and leaned forward earnestly. "One Lieutenant Sheehy, of the Eighty-ninth Foot, flagrantly violated his parole in his escape from Verdun. When the circumstances of his escape became known, the Prince Regent personally insisted that he be publicly reprimanded and sent back to the French!"

"But English officers escape from prison all the time," Arabella protested, having read many accounts of such escapes in her preparations for the journey to Venus. "How can they do so in good conscience?"

"Some officers purposely commit some minor offense, resulting in the revocation of parole, before making their escape. Others write to the prison *commandant* on the eve of their departure, formally rescinding their parole and bidding their gaolers a cordial farewell. To be fair, such a letter may not be *received* until after the officer has absented himself, but it is felt that to *send* such a letter satisfies the proprieties."

Arabella raised an eyebrow. "May I assume that you have already prepared such a letter yourself?"

Fox glanced around before responding in a low tone. "Unfortunately, the appropriate circumstances for such a letter may be some time in coming. My financial dealings have not gone quite so well as I had hoped." He seemed to draw inward for a moment, then continued, "I do have alternatives, but I am loath to employ them. We shall see."

"I did warn you that the gaming-house is little more than a mint for Lefevre."

He inclined his head in acknowledgement. "You did indeed, ma'am. But even a rigged game can be won, if one is willing and able to play the game above the visible game. In fact, a dishonest roulette wheel is actually easier to cheat . . ."

As Fox warmed to his subject, she reflected that he was a bit of a scoundrel, and a tease into the bargain. But he was at least straightforward and open about it . . . in contrast to Captain Singh, who combined unassailable moral probity with a frustrating secrecy about his most important dealings. And Fox's continued efforts toward escape, despite her doubts as to their eventual success, were refreshing by comparison with her captain's stolid devotion to his men's comfort. If only Fox's qualities and Captain Singh's could be combined in a single man!

"... but I am becoming tedious," Fox said, breaking into her reverie. "I do apologize."

"Not in the least, sir." She smiled and met his eye above the rim of her cup as she finished her tea. "Not in the least."

Some days later Arabella and Lady Corey were engaged in a game of piquet in the sitting-room of the *manoir*. Arabella inspected her hand after discarding, finding five spades. "Point of five," she declared.

"Not good," Lady Corey replied, denying her the points.

Arabella's five spades included a sequence of three. "Tierce."

"Not good."

Arabella sighed. "Trio of aces?"

"Good."

"Three points for me, then." Arabella led the king of spades, scoring the point for first lead. "Four."

"Point of six for six, and sixième for sixteen. Twenty-two points." She then laid the ace of spades across Arabella's king, taking the trick. "Twenty-three."

Arabella sighed again. Twenty-three to four already, and the hand had barely begun.

Lady Corey paused before leading. "Really, child, you should not have declared your tierce. *Look* at your cards. Have you any clubs at all?"

Arabella said nothing, but she held just two: the ace and seven.

"You know from the fact your point of five was not good that I hold at least six cards in a single suit. Your paucity of clubs should tell you which suit that is, and as you hold at most the ace and seven you can be certain at least six of mine are in sequence. Your declaration of tierce had no chance of being good, and only gave me additional information."

Arabella set her cards down with another sigh. "I am afraid my attention is not on the game." Indeed, Lady Corey had been trouncing her soundly all afternoon.

Lady Corey, too, folded her hand. "What is the matter, my dear?"

Arabella bit her lip before continuing. "I . . . I fear I am not suited to the role of captain's wife. I assist Captain Singh in his duties, I administer aid and comfort to the men, I dine with the officers, I visit with you . . . I am doing my very best to be useful, but I find the whole thing wearying and lowering. Not," she appended hastily, "that I do not enjoy the time spent with you. But I cannot be happy unless I am *doing* something."

"And I do enjoy your visits." Lady Corey fanned herself contemplatively, though the fan's small motion had little effect on the stupefying heat of a Venusian afternoon. "I appreciate your situation; when I was a child, my family recently arrived on Mars, my mother often complained of boredom despite the constant round of visitations and entertainments." She snapped her fan closed. "You must take up a hobby! Painting, perhaps."

"Perhaps," Arabella allowed, though she found the idea tedious in the extreme. "Or perhaps the study of foreign languages. I have been attempting to teach myself Venusian . . ."

The expression on Lady Corey's face told Arabella she considered the study of the Venusian language even less appealing than the local cuisine. "I cannot imagine why. The croaking of giant frogs? It cannot be other than noise."

"They are *not* merely giant frogs! They are *people*, albeit people with a different appearance, and their craft and culture repay study. We could learn a thing or two from them when it comes to the breeding of animals. And I have observed them carving delightful little figurines, and engaging in games every bit as complex as piquet." She picked up her hand of cards and squared it, tapping it repeatedly on the table. "I have even managed to puzzle out some of their verbs . . . though the language seems inexplicably inconsistent."

Lady Corey's reply was drowned out by a blare of trumpets and rattle of drums from without. Martial sounds such as these were not uncommon in Marieville, but this fanfare seemed louder and more insistent, and was followed almost immediately by the drumming of boots upon floors and frantic shouts in French from throughout the *manoir*. Arabella stepped to the window, where she saw the French officers dashing about like *zoresh* from a kicked-over nest.

"What on Earth has them so put out?" Lady Corey demanded of her. "You know I cannot comprehend their jabber."

"I am not yet certain," Arabella replied, cupping her hands behind her ears.

The agitated soldiers' shouts, in rapid and colloquial French, were difficult for her to make out. But one word—one name—came up again and again.

Fouché.

The Executioner of Lyon.

Joseph Fouché, the Duke of Otranto, had an academic bearing, a high forehead, and a long straight nose. But his mouth seemed very small and hard and pinched, and did not move at all as he paced back and forth, awaiting the rest of his audience.

Arabella had a very good view of him, seated as she was on the *manoir*'s wide verandah along with Lady Corey and the various French officers and adjutants who lived and worked in that building. The rest of the French soldiery were gathered in ranks on the broad lawn below, with Captain Singh and the other English officers behind them. Beyond them, the rest of the prisoners were being driven into untidy squares by their guards. Curious Venusians thronged at the edges of the assembly.

Rescuing Captain Singh before the arrival of Fouché had been her sole goal for months. She had worked so hard, sacrificed so much . . . and failed completely to achieve it. Even worse, now she herself, and Lady Corey as well, would fall under the man's authority. As horrid as the prisoners' life on Venus had been so far, how much worse would it become under the command of the Executioner of Lyon?

"He was a monk once," Lady Corey murmured to Arabella. "But during the Revolution he railed against the Church, and spilled more blood than nearly any one else during the Terror."

"*Silence!*" roared one of Fouché's men—an entire platoon of fresh troops, their uniforms immaculate and their postures rigid, had arrived with him—and Lady Corey obeyed. But her narrowed brows indicated that this merely reinforced her point, and her trembling hands showed that, behind her stoic mien, she was as terrified as Arabella.

Fouché's eyes, drawn by the soldier's command, lit briefly on Arabella. They betrayed an active intelligence, yet showed absolutely no emotion . . . which chilled her blood still further.

Lefevre, wearing a uniform far more ornate than any thing Arabella had seen on Venus until this moment, now ascended the *manoir*'s broad steps, accompanied by his chief lieutenants. "*Tous présent ou dénombrés,*" he reported, with a crisp salute—all present or accounted for. "*Votre commande, Commandant.*" Your command, sir.

Lefevre then turned about, in a single precise motion, and retired with his lieutenants to join the other officers. But though his motions were exact and his bearing upright, Arabella could not fail to notice that his eyes glistened. Clearly the man was less than happy with his loss of command, and she tucked that intelligence away in case it might prove useful in the future.

The new commandant acknowledged the transfer of power with a curt nod, then stepped to the head of the stairs and began to address the assembled men. His voice was high and clear and carried well on the sultry air.

"What is he saying?" Lady Corey whispered. The French troops were giving all their attention to the speaker; none seemed to notice her breach of silence.

Fouché spoke rapidly and with an accent unfamiliar to Arabella, but she understood enough to extract the general sense of his speech. "He brings greetings from His Imperial Majesty," Arabella whispered, keeping her eyes front and moving her lips as little as possible. "The . . . the conquest, I suppose, of Venus continues apace. Your work here is . . . um, essential? . . . to victory, both here and on land. No, on *Earth*. His Majesty has not been pleased with your . . . production, productivity, something like that. Therefore . . ." She swallowed, not wanting to translate the words she had just heard. "Therefore the, the . . . gentle treatment of the prisoners which has been . . . heretofore exhibited, will no longer be tolerated. Production must increase. The foundry will roll— will *run*—day and night. Nothing may make obstacle to the production of iron. Any prisoner attempting escape . . ." Again she swallowed, her mouth dry. ". . . will be shot. Any one, be he English, Venusian, or French, who does not work to his . . . utmost capacity, will be shot. Any one at all who . . . impedes progress in any way, will be shot. No . . . no dissent of any kind will be tolerated."

The silence that followed Fouché's speech was absolute, broken only by the distant chittering of Venusian wildlife. The French officers and men, even Lefevre, seemed as stunned by the address as the Englishmen.

Fouché returned their shocked gaze with a cold and stony glare of his own. "*Retournez à vos devoirs*," he commanded—return to your duties—then turned and strode briskly inside, his boot-heels clacking on the verandah floor and his troops falling in line behind him. The other French officers followed, in rather less disciplined order.

Lady Corey and Arabella looked at each other, appalled. "Go to your captain," Lady Corey said. "He needs your support now, more than ever before." Then she turned and followed the Frenchmen inside.

Her back, Arabella noted, was held quite straight. But the feather on her hat trembled.

———————————————

True to his word, Fouché immediately divided the prisoners into two watches, which the French called *quarts*, which alternated work so that the furnace might run, and be fed with charcoal, limestone, and iron ore, during all hours of the day and night. Following both English and French naval tradition, they were designated the "starboard" and "larboard" watches.

Each watch worked for four hours while the other rested, then rested for four while the other worked. These four-hour periods were also called watches. Arabella was surprised to learn that the French shared this confusion of terminology, calling both the group of workers and the period of work a *quart*. On English ships the watch from four o'clock in the afternoon to eight o'clock at night was divided into two shorter "dog watches" to give an odd number, so that any given airman would only be required to stand the midnight watch every other night. But Venus's twenty-eight-hour day divided naturally into seven four-hour watches. This meant that there were no short watches—every man had to work for four hours, then rest for four, then return to work again for four . . . an unending cycle of misery. And this continual labor ran uninterrupted seven days a week, though church services were conducted during each watch's Sunday morning rest period.

Despite decades of naval tradition, Arabella reflected, four hours of sleep at a stretch was not really enough to sustain an airman, let alone a man doing hard physical labor; furthermore, those four hours of rest must also include eating, washing, mending, and all the other necessities of life. Back on *Diana*, the system of watches had been one thing she had not been sorry to see the back of when her sex had been exposed and she had changed from captain's boy to passenger.

Arabella's services in the role of captain's wife were even more keenly needed now. The continually exhausted men were compelled to perform backbreaking, dangerous work, often in the dark, which led to several deaths and an appalling number of serious injuries. Her old messmate Young, gray-haired and spindle-shanked even when properly used, became nearly skeletal; when he was brought back to the barracks unconscious and bleeding, having collapsed from exhaustion and struck his head on a rock, she was horrified but not surprised. She was kept continually busy folding bandages, washing linens, and otherwise assisting the surgeon as he rushed from one injured man to another.

Captain Singh did as much as he could to improve the men's miserable conditions, but the French officers were so frightened of Fouché that no amount of bribery could now convince them to overlook an infraction of his stringent regulations. The best the captain could do was to purchase food from the Venusian merchants in Marieville—at prices even more offensively inflated than before—and bring it to the men during their watches below.

One afternoon she arrived, carrying a much-desired delivery of fresh meat for the men, to find the Dianas' barracks deserted. This was unusual now—half of them were usually here, while the other watch labored in the forest. She found a French officer on the packed earth of the square where the men assembled for roll-call four times a day, and he informed her that both watches had been called to the forest for some large task; none of them were expected to return for several hours.

Disappointed and disturbed by this turn of events, Arabella cast a worried eye on her basket of raw meat. It was from some local creature, nutritious for human beings but having an unfamiliar flavor. It went bad extremely rapidly in Venus's heat and damp, though, and large green fly-like creatures were already fluttering around it. She thought it unlikely that it would still be wholesome when the men returned.

She decided that the best thing to do would be to bring it to the Touchstones. As the captain's wife, most of her attention was devoted to *Diana*'s crew, but she did see Fox and his men upon occasion, and this was as good an excuse as any—and better than some—for her to pay them a visit.

———————————

The Touchstones' barracks were not quite as tidy or well-maintained as the Dianas', but despite the distressing conditions of their work in the furnace-house they often seemed in better spirits than the Dianas. Arabella attributed this to the fact that the Dianas had been held prisoner for many months longer, but she could not deny that Fox, whose boisterous energy had not diminished, might also play a part in his people's good mood.

In fact, when she arrived at the Touchstones' barracks she found a scene of raucous merriment. Fox, in his shirt-sleeves, was attempting to stand on his hands atop a table, while the men hooted and applauded. Venus's gravity being less than Earth's, this was not as difficult a feat as it appeared, but it still required considerable strength and a keen sense of balance.

A sense which Fox apparently lacked, for on his next attempt he pushed too hard with his feet and went right over, landing on his back on the table top with a considerable thump. "I am unharmed," he gasped, and raised himself to a sitting position, waving a hand. Arabella could not help but notice how well-turned his forearm was. "All is well." The men laughed and clapped him on the back, telling him it had been a good attempt. He winced at the impacts, but continued smiling.

Then Fox spotted Arabella in the crowd of men who had gathered around him. "Mrs. Singh!" he cried. "Always a pleasure to see you."

She did not like the flutter in her breast which rose in response to these words. She was a married woman—or must appear so— and such feelings were entirely improper. "Delighted," she replied, her voice carefully neutral. "I have here a basket of fresh meat, which will go bad if it is not cooked and eaten soon. Would your men like to have it?"

The slavering, enthusiastic cry which came from the Touchstones at this news made Fox's polite nod of acquiescence superfluous. "Of course, madam," he replied formally, stepping down from the table and accepting his jacket from one of the men. "And on their behalf I thank you very kindly for your gift." He took the meat, wrapped in oilcloth, from Arabella and passed it off to Gowse, who stood at his left shoulder. "See that it is properly cooked; none of that French half-raw nonsense."

"Aye aye, sir," Gowse replied, touching a knuckle to his forehead. But rather than taking the meat to the kitchen area, as she expected—the Touchstones had managed to work out an arrangement with the kitchen staff to make use of their ovens—he took it outside.

"Where *is* he going?" she inquired of Fox.

"Ah," Fox replied, a mischievous twinkle in his eye, "you have not yet made the acquaintance of Isambard. Come with me."

Puzzled and intrigued, Arabella took his proffered elbow and permitted him to lead her out the door and around to the back of the barracks. As they walked, she said, "Your antics seem to amuse the men."

"They do." Fox rubbed the back of his head and winced. "Which makes the pain worthwhile. Any thing I can do to keep their spirits up, any thing at all, is justified." He gestured to her empty basket. "Had I Captain Singh's assets, I would provide them with fresh meat myself. But, sadly, Fouché"—he spat the word—"has closed the gaming-house, leaving me over a hundred pounds in arrears. And just when I was on the verge of resuming my winning streak!"

"Hm," she replied noncommittally.

They came upon Gowse, who squatted in the dirt behind the barracks, facing the low open space beneath the barracks floor and clucking his tongue. The meat lay on the oilcloth, skewered on metal rods which presumably had come from the open box nearby. "Isambard," he called gently, making a beckoning gesture. "Isambaaaard . . ."

There came a noise from within. A moment later a creature the size of a large dog, but lower to the ground and with six tentacles, came scuttling out from under the barracks. Its sudden appearance startled Arabella, but delighted Gowse and Fox. "Isambard!" Fox cried, bending down and stroking the beast's head. "Good boy!" He looked over his shoulder at Arabella. "Of course, I have no actual idea whether he is a boy, or a girl, or something other."

"We bought him from one of the natives, before Fouché arrived," Gowse explained. "He were only the size of a cat then. He does a very useful trick, but, what with the lack of meat lately, this is the first time in weeks we've been able to use it." He turned to Fox. "Have ye flint and steel?"

"Of course."

Gowse then leaned down and, to Arabella's surprise and disgust, began tickling Isambard's lower abdomen, behind and between its last set of legs. An orifice in the creature's hindmost end eased open, and a gas hissed out. Unexpectedly, the gas was not fetid; in fact, it had no smell at all.

"Step back, please, Mrs. Singh," Fox said. He bent over and struck the flint against the steel; the resulting spark immediately caught the gas alight. The flame was very wan, nearly transparent, but the heat it produced was considerable; even from five feet away Arabella could feel it upon her face.

Fox and Gowse proceeded to barbecue the skewered meat in the pale flame, turning each rod to cook it on all sides. It cooked extremely quickly, sending up a mouthwatering scent—it smelled better, in fact, than any thing Arabella had eaten in her entire time on Venus.

"How extraordinary," she said.

"When on Venus," Fox replied with a wink, setting a cooked skewer aside and picking up a raw one, "do as the Venusians do."

They set the barbecued meat on a platter from the box, then returned Isambard and the box to the space under the barracks. "Will you join us for supper?" Fox asked.

"I do believe I shall," she replied.

The men cheered when they saw the three of them enter, Fox in the lead, bearing the steaming platter high. "See that it is fairly apportioned," he said, handing a skewer each to the men who pressed in around him. These were, she supposed, the mess-cooks—the men appointed by each mess to bring food from the galley.

Indeed, each man took his skewer back to a group of waiting Touchstones and performed the mess-cook's role. He turned his back to his men, and with eyes closed pulled a bit of delicious-smelling flesh from the skewer and called "Who shall have this?"

One of the other men, facing away from the meat and also with eyes closed, called out a man's name, and the indicated man was handed the hot and dripping morsel, immediately popping it in his mouth and chewing noisily. In this way all the meat was portioned out to the men—if not exactly evenly, then at least fairly.

Fox kept the last skewer for himself, parceling it out to his officers and Arabella. It tasted as delectable as it smelled. "Thank you again," Fox said to her with a bow, "for your generosity."

"Thank *you*," she replied, "for your hospitality."

The barbecued meat, delicious though it was and very welcome for all, was not sufficient for a full supper for every one, so after it was gone they all sat down to a bowl of the usual thin, fishy soup. Arabella sat at Fox's left, with Liddon to his right. On Arabella's left she was pleased to find Mills, whom she had barely seen since their arrival at Marieville, and after consuming their supper they went off to a quiet corner for further conversation.

"How do you fare, sir?" she asked him after the initial pleasantries. Though his shoulders and arms were still robust, his face was haggard and drawn. "Truly?"

He shrugged noncommittally. "Hard work. Not the worst."

"Not the worst? Do you not work in the heat and smoke of the furnace-house? Is it not strenuous and terribly dangerous?"

He nodded. "It is. But no beatings, so far."

Arabella recalled the scars Mills had shown her on his back.

"Guards talk," he continued. "I hear what they say, tell my mates when to work harder. They beat someone else."

"I did not know you spoke French."

Mills shook his head. "Venusian."

Arabella had understood Mills, taciturn though he was, to be extremely intelligent. But she knew from personal experience how very difficult it was to puzzle out the Venusian language without instruction, and was even more impressed with him now. "Perhaps you can help me with a conundrum. Do you know why, for example, the word for those single-wheeled carts they use is sometimes *unguwuggna* and sometimes *manogogla*? There are many such, two or more completely different words for the same concept, and I have not been able to puzzle out when each one is used."

"*Manogogla*," he replied, gently correcting her pronunciation, "is Gowanna language. In Wagala language, *unguwuggna*."

Suddenly Arabella felt extremely stupid. How could she have failed to consider that the Venusians—like Martians and humans—might have many different languages? Thinking over this new intelligence, many of the mysteries she had puzzled over suddenly fell into place. "Of course!" she said. "How foolish of me."

"Not easy to see," Mills reassured her. "Slaves, slavers, both use both. Sometimes mixed together."

"Slaves and slavers?" Arabella was completely taken aback.

Mills nodded. "Guards are Gowanna—slavers. Workers are Wagala—slaves."

Slavery was an abhorrent practice—illegal in England, and not practiced on Mars at all. "But they all look almost exactly alike! How could one possibly enslave a being who looks so much like oneself?"

The expression that came over his face then mingled regret, sadness, and not a little anger. "Many enslave ones who look just the same." He closed his eyes, looked down, and shook his head. "Even me," he muttered to the floor.

Arabella took a moment to find her voice. "I . . . I do not understand."

He looked up again, meeting Arabella's eyes with his own, the irises so dark and the whites nearly yellow. They showed sincerity, trust, and pleading. "I was slaver."

Arabella, shocked, said nothing.

"I was *grumete,* running boats for Portuguese," he continued. "My people, Wolof people—proud warriors. Kept defeated enemies as slaves since time began. Portuguese came, we sold slaves to them. Worked with them." He closed his eyes and shook his head again. "I was good *grumete.* Boat builder, steersman, translator. Never cheated, never stole. But Portuguese . . ." His eyes snapped open, and this time the anger was uppermost. "One day, I brought boatload of slaves. They took me too!"

"How horrid!"

"Thrown in hold with all the rest. Men I captured tried to kill me. I survived. Bound for Brazil, to work in mines. But ship was caught! HMS *Solebay,* Royal Navy Anti-slave Trade Squadron!" He touched a knuckle to his forehead. "Very grateful, joined Navy. Served as waister on *Solebay,* captured many slave ships. Learned English. Reached London, honorable discharge. Worked loading cargo, met Captain Singh. Joined *Diana.* You know the rest."

"What an . . . astonishing story."

"I do not tell many people." A tear ran down the crease of his broad nose. "Ashamed."

"You have nothing to be ashamed of," she reassured him. "Even if you did, you expunged your shame with your Navy service."

He seemed somewhat comforted, yet still the shame remained in his eyes. "Do not tell. Even Captain Singh."

"I will not tell a soul. Not even the captain." For once, she reflected, *she* had a secret to keep from *him.* But something Mills had said tickled at the back of her mind. "You said you worked as translator. You speak Portuguese?"

He nodded.

"How many languages do you speak?"

Mills's eyes rolled upward, his brows furrowed in concentration. "Fourteen. Gowanna and Wagala will be fifteen and sixteen. Still learning."

"If you would be so kind . . . I would like to learn with you. I am certain you have much to teach me."

He gave her a smile. "Yes! We learn together. Better that way."

"Yes," she replied, returning his smile. "Better together."

15

ESCAPEES

Weeks passed—weeks in which the men were worked harder and harder. The officers, too, endured privations; the crews of several additional captured ships were added to the plantation, and many in Marieville were forced to share their already-cramped quarters with the new arrivals. Many leisure activities were cut off; food became even more expensive, and lower in quality. Even the Venusians who reaped the benefits of the inflated prices seemed harried and vexed.

Arabella, short on sleep though she was, tried to match the men's schedules, continuing to offer as much aid and comfort as she could to both watches of both Dianas and Touchstones. The guards learned her face, and no longer checked her papers unless a superior officer was watching.

Injuries became more common and more severe; supplies of bandages and medicines ran low and could not be replenished for any amount of money. Even the surgeon managed to injure himself;

half-dead from exhaustion, he badly cut his own hand during an amputation. This pushed still more responsibility onto Arabella while he healed.

The men's hardships weighed heavily on Captain Singh. He became even more secretive—plainly working hard on his people's behalf, but not sharing his plans with Arabella. She saw little of him during the day, and when she did he was sullen, silent, and moody. At night he slept poorly, tossing and turning so forcefully as to wake Arabella even on those nights when she used the bed and he the floor, and he ate so little she became concerned for his health.

Fox, on the other hand, was filled with manic energy. He did every thing he could to raise his people's spirits, cutting capers on the dirt between the barracks and encouraging the men to tell stories and play card games. He even organized a performance of *Macbeth* in the barracks, with young Brindle playing the part of Lady Macbeth. In Marieville he raced hither and yon, concocting scheme after scheme to regain his fortune or help his people to escape. But to Arabella his schemes seemed desperate and implausible, and none of them came any where near fruition.

And then one day around thirteen in the morning, the cannon on the lawn below the *manoir* boomed out three times. "What is that?" Arabella asked Lady Corey, with whom she was sharing an extremely light collation—little more than weak tea and bread with the crusts cut off.

Lady Corey's eyes widened in alarm. "It means an escape. That sound alerts every Frenchman and filthy native within earshot that three good Englishmen have escaped, and reminds them that there is a bounty of fifty livres upon each of their heads."

"Oh dear," Arabella said, setting her tea-cup down. Ravenous though she was, the news made her lose her appetite. "I wonder who they are?"

"No one we know, I hope."

The two of them sat in silence, regarding each other with anguished expressions as the sounds of pursuit rose on every side.

———————————————

Five hours later Arabella, engaged in negotiations with a stone-faced Venusian over a shipment of badly-needed fresh fruit, heard raucous cheers in the street without; immediately she rushed out to see what was the matter.

A mixed group of Frenchmen, French-uniformed Venusians, and Venusians in native costume cheered and grunted as they pulled a one-wheeled cart through the streets. On the cart, tightly bound to upright stakes, were three Englishmen—their clothing soiled and torn and bloodstained, their faces bruised, the expressions in the eyes above their gags weary and hopeless.

To her horror Arabella recognized them. One of them was Bates, the man she had comforted through the surgeon's work when his legs had been burned. The other two were Touchstones; she did not recall their names, but each of them had been friendly and polite to her whenever she had encountered them during the journey to Venus.

Against her will Arabella was swept up in the crowd who poured from every shop and public house, following the cart up the path to the *manoir*. Shouts from behind drew her attention— prisoners from the barracks, pulled from their duties or rest, being herded along by their guards. No one, it seemed, would be allowed to miss what would follow.

Arriving at the *manoir*, the mob packed itself into the small area of lawn. The scene was even more crowded than on the day of Fouché's arrival, and Arabella found herself crammed shoulder to shoulder with French-uniformed Venusians in a hot, shouting, sweating, seething mass. The stink was appalling.

Fouché appeared on the verandah, and the cheers became even

more enthusiastic. He raised his hands for silence, which came slowly and unwillingly. *"Français, Anglais, Vénusiens,"* he proclaimed, *"amis et ennemis!"* French, English, and Venusians, she translated to herself; friends and enemies. Behold the escapees who have just been recaptured, he continued; see the fate which awaits those who oppose His Imperial Majesty!

The one-wheeled cart full of battered Englishmen was drawn up on the packed earth to one side of the *manoir* steps. The Venusians pulling it set up the stops which kept it upright, and quickly withdrew. Meanwhile, at the other side, Fouché's personal platoon— their uniforms immaculate, their order impeccable—brought up the cannon which had, only a few hours earlier, sounded the alarm of the men's escape. With brisk efficiency they began readying it for action, loading it with grape-shot.

"No!" Arabella cried, realizing with terror what was about to occur. "Dear Lord, no!"

For her trouble she found herself seized by those around her. Clammy Venusian hands clamped her mouth shut; others gripped her head so that she could not look away.

She did what she could: she squeezed her eyes tight shut. But she could not close her ears.

"Armez!" came the command. *"En joue! Feu!"* The last word was nearly obliterated by a terrific boom, the screaming roar of grapeshot cutting through the air, and a great exclamation from the crowd—victorious cheers around her, cries of horror from behind.

She could not stop herself opening her eyes.

The men were not dead, not yet. But they were horribly maimed, writhing in pain against their bonds; hideous whines escaped their gagged mouths.

Blood spattered the *manoir*'s whitewashed clapboards, twenty feet away.

A great roaring filled Arabella's ears, and she fell unconscious.

No further escapes were attempted after that horrific display. All the prisoners seemed cowed, and focused their efforts on meeting the increasingly unreasonable demands placed upon them for more and more work. Even Fox became uncharacteristically subdued.

Captain Singh, for his part, seethed with silent rage. He became even more taciturn, but he carried himself rigidly upright and his eyes burned with intensity. He vanished more often and for longer periods, and refused to share his secrets with Arabella. "It is for your own good" was all that he would say. In response to this her inward sentiments roiled—torn between vexation at his reticence, respect for his devotion to the men, and loving concern for his health.

Whenever Arabella caught sight of her own face, reflected in one of the rare glass windows or a polished knife, it seemed a stranger's—thin and wan and pinched, and horribly downcast. These moments were sobering, and served as reminders that, as Lady Corey repeatedly reminded her, her role as captain's wife included the pretense of calm optimism. Whenever she noticed herself stooping or her brow furrowing—which was very often—she strove to pull her shoulders back and her face into a semblance of composure. As Lady Corey had promised it would, she found that the posture of assurance, even deliberately simulated, served to instill the genuine feeling in her breast.

The great lady herself seemed to glide though life, maintaining her habits of tea, cards, and regular strolls. But even she, Arabella noticed, had dark circles beneath her eyes, and Arabella strongly suspected she was not nearly as composed as she seemed. Nonetheless, her appearance of calm was reassuring to Arabella, and she strove to do the same.

One day Arabella arrived at the *manoir* to take tea with Lady Corey—tea, by this time, meaning literally tea and nothing else, and weak tea at that—and was surprised to find the great lady dressed for a walk in the woods and quivering with excited agitation. "I have discovered some edible mushrooms," she said. "You simply *must* join me in collecting them."

The prospect of this addition to their bland, repetitive diet was, indeed, attractive; even so, Arabella thought Lady Corey's enthusiasm somewhat excessive. "Of course," she said, and accepted the proffered basket and Lady Corey's arm.

She was surprised to find that arm trembling.

"It is this way," Lady Corey said, and stepped off with uncharacteristic vigor, nodding to the door guards as they passed.

They walked in silence—a most atypical silence—into the surrounding woods, until well out of sight of the *manoir*. At this point Lady Corey stopped, peered all about, then turned and took both of Arabella's hands. "I have, in fact, discovered a patch of mushrooms," she said, "but that is not the real reason I asked you on this walk."

"I suspected as much."

They linked arms again and proceeded down the path. "I have been working my way into the good graces of Fulton, the American," she said in a low conversational tone. "It seemed to me from the deference given him by the senior French officers, especially Fouché, that his role here is far more significant than it seems—not only overseeing the technical operations of the iron plantation, which is his nominal position, but something else, even more important. And, by dint of . . . feigned interest in his person, shall we say, I have determined what that is."

Again they stopped, and again Lady Corey looked in every direction. "It is a secret weapon," she whispered.

"What sort of weapon?"

Lady Corey shook her head. "I do not know exactly. It is called"—she closed her eyes and concentrated—"*une navver arian qui razze*."

"That would be . . . a something something that shaves?"

Lady Corey's lips pinched together. "No, that is not quite right. Let me try again. *Un naveer arian qui rassay*."

Arabella employed a tactic which had often proved useful in comprehending foreign languages—she "unfocused her ears" and tried to let the sounds wash over her mind uninterpreted. "*Un navire arianne quirassée*," she muttered to herself, trying to translate Lady Corey's butchered French into the original . . . and then something seemed to click. "*Un navire aérienne*! An aerial ship! But what does *quirassée* mean?"

"I do not know. But Fulton seems to believe it will make Napoleon absolutely invincible."

"*Quirassée, quirassée* . . ." Arabella repeated . . . and again there came a mental click, like a locket snapping shut. "*Cuirassée!*" The word seemed familiar from her reading . . . she had encountered it in stories of the knights of old. "The word *cuirass* is found in English as well. It is . . . it is a piece of armor, one which protects the torso." She blinked. "*Un navire aérienne cuirassée* would be an *armored* airship." The vision that leapt into her head then—an aerial ship of the line, clad from stem to stern in shining steel—brought a chill to the back of her neck. "It would be completely immune to cannon-fire."

Lady Corey positively blanched. "But could such a thing *fly*?"

"You said that Fulton is extremely clever."

"He certainly believes himself to be."

"Well then, perhaps he has found a way to make it fly . . . or, at the very least, he has convinced Napoleon that he has." Even as she spoke, further pieces of information clicked into place. "To the extent of setting up this entire iron plantation to produce the vast quantities of iron needed to build it!"

"This could win Napoleon the war," Lady Corey said, aghast.

In Arabella's mind, a fleet of armored vessels descended on London, the cannon-balls of the defenders bouncing off their hulls like sand from a *shurosh*'s carapace. "Worse than that. He could dominate Europe . . . the world! *All* the worlds!"

The two women looked at each other in silent horror for a time. "We should at least make a pretense of hunting mushrooms," Lady Corey said at last. "But then you must inform Captain Singh."

"Indeed," Arabella replied, and together they set off down the path again.

Again they walked in silence. But this time the silence was charged with anxious thought.

───────────

Arabella did not see Captain Singh again until supper, and even then there was no opportunity to share her information with him privately. She vibrated with agitated tension for hour upon hour, but he was constantly in hushed conference with one officer or another. Finally, when they were just about to go up to bed, she could contain herself no longer. "The heat to-day has been simply appalling," she announced. "I must take the evening air for a bit, or I will never be able to sleep." She put out her arm to Captain Singh. "Will you accompany me, *husband*?"

At first she feared he would not take the hint. But the slight stress she placed on that last word served its purpose, and after a moment's consideration he inclined his head, muttered "Of course," and excused himself from the table.

They passed through the gate—the guards there barely glancing at their papers—and strolled through the gathering darkness for a time, talking of inconsequentialities. When Arabella was certain they were well beyond the guards' hearing, she said, "I have news from Lady Corey."

In response he merely nodded very slightly, continuing his measured pace.

She shared what Lady Corey had learned, and her own speculations about what it implied. To her surprise, he took the information in stride—it seemed that this intelligence was not news to him. Instead of expressing any amazement at the concept of an armored aerial ship, he immediately pressed her for details—how many tonnes displacement, number of masts, crew complement, and most especially how such a massive vessel was to be launched.

She did not, of course, have answers to any of these questions. But the matter-of-fact way in which he had accepted her intelligence, and the entitled manner with which he questioned her for more, caused a resentment which had been simmering in her breast for many weeks to come to a full rolling boil.

"I shall not," she said, coming to a sudden halt upon the path, "divulge any further information unless you reciprocate."

The pale light of the dim, setting sun reflected in his dark eyes, creating two sparks of light which vanished briefly as he blinked in astonishment at her outburst. "How do you mean?"

"I know that I am not truly your wife," she replied, warming to her topic. "But I *am* your fiancée, and I had thought that we meant a great deal to each other. Yet ever since my arrival at Venus, you have treated me with distant formality. You do not take me into your confidences, you keep secrets from me, you make plans and rendezvous without even informing me *who* is involved." She crossed her arms upon her chest. "I shall not put up with this behavior any further. If you desire my cooperation, you must treat me as a full partner in this enterprise. I have come all the way from Mars to Venus out of love for you, and I deserve no less."

Despite her brave words, it was all she could do to keep her voice from quavering. For her anger at the way she had been treated was nearly equaled by the fear that her outburst would drive him away for ever—and that was a thing she did not desire in the slightest.

For a long moment he only stared at her, the light of the waning sun behind her reflecting in his eyes, and she was certain she had overstepped some boundary. He would call her bluff, treat her still more coldly . . . perhaps even break off their engagement.

But then she noticed the twin sparks shimmering, and she realized that her brave captain was experiencing a storm of emotion as great as her own. "I . . ." he began, then stammered to a halt. He took a breath, sighed it out, then took another. "I had not known," he said at last. "I had not understood how deeply you felt about this, and I apologize."

Not trusting herself to say any thing, she kept silent.

"Please believe me when I say that my respect for you is completely undiminished. In point of fact, your impatience with my secrecy is entirely justified, and indeed I have been very impatient with myself. Many times in the past months I have come close to sharing every thing with you. However, a . . . greater responsibility has prevented me from doing so." He sighed again, and took her hands in his. His fingers were lean and strong and warm. "I see now that this has been a mistake. The information you have just brought me, although not new to me, reinforces my understanding of your capability, courage, and discretion."

Wordlessly she embraced him, and in the darkness she felt his heart hammering in his breast.

"I am an agent of His Majesty's government," he said, the words echoing deeply in his chest and thrumming against her cheek.

Astonished, she backed away, holding him at arms' length and looking into his face. But the darkness was now nearly complete, and she could not make out his expression. A thousand questions pressed against her lips, but after a time one pushed its way to the fore: "How long has this been going on?"

"I was approached on Mars, shortly after the insurrection. My contact said that the authorities had been impressed by my handling of the situation, and that they had immediate need of a merchant captain who could keep his head in the direst of emergencies. I attempted to recount your part in the affair, but he dismissed my explanations." A glint of light on his teeth showed that he was smiling. "However, let me assure you that I am keenly aware of how much you have done for every Englishman on Mars, even if the government is not."

"So that is why you postponed the wedding."

He nodded. "Which I regret most profoundly. But my love for my adopted country is such that I could not turn down the request." He sighed. "I had thought it would be a delay of only a few months."

His assignment, he explained, had been to examine and report upon Napoleon's activities on Venus. The tyrant's unexpected departure for that planet, upon his escape from the Moon, had raised questions in the government which could not be answered by the Navy, as the French had quickly moved to control the Venusian airlanes. But, at the time, commercial vessels had still been allowed to approach the planet unmolested; hence the government's need for Captain Singh.

"Upon arrival at Venus," he said, "with Aadim's help I was able to evaluate the French aerial traffic and determine that this location was a center of unusual activity. I waited until no French ships were nearby, then briefly descended below the clouds to investigate the site. I could see from the air that the town and surrounding territory were far bigger, and far more active, than any one in England had known, but not what the object of the activity might be." He sighed. "Unfortunately, my caution was insufficient. We were spotted, pursued, and captured."

Arabella moved in and held her captain tightly. "You could have been shot as a spy!"

"It was a close-run thing," he admitted. "But I was able to

convince the French that we had suffered an error of navigation and seen nothing of import. Nonetheless, they impounded *Diana* and held us prisoner." Again he sighed. "At first we were held at Thuguguruk, but I arranged through careful misbehavior to be transferred to Marieville, in hopes of learning more. Unfortunately *Diana*'s people were transferred to this dreadful place along with me."

Arabella's mind whirled as she attempted to comprehend this new information. "This explains why you have bent all your efforts to the men's comfort, and have not sought to escape."

"Exactly. I cannot depart until I have fulfilled my mission. Only when I have discovered the details of Napoleon's secret project will I attempt escape—and, even then, I will not leave unless I can bring the entire crew with me."

"A difficult challenge."

"Indeed. But I have laid the groundwork, though many details remain to be worked out."

She blinked up into the shadow where his face lay. "Why did you not take me into your confidences before now?"

His warm arms clasped her shoulders even more firmly. "It was for your own protection. Every time I seek more information, or take a step toward escape for the men, I risk discovery . . . and if discovered, I and any confederates would certainly be shot for espionage. I would not expose the least of my crew to that risk, never mind your dear self."

Arabella held her captain strongly in return. "You dear, sweet, brave, foolish man. I forgive you your caution on my behalf. But now that you have shared your secret with me—and I thank you for your trust—I must insist on being included in all future plans."

"You have no idea how much that thought cheers me. This has been such a lonely endeavor . . . but now you are with me, and I have great confidence in your abilities."

Despite the darkness and the peril of their situation, Arabella

smiled. "I am certain that together we will be able to winkle out
Napoleon's last secret."

"And bring the Dianas safely home."

"I hope that we will be able to free the Touchstones as well."

A pause. "We shall see," he said. Then, after another pause: "It
has grown quite late. We should return to the *auberge* before we
are noted as away without leave."

The sun had by now completely vanished, and of course Venus
had no moon. But the wan light of the town's glow-worms reflected from the clouds above to a sufficient extent that they could
pick their way back to the gate.

Much of Arabella's attention was focused on her footing. But
as she walked, grateful for the support of her captain's arm, her
thoughts were bent toward espionage . . . and escape.

16

ESPIONAGE

Some days passed before Arabella and Captain Singh could again speak privately, days during which her existing, public duties of care and support for the men seemed a mere distraction from what she now thought of as her real mission. But without more information from the captain, there was little she could do in that direction, and so she found herself fidgeting in impatience.

Fox, of course, noted Arabella's anxiousness immediately. The man could be frightfully keen . . . except when he was utterly obtuse. "You seem distracted," he observed one day at luncheon. "May I inquire what is the matter?"

"It is . . . personal," she replied.

At once Fox's expression became solicitous. "Has it to do with Captain Singh? I have sensed some tension between the two of you."

"I thank you for your concern," she said, setting down her teacup with a definitive clink. "But, as I said, it is a personal matter."

"Please know that I am always at your service, in case you should require support or comfort."

It was all she could do to keep from rolling her eyes . . . and yet she was also flattered at the attention. "I shall keep your offer in mind."

That evening, when she and her captain again went for an evening stroll, he too acknowledged her agitation. "I apologize for the delay," he said, "but we must not change our behavior overmuch. Such a change would be noted, and would occasion suspicion. I am, to be honest, concerned that even this second outing in a week may raise questions."

"I understand," she said, "but I ache to be *useful*. Please allow me to assist you in your mission, in some concrete manner!"

They walked together in silence for a time, as he considered her request. "It has been so long since I have been able to share my concerns with any one else," he said at last. "Permit me to explain what I do and do not know, and perhaps together we may determine some way in which you can help."

"Very well."

"Your news, from Lady Corey, of Napoleon's project to build an armored aerial ship only confirmed what I have already suspected. The ship is named *Victoire*, by the way, and she is being constructed by Venusian labor to plans provided by the American, Fulton. But I do not feel that this is yet sufficient intelligence. The most important missing piece, which I must determine before I can depart this place, is how they intend to *launch* her. The weight of the iron would require enormous balloons, filled with prodigious quantities of air heated to unprecedented temperatures, to lift her above the falling-line. Yet there is no sign of the vast furnaces required for such an endeavor. The chimneys of such tremendous furnaces would certainly be visible from Marieville; even if Fulton has devised some means of avoiding the necessity of chimneys, the furnaces alone would be so extensive as to be beyond conceal-ment. Indeed, I have been unable to discover evidence of any fur-naces at all, or any indication that such are under construction." He pursed his lips. "All my efforts to gather this intelligence from here have been unsuccessful. I *must* find some way to infiltrate the ship-yard."

"But it is only a few miles from here. I assume there is some reason you cannot make your way there overland? Perhaps by night?"

"The swamps between here and there are prohibited, and dif-ficult to traverse besides. And the ship-yard is protected by a high stockade wall."

She considered the problem from every angle, and an idea be-gan to sprout at the back of her mind. "You have said that no one is ever transferred from the ship-yard to Marieville."

"Indeed."

"But prisoners *are* transferred *to* the ship-yard?"

He paused, raising an eyebrow. "Occasionally."

"And the ship—*Victoire*, did you say?—is being constructed by Venusian laborers?"

"Yes . . ." She had plainly piqued his interest.

"Do you recall Mills? Fox's captain of the mizzen-top, formerly a waister aboard *Diana*?"

"Of course."

"I have recently learned that he has experience as a boat-builder, and speaks the Venusian languages." The plural "lan-guages" did not escape the captain's notice, causing the eyebrow to rise again, but he did not interrupt her. "If we could persuade him to volunteer for a transfer to the ship-yard, he would be in a position to gather the necessary intelligence. I am certain that he would take this risk if you requested it. May I have your permis-sion to approach him?"

The captain considered for a moment, then sighed and shook his head. "I could not countenance such a risk."

"I can personally vouch for his reliability. He was an invaluable ally during the mutiny."

Captain Singh's lips pinched together and he blew out a long breath through his nose. He released her arm and paced up and down the path, head down. Finally he returned to Arabella and took her hands. "After so many months of solitary, secret work it is . . . difficult for me to extend my trust to any one else, even your own sweet self." His chin firmed and he straightened. "But we must take this risk, and soon. Else the tyrant will dominate Europe."

"Or more," Arabella put in.

"Or more," he confirmed. "You may approach Mills . . . but cautiously, very cautiously. We must be *utterly* certain of him before revealing any slightest thing of the mission we will ask him to undertake."

"I assure you my discretion will be absolute."

"Also, under no circumstances may any one know any thing but that which is absolutely necessary for them to know in order to perform their part of the action." He hesitated before continuing. "This applies to yourself as well. Although it pains me to do so, I may continue to withhold certain details from you. This is for your own safety."

Arabella felt her shoulders stiffen at this statement; the idea of her fiancé concealing information from her was extremely discomfiting. But she recognized the necessity of secrecy, to protect the lives of every one involved. "I understand," she said, and embraced him.

Even as she breathed in his warm, familiar scent, she realized she was not entirely satisfied with the situation. But it was, she supposed, the best she could do for now.

Arabella approached Mills after supper the next day, first engaging him in superficial conversation and then gently turning the topic toward Napoleon and the war. She was not at all surprised to learn that he was as opposed to the tyrant as any other British airman, if not more so. Probing further, she discovered that he was, as she had hoped, firmly and personally committed to Napoleon's defeat, and indeed expressed a willingness to put his life on the line if that could make the difference. At this juncture she suggested they take a stroll around the barracks ground, a suggestion to which he readily acceded.

As they walked, she realized that she too was being questioned. Clearly Mills understood that his loyalties were being tested, and his intelligent responses also served to elicit her own. She strove to reassure him of her sincerity and good intentions, without revealing any thing of the captain's secret plans.

After an hour or so of this, they regarded each other with grave solemnity. Arabella's heart pounded beneath her ribs, and despite the languid pace of their walk the usually stoic Mills was breathing hard. The scene reminded her greatly of the moment during the mutiny aboard *Diana* when she had revealed to Mills her allegiance to the captain, and he had reciprocated.

"I am certain you realize that all of this questioning has a purpose," she said at last.

Mills nodded, his expression neutral.

She paused, considering the words she had already composed and rehearsed in her mind for this moment. "Captain Singh has learned that Napoleon is constructing a secret weapon at the shipyard some miles from here. For the sake of Great Britain and her allies, we feel that we must obtain as much intelligence on this weapon as we can and return it to England as soon as possible. But the ship-yard is held in great secrecy." She swallowed, lowered her voice, and leaned in closer. "Would you be willing to accept a transfer to the ship-yard, to discern what you may of Napoleon's secrets?"

"Honored," he replied, closing his eyes and inclining his head. "For England; for Captain Singh. Both so very kind to me."

"Oh, thank you!" she said, releasing a breath she had not known she was holding. "But I must warn you . . . no one is transferred *from* the ship-yard to Marieville. If you accept this transfer, you will likely be there for the duration of the war."

Mills shrugged. "No ship-yard hot as furnace-house." His lips curved in a slight smile.

"Indeed." Arabella felt her own lips curling upward.

But Mills's face immediately returned to seriousness. "How to tell you what I learn there?"

"Oh!" This was a question that she had overlooked, as had the captain—his mind perhaps preoccupied by considerations of secrecy. "I do not know. No person nor thing, other than the most highly placed French officers, travels hence from there."

Mills pursed his lips, considering the question. "My people, the Wolof, we talk by drum. Sometimes over great distance."

At this Arabella was rather taken aback. "*Talk* by drum? Employing some sort of cypher, or code?"

He gave her another smile, and a shake of his head. "No code. *Language.* The beat of it, the high and low. If I want to say"—he spoke a phrase in some musical tongue—"I drum this"—he hummed a few notes—exactly matching the phrase's intonation and rhythm, though lacking its vowels and consonants.

"I see." She considered the implications. "Can you teach me a few important phrases?"

"No, miss. Years to learn the drum language, even if you know

Wolof. It is a kind of poetry." He thought for a bit, then nodded thoughtfully. "Brindle. Fox's steward. He knows the drums. He is Serer—not Wolof, but close. We can talk."

This intelligence made Arabella exceedingly anxious. She knew the captain would firmly resist incorporating even one more person into the conspiracy. "Do you trust him? Truly trust him, with your life? Is there any other person who understands the language of the drums whom you trust more?"

Mills thought for a good long while about that, then again shook his head. "No other. Brindle . . . good man, reliable." He held up a finger. "But . . . *Fox's* man. What he knows, Fox knows." He lowered the finger and gazed steadily into Arabella's eyes. "You trust Fox?"

That was a conundrum indeed. She blew out a breath. "I shall consult with Captain Singh. Do not discuss this with Brindle, or any one else, unless and until I give you leave to do so. Until then . . . I thank you, the captain thanks you, and England thanks you."

"Honored," he repeated, and bowed.

———

"Absolutely not," Captain Singh said. His dark eyes were as hard and serious as ever she had seen them.

They stood at the side of a small pond on the outskirts of Marieville. Small creatures chirruped and splashed at the pond's margins in the gathering dusk, and the breeze across the water was a tiny bit cooler than the sweltering air elsewhere. "We have no alternative," she repeated. "No one other than Mills and Brindle knows the drumming language. In any case . . . would it be so bad to include Captain Fox in our scheme? He hates the French as much as any Englishman I have ever met, and he is intelligent, brave, and an experienced commander. I trust him completely."

Captain Singh scoffed. "He is impulsive, undisciplined, and shallow. And no *privateer*"—he placed a subtle but clear emphasis upon the word—"can withstand comparison even with a captain of His Majesty's Aerial Navy, never mind one of the Honorable Mars Company."

"You would not say those things if you had seen his audacity in taking *Fleur de Lys,* or his steadfastness when the French pursued *Touchstone.* He is a gentleman and an excellent captain, and I am certain he would be an asset to us."

"Mrs. Singh," the captain said mildly, "if I did not know better, I would suspect that your head had been turned."

Arabella turned away quickly, lest the captain see the blush she could feel springing to her cheeks. *It is but the heat,* she told herself. "This suspicion is beneath you," she said.

"I apologize," he said, and placed his hands on her shoulders.

She reached across herself and laid her right hand on his left. The long, strong fingers were dry and warm beneath hers. She took a deep breath to settle herself, then let it out and turned back to him. "I cannot deny that I find Captain Fox agreeable. But do not believe this interferes with a clear-eyed assessment of his merits as a commander. I have experience of him; you do not. Furthermore, though I have given the matter much thought, I have been unable to conceive of any other means by which intelligence may be reliably communicated from the ship-yard to here."

"Nor have I," the captain admitted. "Yet I still find myself reluctant in the extreme to add even one more person to those whom we must trust, never mind two. Each additional person privy to a secret is another hatch which, if not properly battened, may leak information in any storm." He squeezed her shoulder, then released it and stepped back to Arabella's side, the two of them looking across the pond together once again. "Keeping a secret, I have found, is terribly wearing. The creation of plausible fictions, the constant struggle to remember what one has told to whom, the eternal vigilance over one's every word and indeed thought . . ."

"I have experience in keeping secrets," Arabella interrupted softly.

That simple reminder stopped his words completely.

"How long did it take *you*, sir," she continued, already knowing the answer, "to discern that your captain's 'boy' was, in fact, nothing of the sort? Or did I manage to conceal that from you until Gowse removed my shirt?"

"You . . . you did indeed," he said, his voice low and—for perhaps the first time she could recall—somewhat abashed.

"The truth of our marriage, or lack thereof, has also remained a secret known only to yourself."

"You have made your point, Mrs. Singh," he replied, with a semblance of his usual imperturbability, which brought a silent smile to Arabella's lips. He turned to face her, and she faced him as well. "But I must remind you that your . . . previous secret was maintained only because you told *no one*. If you had entrusted the fact of your sex to Gowse, or Mills, or even myself, earlier in the voyage, how long do you suppose it would have remained unknown to any one else?"

"A fair point," she acknowledged. "But we *must* have Brindle, or we can gain no intelligence from Mills. It seems to me that the great value of this arrangement is worth the additional risk of bringing Fox in as well. And time is of the essence."

"Indeed," he sighed. "Very well. But *I* will be the one to approach Brindle; my authority as captain may persuade him not to share what he knows with any one, even Captain Fox."

"We must at least make the attempt," Arabella acknowledged, though she doubted—and she suspected Captain Singh did as well—that the request would make any difference.

Captain Singh folded his arms upon his chest. "Now . . . how are we to arrange for Mills to be transferred to the ship-yard?"

"I have an idea. But you may not care for it. . . ."

"Thank you for agreeing to see me at this early hour," Arabella said to Lady Corey. The great lady was still in her dressing-gown, with her Venusian servant Aglanawamna bustling about laying out her morning clothes.

"Any thing for you, dear child. What is the matter?"

"It is about Mills, one of the topmen from *Touchstone*. You may recall him?"

"Oh yes . . . dear Mr. Mills," Lady Corey replied, almost convincingly.

"I knew him aboard *Diana* as well," Arabella continued undeterred. "He was very helpful to me there, especially during the mutiny. Now it is he who needs help, and you are the only one who can give it."

"How so?"

"It is his lungs, the poor man. The French have him working in the furnace-house, which—as I am certain you are aware—is a place whose air is terribly hot and frighteningly foul."

"It could scarcely be worse than the rest of this horrid planet."

Arabella's eyes darted to Aglanawamna, who continued smoothing out Lady Corey's dress on the bed with apparent equanimity. She did not know how much English the Venusian comprehended, but suspected the servant understood more than she—or perhaps he—let on. "It *is* worse," Arabella insisted, "considerably so, and Mills's lungs cannot withstand the strain."

"I am terribly sorry to hear that, but what help can *I* provide?"

"I hope that you may be willing to impose upon your new

friend Mr. Fulton to have him transferred to the ship-yard. He is an experienced boat-builder—he worked for the Portuguese in Africa—and I am certain that the comparatively salubrious sea air at the ship-yard will do his poor lungs a world of good."

"Mr. Fulton is, in truth, no one's friend but his own," Lady Corey sniffed, "but he certainly does have sufficient influence with Fouché to effect such a transfer." She paused, considering. "I believe I may be able to make the request in such a way that he will see it as being to his advantage to comply. He desires my good favors, as I believe I have told you."

"You have."

Lady Corey dismissed with a brusque gesture the hat Aglanawamna was presenting to her. "Oh no, not that ratty old thing. I could not bear to wear it even one more day. Take it away. Um, *no chapeau!*"

Now Aglanawamna did react, a long slow blink of her broad shining eyes which demonstrated, Arabella had come to understand, annoyance and impatience.

"*Wanagaagna lo gugnula,*" Arabella muttered under her breath to the servant. It was, Mills had learned, a thing that Wagala parents said when their children misbehaved, and meant something along the lines of "be patient with them."

Aglanawamna's eyes snapped open in surprise, fixing themselves upon Arabella's; she saw her own face doubly reflected in the wide black pupils.

"*Ugugla wom guluk,*" Arabella said, enunciating carefully: I am a friend. It was a phrase she had rehearsed many times with Mills, but never before spoken to a Venusian. She hoped it was appropriate in this circumstance.

"*Gumum,*" the Venusian replied, her throat-sac working. It was a statement of acknowledgement—not agreement, exactly, but at least a recognition of the offer. It was a start.

"What on Earth are you gurgling there?" Lady Corey sputtered.

"Just a few pleasantries I have picked up," Arabella replied mildly. "Venusians are people, you know, just as Earthlings and Martians are, and deserve our respect. These servants are as much under Napoleon's yoke here as we."

"Humph," Lady Corey scoffed. "As near as I can tell, they are as happy to work for that murderer Fouché as for me. And, unlike me, they are free to come and go as they please."

Another long slow blink at that, and Arabella reflected on what she knew of the relations between the Wagala slaves and the Gowanna slavers. "I would not be so certain of that. In any case, would you please make that request of Mr. Fulton? I would be ever so grateful on Mills's behalf."

"Of course, my dear. Any thing for you." She turned back to Aglanawamna, regarded the replacement hat she was presenting, and seemed about to snap something disparaging . . . then paused, collected herself, and said with some dignity, "*Un other chapeau, s'il vous plait.*"

As Arabella departed, Aglanawamna raised two fingers to her lips. It was a gesture Arabella did not understand, but she thought— she hoped—it was a positive sign.

———————————

Arabella reported to Captain Singh that she had made the request of Lady Corey without revealing any thing of their secret plans; the captain, in turn, told her that he had approached Brindle about using his drumming skills to communicate with Mills at the ship-yard, and had impressed upon him the importance of keeping the content of those communications secret even from his own captain. "Brindle expressed enthusiasm at the prospect of participating in such an important undertaking," the captain said, "and promised to exercise discretion—though I fear that, at the critical moment, his enthusiasm may outweigh his discretion."

"That is, I fear, a risk that we must take."

"Indeed." He blew out a breath through his nose. "In any case, we have done all we may for the moment . . . now we can only wait for Mills's transfer to occur."

That wait lasted three days—three days full of anticipation, anxiety, and doubt. As Captain Singh had warned, keeping a secret was terribly wearing, even more so when several people already knew part of it. Arabella could barely bring herself to converse with Lady Corey, Fox, or indeed any of the Touchstones, so filled with concern was she over letting some bit of information slip to the wrong person. Yet she knew she could not separate herself from them completely; this would arouse too much suspicion. So she forced herself to continue her rounds of visits and assistance with as little change as possible.

In this she succeeded only partially. Several times Captain Fox or Lady Corey expressed solicitous concern over her drawn expression and the dark circles beneath her eyes; to these entreaties she responded with sincere thanks and a reassurance—not entirely untrue—that her low mood was due to the men's continuing abuse at the hands of Fouché.

The wait ended one evening, in the midst of a language lesson with Mills. The two of them were conferring over the differences in the imperative between Gowanna and Wagala. The slaves' language indicated commands with a suffix, derived from the second person pronoun, while in the slavers' language, as far as Arabella could tell, commands had the same grammatical form as the ordinary third person present indicative but with an added stress on the final syllable. Mills, whose command of both languages was definitely superior to hers, lacked the formal terminology to discuss these fine distinctions, which made it somewhat difficult to be certain they agreed.

Their intense colloquy was interrupted by the sound of stamping boots upon the rough wood of the barracks floor. Arabella looked up to see a detachment of four of Fouché's personal platoon—striding in absolute unison, their uniforms crisp and boots highly polished—marching directly toward her. Her heart leapt into her mouth, but before she could utter a word the leader of the group pointed at Mills. "You," he said in heavily accented English, "come with us."

Mills gave Arabella a look full of anxiety as he stood and meekly presented himself to the French soldiers, who immediately surrounded him and began marching him to the door.

"*D'ou prenez-vous lui?*" Arabella asked—where are you taking him?—recognizing even as she did that, with her mind currently occupied by Venusian languages, she was mangling the French badly.

"*Au chantier aérienne,*" the leader sneered without turning his head. To the aerial ship-yard.

Arabella's sentiments at that moment were so strongly mixed—fading agitation that she might be the French soldiers' object, satisfaction that her request to Lady Corey had borne fruit, fear that their scheme of espionage might yet be found out, anticipation of what they might learn, concern that she might never see dear Mills again, and many others—that she could not frame a reply, and was reduced to girlishly wringing her hands together at her chin, her sweat-soaked handkerchief twisted between them.

But Mills, bless his courage, managed a smile and a wink over his shoulder as he was led away.

17

CONSPIRACY

Several more days passed in anxious anticipation, until to Arabella's surprise the silence was broken from an unexpected quarter.

"Mrs. Singh," Fox said one afternoon with a courteous bow as they encountered one another in the street.

"Captain Fox," she acknowledged neutrally.

"I have recently received some . . . curious intelligence from my man Brindle, which I believe may interest you. Would you care to discuss it over tea?"

She would, she would very much indeed, and shortly thereafter they found themselves ensconced over a pot of dreadful tea in the back room of Fox's club. They were alone, save for a bored young Venusian who provided a fitful artificial breeze by means of a large fan of dried leaves, and to prevent eavesdropping they seated themselves far from him and kept their voices extremely low.

"I came across Brindle just this morning," Fox said, "behind the necessary-house at the barracks, where he stood with eyes

closed and a captivated expression on his face, as though enrap-
tured by some distant piece of music. But, even if he were of a
musical bent, which he has never before shown himself to be,
there was no music to be heard—only the usual hammering from
the ship-yard that lies some miles distant across the swamp."

"I know of it," Arabella put in impatiently.

"Naturally I inquired of him to what he might be listening.
Imagine my surprise when he started as though struck from behind!
I swear that he jumped a good three feet in the air."

"What was the *matter*?"

"Well, he was so startled by my interruption that it was some
minutes until I could extract a coherent answer from him, and
for some reason I found myself forced to exert my full persua-
sive powers before learning the full story. It seems that the Af-
ricans, or certain tribes among them, employ a code consisting
of drum-beats . . ."

"Please do come to the *point*!" she interrupted.

"Mrs. Singh!" he said, raising his tea-cup and his eyebrows.
"This is one of the most extraordinary things which has come to
pass in *weeks* in this benighted prison-camp, and I intend to milk
it to the greatest possible conversational extent."

In reply she fixed him with her steeliest glare.

"Oh, very well," he sighed. "If you insist on taking all of the
pleasure out of it."

"I do insist," she hissed. It was a struggle to keep her voice low
and conversational.

Again he sighed. "In brief, then. Your friend Mills, who as you
may know was recently transferred to the ship-yard, was sending
a message to Brindle by means of drumming!"

"I know! What was the *content* of this communication?"

Fox's attitude, up to that point rather teasing and flirtatious,
suddenly became serious. "As I suspected," he said. "You have been
involved all along."

At once Arabella realized to her shame that she had fallen into a trap. "I, I have no idea to what you might refer," she stammered.

Fox's mien was now as hard as it had been just before the attack upon *Fleur de Lys*. "Do not pretend innocence, Mrs. Singh. I am quite aware of the fact that you and Mills have been making a study of the Venusian language for these last few weeks, and that his transfer to the ship-yard—a quite unprecedented transfer—was the result of a request from Lady Corey to the American Mr. Fulton. The only point of commonality between Mills and Lady Corey is yourself, and the obvious conclusion is that you have engineered this transfer for the express purpose of obtaining some information from the Venusians at the ship-yard." He leaned toward her across the tea-set now, his eyes burning into hers, and spoke low and very intently. "You have deprived me of one of my people, Mrs. Singh—possibly putting him in grave danger—and attempted to suborn another, all without consulting me. And despite the fact that we are guests of dear Monsieur Napoleon—and although I have great respect for you, and your husband—I am still the captain of my crew and I will no longer brook such interference." He sat back and took up his tea-cup, abruptly genial again . . . at least, to all appearance. "So, my dear Mrs. Singh. Do you wish to know what news has made its way from the ship-yard to Brindle's ears, or do you not?"

"I . . ." She paused, swallowed. "I do."

"Then you will inform me of your larger plan—for I know you well, after all these months, and I know that you do have a larger plan—and, if I agree with it, I will instruct my man Brindle to cooperate with you. Otherwise, you must do without him."

Arabella covered her consternation by pouring herself another cup of tea—though, to her dismay, her hand shook sufficiently that the tea-pot lid rattled—as she considered her options. Captain Singh would be furious if she told Fox any thing without consulting him first. Yet she knew and trusted Fox; his perspicacity in deducing the facts of the situation provided further confirmation of his powers of mind and observation; and his hatred of Napoleon would certainly guarantee his whole-hearted cooperation in any scheme of espionage.

And, she was forced to admit to herself, inviting Fox into their conspiracy would require her to spend more time with him . . . which did not displease her in the least.

"I am waiting," Fox said.

"It is a . . . delicate situation."

"I am certain that it is."

Arabella glanced over at the young Venusian, who sat more than fifteen feet away and appeared to be nearly dozing as he lazily wafted the fan. Even so, she leaned in close to Fox and spoke very low as she explained the whole matter: Captain Singh's secret mission, Fulton and the armored airship, how Arabella had engineered Mills's transfer to the ship-yard, and Brindle's role in the affair. "Lady Corey has no knowledge of any of this," she emphasized. "She believes the transfer was done for Mills's health, and under no circumstances may she *or any one else* learn any of the true details."

"I understand," Fox replied in an equally low tone. "You may rest assured that my discretion in this matter will be absolute." A small smile quirked one corner of his mouth. "I must confess myself pleased and honored that you have chosen to include me in your scheme."

Once again Arabella was required to take a sip of tea to hide her reaction. But she could not suppress her own smile as she set the tea-cup down. "Now, what *was* the content of Mills's communication to Brindle?"

"He has arrived safely at the ship-yard and has been put to work at the rope-walk. It is wearisome work, and offers few chances for gathering intelligence, but he hopes to demonstrate his skills at ship-building and be promoted to a position of greater opportunity soon."

Captain Singh was, as Arabella had expected, not at all pleased that she had included Fox in the conspiracy without his counsel. But what had been revealed could no longer be concealed, and eventually, grudgingly, even he was forced to admit that Fox was a worthy addition to their small company.

Fox, as an officer, was free to come and go where he pleased—within limits, of course—and as Brindle's commanding officer and employer was naturally able to meet with him frequently without raising any suspicions. Thus communications with Mills became far easier than they had expected. Furthermore, Fox had accumulated knowledge of the French guards' and officers' movements, which he now shared with Arabella and her captain, and was willing and able to essay some rather risky excursions, such as into the swamps beyond the barracks, in order to obtain more information.

Despite this, their meetings—infrequent and irregular, due to the necessity for secrecy—often grew quietly heated, as the two captains differed so greatly in their ideas of what should take precedence. Captain Fox was still centered upon escape for himself and his people, a concentration which he now extended to the Dianas, while Captain Singh continued to emphasize espionage, refusing to consider escape until further critical details of the armored airship could be discerned. For her part, Arabella felt compelled to take Singh's side when the three of them were together. When she was alone with her own captain, though, she continued to press him to at least begin laying plans for escape, which could then be put in motion once the necessary information had been obtained.

But even if they could all agree to attempt escape, the success of such an enterprise was far from guaranteed.

The most difficult part of escape was not leaving the plantation, but remaining free while traversing the vast distances to English-controlled territory. Even if the difficulties of food, water, and transport could be overcome, the unavoidable fact was that the least astute passer-by could tell at a single glance that they were not Venusians. And, as every Venusian and Frenchman for a hundred miles would immediately be informed of any escape by the sound of the cannon, if the fleeing Englishmen were observed at all recapture would inevitably follow. Despite the best efforts of the three of them, they had been unable to arrive at a solution to this thorny problem.

Arabella, thinking back to her several conversations with Mills on the topic of slavery, reflected that this same situation was faced by African slaves in America and Brazil. How horrible it was to be so easily identified, and judged as less than human, simply by one's appearance.

But the same, of course, was true of one's sex, and yet she knew from her own experience that that could be overcome. So she continued to worry at the problem whenever she found herself with a moment for contemplation.

———————————

Arabella and Captain Singh had just sat down to breakfast—the butter, she noted, was rancid again—when, to every one's surprise, Fox came clattering in the door, sweating and out of breath, his collar undone. Two Venusian waiters protested his untoward appearance, but he brushed them off and strode directly to Arabella's table.

"I have urgent news," he said, sketching a bow to Captain Singh and Arabella. "Please, you must both accompany me to the barracks immediately."

"Of course," the captain said, rising and folding his napkin. "Shall we bring the surgeon?"

"No. This is . . . personal. I shall explain on the way."

Arabella, anxious though she was to hear this news, took a moment to wrap several bread rolls and some cheese in a napkin and stow them in her reticule. Whatever the situation might be, none of them would be in a good position to take it in hand without sustenance. She swallowed a gulp of coffee and hurried to follow the two captains, who were already out the door.

All eyes followed her as she swept out of the dining-room.

Conversation was impossible as the three of them dashed through the Marieville streets, Arabella scurrying to keep up with Fox's mad rush and her captain's smooth long-legged gait. Soon they reached the gate, presented their papers, and hurried down the well-trodden path to the barracks.

But after just a few minutes on the path Fox slowed, looked around, then stopped. He stood panting, hands on knees, for a moment before straightening and looking around again. No one else was about at this early hour, and the gates with their guards were well behind them. "Forgive me . . . for this intrusion," he puffed. "But I have just had the most *extraordinary* news from Mills, by way of Brindle, and I knew you would want to know immediately. This was the most expedient means I could contrive to extricate you from the guards' attentions." His expression mingled pleasure and anxiety.

"Go on," Captain Singh replied. He had already regained his usual calm demeanor, though Arabella's breast still heaved from the exertion and the day's already-rising heat.

"The news concerns *Diana*," Fox said.

At that single word Arabella's rapid breath caught in her throat, and Captain Singh's tranquility completely shattered. His eyes widened and he took a half-step forward, as though about to grasp Fox by his lapels. "Out with it, man!" he spat.

"Mills," Fox continued, "has just been assigned to work on *Diana* at the ship-yard. She is in the process of being refitted into a French warship!"

This news forced the words "What of Aadim?" from Arabella's lips, almost without her volition. The name *Diana* had brought to her mind a rush of emotion and memories, foremost among which were thoughts of the ship's automaton navigator—a beloved figure whose finely crafted wooden face she had not expected ever to see again.

The captain glanced to her at that, then fixed his gaze on Fox's face. "Yes, have you any news of him?"

Fox shook his head. "I have heard nothing about any one of that name. Is he a member of your crew?"

"After a fashion," Captain Singh replied, betraying nothing.

"In any case . . ." Fox raised his hands, fingers spread. "Though I knew that news of your ship would be of great interest to you, I do not believe it is the most important item in Mills's report—that would be the status of *Victoire*, the armored airship. His intelligence of her is less detailed as of yet, but he has been able to ascertain that she is far from complete, lacking landing-furnace, cook-stoves, and lanterns among other necessities; nor is there any sign of the launch-furnaces you asked him to look for. So it seems we have some weeks at least, perhaps months, before she is ready to launch."

Captain Singh breathed deeply, stroking his chin, as he absorbed this news. "Although I greatly appreciate your zeal in bringing us this intelligence so quickly, I wish that you had not created such a scene in doing so. Now every one, including the French, will be keen to know what the matter was."

"Ah," Fox replied, his face falling. "I had not considered that."

This reaction did not soothe the captain at all. "We will think of some story," Arabella said, placatingly.

Captain Singh nodded. "I suppose we shall. And we must also consider how best to make use of *Diana*'s presence at the ship-yard." He proffered his arm to Arabella. "Let us continue to the barracks. It will, if nothing else, correspond with our supposed destination, and will provide us some time for private conversation."

On the way to the barracks they concocted a tale of misunderstanding about a personal matter, which seemed implausible to Arabella but proved sufficient to satisfy any queries they received regarding Fox's sudden appearance at breakfast, and began sketching plans to make use of *Diana*'s proximity. Over the following few days Arabella and her captain mulled over these plans, together and separately, until the three of them could again meet together in private. This opportunity was provided by a mushroom-hunt in the forested hills above Marieville.

"The distance to the ship-yard is only a few miles," Captain Singh summarized as he strolled along with his mushroom-basket swinging at his hip. "It would not be difficult for a small group to depart the barracks by night and make their way thence. But in order for this scheme to succeed, we require a sufficient crew of able airmen to seize *Diana* from her captors, launch her, fly her, and fight her. How can we possibly assemble so many men in one place without arousing suspicion?"

"I have been considering this very issue," Fox replied. "I propose that we gather, in secret, large quantities of the native foliage. At the appointed moment, each man shrouds himself in leafy branches, and makes his way to some rendezvous in the forest thus disguised." He permitted himself a satisfied smirk. "Rather like Birnam Wood in the Scottish play, if I do say so myself."

This idea seemed to Arabella entirely ridiculous, and Captain Singh's face showed that he was just about to make some scornful comment upon it. But something in Fox's words connected with her memories of him painted and caparisoned as the goddess Gaia at the ceremony of crossing the line. "I saw your performance of *Macbeth* at the barracks," she put in quickly, before Captain Singh could speak, "and it was very good, particularly your turn as the Scottish Lord."

"Thank you, ma'am."

"It seems to me," Arabella said, continuing to interrupt her captain, "that you and your company deserve a larger audience."

Fox inclined his head, acknowledging the compliment. "Do go on."

Arabella turned to Captain Singh, whose brows were lowered in an expression of confusion and stern rebuke. "If we were to stage a play," she explained, even as the idea was continuing to form itself in her mind, "a very popular play, perhaps *Romeo and Juliet* . . . we would be compelled by the size of the audience to perform outside the palisade. This would provide us a ready excuse to gather the Dianas and Touchstones together in one place . . . in a convenient position for a mass break! And the . . . the production of the play—the gathering of properties, manufacture of set-pieces, and so forth—would provide a pretext for our escape preparations. Once every one is gathered together for the performance, at some prearranged signal we dash across country to the ship-yard, take *Diana* by surprise, and escape in her."

"I like this plan!" Fox said.

"I am not surprised that you do," Captain Singh said, "especially as I imagine you view yourself as Romeo."

"Of course," Fox replied, as though astonished at the very

concept of any alternative. "A part which, indeed, I have played several times before."

"In more than one way, I am certain," Captain Singh murmured.

But Fox, not hearing the other captain's comment, turned his attention to Arabella. "And naturally, our Juliet must be—"

"We can put off questions of casting until later," Arabella interrupted. "Our most immediate concern is to obtain permission from the authorities for the production. I will approach Lady Corey, proposing it as a humanitarian project; her influence with Fulton, the architect of Marieville, will surely carry some weight even with the demon Fouché."

"We will require food and water for the escape," Fox said. "These can still be obtained, for a sufficient fee, and I will begin assembling those supplies immediately."

Captain Singh did not seem entirely convinced. Nonetheless he nodded slowly. "This plan may succeed . . . *if* we can arrange it so that the performance is lightly guarded, and if we can obtain some small arms." He stroked his chin. "I have been cultivating connections for some time with the sort of men who can provide pistols and boarding-axes, and I believe that now is the time to exploit those connections. However, I am afraid that their price may be more than I can pay." His eyes met Arabella's. "I believe you retain some portion of the four hundred and eighty livres in gold we obtained earlier?"

"I do. Nearly seventy livres remain."

"Fifty livres of that should, I think, procure sufficient arms for our escape."

Arabella hesitated; she had been saving that money in case of some unforeseen crisis. But if this plan failed, for want of pistols or any thing else, they would likely all be shot.

"Of course," she said, though her mouth suddenly went quite dry.

"Well then," Fox said, rubbing his hands, "it is settled. Now let us discuss casting."

———————————

That evening Arabella trudged wearily up the *auberge* steps and collapsed on the bed. "Why must it be so impossibly *hot* on this planet," she said, fanning herself uselessly with one hand, "even after sunset?" She and Captain Singh were alone, Stross and Richardson having not yet returned from their club.

"It is the proximity of the sun," he replied mildly. "As you well know."

She fixed him with a baleful glare. "Help me with my shoes."

Without a word the captain knelt and began unlacing Arabella's shoes—the very same sturdy Martian-made half-boots which had accompanied her from Mars to Earth and back, and now from Mars to Venus. They were in remarkably good shape, for all their tens of thousands of miles, and fitted her like gloves. "What news from Lady Corey?" he asked.

"She was quite keen on the idea, and seemed certain that Fulton would be able to convince Fouché to permit the performance, on the grounds of encouraging morale and greater productivity among the prisoners. So keen was she, in fact, that she insists that she must play the Nurse. 'I was very active in the amateur theatricals in my younger days, you know,'"—Arabella's accurate imitation of Lady Corey's haughty tones brought a smile to even the usually staid Captain Singh's face—"'and I welcome the opportunity to tread the boards again.' Of course, I am certain her true aim is to keep close watch on me, to prevent any impropriety." Arabella sighed and shook her head. "I begin to fear that the theatrical production itself may be more vexing to arrange than the escape."

"Her involvement will be all to the good," the captain said, setting Arabella's shoes neatly aside at the foot of the bed and rubbing her feet. "It will make the theatricals more believable to the French. And we may be able to devolve some of your tasks regarding the play to her, thus freeing up your time and attention for the escape attempt."

"I had also thought that it would put her in a position to escape along with us. I should not like to leave her behind."

Captain Singh frowned. "Indeed. Especially as Fouché's treatment of any one thought involved in a successful escape, after the fact, will be quite harsh." He tapped his chin with one long finger. "Let us not inform her of the escape plan until the last moment, though. What she does not know, she cannot let slip."

"I quite agree. And what of yourself? Have you made any progress in arranging for a reduced guard on the performance?"

"Some progress. As you may be aware, Lefevre has been rather nettled by his loss of command. And, though he and I have never seen eye to eye, after the amount of time we have spent together in his office we do have an . . . *entente*, shall we say, and a certain shared dislike of Fouché. I think that I understand his priorities and motivations . . ."

"Money," Arabella put in.

"Indeed. And though his price for co-operation is high, I suspect that he looks forward to the black eye a mass escape would give to Fouché. I hope to be able to negotiate him down to an amount we can actually afford." But though this news was promising, he still seemed troubled.

"Is something the matter?"

The captain sighed. "Though plans for the escape itself are proceeding apace, I am concerned that they may all come to naught."

"I am sure that all will be well," she said. Though she was, in fact, far from certain.

He nodded in acknowledgement of her reassurance, but paused

before continuing. "We have had some very bad news to-day, which I have been reluctant to share with you. You recall John Bannatyne, one of *Diana*'s young gentlemen?"

"Of course." She had shared navigation lessons with him when she had been captain's boy. He was a rather thin and spotty young man, and quite reticent because of a severe stutter, but always cheerful and affable for all that.

The captain hesitated still further, looking down into his folded hands. "He collapsed from exhaustion to-day, in the midst of cutting down a tree for charcoal. The other men, defying the guards, rushed him back to the barracks, but despite the surgeon's best attentions he could not be roused. He was buried immediately; you know how quickly every thing goes to rot on this horrible planet."

Arabella, appalled, put a hand onto her captain's shoulder. "Oh dear."

"*Diana* requires a full complement of able airmen to launch and fly her," he continued, "never mind to fight, and after the depredations the people have suffered in their months of imprisonment I fear we may not have a sufficient crew."

"We will have the Touchstones as well."

"We will. Yet they, too, have suffered . . . and I do not know how many of us will succeed in escaping and reach the ship."

Arabella was taken aback by his pessimism. "Surely all, or nearly all."

The captain's expression as he returned her gaze was solemn. "Let us hope so. But even a reduced guard will take a toll, the swamps between here and the ship-yard are treacherous, and we will certainly suffer some casualties in taking the ship back. We are merchant airmen, after all, not men of war."

Arabella reached down and took his hands. "*Diana*'s crew are the finest in the Honorable Mars Company, and they have the bravest and most capable captain. With the help of the Touch-stones, I have no doubt that we will win through."

"Your confidence is an inspiration."

The next morning Arabella and the two captains were prome-nading the bustling high street of Marieville, quietly discussing amongst themselves the import of the latest communication from Mills. The street was, as it happened, far more heavily peopled than usual, and they found themselves forced to dodge hurtling carts and rushing platoons of French soldiers. But Arabella had no attention to spare to the origins of this tumult, because of the news they had just received.

It seemed that *Victoire* was not alone at the ship-yard; in fact, an entire fleet of armored airships was a-building. Seventeen more keels had already been laid, with plans for a further five. No wonder Fouché had been driving his prisoners so very hard to produce more and more and more iron. The only good news in this disturbing missive was that *Victoire,* the exemplar upon whose model the whole fleet would be built, was the only one near com-pletion; the others were awaiting her successful launch to prove some troublesome questions of design.

"This makes our curtain," said Fox, *curtain* being the word they had agreed to use instead of *escape* when speaking in public, "still more urgent. We must raise the curtain immediately, before this exemplar proves herself!"

"This changes nothing," Captain Singh countered. "We will raise the curtain only when the details upon which we have agreed have been discovered, and there is no indication the exemplar is any closer to completion than before. Furthermore, the prepara-tions for the performance are already quite rushed, and cannot be hastened further." Though his outward attitude appeared composed, to Arabella it was clear that considerable heat seethed below his placid words.

Arabella was seeking to formulate some comment which might redirect the two men's words in a calmer and more productive direction when she noted they had both fallen suddenly quiet. Following their gazes, she saw a detachment of eight of Fouché's personal platoon marching directly toward them.

"I will answer their questions," Captain Singh murmured, reaching into his coat pocket for his papers. Fox bristled at his arrogation of authority, but with only moments before the soldiers arrived he held his tongue.

The eight drew themselves up before the three with a crash of boots upon the street's hard-packed earth. "*Vous viendrez avec nous*," said their leader, inclining his head fractionally to Arabella.

Captain Singh's calm demeanor appeared unruffled as he stepped forward. "I shall comply," he said, "though I have other business . . ."

"*Arrêtez-vous!*" interrupted the soldier, raising an immaculate white-gloved hand. "*Seulement la madame.*"

Arabella glanced briefly at Captain Singh, and then at the nervous Fox, before setting her jaw and stepping forward. Her heart pounded—had they been incautious? Had they trusted the wrong person? Or was this demand unrelated to their escape plan? "Where are you taking me?" she replied in French.

"*Au commandant Fouché*," the man replied, and without another word the eight men formed up around her and marched her quickly away.

The tumult Arabella had observed in the streets of Marieville grew still more agitated as she and her silent escort approached the *manoir*; French officers and Venusian collaborators rushed hither and yon with what seemed to her to be expressions of near-panic.

The soldiers delivered her to another group, these still more immaculate and ornamented with braid and gilt, who conveyed her rapidly down carpeted halls to a room she had never before entered: Fouché's private office. Here the man himself sat writing behind a great desk, rococo with gold leaf, but when she entered he did not rise—he merely nodded to his men, who bowed and retired, leaving Arabella stranded in the middle of the broad and empty floor before it.

For an endless minute Fouché examined her silently, elbows on the desk, fingers steepled unmoving before him. His eyes, as she had noted before, betrayed a keen intelligence but no emotion whatsoever—they might have been the eyes of some ancient tortoise, one who had seen a thousand empires rise and fall and cared nothing for any of them.

Fouché then rose and walked around Arabella, still not speaking, examining her quite closely as though she were a prize *huresh* whose purchase he was considering. Finally he came to a halt before her and spoke without preamble.

"*Sa Majesté Impériale et Royale, Napoléon le Premier, va nous rendre une visite,*" he said. "*Il souhaite un dîner intime pour lui et son impératrice Marie Louise, qui a donné son nom à Marieville.*"

Arabella's mind whirled, barely able to comprehend Fouché's words, never mind their import. Napoleon, the Great Ogre, was coming *here*, to this shabby prison-camp? An intimate dinner? And the empress Marie Louise, after whom Marieville was named, would accompany him?

"*Je ne comprends pas,*" was all she could manage. "*Pourquoi suis-je ici?*"

"*Fille idiote!*" he snapped. "*Certainement vous n'y penserez pas que l'Impératrice des Français dînerait seulement avec des soldats! Il doit y avoir un nombre égal d'hommes et de femmes!*"

At this she could only stare stupidly, as though to confirm his assessment of her as an "idiot girl." Something about the Empress of the French not dining with only soldiers, and how there must be an equal number of men and women.

"*Vous serez ma compagnon de table!*" Fouché continued. "*Ce soir!*"

His eyes upon hers were cold and hard and unmoving as the meaning of his words penetrated her dumbfounded brain.

She was to be *Fouché's* dinner companion.

At an intimate dinner with the Emperor Napoleon.

That very evening.

18

AN INTIMATE DINNER

Though her ability to speak French nearly deserted her in the wake of that revelation, Arabella did manage to make clear in stammering fashion that she understood what was being asked of her. But before she could reject his demand—and she did wish to reject it, in the strongest possible terms—Fouché dismissed her brusquely from his presence.

With a rapid stream of French in his unfamiliar accent, Fouché handed her off to some aide-de-camp in a powdered wig, who conducted her—with a strange combination of fawning politesse and iron-hard military discipline—down the hall to a large and well-lit dressing-room.

Her first impression was that the room was crowded, a teeming mass of Frenchmen and Venusians. But in a moment she realized it was merely mirrored—an enormous triple glass stood in the corner, reflecting and redoubling a French officer, a trembling boy, two guards armed with rifles who stood rigid by the door, and three Venusians in the costume of French maids.

The officer was a man she had never seen before, and from his bearing and accoutrements he seemed to be some sort of military tailor, pressed into this service rather against his will. He looked her up and down and commanded the boy to bring forth dress after dress from a large trunk in the corner. Never before had Arabella even seen such a collection of fashionable confections, never mind having them draped upon her, one after another, as though she were some witless mannequin. Her protests were ignored, or drew a sharp *"Ne bougez pas!"*—the command reinforced by the Venusians' firm, clammy grip upon her upper arms and the glares of the armed guards.

Eventually the officer settled upon a voluminous court dress of shining white Venusian silk, with a Grecian front, long sleeves, and enormous train, all bound with embossed ribband and trimmed with tulle. It was absurdly impractical, and far more ostentatious and old-fashioned than any thing Arabella would have expected even for a formal dinner party. Perhaps this was the latest French court fashion, or perhaps it was merely a reflection of Napoleon's execrable taste and addiction to the trappings of royalty. The officer handed the dress to the Venusians; then, with a curt bow, he and the other men retreated to the hall and shut the door behind themselves.

The Venusians, she realized at once, were as uneasy with the situation as she was. Though they were costumed as women, Arabella was privately coming to the conclusion that among the Venusians the sexes were not divided quite as they were among Earthlings—their concepts of grammatical gender were quite confusing—and the awkwardness with which they carried themselves in female dress showed that they were even less familiar, and less comfortable, with French courtly fashion than she was.

She turned to the Venusian who held the dress. "I will do it," she said in Venusian, or something approximating that. She had no idea of the verb "to dress oneself," at best a partial understanding

of the future tense, and little command of the niceties of Venusian etiquette, but she held out her arms to receive the dress and
gave the best gentle smile she could manage.

Trembling, the Venusian laid the dress in Arabella's arms. The
brilliant white Venusian silk slid along her forearms like water—
it was the finest, smoothest fabric she had ever felt, and despite
the circumstances her skin thrilled at the touch.

Arabella nodded her thanks, swallowed, then—doing her best
to make it a friendly request rather than an imperious command
as she had seen from the French officer—she gestured to the
Venusians to turn around.

It seemed to her that there was relief in their broad, shimmering eyes as they did so.

Divesting herself of her ordinary clothing was nearly a pleasure, given the heat of the day and the close stillness of the
dressing-room, but then she had to work her way into the voluminous silk dress without assistance—which was a struggle, though
she would still rather struggle on her own than with the questionable help of the Venusian maids—and soon she found herself
perspiring to an embarrassing extent. The dress was far more vast
and elaborate than any thing Arabella had ever seen, even at the
most fashionable balls, and she supposed the enormous quantities
of silk involved must be intended to ostentatiously display the own-
er's wealth. But, eventually, she did manage to dispose the mountain of fabric upon her body sufficiently for decency, and with a
gentle "*gogalla*"—a request for help—she called the maids to assist
her in arranging it to better effect.

Soon the tailor returned, along with the boy and the guards.
He made a disgusted sound, a sort of "*bouf*," with his lips, and
immediately gestured her to stand upon a small ottoman before
the mirrors. There he twitched and tucked, pinned and stitched,
and poked at Arabella and the dress until he stood back, sighed,
and sniffed "*Ça ira*."

One question nagged at her. "*Combien coûte la robe?*" she asked—with some trepidation, for the gown was so very fine that she was certain the price was quite beyond her current means.

"*C'est un cadeau de Sa Majesté Impériale.*"

A gift from Napoleon himself?

She was not certain how she felt about that.

After one final twitch of the fabric at Arabella's shoulder, the tailor shooed Arabella into the hall, where she was surprised to encounter an even more startled Lady Corey.

"You look utterly divine!" Lady Corey exclaimed, but they had no time to exchange any further words; the great lady was immediately whisked away into the dressing-room. Two guards, who had apparently accompanied Lady Corey, took Arabella in hand and ushered her down the hall to a sitting-room, where she was at least permitted to seat herself and rest for a bit. The guards remained, standing stiffly by the door.

Arabella sat, awaiting she knew not what, for what felt like several hours. There was no clock in the room, and nothing to read or otherwise occupy her time. She did her best not to wrinkle or sully the dress; Venusian silk of this quality must surely cost the Earth.

Captain Singh, and probably Captain Fox as well, must be frantic with worry. She had no way to send a message to them; if Fouché had not deigned to inform them of her situation they would not learn of it until she returned. If, indeed, she were allowed to return! Would she be required, she wondered with a shudder, to continue as Fouché's companion for the duration of Napoleon's visit . . . or for the duration of the war?

Her distraught musings were suddenly interrupted by the reappearance of Lady Corey, who rushed in the door and immediately embraced her. "Oh, it was horrid!" Lady Corey cried. "Those beastly frogs kept *pawing* at me, and that terrible Frenchman would not stop *shouting!*"

"There, there," Arabella said, though her attempts at comforting Lady Corey were somewhat hampered by their voluminous dresses. "It is over now. And, however horrible the fitting, that dress is lovely." It was a round robe, of finest white Venusian silk, with demi-traine and military front; though not quite so vast as Arabella's, it was equally sumptuous, and very flattering to Lady Corey's generous figure.

"Thank you, my dear," Lady Corey sniffed, dabbing at her eyes with a silk handkerchief. "But I must confess I feel rather like a lamb ritually cleansed and beribboned before the sacrifice."

"I am certain no ill will befall us," Arabella said, though she was in fact not certain of any such thing. She glanced to the two guards, who stood rigid and unmoving.

Once she had resumed her composure, Lady Corey stepped back and examined Arabella with a skeptical eye. "Exactly the sort of pretentious show of wealth I would expect of that *parvenu* Napoleon," she pronounced, "but the color does suit you wonderfully. Might I see the back?"

Arabella tried to turn about, but the dress's grand train twisted about her feet. "How am I supposed to *move* in this? It feels as though I am wearing a main-sail!"

"You must move with deliberation and grace." She guided Arabella through the motions, reminding her of the importance of an easy, graceful deportment suited to her youth and pliancy, and advising her on the proper use of the train.

Then a peremptory knock at the door interrupted their conversation. It was Fouché, in the most elaborate uniform Arabella had yet beheld, accompanied by Fulton—in comparatively restrained evening dress—and a half-dozen of Fouché's personal troops.

"*Mesdames,*" Fouché said, bowing. "*Si vous voudrez nous accompagner . . .*"

His manners were impeccable, but still his eyes were cold and dead and calculating.

As they proceeded down the hall Fouché instructed them all, Fulton included, as to their proper conduct in the presence of the emperor and his wife. They were to bow or curtsey when introduced, not speak until spoken to, and to address them as *Votre Majesté Impériale*. The empress, in particular, was to be given every deference and courtesy—the slightest offense to her would be counted as a very grave transgression and would be subject to severe penalties afterward. This last was accompanied by a significant look to Fulton, whose glare in return combined American assertiveness with a certain amount of abashed contrition.

This was the first occasion upon which Arabella had spent any significant amount of time with Fulton, a handsome man aged about fifty. Though, as an American, his manners suffered from a lack of refinement, he was clearly a man of great intelligence, and despite the pressure of the forthcoming meeting with Napoleon he displayed a charming degree of ease and good humor. And though his accent in English was flat and grating upon the ear, his French was excellent; it was he who provided translation to Lady Corey. Arabella, for her part, found herself depending upon his translations more than she cared to admit even to herself.

They arrived at the end of the hallway, where a grand pair of doors stood closed; two pristine and identical soldiers in ornate uniform stood like ram-rods at either side. Fouché paused, cast an appraising eye over the party, then nodded to the soldiers. Moving in absolute unison, they drew the doors open.

The room beyond was the largest Arabella had beheld since coming to Marieville, though—like every other structure in the town—it had plainly been thrown up recently and with little attention to detail. But the furnishings were of the highest order: a large round table set for six, chairs of gleaming dark wood enhanced with gilt and embroidered cushions, a glittering chandelier, and a broad sideboard heavy with ornate china. Soldiers stood like chess pieces, evenly ranged along each wall, each with a bayoneted rifle precisely vertical at his side. And at the sideboard, sipping from a glass of wine . . .

Napoleon Bonaparte. The Tyrant, the Dictator, the Great Ogre; sworn enemy of all that was right and good. It was his personal ambition and pride that had kept first Europe, then all the worlds in a state of nearly continual warfare for the past fifteen years. Millions had died at his order. Yet here he stood, no beast at all but an ordinary human man. And yet, somehow, he seemed to fill the room.

At his side was a quiet young woman, plump and buxom—a *very* young woman, barely more than a girl in fact; she seemed half Napoleon's age and indeed not much older than Arabella herself.

"*Mesdames et monsieur,*" Fouché said, bowing, "*permittez moi de vous presenter Sa Majesté Impériale Napoléon Premier, et Sa Majesté Impériale Marie Louise.*"

Arabella, Lady Corey, and Fulton paid their obeisances to Napoleon and his empress as they had been instructed. Then, as they were being presented in turn, Arabella inspected the emperor.

Despite his reputation, Napoleon was not particularly short in stature. Shorter than Arabella, to be sure, but due to her upbringing on Mars this was far from unusual; he seemed of average height, accounting for the rather substantial heels of his boots. Nor was he as ugly as he was portrayed in the gazettes; in fact, though his features were swarthy and his mien was rather weary and preoccupied, he was more than passing handsome and his dark eyes burned with keen interest in every thing around him. Indeed, when those eyes met Arabella's, she felt herself pinned to the spot. "*Madame*," he acknowledged with a slight nod, and she found herself unable to respond with either word or gesture.

Had he not been the sworn enemy of all Arabella held dear, she could perhaps begin to understand why so many had pledged their lives and fortunes to his cause.

To Arabella's surprise, the Emperor of the French was not adorned with silk, satin, furs, gold, nor jewels; instead, he wore a simple colonel's uniform, with only a silver medallion on the breast to distinguish him from any ordinary officer. In this he stood in sharp contrast to his empress. Her gown of pristine Venusian silk was actually somewhat less ornate than Arabella's, but exceptionally fine, and she wore it with such natural grace and poise that she outshone every one in the room for quality and elegance. Only Napoleon's galvanizing presence, Arabella realized, had prevented her from being the very first thing to which Arabella's eye had been drawn upon entering the room.

The introductions concluded, the party adjourned to the table. Six soldiers stepped away from the walls to draw out their chairs, and to push them back in as the guests seated themselves. A veritable army of servants then appeared, bringing course after course of delectable foods.

The guests were seated in alternation of men and women about the round table. The empress sat to the emperor's left, of course, followed by Fulton, Lady Corey, Fouché, and finally Arabella—which put her immediately beside Napoleon, who consumed her entire attention.

No matter how inconsequential the conversation—even a simple request to pass the salt—the least remark from his lips to her made her heart pound and her insides roil. Not only could a single word from him condemn her and every one for whom she cared to speedy death; not only was she desperate to glean any vital intelligence he might accidentally let slip in his conversation;

not only did the slightest glance from his extraordinary dark eyes seem to pierce to the depths of her soul; but his French was *terrible*, and she was required to employ every bit of her concentration merely to understand it.

His native language, as she understood it, was that of Corsica—wherever that might be—and his accent in French was closer to a rough Italian than the cultured Parisian French she had learned from her tutors, making him sound as though he were speaking through a mouthful of gravel. His grammar was equally atrocious, barely literate and full of uncouth contractions, and sometimes several additional sentences would go by before she was able to parse out what he had meant by the first. Even Fulton, whose murmured translations of Fouché to Lady Corey were so helpful to Arabella, seemed daunted by Napoleon's mutilation of the French language.

Marie Louise, to the far side of Napoleon from Arabella, was in some ways equally difficult to understand. Her French was cultured, grammatical, and precise, but her accent was German—no doubt equally genteel, but unfamiliar to Arabella—and her voice was quite small and high. She also seemed extremely subdued in manner, quite shy and self-effacing.

But despite the young empress's diffidence and the difficulties in communication, Arabella found herself kindly disposed to her.

———

As the first fish course was being cleared away, Fulton spoke up from his place across the table, between Marie Louise and Lady Corey. "Lady Corey tells me," he said to Arabella in his flat American English, "that you are preparing a performance, to be presented this Tuesday. Would you care to tell us about it?"

As Fulton translated his own words into French for the benefit of the rest of the table, Arabella's mind raced. The play was set for just three days hence, and preparations were not going well. Nearly all of the arrangements for the escape were in place, thankfully, but the play itself had received very little attention. Just last night she had insisted to Fox that he must make time for additional rehearsals.

"It is only a small entertainment for the prisoners," she stammered in something approximating correct French. "An amateur performance of *Twelfth Night.*" They had changed from *Romeo and Juliet* to *Twelfth Night* after one too many arguments between Fox and Singh over Fox's overly attentive performance as Romeo to Arabella's Juliet. Arabella was much happier playing Viola than Juliet in any case, especially as the part permitted her to wear breeches for much of her time on stage.

"*Cela semble délicieux!*" Marie Louise cried. It was the first expression of interest or enthusiasm Arabella had seen from the young empress, and Arabella's delight at seeing her pretty face so animated immediately collided with a new and distressing realization: if Marie Louise were to attend the play—or, even worse, if Napoleon attended along with her—Fouché and his crack troops would certainly come along as well, for the protection of the imperial couple. All the conspirators' hopes for a light and inattentive guard would be for naught.

"I doubt it would be of any interest to Your Highness," Arabella prevaricated in French, realizing as she did that she had mangled the empress's French title. "We lack professional actors; it is only for the amusement of the players."

"*Je déteste votre Shakespeare,*" Napoleon spat . . . but then Marie Louise touched his arm, and gave him such a poignant pleading look that even the Great Ogre's heart melted. "*Eh, bien. Si ma impératrice désire,*" he said, inclining his head indulgently.

Fulton and Lady Corey both smiled at this, but Fouché—never a cheery man—looked as though he had swallowed an unripe plum. Nevertheless, he bowed his head and said that he would make the appropriate arrangements for Their Imperial Majesties to attend the performance.

Every one looked to Arabella. Though her heart had collapsed to a small, leaden lump somewhere in the vicinity of her stomach, somehow she managed a smile. *"Nous nous félicitons de la visite des Majestés Impériales."*

The dinner wore on—course after course of delightful morsels which might as well have been ash in her mouth; hour upon hour of conversation inconsequential in meaning yet freighted with implication—until, just as the soup course was being served, the young empress murmured a quiet request to her husband. After Napoleon replied in the affirmative, she said to the company, *"Veuillez m'excuser."*

Clearly, the young woman merely needed to relieve herself. But when the empress rose, all must rise. Soldiers immediately scurried from their places at the wall to pull out every one's chair, and with a scrape of wood on wood and a clatter of cutlery the entire party rose to its feet—somewhat unsteadily on Arabella's part, as she was unused to the quantities of wine she had been consuming.

Indeed, even as she stood, Arabella realized that she, too, required the necessary. Catching Marie Louise's eye across the table, she spoke just loud enough for the young empress to hear her. *"Excusez-moi, Votre Majesté Impériale, pourriez-je vous accompagner au chambre du toilette?"*

"Bien sûr, madame," the empress replied in her cultured German accent.

The two women curtseyed to the table—Arabella, despite her best efforts, knew herself thoroughly surpassed in elegance—and walked together toward the double doors, a retinue of imperial guards forming up around them as they did so. But as Arabella passed Lady Corey's chair, she spotted something that brought her heart to a sudden stop.

The trembling gleam of candle-light on steel.

The steel was an oyster-knife, which had been employed in the second fish course to pry some local mollusk from its stony shell. Somehow Lady Corey had managed to retain it when the course had been cleared away. The light gleamed because, although the blade was quite short and thick, it was wickedly sharp, and it trembled because Lady Corey's fingers, which held the knife in a death grip, were nonetheless shivering markedly.

One glance at Lady Corey's face told Arabella all she needed to know. The older woman's gaze was fixed on Napoleon, and her skin showed the pallor of heartfelt terror, but her eyes were full of hate and her jaw was set in firm determination. The plume on her silk coif quivered, whether from fear or barely-contained rage Arabella could not tell. Napoleon, for his part, was distracted, all his attention upon his young wife, and the guards were occupied in readjusting their positions for the protection of the departing empress and the emperor simultaneously. It was the perfect moment for Lady Corey to strike.

But Arabella knew she could not succeed.

Lady Corey might be armed, determined, and have the advantage of surprise, but she was nonetheless a woman of middle age, inexperienced in combat, and lacking strength of limb. She would have to leap across the table, or push past both Fulton and the empress's just-vacated chair, to reach Napoleon, and armed guards— men no doubt pledged and fully prepared to give their lives for the emperor—were mere steps away. At best she might injure Napoleon slightly before being seized and dragged to the ground by

Napoleon's guard. After which not only she but any suspected co-conspirators, including Arabella, Singh, and Fox, would surely be jailed or executed.

All of this ran through Arabella's mind in an instant as soon as she saw that flash of candle-light on steel, and a moment later—almost without volition—she acted.

"Oops!" she cried, pretending to trip upon her dress's ridiculous train, and pitched forward. Sprawling across the table, she shoved the soup tureen with both hands directly into Lady Corey's lap.

It was an awkward performance, unconvincing even to Arabella herself, but it had the desired effect.

Lady Corey shrieked—the soup, fortunately, was not extremely hot, but the surprise, especially given Lady Corey's heightened state of excitement, was profound—and fell backward, sending the chair clattering to the floor behind her. Fine porcelain shattered left and right, the silver tureen rang like a bell as it struck the ground, and orange-red bisque splashed everywhere.

"Oh!" Arabella cried in English. "Oh! Oh! I am so terribly, terribly sorry, Lady Corey! Please permit me to—"

But Lady Corey would have none of it. Livid with anger, she slapped Arabella's helping hand away, making an incoherent noise of rage and disappointment as she tried to wipe the thick, clinging soup from her robe and pelerine. The dress, though, was as ruined as her assassination attempt.

Arabella hoped that, some day, Lady Corey would find it in her heart to forgive her. Though she doubted that she ever would, still she knew that her action, though intemperate, had been absolutely necessary.

As the table was set right, and the empress and two of the guards escorted Lady Corey away to change her dress, the men muttered amongst themselves in French. Arabella, feeling her face flushing hot with humiliation that was not in the least pretended, sank into her chair and stared down at the disheveled table.

A small sound brought her attention from her own misery. To Arabella's surprise it was Fouché, clearing his throat and holding out a silk handkerchief. Confused, she followed his gaze to her shoulder, where a small spot of bisque stained her dress. Nodding her abashed thanks, she took the handkerchief and cleaned the stain away. It appeared to be the only such smudge.

She returned the handkerchief to Fouché, who accepted it unsmiling and dropped it into the soup still puddled on the floor beneath Lady Corey's fallen chair. He then bowed to Napoleon and Fulton, gesturing toward the adjacent smoking-room. "*Messieurs?*"

"*Avec plaisir,*" Fulton replied, smiling and drawing a cigar from his pocket. "*Contrairement au chantier, ici je peux fumer sans souci!*"

To Arabella's surprise, Napoleon reacted to Fulton's off-hand remark with incandescent fury. "*Silence, imbécile!*" he growled through gritted teeth.

Fulton cringed at the rebuke, ducked his head in embarrassment, and begged Napoleon to accept his apologies, promising that the indiscretion would not be repeated.

"*Ça ne devrait pas!*" Napoleon snarled, and stamped away through the indicated door, not in the least mollified. Fulton and Fouché followed, neither of them favoring Arabella with even a backward glance. Plainly, she was dismissed.

She sat, uncertain what to do with herself, for only a moment before two of the soldiers approached her, offering to conduct her back to her lodgings. Numbly, she allowed them to lead her out of the room.

As Arabella trudged back to the *auberge*—head down, disconsolate, and unconcerned with the soldiers marching beside her—the horrible events of the evening ran through her mind again and again. She had jeopardized the escape attempt, saved the tyrant Napoleon's life, and destroyed her friendship with Lady Corey.

Yet, despite her great misery, one nagging detail of the evening's disastrous end would not let go of her mind. Fulton's inoffensive remark "*ici je peux fumer sans souci*"—which she was certain meant nothing more than "here I can smoke without concern"—had driven Napoleon into a rage. Why?

No. Wait. Fulton's words had not merely been "*ici je peux fumer sans souci.*" He had also said "*contrairement au chantier*"—as opposed to the ship-yard.

It was not, perhaps, a surprise that smoking might be prohibited at the ship-yard. It was a place of saw-dust, wood-chips, tar, and other highly inflammable substances. Yet that alone could not explain Napoleon's great ire at Fulton's statement. The emperor had reacted as though the American had betrayed a state secret.

Could it be that he *had*?

She let her mind drift across all that she knew about the ship-yard, and the fleet of armored airships a-building there. All the secrets of this place seemed bound up with that infernal airship *Victoire*, which was, they knew from Mills's reports, nearly ready to launch, except for the lack of such vital equipment as cook-stoves, lanterns, and of course the necessary launch-furnace.

Cook-stoves. Lanterns. Furnaces. All of them concerned with fire or flame.

And the ship-yard prohibited smoking.

Might there be something aboard the armored ship that was especially inflammable? Something, perhaps, unique to Venus? For the questions of why the ship-yard was here, and why Napoleon had immediately fled to this planet upon his escape from the far side of the Moon rather than returning in triumph to France, remained open.

Thinking of inflammable materials led her to recall Isambard, the creature who lived beneath the Touchstones' barracks and which they sometimes used to cook their food. He produced a highly inflammable gas from his abdomen.

Might this gas, in some way, form the connection between the several mysteries of the armored airship?

The answer, she felt, was very nearly within her grasp. Yet some vital point was missing.

19

FINAL REHEARSALS

When she returned to the *auberge*, she found Captains Singh and Fox, and all the principal officers of both *Diana* and *Touchstone*, gathered in something very like a council of war. "My dear, *dear* Mrs. Singh," Captain Singh cried, rising from his chair. "We were sick with worry!"

Heedless of all social graces, Arabella rushed to her captain and embraced him passionately, to which he responded by decorously patting her shoulder. Eventually propriety triumphed, and the two of them stepped away from each other, holding hands and blinking tearfully.

Captain Fox, less restrained, whooped aloud at her appearance. "You are a veritable fashion-plate!" he cried. "Wherever did you obtain that extraordinary gown, especially in this benighted backwater?"

"It was given to me as a present by Emperor Napoleon," she replied, and the expression on Fox's face was positively delicious.

"I will explain later," she said, smiling through her tears. "For now, I must speak privately with my husband."

She and Captain Singh adjourned to their chamber, where— after a heartfelt embrace and expressions of affection inappropri- ate for a more public place—she quickly explained the disastrous events of the day and her conjectures upon the inflammable gas, to which he replied with one mysterious word.

"Hydrogen," he said.

"Hydrogen?" Arabella repeated in confusion. The word was unknown to her.

"Tell me more of the creature Isambard," he said, waving aside her questions. "You say he produces this gas from his abdomen. Does it have any smell?"

"No," she replied. "None at all."

"And it burns with a colorless flame?"

"Very nearly. And quite extraordinarily hot."

The captain nodded vigorously, stroking his chin with a finger, his thoughts clearly directed inward. "Hydrogen, then. I am cer- tain of it. This explains every thing."

Vexed, Arabella stood back from him and planted her fists upon her silk-clad hips. "I shall give you no more intelligence until you explain this word."

Captain Singh blinked once, then said, "Very well. Hydrogen is a gas: colorless, odorless, and highly inflammable. It does not exist in nature, but may be artificially produced by several methods in- cluding the dissolution of iron filings in acid. When burned, it produces water, hence the name. It is the lightest in weight of all known gases."

Arabella tried, and failed, to imagine what the phrase "weight of a gas" might mean. "I do not understand. Gases weigh nothing! They simply drift about in the atmosphere."

"Gases weigh very little, but some are heavier than others.

Consider, please, Newton's Laws of Universal Buoyancy. Do you recall the First Law?"

"The upward force upon any body suspended in a medium in gravity is equal to the weight of the medium displaced by the body," Arabella quoted. "This is the principle by which airships ascend to the interplanetary atmosphere, and is also known as the Law of Archimedes."

"Exactly. Now consider the *net* upward force, which is the buoyant force reduced by the weight of the body in question."

Arabella considered. "What has this to do with the weight of a gas?"

"A modern airship ascends because her envelopes are filled with hot air, which is a gas whose weight is less than that of unheated air. If an envelope filled with hot air weighs less than the same quantity of cold air, what does this imply about the net upward force? Imagine only the filled envelope, please, without the airship. You may assume that the envelope fabric weighs nothing."

Why did the captain always answer her questions with more questions? She thought the problem through before replying. "An envelope filled with unheated air weighs exactly the same as the medium—the unheated air—around it. Thus, the net upward force is . . . zero. Whereas an envelope of the same size filled with hot air weighs less, hence its net upward force is positive."

"Precisely. Now imagine that the hot air is replaced with a different gas whose weight is even less. What effect does this have?"

She understood immediately. "The upward force is increased, by the difference between the weight of hot air and the weight of an equal quantity of the new gas."

"Now you see the significance of hydrogen and its weight. Hot air at one hundred degrees weighs one and one-eighth ounces per cubic foot, while hydrogen, even at a cool temperature, weighs just three thirty-seconds of an ounce per cubic foot. For this reason, the lifting power of a cubic foot of hydrogen is as much as four times that of hot air."

"Could it lift even more," Arabella cried, excited, "if it were heated?"

Captain Singh smiled indulgently. "Perhaps, but recall that hydrogen is highly inflammable. Any attempt to heat it would be very likely to result in disaster." He shook his head. "The use of hydrogen for aerial ascent has been known to aeronauts for decades; in fact, the French made use of it as early as 1783. But even the French very quickly realized that the danger of fire or explosion with hydrogen was so great—even without heating it—that no sane airman would even consider it."

Arabella paced the short length of the chamber's open floor, thinking rapidly. "But that risk of fire or explosion could be eliminated if the airship carried no cook-stoves or lanterns."

"Reduced, never eliminated. And a ship of war must, inevitably, carry cannon and other sources of combustion."

"But consider this: a ship lifted by hydrogen rather than hot air would require no launch-furnaces, nor coal-stores for landing. She could launch and land at will, any where at all. And she could float in the planetary atmosphere for ever, if desired, with no concern for her envelopes cooling. Napoleon might consider those advantages worth the risk of fire."

Captain Singh nodded slowly. "Indeed, if he were desperate enough. And hydrogen's much greater lifting power would be valuable—nay, *indispensable*—in overcoming an armored ship's great weight."

Arabella felt her eyes widening in shock then, as the implications of the captain's words and her own suddenly became clear. "If *Victoire* is indeed lifted by hydrogen . . . she will *never* be equipped with lanterns or cook-stoves, and she requires no launch-furnaces! She could launch *to-morrow!*"

The two of them looked at each other, the expression of dismay

DAVID D. LEVINE

upon the captain's face matching the one Arabella felt upon her own.

They *must* escape, and *immediately*, to bring word of *Victoire* to England before the indestructible airship could be launched.

But with Napoleon, and all of Fouché's crack troops, attending the play, how could they possibly escape now?

———————————

After considering this thorny problem, and utterly failing to find a solution, Arabella and the captain agreed that the time had come to expand the conspiracy.

They had known that this time was coming. Even though, for the sake of keeping the plan a secret, they had decided not to inform the crews of the escape plan until nearly the moment it sprang into action, they had known that they would need a set of trusted partners to help spread the word when that moment came. But now, when a pivotal aspect of the scheme had been compromised and the urgency of its execution was the greatest, those trusted partners—Stross, Richardson, Liddon, Gowse, Faunt, Young, Brindle, and the little midshipman Watson—were the ones who might possibly be able to devise some means to salvage the plan. And Fox, of course, who had been excluded from this current conference only as a matter of propriety.

One of their planned partners, though, was now very much open to question. "Lady Corey will never trust me again," Arabella sighed. "I am certain she understands I ruined her assassination plan deliberately; even if she believes it was an accident—and she is far too smart and observant for that to be the case—she will still be furious with me for spoiling her opportunity with my clumsiness. Not to mention the destruction of her dress." She gestured at her own dress, the fine smooth silk still gleaming white.

"I will approach her, then," said the captain. "We can no longer exclude her from our plans; if nothing else, we are obligated not to leave her behind when we escape. The consequences to her, as a presumed conspirator, would be severe."

"Indeed," Arabella sighed miserably. "I hope that you can persuade her to come along, despite the grievous harm I have done her."

"I am certain she will understand."

Arabella was far less sanguine on that matter. "Even if she does, I fear the whole attempt will go for naught. With Napoleon, Fouché, and all Fouché's men at the performance, it becomes the very opposite of the distraction we had planned. We will have to find some other way to gather the people together, away from the majority of the guards, and very soon."

The captain's face displayed his pessimism as to the possibility, but his voice was reassuring. "We will find a way," he said. He paused for a moment, then spoke again. "In the meantime, I have a special request of you. It may be a thing you do not wish to provide, but I assure you it is of the utmost importance to our escape."

"You know that I will do any thing I can to benefit the escape."

Captain Singh nodded his thanks. "It concerns your dress." Again he hesitated. "I wish to requisition it."

Arabella laughed aloud. "By all means!" Though the gown was exceptionally fine—the fabric was lighter and yet tighter than the best balloon envelope—it was freighted with unpleasant memories and she really had no desire ever to see it again. "You may do with the wretched thing whatever you wish."

———

After Arabella had changed into her ordinary clothes, she and Captain Singh returned to the *auberge*'s sitting-room. Fox, Stross,

Richardson, Liddon, and Watson were still present, having been among the group who had gathered that afternoon out of concern for the missing Arabella. Arabella and Captains Singh and Fox pulled the other trusted officers together in a quiet corner and, after bribing the hotelier Gugnawunna with some of Arabella's last few gold livres to insure privacy, quickly conveyed to them in quiet voices the key elements of the escape plan.

As Arabella had expected, Liddon and Stross were cautiously optimistic, Watson displayed the enthusiasm of youth, and Richardson was doubtful of the scheme's chances of success but willing to follow his commander's orders.

"So," Captain Singh said, "do we all know our parts?"

All the men nodded their assent, except little Watson. "What am I to do, sir?" he piped.

"I have a special assignment for you," Captain Singh said, "which I will convey to you privately." He looked around at the others. "Now . . . do any of you have any thoughts on how we might best escape the much heavier than anticipated guard, given the presence of Napoleon at the performance?"

The officers exchanged glances, but none of them spoke up. Finally Watson tentatively raised his hand. "We might ask the people to wait until Napoleon and his entourage have departed, then make their escape?"

Captain Singh shook his head. "The presence of so many prisoners loitering after the performance would surely arouse suspicion."

"Oh."

"Could we bribe the soldiers to let us go?" asked Stross.

"Our finances have been nearly exhausted by the preparations for escape," Arabella said. "Though Lefevre is certainly susceptible to bribery, now that Napoleon will be in attendance I fear that his price for such a significant service is well beyond our means."

"I see," said Stross.

The uncomfortable silence stretched out, to the extent that Arabella was nearly ready to concede that they would have no choice but to attempt to escape from beneath the very noses of Fouché's best soldiers. But then she noticed Fox and Liddon casting significant glances at each other. "Have you any thing to contribute, sirs?" she asked them.

The two men looked at each other, and Liddon nodded fractionally. "We might," said Fox. "We just might. But we must consult with the rest of the Touchstones before we can say."

After another long silence, Captain Singh said, "Well then, gentlemen, I suppose we are as prepared as we are likely to be for the moment." He folded his hands. "The performance is in three days, and every one knows their part."

"May Providence smile upon us all," said Richardson.

"Break a leg," said Fox.

—————

The following days passed in a blur. With Singh, Fox, and most of the officers now fully engaged in escape planning, responsibility for the play itself fell almost entirely upon Arabella. She called together as many rehearsals as she could manage, but that was fewer than they needed, and when the cast and musicians did meet they inevitably wound up with so many interruptions and repeats of the material that they never made it all the way through to the final act. Arabella herself, stage-managing the production as well as playing the part of Viola, was constantly forgetting her own lines; some of the musicians could barely carry a tune; and little Watson, playing Olivia's gentlewoman Maria, kept tripping on his dress.

"Act well your part," Fox said to her at the end of yet another incomplete rehearsal. "There all the honor lies."

"I suppose it will have to do," she sighed. She glanced around; finding the two of them momentarily well away from any one else, she muttered, "We may be the first theatrical company in history for whom the presence of an emperor and his empress in the premiere audience is the *least* worrisome thing about the performance."

Fox too looked around, then replied in an even lower voice, "Patience, Mrs. Singh. I believe I am very nearly ready to reveal a solution to our most pressing problem. Just two more signatures are required."

"Oh?" Arabella replied, raising an eyebrow, but Fox refused absolutely to say any thing more about the matter.

Captain Singh came up to them then, and after a brief inconsequential conversation Fox bid them a polite farewell.

After Fox departed, the captain spoke quietly. "I have met with Lady Corey and carefully sounded her depths." Arabella looked to where the great lady stood at the other side of the room, going over her lines with Watson. Though she had continued to participate in rehearsals, her relations with Arabella had become entirely formal; they had barely exchanged a single word, other than their scripted lines, since the disastrous dinner with Napoleon. "Though she is, as you suspected," the captain continued, "extremely upset with you for ruining her dress, she did not know that you deliberately disrupted her assassination attempt—which was entirely unpremeditated and opportunistic, by the way; she would not even have considered it had her knife not happened to be left behind when the fish course was cleared away. In fact, I believe she now considers your spilling of the soup as a fortunate accident, and that if she had actually carried through with her attempt she would very likely have failed, and wound up imprisoned or dead. So she has agreed to join our conspiracy, and I expect that you will return to her favor sooner rather than later."

"That is very reassuring news."

Monday morning came—one day before the performance—and all was in readiness, or very nearly so. All save one very important detail: how the escapees would evade Fouché's numerous, disciplined, and loyal troops.

So far they had no plan other than to dash en masse to the swamps the moment the curtain closed after the players' final bow, counting on surprise and numbers to permit a substantial fraction of the men to escape. But every one knew that many would be captured or killed, and they all still held out hope that some other solution could be found.

Captain Singh had cautiously probed at Lefevre, in the hopes that his dislike toward Fouché might be fanned into a flame of outright rebellion. But even Lefevre was afraid of Fouché. "Not for five thousand livres would I oppose that man," he had said. "Not even for ten thousand. Now, if you had twenty thousand . . . ah, but you do not have twenty thousand, do you?"

After roll-call that morning, Arabella and Captain Singh were just leaving the square—quietly and worriedly discussing whether the number of airmen who would survive and reach *Diana* would be sufficient to capture, fly, and fight her—when Fox, Liddon, Gowse, and several of the other principal Touchstones approached them as a party. Their mien was serious, but they seemed determined rather than concerned. "A word, if you would," said Fox. "It is a matter of some urgency."

They adjourned to the back room of Fox's club, with several Touchstones standing guard outside to ensure complete privacy. Once they were seated, Fox reached into a pocket in the tail of his jacket—a hidden pocket, carefully shut with three buttons—and pulled out a thick sheaf of rather battered papers. "Please know that this is not offered lightly. This is a great sacrifice, but after much discussion we have all agreed that there is no alternative." He handed the sheaf to Captain Singh.

Even upside down, Arabella recognized it. It was the "plunder contract" Fox had signed with the captain of the *Fleur de Lys*—a promise from the captured ship's owners to pay Fox for her release and safe passage. Arabella's mind began to whirl at the implications.

Captain Singh gave Fox a puzzled look, then turned his attention to the papers. He skimmed quickly through the sheaf—it was in two parts, the second being a French translation of the first—until he came to the last page, a hand-written addendum legally conveying the document, and the money which it promised, to Capitaine Lefevre. It carried several signatures—Fox's being the first, largest, and most ornate—and dozens of X's with names printed beneath, clearly representing the entire officer corps and crew of *Touchstone*, jointly and severally pledging their shares of the plunder.

"Thirty thousand livres," Captain Singh said in a wondering tone.

"We actually negotiated forty-five thousand," Fox admitted, "but the other fifteen were provided as cash in advance. Which was, of course, captured along with the ship. Fortunately, I was able to retain the contract." He patted the tail of his coat.

A coat which, Arabella recalled, Fox had offered to her to shield herself from the downpour as they had walked from the port to Marieville. No wonder the contract seemed battered. It was very fortunate that it was still even legible!

At that moment her estimation of Fox's bravery, intelligence, discretion, generosity, and selflessness was raised a hundred fold. "My *dear* Captain Fox!" she cried, clasping her hands on her breast. Her eyes filled with tears. She wanted desperately to kiss him. "Thank you so much!"

"Indeed," said Captain Singh, clasping the other captain's hand warmly. "My most heartfelt thanks to you and your entire crew seem entirely inadequate."

"It is nothing that any loyal Englishman would not do," Fox replied modestly. "Besides, we hope that His Majesty will compensate us for our sacrifice . . . should we survive."

"Indeed," Captain Singh repeated, this time far more soberly. He looked around at the assembled Touchstones. "And I have every expectation that this donation will markedly improve our chances of doing so. I shall approach Lefevre immediately."

"Best of luck," said Fox.

"To all of us," Arabella added.

Captain Singh nodded his thanks for the sentiment. "But whatever happens, by to-morrow evening we shall be quit of this place . . . one way or another."

20

PLACES, PLEASE

On the morning of the performance Arabella woke long before the gray and muggy dawn. Perspiring upon the bed in the already-unbearable morning heat, with Captain Singh breathing gently in the chair and snores coming from the other side of the curtain, she lay with her mind racing. What would the day bring?

Eventually the sky outside the window brightened, to the extent it ever did, and Captain Singh roused himself. From the dark circles beneath his eyes she realized that he had lain as sleepless as she, though they had both pretended otherwise. For a longing moment she wished that they had spent that time in something other than fruitless worry, but the opportunity had passed, and all she said was "Good morning." They washed and dressed in anxious silence, then descended to breakfast.

When the bell rang for roll-call, Arabella noticed that her breakfast, small and poor though it might be, was still only half-eaten. She sighed and began to rise from her place, taking a scrawny bread roll from her plate to eat on the way to the square. But before she could reach her feet, Captain Singh—still seated—stopped her with a touch on her wrist. "Stay a while," he said, "and enjoy your tea."

She looked down at her tea-cup. The fluid within—which looked and tasted like nothing other than warm, filthy water—was scarcely something she could enjoy. But Richardson and Stross, she noted, were also not moving from their places.

Suddenly she understood, and sat down again.

The other officers all finished their breakfasts, stood up from their chairs, and departed for roll-call. Several of them looked askance at Arabella's table as they left, but said nothing. A few, puzzled, asked why the Dianas remained at their table, queries which Singh waved off with some vague comment. Even the Venusian servants seemed perplexed, and stood indecisively in the kitchen door, uncertain whether to begin clearing the tables or not.

Eventually Arabella, Stross, Richardson, and Singh were the only ones in the room. They sat silently at their table, occasionally picking at the remains of their breakfasts.

Half an hour passed before the sound of boots in the hall announced the arrival of four French soldiers. "You have missed *appel*," said their leader.

"We overslept," Captain Singh replied mildly, buttering a piece of stale toast, "due to a late rehearsal last night." There had been no such rehearsal.

"This is a serious infraction," the soldier continued. "You do realize this will cause your parole to be revoked."

"Oh dear." He took a bite of the toast. "What a terrible hardship. Still, you do know that we are presenting a performance of *Twelfth Night* this evening, to an audience including Commandant Fouché, His Imperial Majesty Napoleon, and Empress Marie Louise. Given the importance of this occasion, may we request leave to perform as planned?"

"This is . . . this is quite irregular," the soldier stammered. "I must consult with Lefevre."

"Please do. I am certain he will acquiesce."

The soldiers looked at each other, quite baffled by the Englishmen's behavior. Finally, with an expressive Gallic shrug, the leader departed, taking his men with him.

"Well," Richardson said, "we're in it now."

Captain Singh set down his toast, missing only that single bite, and wiped his mouth. "Come, gentlemen," he said. "We have a play to perform."

That afternoon, Arabella was shifting some scenery to hide from view a stack of panniers which would be used in the escape when Captain Singh approached her. "Three hours to curtain," he told her.

"Thank you. Would you please assist me in this?"

He did so, with strength and grace, and after they finished—panting in the heat of the late afternoon—he glanced about, saw that they were momentarily alone, and murmured low, "A word, if I may?"

They ducked behind the scenery they had just moved into place, finding themselves in cluttered shade, and sat upon one of the panniers. "My dear Arabella," he said, taking her hand and speaking uncommonly quietly. His long, strong fingers trembled slightly. "I know that I have not been the best of husbands to you, these past weeks and months."

"You have done your best, under the very difficult circumstances." She lowered her voice still further. "Besides, you and I both know that you are, in fact, no husband at all."

He shook his head. "I have kept secrets, been cold and distant, and failed to grant you the love and respect due to you—due to

your pretended position, if nothing else. And for this I apologize." He took a breath and closed his eyes. "It is only that . . . for
my entire career as captain, loyalty to Company and Crown, and
the safety of my crew, have come before any thing else, and this
habit has been difficult for me to break." He opened his eyes again,
and took her other hand. "But we may . . ." He blinked rapidly
several times. "We may not survive this day, and I wanted you
to know that my feelings toward you are very strong, very strong
indeed."

Arabella's heart beat low and hard, and her mouth suddenly
felt dry. "As are mine toward you."

"I thank you for that assurance."

She extracted her hands from his grasp and laid them against
his warm brown cheeks. "A kiss for luck?"

"For luck," he said.

But the kiss he delivered to her was far from a chaste good-luck
charm.

Seven o'clock. Arabella peeked out between the curtains—two
stretches of sailcloth salvaged from captured ships, perhaps including *Diana* and *Touchstone*—and saw that, though the performance was not scheduled to begin until eight, the audience of
prisoners had already begun to filter in, taking the best places on
the long logs laid out across the clearing as seating. In the center
of the front row, four ornate chairs, dragged down from the *manoir*,
were reserved for Napoleon, Marie Louise, Fulton, and Fouché.
Napoleon's, of course, had a high back; this would obstruct the
view for those seated behind him, but Arabella supposed that was
entirely what one should expect from the Great Tyrant.

She twitched the curtains shut and turned around, beholding
a scene of nearly complete chaos. Watson's dress was on entirely

backward; Quinn had broken a string on his violin and was casting desperately about for a replacement; Lady Corey, who had suffered a sudden attack of stage-fright as soon as the audience had begun to arrive, stood pale and rigid with her costume only half-arranged; and Richardson and Stross were arguing strenuously—though in hushed voices—over whether the painted canvas representing Duke Orsino's palace should be placed stage left or stage right. Far upstage, Fox and Gowse were frantically shoving a heavy, lumpy sack behind a piece of scenery.

But, still, she told herself, the truly important things were well in hand. Three duffel-bags full of pistols, swords, and boarding-axes lay safely hidden beneath the stage platform, ready to be brought out and carried into the swamp when the time came. Other duffels of necessary equipment awaited in the wings. All the officers had by now been brought into the conspiracy and knew their parts in the escape; the captains of the divisions were keenly aware that action was in the offing, and though they knew not what it would be, they stood on high alert, ready to pass the word to their men at a moment's notice. Even the ordinary airmen, at least the more attentive of them, knew that something was afoot.

All she had to do was to survive the performance itself, she thought, and all would be well. Or, at least, once the final curtain fell they would all be in the midst of action, and at that point events would take whatever turn they would, without any further help from her.

At least her part in this farce would be discharged.

She clapped her hands. "Places, please!" she called. "Places! One hour to curtain!"

Stross and Richardson left off their whispered argument and looked at her for a moment, then returned to their debate even more vigorously. No one else paid any attention at all.

"Act well your part," Arabella muttered to herself, then hurried to help Watson turn his dress around.

Arabella was still rushing about, doing her best to make sure every thing was in place for the play to begin, when a distinct change in the sound of the audience came to her ears: a sudden rise in the susurration of the crowd, followed by mutters and gasps, followed by astonished silence punctuated with occasional growls and shouted commands in French.

In the midst of that noise one word was clearly audible again and again: *Napoleon.*

"The emperor has arrived," she muttered to Fox, who happened to be nearby.

"May God have mercy on us all."

A moment later the strains of the overture could be heard from the other side of the curtain, indicating that the curtain was just about to rise. "What!" she cried aloud. It was easily twenty minutes early. Well, no help for it now. "Curtain!" she told all the players, dashing from one side of the stage to the other and whispering it to each in turn. "Curtain in five!"

Somehow the players managed to get off the stage and arrange themselves for their entrances before the curtains were pulled aside by a pair of midshipmen. The audience applauded lustily, whistling and hooting, then fell into expectant silence.

Captain Singh, playing Duke Orsino, entered, accompanied by his second mate and the musicians. Quinn, she could plainly hear, had not managed to find a replacement string for his violin and was gamely attempting to continue with three. It was not the worst part of the sound.

The captain stopped, commanding the stage with his presence, and looked out over the audience. Arabella, following his gaze, noted that it paused only briefly as it passed across Napoleon and his party. The emperor, for his part, leaned on one elbow as though he would really rather be elsewhere. Beside him Marie Louise sat straight, politely attentive, as did Fulton; but Fouché's eyes flicked all about, scrutinizing every thing in sight except the play before him.

Captain Singh drew himself up, took a breath, and paused.

The pause continued.

And continued.

Arabella realized that her captain—the brave, resourceful, intelligent Captain Singh, leader of men and inventor of the finest automaton in human history—had forgotten his very first line.

"*If music be the food of love,*" she hissed.

"If music be the food of love, play on!" the captain immediately repeated, in a voice pitched to carry across a heaving deck in the midst of the worst storm. "Give me excess of it! That, surfeiting! The appetite may sicken! And so die!"

He might be overplaying it a bit, she thought, but at least the audience would be able to hear him. Unlike Lady Corey.

And so it went, until the captain uttered the rhyming couplet that ended the scene and exited, to a smattering of applause.

Arabella, too, applauded from her place in the wings, pleased that the first scene had gone off almost without impediment, while Fox—in this scene playing, appropriately enough, the minor role of a captain—entered, and waited.

With a start she realized he was waiting for *her*. It was the shipwreck scene already.

"What country, friend, is this?" she said as she rushed onstage.

———

And so it went, this madcap, ribald tale of shipwreck, romance, disguise, deception, and mistaken identity. Arabella soon found herself wearing trousers again—and what a relief that was!—playing the role of the girl Viola, disguised in turn as the young man Cesario.

Whenever she was on stage, she did her best to observe Fouché as closely as possible without seeming to do so. It was not easy—the man's eyes went everywhere and seemed as keen as a hawk's. There seemed to be no chance that the escaping prisoners might avoid his gaze, or that of the numerous and disciplined soldiers who ringed the audience with bayonets fixed. But Captain Singh had said that Lefevre, more than pleased with the plunder contract's thirty thousand livres, had promised an effective distraction at the key moment.

The play, under-rehearsed at best, did not go well. Lines were forgotten, set-pieces fell over, curtains closed too early or failed to close at all. But the audience was greatly entertained, laughing and clapping at every mistake. Even Napoleon emerged from his pensive mood, sat up, and applauded with a genuine smile upon his face. With every fresh blunder his merriment grew, and he clapped and whistled lustily with unfeigned, rustic glee.

Even the worst problem of the night was not a complete disaster. It occurred late in the play, in Act IV Scene II, when Watson tripped on his gown while exiting the scene. He fell offstage with a crash and a cry, and Arabella immediately rushed to him. "Are you injured?" she whispered.

"No," he replied through clenched teeth, clutching his shoulder.

Captain Singh, just arrived, looked on the prostrate young man with a skeptical eye. "We will let the surgeon be the judge of that," he said, and set off to fetch Withers from the audience.

"I am most terribly sorry," Watson said, wincing.

"No matter," Arabella said. "It was your last scene."

Watson seemed not to be put at ease by this reassurance. Nonetheless, Arabella left him then, as she was required to help Captain Fox with a costume change before the next scene began.

From that point the play continued to its uproarious end without further serious incident. Viola's twin brother Sebastian appeared on the scene, and the siblings were so alike in appearance—this was a bit of theatrical make-believe, as Fox and Arabella looked not at all similar—that Countess Olivia, thinking Sebastian was "Cesario," ran off and married him. The revelation of the offstage marriage of the characters played by Fox and Lady Corey was greeted by many boisterous snickers from the assembled airmen, and the two cast rather embarrassed glances at each other. Then, after the twins' true identities and sexes were revealed, Duke Orsino and Viola, too, became engaged to be married.

"Here is my hand," Captain Singh as Orsino said to Arabella as Viola—now revealed as a girl, though still in trousers. "You shall from this time be your master's mistress." This drew a rousing reaction of "aww"s and whistles from the audience.

But as they were about to kiss—a pretended kiss, to be sure, but still it had gladdened Arabella's heart every time they practiced it in rehearsal—the play was suddenly interrupted by the sound of cannon. Nine shots boomed out from the gun on the *manoir* lawn, and every person on stage and in the audience stopped and looked around.

"*Neuf évadés!*" came the cry from all around. *Nine* escapees! It was an unprecedented number.

Arabella looked into Captain Singh's eyes, terrified. Had some one jumped the gun, started the escape early? Or was this a coincidence, some other group of escapees on the same evening? But, after the initial shock from the noise and the interruption, the captain's face relaxed into a quiet grin. "Lefevre," he whispered, and Arabella immediately understood.

Shouts soon came from the darkness beyond the lights of their improvised theatre: Lefevre's troops, demanding assistance in re-capturing the escapees. Fouché abandoned his seat and rushed to the back of the house, calling for his men to follow. Only a few of Fouché's troops remained.

"There are, in fact, no escapees for them to pursue," the captain murmured in Arabella's ear. "It will take them some time to realize this."

"We must make as much use of this opportunity as we can," Arabella whispered back, then stepped away from him to downstage center, facing the muttering and fractious crowd. "Ladies and gentlemen," she called, raising her hands, and repeated the call until the audience quieted somewhat. "We apologize for this interruption, but as the play is nearly complete, we will proceed directly to the curtain call."

The players all looked at each other—surprise, concern, disappointment, and excitement all mingled together in their faces—then began shuffling into a line at the front of the stage, while those not involved in the current scene began moving in from the wings. Other officers, not members of the cast, made ready to pass the word to the captains of their divisions: the mass break would occur the moment the curtain closed after the cast's third and final bow.

But before they could take even their first bow, a voice rang out from the crowd: *"Non!"*

It was a strong and strident voice.

It was a voice accustomed to command, and to being obeyed.

It was a voice in Corsican-accented French.

Arabella stood in the middle of the line, holding Captain Singh by the left hand and Captain Fox by the right . . . frozen at the beginning of her bow, mouth agape, stunned into silence.

"Non, non, non!" came the voice again—clearly Napoleon's. *"Le spectacle doit continuer!"*

Arabella's eyes focused on Napoleon, standing before his high-backed chair. Grinning broadly, he rattled off a long proclamation in highly colloquial French, the gist of which seemed to Arabella to be "I hate plays, but your stupidities are amusing." Then he waved a hand: "*Continuer! Continuer!*"

Only a half-dozen of Fouché's troops remained in the theatre, but they raised their rifles to a ready position. Every one seemed aimed directly between Arabella's eyes.

The spectacle, apparently, *must* continue.

Arabella exchanged a panicked glance with Captain Singh, then bowed to the inevitable. "Very well," she announced to the audience with as much of a smile as she could muster. "By imperial command, we shall continue with the performance."

Awkwardly the cast rearranged themselves on the stage as they had been before the cannon spoke. Arabella remained downstage center, her back to the audience, until she saw that they were properly positioned, then spoke low to Captain Singh: "Take it from 'Here is my hand.'" Then she stepped into position beside him and did her best to put herself back in character.

"Here is my hand," Captain Singh said again. "You shall from this time be your master's mistress." Again they embraced; again they pretended to kiss. This time there was no reaction from the audience.

Lady Corey was late with her following line: "A sister! you are she!"

Richardson entered now, and he and Lady Corey played out their final scene together . . . as quickly as possible, and with many nervous glances to the tall chair at front row center.

Arabella, too, kept glancing anxiously at the audience from where she stood upstage, gripping her captain's hand painfully. But she was not as concerned with Napoleon himself—he continued to laugh uproariously at every rushed, bungled line—as with the darkness beyond the last row. How long would it take for Fouché's men to discover that there were, in fact, no escapees, and return to their emperor's side?

After endless minutes only Brindle, playing the fool Feste and wearing a costume modeled on *Touchstone*'s figurehead, remained alone on stage to sing the play's finale. It was a lovely song, delivered in a remarkably strong high clear voice, and the whole audience, even Napoleon, plainly enjoyed it tremendously. But it seemed to Arabella to go on and on, and from her position in the wings she waited, heart pounding, to see whether the song should conclude or Fouché's soldiers return first. She clutched the strap of the satchel containing her reticule, a change of clothes, and other necessities, which she now carried slung over one shoulder, ready to run with it as soon as the opportunity presented. She still wore her "Cesario" trousers.

"But that's all one, our play is done," Brindle concluded at long last. "And we'll strive to please you every day." He bowed, to tumultuous applause.

Finally—finally!—the cast could take their curtain calls, and begin the escape. They all stepped to the edge of the stage, and with a genuine smile Arabella gripped her fellow players' hands and took her bows. Once they bowed, and again.

As they straightened from the second bow, Arabella glanced left and right. The midshipmen were poised to whisk the curtains closed. The word had already been passed to the men in the audience: when the curtain closed after the third curtain call, run for the swamp!

This was it: the final curtain call. Arabella led the third bow, the whole line of players bending low along with her.

But before she could rise from her bow, a familiar Corsican-accented voice called again from the audience: *"Bravo! Bravo! Encore! Encore!"*

Arabella glanced up from where she stood bent. Napoleon was actually standing on his chair, hammering his hands together with great vigor and showing no sign of stopping. Marie Louise was standing as well, applauding with a more ladylike enthusiasm,

as was Fulton. The airmen to either side of them were also continuing to applaud, glancing nervously at the emperor and the armed
soldiers all around.

She looked left and right. Both midshipmen were giving her
questioning looks.

Napoleon continued to applaud energetically.

Arabella caught the midshipmen's eyes and shook her head
fractionally, then straightened and immediately bowed again. The
line of performers followed her lead—raggedly, but they followed
nonetheless.

The curtains did not close.

Napoleon kept applauding.

So did the airmen. They seemed terrified to stop.

Four bows. Five. Six. Seven. The applause went on and on.

Eight bows. Nine. Ten.

As Arabella straightened from her tenth bow, she saw the thing
that she had been awaiting with anxiety and dread: uniformed
soldiers reappearing at the back of the audience. Many of them.

And in the lead: Fouché.

Arabella released the captains' hands and took a step forward,
raising her arms for silence. "*Merci, merci, merci beaucoup!*" she
called, speaking directly to the imperial couple, as the applause
stuttered to a halt. "Unfortunately, we must now conclude our
show!"

With that, she gestured firmly to both sides, and the curtains
at once whisked closed.

But, as she had stepped out of the line of players, the curtains
closed behind her, and she found herself standing alone on the
visible side of them.

Pandemonium immediately erupted in the audience, as the crowd
of airmen rushed all at once and in every direction from their
seats, heading for the swamps behind the theatre.

Napoleon let out a squawk of surprise.

Fouché reacted immediately, calling, "*Tirez! Tirez-les tous!*" Shoot them all!

The recently-arrived soldiers raised their rifles.

Arabella stood frozen, realizing that she was about to see her friends and shipmates slaughtered.

And then an enormous *bang*, a gout of flame and smoke, and a great rush of wind erupted from behind the curtain, sending Arabella sprawling in the soft dirt between the stage and Napoleon's chair.

For a moment her eyes met the emperor's. He seemed as stunned as she, but thanks to her youth she recovered first. She leapt to her feet, ears ringing, and jumped back behind the curtain line—the curtains themselves now flapped in smoldering tatters.

The chaos on the stage and in the audience now made the previous confusion seem positively tidy by comparison. The stage-floor was broken into jumbled, charred flinders. Small fires guttered here and there; bits of flaming canvas and silk drifted down from a smoke-blackened sky. Fouché's men lay scattered like discarded toy soldiers among the logs, momentarily stupefied by the noise, smoke, and flame which had struck them in the face. But the airmen, who had been running with their backs to the explosion, had merely been pushed hard in the direction they were already going; most of them had fallen over, but they were already scrambling to their feet and heading off into the darkness.

Of Fouché himself there was no sign.

Arabella shook herself and stumbled upstage, seeking the basket of supplies she had been assigned to carry for the escape, which had been hidden behind scenery. But before she could find it in the wreckage, she nearly collided with Captain Singh. His eyes were wide and white in his smoke-blackened face, his costume was singed, and he struggled under the burden of two large duffel-bags. "Change in plans!" he shouted into her face—the sound was muffled, and she realized that she was somewhat deafened by the blast. "Take this!" He thrust one of the two duffel-bags into her arms—it was large and extremely bulky, but weighed little—then gave her a brief passionate kiss, seized her hand, and ran off toward the swamp.

Between the pounding speed of his long legs and the lingering effects of his kiss, she found herself quite out of breath.

They dashed into the darkness, fitfully lit by the still-smoldering wreckage of the stage and scenery behind them. As she ran, Arabella's ears began to clear and she heard groans, shouts in French and English, and the occasional *crack* of small-arms fire. Barely-visible figures rushed here and there among the trees; whether they were escaping Englishmen or pursuing Frenchmen she could not say.

They ran until they had passed so far from the light that they risked running into a tree or stumbling into a swampy hole, then paused for a moment. Arabella stood bent over with hands on knees, gasping for breath, while the captain dug a dark-lantern from his duffel, along with a pistol which he tucked in his belt and a knife which he gave to Arabella. They lit the lantern and looked cautiously about until they had their bearings and were certain they were not pursued, then headed off again—still rapidly, but more prudently than their previous headlong flight.

As they went they kept a sharp eye out for paint marks left on trees by Fox—blazes indicating a safe and rapid passage through the hazards of the swamp. Several different routes had been planned out, in addition to deliberate false marks designed to lead pursuers off the trail, so they were compelled to pause and be certain of the marks before continuing. Nonetheless, they made very good time, avoiding any encounters with mud pits, tangling vines, or carnivores.

The French, however, were not so obliging.

On several occasions the sound of tramping boots through the muddy undergrowth reached their ears, and Arabella and the captain were compelled to shut the lantern-slide and secrete themselves in the bush. Once the searching troops came close enough that she held her breath, heart pounding, and gripped her knife with sweating fingers . . . but they passed by, muttering amongst themselves. Another time the pursuers were distracted by a noise nearby, and set off in a different direction—which was followed by a tumult of thrashing foliage, rifle shots, and shouts in French and English. Arabella and the captain cast worried glances at each other as they fled the scene. Had the French surprised and arrested the Englishmen they encountered? Or had both groups stumbled into a nest of some native predator?

There was no telling. They pressed on toward the rendezvous.

21

OVER THE WALL

Eventually they arrived at the small clearing which Fox had discovered for their rendezvous, not far from the palisade which divided the swamp from the ship-yard.

As Arabella and the captain had been among the last to leave the theatre, and as they had been delayed several times on the way, she expected to find most of the people here already. But the group of fatigued, mud-spattered airmen that she beheld in the clearing numbered no more than forty-five—forty-five out of over a hundred who had presented and attended the performance, and very few of them officers. Stross was here, as was Liddon, but Richardson was among the missing—he was reported to have been shot in the head before even leaving the theatre.

The loss of Richardson saddened Arabella to a degree surprising to her. He had proven himself worthless as a commander when Captain Singh had lain unconscious after *Diana*'s battle with French corsairs on the way to Mars, but he had never had any thing but the best of intentions. She wondered now what he might have made of himself had he lived.

Diana's usual complement was over sixty. Forty-five might be sufficient to launch and fly her—but how many to fight her, if it came to that? And how many more would they lose in recapturing her?

Captain Singh waded into the ragged crowd of men, leaving Arabella momentarily alone. She sank wearily down onto a muddy rock, panting from exhaustion and heedless of the filth which soiled her breeches—though glad, yet again, that it was breeches she was wearing and not a dress. More than once in her headlong flight through the swamp she had dodged through brambles or thorny vines, which would surely have caught her up if she had been dressed conventionally.

Stross, she saw, was doing his best to marshal the mixed group of Dianas and Touchstones into some kind of order, and distributing the rifles, boarding-axes, and other supplies as men arrived with duffels. Brindle, too, had arrived ahead of them, as had little Watson . . . his arm in a sling and his face wet with tears. Arabella roused herself from her rock and went to him.

"Oh, Mrs. Singh!" Watson gasped as she approached. "I am so very, very sorry!" His sling, she saw, had been quickly assembled from torn fragments of his costume—the very costume which had tripped him. Arabella imagined that tearing it to bits must have been quite satisfying.

"Do not apologize, sir. We have come this far; all will be well."

"Oh, no, ma'am!" he cried, tears gushing anew. "For my collarbone is broke, and I cannot perform my part in the escape!"

Before she could gain any clarification on this statement, a sudden shout from the other side of the clearing drew her attention. It was Fox, half-carrying a scorched, sodden and prostrate Lady Corey! They were accompanied by Gowse, leading Isambard on a leash, and several other Touchstones. She and Watson dashed over to welcome the new arrivals.

Isambard, she noted, was nearly half again as large as he had been the last time she had seen him.

Arabella took the insensate Lady Corey from Fox's arms and helped her slide to the ground without injuring herself. Someone pressed a water-skin into Arabella's hand; she nodded her thanks and encouraged the great lady to sip from it.

Captain Singh, meanwhile, embraced Fox, whose grin was broad and white in his filthy face though his shoulders sagged from exhaustion. "Was it you," Captain Singh asked, "who produced the explosion?"

"It was Isambard," Fox replied, gesturing at the creature. "Gowse and I conceived a distraction, in case one should prove necessary; we brought Isambard backstage and encouraged him to fill the space beneath the stage with his gas. When Fouché and his men reappeared, I dashed upstage with my little flint and steel and—" He gave a small gesture with his fingers. "Boom. Perhaps a somewhat larger boom than we had anticipated."

"A very effective plan, sir, in any case, and I am very glad to see you . . . and Isambard."

"And I you. Did the dress arrive intact?"

Captain Singh glanced at the confused Arabella, and at the duffel which still rode on her shoulder. "It did, but there is a complication . . . Watson has broken his collar-bone."

Fox and Singh looked at each other for a moment, then both turned to Arabella. Their gazes were intense, and combined concern, fear, doubt, and desperation.

"Sirs?" she queried, worried and uncertain. "What is the matter?"

The two captains exchanged another glance; then Captain Singh bent down to where Arabella knelt with the half-conscious Lady Corey. "Watson—and Isambard—had been a key element of the next stage of our escape. But with a broken collar-bone he cannot perform his part." He stopped and looked down for a moment, then returned his gaze to her face. "None of us had wanted to ask this of you, but now we must. Will you take a great risk for the sake of our escape?"

"Any thing," Arabella replied, though her heart pounded and her hands, despite the oppressive heat of the evening, suddenly felt chill. "Any thing at all."

"Very well. Here is what you must do. . . ."

The duffel-bag which Arabella had carried through the swamp proved to contain her own Venusian silk dress, along with Lady Corey's stained one. They had been carefully picked apart and reassembled with tight, delicate stitches into a new shape: a teardrop-shaped balloon envelope, about twelve feet across. This was enclosed by a net of silken ropes, which converged on a harness like the one from which Arabella had been suspended during the falling-line ceremony on her departure from Earth so many months ago. The whole assemblage formed a balloon for one person—a vessel of extremely low tonnage. And Arabella, despite her height and the muscle she had gained from pedaling, weighed far less than any of the other airmen or officers who had reached the rendezvous.

Arabella now stood tethered to the balloon, which swelled gradually behind her. Gowse was engaged in tickling Isambard, encouraging him to produce his gas, which Stross was shepherding into the envelope through what had once been the sleeve of Arabella's dress. The process was made far more difficult by the necessity of utter silence and darkness, for fear of attracting French attention.

Above them, at a remove of some hundred yards, loomed the palisade marking the edge of the ship-yard. This sturdy wall of wood, some fourteen feet in height and topped with pointed stakes, stretched the entire width of the neck of the peninsula upon which the ship-yard was located, and had but a single door in it. Guards, carrying lanterns, paced the wall's top.

"Your weight will be greatly reduced," Captain Singh whispered to her as he looped a coil of rope over her shoulder, "but not canceled completely. You will need to jump as hard as you can in order to achieve the top of the wall. Watson, with practice, was able to reach fifteen feet in this gravity, but he weighs somewhat less than you."

"I will do my best," she said. Her teeth chattered as she spoke; she clenched them together again. She would *not* show fear.

"Above all else, you must take care to keep the balloon away from the guards' lanterns. Hydrogen, as you know, is highly inflammable."

"I am keenly aware of that." Her hair and clothing still stank of smoke from the explosion which had scattered Fouché's men.

Arabella felt a tug on the ropes which connected her to the swelling balloon. She looked over her shoulder and saw that three men were now required to hold it down. "Not much longer," said Stross. Captain Singh went to help him manage the ungainly thing.

Fox approached her then, holding a boarding-axe more than two feet long, whose wickedly sharp blade was balanced with an equally cruel spike. "Do not hesitate to use this," he said, pressing it into her hands.

Perhaps Fox misjudged her expression of hesitation—despite her several hand-to-hand fights, firing of cannon, and too much experience having pistols aimed at her, she had never directly attacked another person with any sort of weapon—for cowardice, for he suddenly grabbed her shoulders and gave her a firm, encouraging kiss on the lips. "Good luck," he whispered, and before she could recover from her shock he vanished away into the dark.

Surely her pounding heart, her tingling lips, and the burning flush she felt upon her face were the result of anxiety over the coming action. Surely.

Captain Singh returned then. "The balloon is as full of gas as we can make it. We will give you a push in the necessary direction, but you must thrust with your legs as hard as you can, and you may need to swing yourself to one side or the other to avoid the guards. Are you ready?"

She was not in the least ready. "Yes."

"Cheerly now . . ." Captain Singh whispered harshly to the men holding the balloon, while he, Stross, and Fox all laid hands— quite firmly and improperly—on Arabella's breeches-clad legs and bottom. "Make ready. . . . *Shove off!*"

The balloon snapped upward, jerking Arabella's harness sharply, while the men holding her lower limbs pushed her up and forward. She met their thrust with a firm shove of her legs . . . and in a moment she was sailing upward!

Her passage into the air was as unlike the stately ascent of an airship as could be imagined. The balloon wobbled above her like an undercooked pudding, and she swung wildly forward, then back as she ascended. It was all she could do to retain her hold upon the boarding-axe.

The top of the wall, with its pointed stakes reaching upward like claws, loomed closer and closer. Vicious though those spikes appeared, she feared that her trajectory, which in its swaying, ir-regular fashion was beginning to curve into a parabola under the inexorable assault of Venus's gravity, might terminate below them. Gripping the axe in her left hand, she pulled herself upward with her right, hauling on the balloon's silken ropes with all her strength. It did only a little good.

The wall drifted closer. The guards, fortunately, did not seem to have yet noticed her silent, unprecedented aerial approach . . . but that would avail her little if she did not achieve the wall's top.

She was now about four feet from the wall. The palisade's rough, unpeeled logs hovered before her at eye level . . . then began to slip slowly upward. She was drifting down!

Acting almost without thinking, she pulled hard on the balloon ropes with her right hand while swinging out with the axe in her left. A most unladylike grunt of effort escaped her lips, but the axe's spike bit deeply into the wall!

The sound of her exertion and the *thunk* of the axe immediately brought cries of alarm in French, and the sound of boots pounding on wood.

Abandoning her hold on the balloon ropes, Arabella hauled herself up with both hands on the axe handle. That effort, combined with the balloon's lifting force, propelled her rapidly upward—so rapidly, indeed, that the axe, firmly embedded in the wood, was pulled from her hands as she ascended! A moment later she found herself staring into the astonished eyes of two French soldiers, who looked at her with utter bafflement as she rose before them like some unprecedented moon.

Arabella pulled with both hands on the ropes, brought her knees up to her chest, and kicked both of them in the face.

With a strangled cry of "*Merde!*" they went over the low railing behind them, plummeting twelve feet or more to the dirt below. But other guards were already dashing toward her, as she sailed in a gentle arc over the top of the wall. It looked to be a near thing whether they would reach her before she could drift past their reach.

There was nothing she could do to move any faster. And as for striking back, she had lost the axe.

Up, up, she sailed, over the wall and its walkway, then began to drift downward—already her feet were only six feet from the ground within the palisade. Shouting to each other in French, the guards converged on her position. One of them held his lantern high.

Too high.

"No!" Arabella cried, but it was too late. The lantern's flickering flame seemed to reach out to the gas leaking from her balloon envelope.

With an enormous flash and a brief sudden blast of heat and noise, the balloon exploded, leaving a shocked Arabella to plummet to the earth. But the fluttering, flaming fragments of her Venusian silk dress slowed her passage somewhat, and the ground was soft. Though she struck hard, she did not feel any thing break. The guards nearby seemed as stunned as she.

Shaking her ringing head and struggling free of the harness, she ducked out from beneath the falling shreds of smoldering fabric and ran at the best speed her wobbling legs could manage toward the gate in the wall. Shouts in French sounded behind her, far too close.

The door was shut with a bar. She slammed into the wall beside it, put her shoulder under the bar, and pushed upward with her legs.

Immediately the door erupted inward, admitting a mob of shrieking English airmen armed with pistols, cudgels, axes, and the righteous anger of men long imprisoned. "For the King!" cried Gowse, in the lead, and fired first one pistol and then another with deadly effect.

The escaped prisoners were fewer in number than they had hoped, but they far outnumbered the light guard which had been placed upon this stretch of wall. In mere moments all the French lay dead or insensible.

"To *Diana!*" Captain Singh cried, pointing.

"*Diana!*" the men echoed—Arabella along with them—and they all charged off in the indicated direction.

Making the best speed they could across unfamiliar terrain in the dark, the small party of Dianas and Touchstones moved quietly toward *Diana*, whose location within the ship-yard Mills had previously communicated to them via Brindle. Watson and Lady Corey, helping each other as best they could, followed, accompanied by one stalwart airman for their defense.

Masts, hulls, and spars loomed about them on all sides, the armored airships under construction packed tightly together. Here stood the bare ribs of one awaiting its planking, like the carcass of a slaughtered wind-whale; there lay the long keel of another, freshly laid. If Napoleon had his way, these skeletons of ships would soon be clothed in flesh of wood and iron, a vast and invincible aerial navy before whose might even the vaunted English fleet could not stand.

No Frenchmen, fortunately, accosted them; the troops at the wall had been vanquished swiftly enough that they had raised no alarm. The slaves and workers, they knew from Mills, would all be in their beds—all, they hoped, save Mills himself, who was supposed to await their arrival aboard *Diana*.

Suddenly the mass of creeping Englishmen bunched up upon itself, and whispers of *"Diana! Diana! There she is!"* could be heard from the men in the lead. Arabella forced herself to the fore and looked upon the beloved ship.

She floated serenely in a flat stretch of black water, with crates and barrels of supplies and stacks of lumber heaped up on the docks on both sides. They had arrived near her aft end, and what they could see of her seemed fit and ready for flight; her pulsers were stepped and set, her masts and stays cleared for action.

"Grapnels," Captain Singh whispered to Gowse, who passed the word to the other airmen who held the needed equipment. "We will board through the great cabin."

One, two, three, the grapnels sailed upward, each trailing a silken line and catching firmly upon the aft rail. Gowse and two other burly airmen shinnied up them, pistols in their belts and cutlasses in their teeth, then slipped silently through the great cabin's broad stern window. A moment later Gowse waved the all-clear and the rest of the party followed them.

It was the first time Arabella had climbed a line in gravity since her very earliest days aboard *Diana*, before she had even left Earth, but desperation and fear gave strength to her arms and legs. Lady Corey and Watson, she knew, would secrete themselves nearby, to be hoisted aboard as soon as the ship was taken . . . assuming she was.

Arabella clambered through the open window, with Stross's assistance, and stood panting within. The great cabin, which she had not beheld in nearly a year, lay dark and silent, illuminated only by a flickering dark-lantern held by Captain Singh.

Captain Singh's fine furnishings had all been cleared away, replaced by a clutter of saw-horses, tools, and papers. The once-familiar space loomed strange and empty . . . save for a large, lumpy form in the corner, shrouded by a sailcloth tarpaulin. Dare she hope?

The captain was obviously even more anxious than she on this point, for he literally leaped the short distance to the object and whipped the cloth from it. This raised a great cloud of saw-dust, making every one cough . . . but despite her watering eyes and heaving lungs, Arabella's heart leapt with joy.

The shape beneath the cloth was Aadim, *Diana*'s automaton navigator. And though he sat unnaturally still, unlike the constant quiet hum and tick to which she was accustomed, he seemed in good repair. "Wind him!" Captain Singh whispered to her. "Quickly!"

"Aye aye, sir!" Arabella responded automatically.

As she jumped to her assigned task, the captain directed other men and officers to fan out across the ship and take her under control. Then, after checking the two pistols he had thrust into his belt, he too left the cabin, leaving Arabella alone with Aadim.

Arabella opened the door at the side of Aadim's desk and began

DAVID D. LEVINE

to turn the handle there. In all the thousands of times she had wound the automaton's mainspring, the task had never been so difficult—the spring was completely unwound, and each turn of the crank took all her strength—nor so urgent, nor so uncertain. After so many months in the not-so-tender care of the French, would Aadim even function? Would his many connections with the rest of the ship be intact?

As she began to wind, shouts and pistol-shots came to her ears from elsewhere on the ship. Part of her desired fervently to join the other Dianas and Touchstones in freeing the ship from French control, but her captain had ordered her to wind the navigator.

After the thirtieth turn of the handle, a whir and ticking sounded from deep within Aadim's desk. But there was no further sign of life, and she kept cranking.

After the fiftieth turn, Aadim's head began to tremble and stir. It turned to one side and then the other, as though he were shaking his head to clear it, but otherwise showed no volition. She kept cranking.

And then, after the one hundred and twentieth turn, when Arabella's weary arms felt as though they were just about to drop off at the shoulder, Aadim suddenly shuddered to life, his slack arms rising into a more life-like position with an audible *click*. His head swiveled to Arabella, the unseeing green glass eyes seeming to fix upon her with an unspoken question.

Arabella smiled and glanced to the lens, fixed in a corner near the broad window, which she knew to be Aadim's true "eye" in the great cabin. "The captain is safe," she said, not caring if any one heard or wondered at her speaking to a clockwork mechanism. "We are in the process of taking the ship back from the French."

Aadim's finely-carved wooden hand tapped the desk before him, then gestured behind Arabella. She turned, following his pointing finger, and saw a plan of the ship spread out on a plank laid across a pair of saw-horses. Immediately understanding, she pulled the plan from the plank and laid it before Aadim, fastening down the corners with the clips built into his desk.

With a whir and a ratcheting sound, Aadim's arm swiveled through an arc; then the hand tapped repeatedly at a point on the map. Arabella peered at the indicated location: it was the base of the ladder which led from the lower deck up to the very doors of this cabin. "The French?" she asked. "Are they on their way here?"

Aadim only rapped firmly on the desk—as though in a demand for immediate action—and pointed to the door.

Arabella drew the little knife from her belt. Clutching it in her hand, she crept cautiously out the cabin door.

———————

The ladder—which was not what she had formerly considered a "ladder" at all, more a very steep flight of stairs—led from the great cabin's door down into the darkness of the lower deck. Grunts and sounds of struggle came distantly to her ears from below, but the peculiar echoes of the near-empty ship's inner hull made it impossible for her to tell from whence, exactly, they came, or even how far.

Gently, silently, she shut the door behind herself—cutting off even the tiny amount of light from the dark-lantern, which she had left behind—and stepped onto the ladder. Keeping one hand on the ladder's rope railing, gripping her knife in the other, she slipped quietly downward.

The darkness of the deck below seemed absolute at first, but her eyes soon adjusted; there was enough light from the torches and lanterns that illuminated the ship-yard outside for her to find her footing. Still, all was gray and vague, with many a dangling line or loose board to catch an unwary foot or neck.

Then another grunt, this one from very close, caught her attention. At the bottom of the ladder, just where Aadim had indicated, two indistinct forms wrestled together. So intent on their combat were they that they had not yet noticed Arabella. Heart pounding, she moved toward them as quickly as she could without alerting them to her presence.

The two men were plainly evenly matched, the eerie near-silence of their struggle emphasizing the concentration and effort they brought to the fight. For long moments they strained against each other, then suddenly one or the other would gain a temporary advantage and they would shift position. But then the other would recover his grip and they would struggle, shivering but unmoving, against each other anew.

Closer and closer she crept, the sweat-slick knife threatening to squirt from her clutching hand like a wet pumpkin seed.

She would have one chance to strike, no more. Both men—surely one of them French, the other English—were far larger than she, and if by her interference she allowed the wrong one to gain the upper hand it would surely be the end of her. But which one was which? In the darkness, and with their frequent shifts and tussles, she could not make out their clothing or complexions.

Nearly close enough to touch, now. If the two men were not so occupied by their struggle they would surely have noticed her by now. Yet still, even so close, she could not tell one from the other.

Both men were tiring. Their fight would end soon. She could not afford to let the Frenchman win. But which was which?

Then, with a grunt and a muffled curse, the two men tumbled over each other, nearly striking Arabella where she crouched in the blackness nearby. As they rolled past her, she noted that one—the one on the bottom as they slammed against a bulkhead—had his hand clamped over the other's mouth.

Of course! The Frenchman would be seeking to raise the alarm, the Englishman to stop him! She rushed into the fracas and stabbed her little blade into the back of the man on top.

He snarled *"Putain!"* and, swift as thought, reached behind himself, seizing Arabella's wrist in an iron grip—crushing it until she cried out and released the knife. But to do so he was forced to let go his hold on the man beneath him, and a moment later that other man struck upward—a sudden forceful blow with both hands to the Frenchman's chin.

The Frenchman's teeth *clacked* together like billiard balls and he collapsed, unconscious.

The three of them fell in a heap, all panting with exertion and agitation. "Are you . . . are you injured?" Arabella gasped to the Englishman, who lay beneath the insensate Frenchman, who lay in turn beneath Arabella.

"I . . . am not," the Englishman replied. "Thanks to you, my dear."

It was Captain Singh! "You can thank Aadim," she panted, "for alerting me to your circumstances."

"I shall. But first you and this fellow must get off of me."

They tied and gagged the Frenchman, and Captain Singh retrieved the pistols which had fallen from his belt in the struggle. Checking that they were still properly primed and cocked, he informed Arabella of the situation. "We have taken the ship," he said. "I was in the process of checking for any remaining guards on board when this fellow leapt upon me from behind. But Fouché's men will be here momentarily. We must launch as quickly as we may."

They made their way to the top deck, where the surviving Dianas and Touchstones—they seemed so few!—were engaged in unpacking the ship's balloon envelopes from the great chests in which they were stored. Lady Corey and Watson, Arabella noted, had joined the boarding-party and now stood watch on the starboard and larboard rails. "We'll have these balloons ready to inflate in a trice, sir," Stross reported. "And we *might* have just enough men for the launch . . . though rounding Venus's Horn is another matter, and fighting even more so." He shook his head. "But without a launch-furnace, the whole question is moot."

"This ship is plainly nearly airworthy," the captain observed, gesturing about. "They would not have gone so far in her reconstruction without a way to launch her."

"Aye," Stross agreed. "The coal-stores and landing-furnace have been replaced with enormous iron tanks. Higgs the boatswain guesses they are full of hydrogen, and I concur. There must be some means to transfer it to the balloon envelopes, but we have not been able to identify it. Mind you, the frogs have rebuilt *Diana* almost entirely . . . there is much equipment on board whose function we have not yet been able to fathom."

"I saw her draughts in the great cabin," Arabella said, referring to the ship plans which were now clipped to Aadim's desk. "Perhaps there may be some clues there."

"Go and get them," Captain Singh ordered. "Smartly, now!"

"Aye aye, sir!"

But the draughts, once retrieved, proved incomplete, and what there was of them was written in obscure symbols and dense technical French. "We must try whatever we can," said Fox, peering at a network of lines that converged upon the forward balloon chest, "and at once. Fouché could arrive at any moment."

"We must," Captain Singh agreed, but the tone of his voice showed he was deeply disturbed by this necessity. "But I fear we may only succeed in blowing ourselves up."

"I will attempt to route the gas to the balloons," Fox said, straightening . . . but plainly neither he, nor any one else in the group, had much confidence in his ability to do so safely. Arabella's own experience with hydrogen had shown her how dangerously explosive it was. "I will go alone. Our crew is already too reduced to risk any more."

But just as Fox was headed belowdecks to try his hand at the incomprehensible French equipment, a cry from Lady Corey drew their attention to the starboard bow. "Oh! Oh!" she called. "Oh . . . drat! I forget how to say it in naval language, but *someone is coming!*"

Every one took up pistols, rifles, and cutlasses and rushed forward. Captain Singh clapped Fox on the shoulder; the two men looked each other in the eye for a moment, then Fox nodded and dashed below. Arabella swallowed hard, took up a cutlass, and followed the rest of the men to the bow.

"There!" Lady Corey cried, pointing.

Gowse immediately raised his rifle and sighted along the barrel.

But the group that was approaching *Diana* lacked the forceful rush and disciplined stamp Arabella would have expected of Fouché's men, or even of the ship-yard's less disciplined guard. They were, instead, a ragged and slow-moving crowd, and as they drew closer, the gathering dawn light showed Arabella that they were not even human.

Venusians. Nearly fifty Venusians were advancing with cautious and hesitant step toward *Diana*. They wore shabby workers' garb and carried only lanterns, pry-bars, and other tools; not a rifle nor pistol was to be seen. And in the lead . . .

"Mills!" Arabella cried, waving both hands above her head.

Even from this distance, and in this feeble light, she had no difficulty recognizing Mills's wide white grin. He waved back at her, just as enthusiastically, and began running toward *Diana*'s gangplank.

Captain Singh turned to Higgs. "Run below and stop Fox from tinkering with the gas-valves, before he kills us all."

Mills and the Venusians dashed up the gangplank and immediately began pulling it up after themselves. Gurgling to each other in their own language, they swiftly divided into groups, which hurried to different parts of the ship . . . all save one Venusian, who accompanied Mills to meet with Captain Singh and the rest of the Dianas and Touchstones. Though, Arabella supposed, they were all Dianas now.

"This is Ulungugga," Mills said. "He leads the work crew. They know *Diana*, stem to stern."

"Not the way we do," said Chips the carpenter, and Stross's face showed he concurred with this assessment. "*Diana* is *our* ship, and no bunch of squishy froggies can say different!" Several of the other airmen growled their agreement, which raised Arabella's ire.

But before Arabella could spit out a heated comment on the men's prejudice, Mills gave a measured response. "No, not like you," he agreed. "They cannot set sails, plot course, fire cannon. But they rebuilt her. They know the new gas equipment. They are strong, and ready to learn."

"But can we *trust* them?" Stross said, and his question was directed equally to Mills and Captain Singh. "They've been collaborating with the French for years!" The captain, for his part, waited patiently for Mills's response.

"They have been slaves," Mills replied simply. "First to Gowanna, then the French. We are leaving. They will help us, if they can leave too."

"We will be leaving your planet far behind," Captain Singh said, addressing the Venusian directly. Mills translated his words. "We may not return soon. Are you prepared to abandon all you know?"

Ulungugga's croaked response surprised Arabella greatly, to the extent that she questioned her own understanding of it, and even Mills hesitated before translating. "He is pregnant," Mills said. "He does not want his tadpoles born slaves."

"*He* is pregnant?" Captain Singh's eyebrow raised at this. "You are sure of this translation?" He seemed uncertain, even disquieted, by this news; some of the other Dianas appeared actively disgusted.

Mills shrugged. "They are not like us."

This new information answered some questions Arabella had had concerning grammatical gender . . . though it raised others about Venusian biology. "We have every reason to trust them, sir," she said, "and little alternative in any case."

Captain Singh seemed to be considering the question, but suddenly their colloquy was interrupted by a shout from Watson, stationed as lookout at the larboard quarterdeck. "Man ho!" he cried. "French troops, coming fast!"

A subtle shift in the captain's face told Arabella he had come to an immediate and firm decision. "Very well. Mills, direct the Venusians to fill the envelopes with greatest haste. Mr. Stross, choose ten men and prepare to cast off, again with greatest haste. And Mr. Fox"—for Fox and Higgs had just reappeared, panting, from below—"take the rest of the men and prepare to repel boarders . . . but for God's sake keep all fire, flame, and gunshot away from the hydrogen."

"But we cannot even *see* the hydrogen!" Higgs protested.

Without hesitation Captain Singh turned to Arabella. "Mrs. Singh, you are to work with, ah, Mr. Ulungugga to identify all fire hazards and communicate them to Mr. Fox's party." He cast his eyes swiftly about the group. "Is all clear?"

"Aye aye, sir!" they chorused, and ran to their assignments.

————————

Arabella's command of the Wagala language was, she discovered, not as strong as she had hoped. But with that, a few bits of French

340 DAVID D. LEVINE

she and the Venusian shared, and many gestures, sounds, and facial expressions, she managed to communicate the question to Ulungugga . . . and, she fervently hoped, comprehend the answer. "The hydrogen tanks in the hold are quite tight," she told Fox, "but when the . . . gate, I suppose you would call it, is opened to fill the envelopes, the . . . channels that carry the gas to the balloons are subject to leakage. The envelopes themselves are somewhat permeable to hydrogen, and furthermore quite flammable in themselves."

Fox cast his eye down the length of the ship from where they stood on the quarterdeck. Stross and his crew, assisted by a dozen or more Venusians, were managing the envelopes as they began to swell rapidly from their chests; meanwhile, the rest of the men were taking shelter behind capstans, climbing into the rigging, and otherwise dispersing themselves for the ship's defense. "Doesn't leave a lot of room to maneuver. How far from the gas must we be in order to fire a pistol safely?"

"I am not certain. Five feet at least, at a guess." Here she was proceeding not from Ulungugga's words but from her own experience with the small balloon at the palisade. "And if an envelope should be punctured, I imagine the pressure within will produce a spray of inflammable gas that could reach twenty feet or more."

Fox sighed, tucked his pistol in his belt, and drew his sword. "It's cutlasses and boarding-axes for us, then, unless the situation turns desperate." He took one step away, then turned back. "A kiss for luck?"

Arabella's hesitation before complying was, upon reflection, rather indecently brief.

The slowly waxing light of the dim Venusian sun revealed the French arraying themselves along the docks, disciplined squadrons dashing from one stack of lumber to another. But, to every one's surprise, though they had the advantage of good cover and greater numbers they did not employ their rifles. "What are they *waiting* for?" muttered Fox through gritted teeth. He and Arabella crouched behind the larboard bulwark in the waist, peering out over the gunwale at the docks. All around them, Dianas waited grimly for the French assault, clutching their weapons and breathing heavily.

Arabella spared a brief glance for Captain Singh, who stood exposed on the quarterdeck, directing Stross's men and Ulungugga's Venusians in making the ship ready for launch. Mills stood by his side, translating his commands to Ulungugga; Arabella had been stationed with Fox to perform the equivalent task in case the Venusians should be called upon to assist in the ship's defense. She fervently hoped that her services in this would not be required in the midst of a battle.

The envelopes now stood tall, straining at their ropes, and the ship rocked in the light and queasy fashion that indicated she was nearly ready to leap into the air. Surely only a few more minutes would be required before *Diana* could cast off. What, indeed, were the French waiting for?

"They cannot use their rifles either!" she suddenly realized. "They do not wish an explosion in the midst of their ship-yard!"

"At least we are evenly matched, then," Fox growled.

Suddenly there came a shouted command, and a squad of fifteen or twenty Frenchmen charged from cover, the men in the lead carrying long planks with great iron hooks on the end. These they swiftly fastened onto *Diana*'s gunwales near the quarterdeck, which the men behind—bearing cutlasses, boarding-axes, and other small arms—began to scramble up.

"Larboard, amidships, abaft!" Fox cried to his men, raising his sword and charging to the defense. "Gowse, watch the bow!"

In a moment the first of the Frenchmen reached the rail, but even as he rose from his plank Fox struck him aside with his cutlass.

He fell into the water below with a cry and a splash. But there was another behind him, and another and another, and three more planks fastened to the gunwales nearby; soon a great shouting brawl of Englishmen and Frenchmen had formed at the rail.

Arabella, far outmatched in strength and reach, dashed about at the edges of the melee, doing her best to watch for French surprises and call the defenders' attention to them. On one occasion she subdued a French soldier whose back was turned, using a two-handed blow of her cutlass hilt to the head. But though he fell, the jarring impact made her drop her sword, and as she fumbled for it a second Frenchman sprang up before her, eyes wild and teeth bared, his boarding-axe raised for a killing blow. Disarmed, defenseless, all she could do was cower before him . . . but then a blade slashed him down from behind, spraying Arabella with blood, and he too fell to the deck.

It was Fox who had saved her. But he could spare no more than a moment's attention for her, as two more French soldiers assaulted him from behind. He fought them fiercely, eventually beating both of them down, but sustained a grievous gash to his left forearm in the process.

While Fox fought the two Frenchmen, Arabella scrambled to retrieve her fallen sword. All around her the combat raged in fierce, deadly earnest; blood pooled upon the deck, and soaked the sleeves and breeches of her "Cesario" costume.

Then a hoarse cry from her right called her attention. It was Gowse: a second party of Frenchmen was attempting to board at the bow, using grapnels and boarding-pikes. She glanced back and forth, and quickly realized that while Gowse's people were outnumbered, Fox's party could spare no men either. Without hesitation she rushed forward.

A moment later she found herself straining to remove a grappling-hook from where it had lodged at the rail. But it was deeply embedded in the *khoresh*-wood of the bulwark, and the weight of the ascending Frenchmen pulled it still deeper. She peered over the rail . . . and her eyes met the fierce, angry gaze of a French soldier. The man was hatless, with dark eyes in a red face; clutched a dagger in his teeth; and was clambering up the boarding-rope like a swift and agile monkey. He was no more than four feet away.

Arabella chopped with her cutlass at the French line where it fastened to the grapnel; the tough cordage frayed, but refused to part. Again and again she hacked at it, cursing with vehement passion.

The Frenchman had climbed to within arm's reach. He pulled the dagger from his teeth . . .

Just at that moment the rope parted. "*Salope!*" the man cried, and he and the others on the line fell into the black water between *Diana* and the dock.

But two more lines nearby still held strong, and the Frenchmen upon them were already battling with Gowse's men. Arabella did what she could with her cutlass to fend the climbers off.

But there were too many, too strong, too disciplined. The defending Englishmen were weary from lack of sleep and the long run through the swamp. One after another the Frenchmen won through to the deck, and though Arabella and the rest of Gowse's people managed to defeat each one as he arrived there were always more fresh troops behind him. The cause seemed lost, but they had no alternative—they battled on, would keep fighting until the last of them fell.

Just then there came a cry—a command repeated down the deck in English and translated into Venusian. "*Cast off!*"

The deck lurched beneath Arabella's feet, sending her stumbling . . . just as a French cutlass swished through the space where her head had been. But before the Frenchman could press his advantage, he too, was thrown from his feet by the tilting deck. Ten, twenty, thirty degrees to larboard the ship heeled, and all about Arabella defenders as well as attackers cried out, clutching at

whatever they could to prevent themselves from falling overboard . . . or failing to do so, and tumbling into the void.

Clearly something had gone wrong with the ship's launch. But
from here there was nothing Arabella could do about it; it was all
she could do to hold tight to the pinrail at the mainmast's base.

Diana rose from the water like the infant Achilles, drawn up
by one heel with his baby arms flailing. Beyond the rail Arabella
saw the ship-yard, dozens of half-built ships spread out beneath
them in the gray dawn light like fish on saw-dust in a fishmonger's
stall.

And there—not far at all from where *Diana* had lain docked—
that ship, well away from the rest, must be *Victoire*. Her hull
gleamed, clad all in shining steel from a prow like an axe blade to
a stern that bore *two* enormous sets of pulsers; amidships she resembled a castle, a great rectangular fortress with steel walls, a
peaked steel-clad roof, and four rounded turrets at the corners.

But before Arabella could discern any further details, a further
torrent of shouted commands came from the quarterdeck and
the ship lurched to the right, dashing many men who had just
regained their footing to the deck again. Several of them fell
screaming over the rail, their voices swiftly descending to be lost
in the distance below.

The ship righted herself then, wobbling and trembling to a
proper vertical, and Arabella rushed to the larboard rail, peering
to either side. Only one of the boarding-planks at the gunwale
amidships was still attached, and even as she watched Fox kicked
that one free, sending it and the screaming Frenchman who clutched
to it tumbling down to the water. To her right, a good number of
attackers still clung to the ropes, desperately clambering upward
but meeting fierce resistance at the top. She dashed forward to
assist in the defense, but by the time she reached the bow Gowse
and his men had dealt with the last of them.

Gasping, Arabella slumped to her knees, then pitched forward to the blood-soaked deck; her cutlass fell clattering beside her. She lay prostrate and panting, the smell of blood and steel filling her nose and her ears roaring.

It seemed she had barely caught her breath when a toe nudged her and she opened one eye. It was Faunt, the captain of the waist, who looked nearly as bad as she felt—his clothing was slashed and bloodstained, and one eye was bruised and nearly swollen shut—but his face bore a fierce grin nonetheless. "Captain's compliments," he said. "Yer wanted on the quarterdeck."

Arabella groaned and dragged herself to her feet.

22

AN UNUSUAL COURSE

Once she managed to haul herself up the ladder to the quarterdeck, Arabella felt herself an intruder—ragged, blood-soaked, and bone-weary, while the men on the deck were nearly unmarked by the recent fighting. But Captain Singh immediately embraced her, heedless of both propriety and of the blood that smeared his already-stained uniform coat. "I am so glad you are safe," he murmured into her ear.

"No gladder than I am to find you safe as well," she replied, closing her eyes and resting her head briefly on his shoulder. She was so very tired.

"We have lost too many this day." He squeezed her shoulders, then released her and returned to his usual composed and confident mien. "But we cannot rest now. Observe." He handed her a telescope and pointed aft and starboard.

Arabella extended the glass and peered over the taffrail. The docks below now blossomed with balloons, inflating as she watched like so many poisonous mushrooms. Soon there would be eight, ten, perhaps even twelve ships rising in pursuit.

And, unlike their recent escape, once they were no longer above the ship-yard these pursuers would not hesitate to fire cannon upon them. An explosion at this height would be unlikely to do damage to any ship other than *Diana*.

"I see," she said, returning the glass to her captain. "What can we do?"

"I have already ordered all hands to the pedals." Indeed, behind him the great pulsers were already beginning to turn. "*Diana* is the fastest ship in the Honorable Mars Company's fleet, but with a weary, inexperienced crew and so many determined ships in pursuit our advantage is diminished. Therefore, I desire you to consult with Aadim and find the swiftest route to English-controlled airlanes." A small, strange smile quirked one corner of his lip then. "You have always been a most . . . *unconventional* young woman, Mrs. Singh, and I encourage you to indulge your most atypical tendencies. An unexpected course change or unprecedented maneuver may be our only hope for escape."

"I shall do my best, sir."

"I expect nothing less."

———————

Giddy with exhaustion, alone in the great cabin with Aadim, she found herself speaking aloud to him . . . though, in truth, she had no idea whether or not he could even hear her, never mind understand her words. He had "eyes" that reacted to light, and instruments for the detection of wind speed and the ship's location and orientation in space, scattered throughout the ship, but no "ears" that she knew of, and the inner workings of his inhuman consciousness were as mysterious to her as the distant songs of angels. But, as Captain

Singh had often said, describing her problems to Aadim helped to focus her own thoughts if nothing else.

"We are *here*," she said, tapping Aadim's wooden finger on a chart of the wind currents near Venus, which she had clipped onto his desk. "And we must make our way *hence* as quickly as we may." She adjusted the dial indicating displacement in the vertical direction, then tapped the finger in a second location.

She was not happy with her observations of their current position, but they would have to do. She had had time for only two sightings by sextant—Saturn and Polaris, which were not the ideal—and those had been made hurriedly, and in terrible conditions.

Their destination, too, was no more than an educated guess. The indicated location was a largish asteroid called Xanthus, which orbited between Earth and Venus and had only entered Venus's vicinity in the past month; to the best of their intelligence it was still held by the English, and they had chosen it as the closest and best destination to which to escape. But if Napoleon had captured Xanthus recently, they might be sailing directly back to captivity.

"Now, we have the advantage of carrying no cargo." She moved one of the levers on the side of Aadim's desk to the furthest extremity of its range. "But many of the crew are exhausted, and the Venusians' abilities at the pedals are an unknown quantity." She moved another lever to the three-quarter point, then after further reflection back to two-thirds.

A rattle and a thump sounded from the deck above, accompanied by shouting, and briefly she was paralyzed by alarm. A moment later, though, she recognized the sounds of the larboard mast being swayed-out and set in its socket in the lower hull. This was a normal part of departure from any planet . . . but in this case it was far earlier than usual, and many of the shouts she heard were in Venusian language. Clearly there would be no falling-line ceremony on *this* voyage. She shook her head and tried to concentrate upon her navigation, as with a sliding *thump* the lar-board mast was seated and the action shifted to the starboard side of the ship.

One after another Arabella puzzled out the proper settings for the fastest possible transit. Wherever there were two or more plausible alternatives, she deliberately chose the least obvious one; in one case, having no solid information, she closed her eyes and set the dial by hazard. And, always, she let herself be guided by the navigator himself; if the purring clockworks within the desk seemed to resist the motion of some lever, or encourage a different setting, she accepted the hint without question.

The question of how to account for the hydrogen was the most difficult one, and she spent some time puzzling it out. Finally she set the lever indicating coal supplies all the way to the right. "You should imagine that the coal supplies are infinite," she said as she worked. "I wish there were some way I could indicate that the weight of the hydrogen tanks is much less than that of the coal-stores and launch-furnace they replace."

She had no idea, of course, if her words had any effect. But she took some comfort in the fact that Aadim's mechanisms did not seem to protest her settings.

At last, all being as much in readiness as she could manage, she held her breath and pressed down Aadim's finger for a third time. At once the works beneath the desktop began to whir and ratchet—a very familiar and welcome sound, yet also somewhat different than she recalled; a bit noisier, perhaps, and somehow more urgent. Perhaps, she reflected, there was a bit of saw-dust in the gears. Or perhaps the seriousness of the task, which she had communicated to Aadim through the settings of his levers and dials, had encouraged him to think even harder than usual, and this thought was audible in the sound of his works.

As she waited for the calculations to complete, lulled by the sound of Aadim's gears, she closed her eyes for just a moment. . . .

"I had worried about you," Aadim said. His voice was very like Captain Singh's, and for some reason she was not in the least surprised to hear it, though he had never spoken before.

"And I about you," she replied.

He turned to her and tilted his head to one side, a movement of which she had not even been aware he was capable. "The French were not kind to me. But I am not without my resources, and I was able to maintain my integrity." His lips did not move as he spoke. "I must say that some of the changes they have made to the ship are quite intriguing." He paused, whirring. "This man Fox is also intriguing."

"He is." Arabella sighed. "Also maddening."

"Many of the best are."

Suddenly the sound of a bell announced the completion of the calculation, and Arabella raised her head from a sleeve wet with saliva. She had fallen asleep on the deck while awaiting the result.

She sat up—the force of gravity, she noted, had diminished perceptibly—and wiped her mouth with her hand. Aadim sat as he ever had, vibrating slightly from the turning clockworks within. His green glass eyes were fixed straight ahead, as usual, and he showed no sign of having moved—and certainly none of having spoken—since she had initiated the current set of calculations.

"Are you navigating my dreams now?" she asked him.

No reply.

For a long moment Arabella gazed into Aadim's blind green eyes, which did not shift or acknowledge her in the slightest. Eventually she shrugged, shook her head, and took up a scrap of wood and lead pencil with which to copy down the course displayed on the dials at the front of Aadim's desk.

As she began to understand what Aadim had come up with, her eyes widened. But her busy pencil did not hesitate.

"This is an . . . unprecedented course," Captain Singh said as he read over the figures on the plank.

"That is, as you may recall, what you requested."

"I did. Still . . . to dive so deeply into Venus's planetary atmosphere, especially when we have just worked so hard to escape it, seems a very great risk indeed."

Arabella glanced up at the great turbid ball of Venus, shielding her eyes from the Sun beyond. Unaccustomed though she was to the Sun's glare, it was still a great relief to see his face unshrouded by clouds. And though his light struck her skin with exceptional heat, it was at least a *dry* heat.

"I have compared this course with our maps of the planet," she said, "and it does make a certain amount of sense. There is a large rocky area near the equator, corresponding with the location of this instruction here." She tapped an indication of a quite dramatic course change, conducted at a frighteningly low altitude. "The area may be very hot, even by Venusian standards, and rising air currents there could be sufficient to push us quickly into a much higher orbit. From which we can perhaps achieve the de Ruyter Current, which will bear us swiftly to Xanthus."

"May be," the captain repeated. "Might be. Perhaps."

Arabella shrugged and pointed aft, where four French ships were plainly visible to the eye; a half-dozen more were concealed by the scudding clouds of the planet's Horn, and all were drawing nearer hour by hour. "If we continue on our present course, or indeed any predictable course, the French *will* overtake us."

Captain Singh said nothing, merely stroking his chin as he stared at the peculiar figures upon the plank. Finally he firmed up his jaw, raised his head, and called, "All hands about ship!"

Among the chaotic, tempestuous winds of Venus's Horn they soon found a current which carried them swiftly southward, at a sharp angle to their original course, and into an orbit which would bring them above the rocky desert labeled ULUUMNA on the map. But their French pursuers, observing the maneuver, were able to catch the same wind, cutting the corner of *Diana*'s course and drawing still nearer.

Captain Singh employed every bit of his skills in navigation and command to increase the distance between *Diana* and the French. The course provided by Aadim, with its numerous unexpected twists and turns, proved helpful, but the winds of the Horn were, as always, so wild and unpredictable themselves that no course could be any thing more than a guideline.

Fox took on the role of chief mate, in place of the fallen Richardson. Though it seemed to Arabella that he rankled somewhat at the diminution in authority, he seemed content enough for now. He was also favoring his bandaged left arm, but never uttered a word of complaint.

Stross, as always, was a capable and decisive sailing-master, and quickly sorted out the surviving men into divisions; Faunt, Higgs, Gowse, and the other captains of divisions soon got their people organized. But the many months of imprisonment, the chase through the swamp, and the ferocious violence of the launch had taken a heavy toll.

"We have no alternative," Stross sighed to Arabella and Mills. "We must employ some of the Venusians." Clearly the prospect brought him no joy.

They stood on the quarterdeck, their stained and ragged clothing fluttering in the artificial wind of the whirring pulsers. Their weight, having fallen to less than half its Venusian value at the height of their escape, was now beginning to return as they drew nearer the planet they had just departed. "They are strong and willing," Mills said. "In ship-yard, work together. Haul and lift and place. They will serve well."

"They have done well at the pedals, so far," Stross acknowledged with little grace. "But we have no common language! Can we get our point across as to what they must do, in the midst of maneuvers . . . or even battle?"

Mills said simply, "Yes," then glanced to Arabella.

Arabella swallowed. "I believe so," she said, trying to project a confidence she did not feel, "with Mills's help."

Stross was obviously not reassured, but he nodded. "Very well. I will put most of them in the waist—they can do the least damage there—and distribute the rest among the main-top and after-sails where we can keep an eye on them."

Arabella met Stross's eye. "I am sure they will acquit themselves well, sir. Even I managed not to make a hash of it, when I served in the waist."

"I certainly hope so. I am seconding you to Faunt, as interpreter for the Venusians in the waist." Arabella gulped, but Stross seemed not to notice—or deliberately ignored it—and turned to Mills. "You'll be captain of the main-top. I shall do my best with the after-guard. Now look alive!"

"Aye aye, sir," they replied automatically, saluted, and departed the quarterdeck.

"You will serve well," Mills said to Arabella as they descended the ladder, their steps high and drifting in the diminished gravity.

"Thank you," Arabella replied, grateful for the reassurance . . . but still not reassured.

In the next few hours Arabella, Faunt, and the Venusians—whose wide, shining eyes made them look rather startled even when they did know the command that had just been issued—somehow managed to work out a vocabulary of mutually intelligible phrases covering the most common actions: go there, haul on that, make that line fast, for Christ's sake stop whatever you're doing this instant. One English phrase the Venusians had no trouble with was "aye aye"—its vowels suited their tongues well, and they seemed to take pleasure in the very utterance of it. Unfortunately, it sometimes meant "I have no idea what you just said, sir."

While they drilled and trained, the cloudy ball of Venus drew nearer and nearer, growing from a huge mottled globe to a roiling curved plain. Even as it did, though the men and Venusians at the pedals worked themselves to exhaustion, the pursuing French continued to narrow the distance between them. Arabella felt as though *Diana* were about to be crushed between the two.

The clouds below grew still closer, gaining definition, turning from a hazy mass to a heaving, mountainous cloudscape. Then the ship slipped beneath the cloud-tops. Soon she was completely embedded in seething gray blankness, the French ships vanishing from view. The sudden dampness of the air struck Arabella like the slap of a hot wet towel in the face.

Suddenly, and far earlier than Arabella had expected or felt prepared for, Fox began to bellow a barrage of commands from the quarterdeck. "'Vast pulsers! Heave to!" he cried, and the captains of the divisions, including Faunt, quickly translated this into specific commands to haul on lines, set sails, and so forth to retard the ship's forward progress. This was swiftly followed by "Strike the jib!" and "Brace all up on a larboard tack!"

Slowly, majestically, the ship yawed one hundred and eighty degrees, swinging about until she was sailing pulsers-first, the hot foggy breeze now coming from abaft. The sensation was remarkably disorienting, and Arabella hoped the French would be equally disoriented by this maneuver—one which Aadim had apparently devised himself. It certainly did not match any thing she recalled from the sailing manuals she had studied.

"I don't like this," Faunt muttered through clenched teeth. "Feels like we're falling into our own grave."

"I have confidence in Aadim's course," Arabella replied, though in truth she had her misgivings. Still, what they had seen so far showed that Aadim seemed to understand the ship's new capabilities; this maneuver, in which they returned immediately to the planet they had just left only to depart again, would not even have been possible without hydrogen. A coal-fired ship would never have been able to re-inflate her balloons for a maneuver such as this without expending the coal needed for a safe landing at the end of the voyage. But, with the Venusians' help, they had drawn the lifting gas back into its tanks upon achieving the Horn, and used the same gas a second time for their current descent; they would use it again, for a third time, if they reached Earth.

When they reached Earth, she corrected herself.

Suddenly they fell below the clouds. The landscape revealed below was gray and black and lifeless, a broad rocky desert, and a blast of furnace-hot air immediately struck the ship. *Diana* shuddered and rocked as though held in some ancient's trembling hand.

"Idlers and waisters aft!" Fox called. "Set all sails!"

At once Arabella, Faunt, and every other hand not directly involved in the management of the sails rushed to the quarterdeck, crowding against the taffrail in an overheated, gasping mob. The ship pitched back; the rising air from the baking rocks below filled her sails; and she leapt forward, up, and back into the clouds in a great rush that pressed Arabella, the Venusians, and all the others together most uncomfortably.

A moment later they burst out of the clouds again . . . and nearly collided with a descending French warship! Arabella had a glimpse of the French airmen's startled faces as they flew past, but it was over in a moment; in any case, Fox's and Faunt's bellowed commands sent her and her Venusian comrades scrambling back to the waist, to help set the sails and catch the winds of the Horn to make good their escape.

Days passed. Endless days—literally endless, in that the sun never set—of pedaling, pedaling, pedaling, with little to eat, less to drink, and only the occasional snatch of sleep. And always the French drew nearer.

They had lost many of the pursuers with their dramatic maneuver over the Uluumna desert; some of them, Fox claimed, had surely smashed to flinders on the surface, while others had simply fallen behind. But four still followed, their pulsers turning with steady persistence. *Diana* was the Mars Company's swiftest ship, and lightly loaded, but her people were battered and weary; the French warships were fully crewed with rested, well-fed airmen, and in a duel of pedals they must, inevitably, win. *Diana*'s only hope—a hope which seemed slimmer by the day—was to reach English-held Xanthus before the French intercepted her.

Water was their most critical lack. Their stolen ship had not, of course, been provisioned for a long voyage, and for water they had only what small amount the Venusians had brought with them. So they were on short rations, and in the dry heat of the interplanetary atmosphere—the dry heat which had been so very welcome after months on Venus's muggy surface—every one was parched and irritable.

Arabella still wore her tattered, bloodstained "Cesario" breeches, though she had found a better shirt in the small collection of clothing the escapees had brought with them. The dress from her satchel she had given to Withers to make into bandages.

"I am sorry to interrupt your sleep," Captain Singh called up to her one day, "but your services as translator are required." She blinked and pushed herself away from the dark nook between the bulkhead and the deck above where she slept, drifting down toward the captain in a state of free descent.

There were no watches—each member of the crew simply worked until they could work no more, then slept until they were required to work again—and, lacking hammocks, every one was compelled to find a place to sleep wherever they could. In Arabella's case, that was a corner of the great cabin, one that was out of the way when the captain required the cabin for navigation or for meetings with his staff. She had no difficulty sleeping through any conversation; indeed, she felt she could sleep through a full-blown aerial battle.

Still blinking and rubbing sleep from her dry eyes, Arabella pushed off the aft bulkhead of the upper deck and sailed with Captain Singh along its echoing length. The space was empty of cargo, though gently snoring bodies occupied most of the corners.

They came to the gun deck, undogged the hatch, and slipped within. Fox, Mills, and Ulungugga floated there. "Sorry to wake you, Mrs. Singh," Mills said. "The science is beyond me."

The gun deck was vastly larger now than it had been when Arabella had served as powder-monkey. Where before it had held three four-pounder cannon, the space was now crowded with twelve eight-pounders—three groups of four, fresh-cast, still shining and smelling of hot brass. Each cannon, Mills pointed out, was connected by a flexible lead pipe to a small cylindrical device perforated with holes; there was one such for each group of four. This was the item for which her translation services were required.

Between Ulungugga's understanding of the devices, Mills's superior command of the Wagala language, the captain's scientific knowledge, and Arabella's attempts to put the others together they managed to come to a mutual comprehension of their function: they were fire-safes—or so she translated from Ulungugga's pronunciation of what she believed was a French term—designed to replace the function of the slow-matches which other ships kept burning for the ignition of the cannon during battle. These devices, apparently invented by Fulton, were intended to provide a source of ignition to the cannon without risking a hydrogen explosion.

"But surely," Arabella said when she understood this, "the detonation of the cannon itself is an even greater danger?" She knew from experience that each cannon shot resulted in a great lance of fire and smoke being expelled from the gun's muzzle along with the projectile.

The guns, Ulungugga explained, were only to be fired while the pulsers were in use; their rushing wind would draw any stray hydrogen aft and away from the guns. The fire-safes were intended to prevent explosion while the ship was not under way.

At least, she gathered, that was the theory. *Diana* and *Victoire* were among the first to be equipped with this device—Arabella realized that Napoleon must be furious that the honor of this invention's debut had been stolen from his wonderful secret weapon by a ragged mob of English prisoners-of-war—and their weapons had never yet been fired in anger.

"So," Fox said, "if we fire at the French, we run the very real risk of blowing ourselves up in the process."

"So it seems," said Arabella. "However, I gather that the French ships—lacking the benefit of this new device, and having to make do with slow-match—are even more likely to explode."

"This may explain," Fox mused, "why they have not even lobbed any ranging shots in our direction."

Captain Singh straightened in the air and clasped his hands behind his back. "Still, we must make a decision. If it were to come to battle, would we fight, or would we surrender?"

"Fight," said Fox immediately, and Mills and Arabella echoed him without hesitation. Ulungugga merely blinked, uncomprehending.

"And if we fought without practicing first, would we win?"

They were all stunned into silence by the implications.

"Exactly," the captain said after the silence had gone on long enough. "Mr. Fox, select your gun crews and begin drill at your earliest convenience."

Fox's eyes widened, but he touched his forehead and said, "Aye aye, sir."

But in order to exercise the guns, they had no choice but to take some men from the pedals, and as they prepared for the first round of drill the French gained still more quickly. Arabella, serving once again as powder-monkey, peered glumly through the gun-port at the air ahead. Xanthus was still invisible somewhere in the distance.

It seemed more and more likely they would have no choice but to turn and fight. Four ships of the line full of well-fed, well-rested, well-trained Frenchmen against one refitted Marsman whose crew was ragged, exhausted, thirsty, and barely practiced. But they owed it to the King, and their own pride and dignity, to make the attempt.

They had only enough crew to man three guns, one in each group of four. Each gun crew was half human and half Venusian. The Venusians, who had installed the guns, took to the handling of them quite quickly, and proved strong and able in their initial practice of running them in and out in dumb-show. But now the crews would fire the guns in earnest for the first time . . . and they would learn whether or not there were any substantial hydrogen leaks nearby.

Arabella passed a bag of powder to Gowse, the captain of her gun; he tossed it through the air to one of the Venusians, who rammed it down the barrel with a stout oaken ram-rod. Gowse, who held a priming-iron in the touch-hole at the cannon's butt, called "Home!" as he felt the bag arrive. The bag was followed by a ball and a wad, again packed tightly down with the ram-rod, and the gun was snugged up tightly against its port.

Now came the moment of truth. All three guns were loaded and ready.

Arabella covered her ears, as did every one else—the Venusians, lacking visible external ears, held their hands much further back on their heads than she had expected.

Fox looked them all over, hesitated a long moment, then called "Fire!"

Gowse and the other two gun-captains pressed the firing-studs on their fire-safes.

The *bang* which followed was so great that Arabella feared the hydrogen had exploded. But it was merely unfamiliarity, after so many months away, and the fact that even three eight-pounders were so much greater in force than the four-pounders *Diana* had formerly carried. She could not imagine the sound which would result from all twelve guns firing simultaneously.

Fox leaned into the gun-port, shading his eyes, and Arabella leapt to another and likewise peered through the sulfurous smoke. Two of the barrels soon flew into splinters; the third shot missed, but it was still a promising start.

The gun crews gave a ragged, coughing cheer. But amidst the cheering and the ringing of her ears, Arabella thought she heard another sound. Others did as well, and the cheers quickly stuttered to a halt.

There it came again: a distant, echoing *boom*.

Were the French firing at them? Had they come so close already? Was this, suddenly, to be *Diana's* last stand?

But no: the *boom* came again, this time distinctly from ahead.

Arabella looked to Fox, who peered intently forward, waving his hat in frustration at the smoke which clouded his view. But then came a cry from without: it was Watson, stationed as look-out at the bowsprit-head: "Sail ho!" he called in his high, carrying voice. "Thirty . . . no, thirty-*three* sail of ship!"

"Whose, d—n it, *whose?*" Fox shouted in frustration. Arabella, for her part, felt her already-parched tongue go even drier in her mouth. If this were a French fleet—perhaps returning from a successful conquest of Xanthus—they were surely doomed.

It was Arabella's old messmate Taylor who broke the spell. Peering forward through another gun-port, he suddenly whooped in glee and threw his hat upward, whence it bounced off the deck above and drifted gently down again. "Square formation!" he cried. "Lookee there! Square formation, by God!"

Most of the other airmen, including Fox, immediately joined Taylor in joyful exclamations, while Arabella and several others seemed perplexed. "What does this mean?" she shouted to Fox above the tumult.

"It can be none other than His Majesty's Aerial Navy!" Fox shouted back. "The French employ a hexagonal formation."

Grinning, Arabella stuck her head out the gun-port. Through the clearing smoke could now plainly be seen an orderly array of white sails, laid out with mathematical rigor in a square grid.

Never had she been so glad to see such a tidy sight.

23

COUNCIL OF WAR

The great grid of the English fleet grew and grew until *Diana* lay embedded in it, mighty ships-of-the-line above, below, and to every side in pristine rank and file. The four pursuing Frenchmen, meanwhile, turned and ran as soon as they caught sight of the fleet, pedaling at top speed due west. The English did not pursue them; Captain Singh explained that the distances and currents were such that even a swift frigate could not intercept them before they reached the Nalbach Current, which would carry them rapidly back to Venus.

No sooner did Fox cry "Back pulsers!"—bringing *Diana* to a tidy halt alongside the flagship in the very center of the formation—than an aerial cutter set off from the flagship toward them. This was a lightweight affair of bamboo and rattan, equipped with eight pedaling airmen, a four-sail pulser at the rear, and three small sails for direction.

The cutter soon drew alongside and Watson hailed it: "Ahoy the boat!"

"Aye aye!" the boat replied, meaning that an officer was aboard. "Permission to come aboard?"

Permission was granted, most enthusiastically granted indeed, and the cutter's captain kicked off from his boat, drifted down to *Diana*'s deck, and landed with a very neat touch of one toe. "First Lieutenant Thomas Townsend," he introduced himself, "of the Royal Aerial Navy flagship *Bucephalus*."

"Captain Prakash Singh, of the Honorable Mars Company airship *Diana*."

"Very pleased to meet you, sir."

They shook hands, and Captain Singh proceeded to introduce Lieutenant Townsend to Fox, Stross, and the rest of his quarterdeck crew, not omitting Lady Corey and "my dear wife."

"Charmed," Arabella said.

Captain Singh quickly summarized *Diana*'s situation and recent history to Lieutenant Townsend, speaking loudly enough that the cutter's crew could plainly hear him. Every member of *Diana*'s crew—longstanding Dianas, former Touchstones, and Venusians all mingled together—floated now in untidy lines across the deck, and though their clothing was shabby and their faces were haggard from exhaustion and thirst, their expressions were joyous, their chests puffed out with pride, and many an eye glistened with barely suppressed tears.

"Well!" Lieutenant Townsend exclaimed. "You certainly have been through quite a bit!"

"We have," the captain acknowledged, "but our journey is not yet complete. We carry critical intelligence which must be reported to the highest levels of naval command at once."

"You are in luck, then, sir, for the admiral of our fleet is none other than Nelson himself!"

"Nelson!" exclaimed Fox, and the name was echoed by many across the deck, an awed reiteration of "Nelson . . . Nelson . . . Nelson . . ." that raised the hairs on the back of Arabella's neck.

"Who is this Nelson?" Lady Corey asked Arabella.

Arabella was astonished. Even she, who had paid as little attention as she could to the war before Napoleon's escape from the Moon, knew of Nelson. "Have you not heard of Lord Nelson, the admiral who smashed Napoleon's aerial fleet above Brussels in 1805? And the Battle of the Nile? Surely you have heard of *that*?"

"Oh! Of course! We have a tea-pot in Egyptian style commemorating that victory." She raised her eyebrows. "I thought I had heard that he died."

"Very nearly," put in Fox, who had been listening. "He was shot at the Battle of Brussels and took nearly a year to recover. But he is a tough old bird; lost an eye, lost an arm, still going." He rubbed at his own arm then; the bandage was stained with blood and less salubrious fluids. "I hope that I will not be required to emulate him in this."

Captain Singh cleared his throat pointedly, returning the attention of all three of them to himself. "The lieutenant has invited me to the flagship to present our intelligence on *Victoire* to the admiral," he said. "Mr. Fox, you will remain in command here."

"Aye aye, sir."

"Lady Corey," the captain continued, "will you join me? I would like you to personally report the information you have prised from Fulton."

"I would be honored."

"Thank you. Mr. Fox, pass the word for Ulungugga. He worked on *Victoire* and may be able to answer questions as to her construction and capabilities." He paused, considering, then turned to Arabella. "Mrs. Singh, will you accompany me to the flagship, to translate for Ulungugga? Mr. Mills is needed here, in case of action."

Arabella felt herself entirely inadequate to the task, but she could not disagree that if *Diana* should find herself in battle she would be better defended with Mills in charge of the Venusians at the main-top. "Aye aye, sir."

"Very well." He nodded. "Mr. Fox, the ship is yours. Take good care of her."

"Absolutely, sir." Then, as Captain Singh departed the quarter-deck with Townsend, Fox touched Arabella's shoulder and smiled. "Give the admiral my very warmest regards."

At the touch a warm blush rose in Arabella's cheeks, and she quickly turned away before she could be tempted to offer Fox any more encouragement.

She owed her heart, her loyalty, her very life, to Captain Singh. Why did Fox, that vexatious man, hold so much attraction for her?

———

The cutter quickly carried them across the short distance to *Bucephalus,* the eight strapping Navy men pedaling in crisp unison to Townsend's commands, and soon Arabella, Captain Singh, Lady Corey, and Ulungugga floated down to the flagship's deck.

Where *Touchstone* had seemed small and shabby by comparison with *Diana*, even before the latter's recent refurbishment—a bantam rooster set against a sleek racing *huresh*—*Bucephalus* was more a proud and snorting bull. Though *Diana* was greater in length and breadth, *Bucephalus* had one more deck, sported twenty-one cannon and six masts, and was positively crowded with crew. So many men, indeed, were crammed aboard that there seemed scarcely space on the deck for the four Dianas to alight.

Those numerous airmen were plainly kept very busy aboard. Every inch of the flagship's *khoresh*-wood was scrupulously clean, gleaming nearly as bright as her shining brasswork. Every line was meticulously coiled, every bit of rigging spruce and clean and properly tarred.

The moment Captain Singh's foot touched the deck, a bosun's pipe sounded and every airman present saluted in crisp unison.

A group of men in very impressive Navy blue drifted up to them, halting all at the same time with an expert touch on the deck. The one with the most impressive epaulets—though his uniform was far inferior in quantity of gold braid to even a middling French officer—introduced himself: "Vice-Admiral Thomas Hardy, sir. Captain, HMAS *Bucephalus*." Once the usual round of introductions and a brief summation of the situation had been dispensed with, they were immediately ushered into the great cabin to meet with the admiral.

Bucephalus's great cabin was very great indeed, the overhead being more than high enough to stand erect, and exceptionally finely appointed. Brass and crystal lanterns illuminated a substantial collection of rolled charts and a varnished, gilded map-desk of fine Venusian blackwood.

Floating behind that desk, peering very intently at a map of Venus, was a man whom Arabella immediately recognized from his portraits in all the gazettes: Admiral Lord Nelson.

He was not a large man; in fact, he was slightly shorter than Napoleon. And, unlike Napoleon—who was stout, florid, ill-shaven, and full of energetic bluster—he was slightly built, stooped, and rather sunken of cheek, with unruly gray hair. His right coat-sleeve was empty and pinned up. But his eyes, when he looked up, glittered with a keen intelligence. One of them, she knew, was blind, but she could not tell which. "And who do we have here?" he said, the remark directed equally to Captain Singh, Lady Corey, Arabella, and Ulungugga. Arabella suspected that the four of them were probably the most unusual set of visitors the admiral of this well-ordered ship full of Royal Navy airmen had received in a long time.

Captain Hardy introduced them. "Captain Singh says he carries vital intelligence."

"Indeed, sir," Captain Singh said to Nelson. "I am a secret agent of His Majesty's government, tasked to examine and report upon Napoleon's activities on Venus."

Nelson straightened at that. "You have my full attention, sir."

"My people and I have just escaped from a prison-camp on the surface of the planet, where Napoleon is currently engaged in the construction of a fleet of armored airships. These ships are entirely clad with steel plate, and are very likely impregnable to ordinary cannon-fire. They are very heavily armed, having twenty-four ten-pound great guns and four six-pound swivel-guns. The first of these ships, called *Victoire*, is ready for launch, or nearly so. They must be disabled or destroyed before they launch, or Napoleon will be unstoppable."

When the situation was stated so concisely, even Arabella, to whom it was no surprise, found it exceptionally daunting. But Nelson did not hesitate one moment before asking, "What is your source for this intelligence?"

"The ship is being built at a ship-yard adjacent to the prison-camp where my people were engaged in the mining and refinement of iron for her construction; we were in a position to learn important aspects of her design and operation during our confinement there. Lady Corey has been in close personal contact with the ship's designer, an American by the name of Robert Fulton. Ulungugga was one of the Venusians tasked with building *Victoire*, and Mrs. Singh speaks his language. I myself have managed to discover a few details through patient investigation and questioning."

Nelson held up one finger to pause Captain Singh's explanation. "A moment, sir." He turned to Lieutenant Townsend—he, Captain Hardy, and two other lieutenants had been listening with wide-eyed astonishment—and said, "Pass the word for my secretary." Townsend saluted and departed. "I apologize for the delay, sir," Nelson said to Captain Singh, "but I am right-handed, and even after many years of practice with the left my handwriting is entirely inadequate." To the other lieutenants he said, "I must ask you to leave us; this information must be held in the utmost secrecy. Tell no one what you have heard, and tell the Marine on duty to admit no one else to the cabin without my express permission."

"Aye aye, sir," they replied in chorus, and departed.

"Some tea, while we wait?" Nelson asked Captain Singh.

"I should be honored to take tea with you, sir, but first I must ask that you send food and water, and a physician if you have one, to my ship. My people have been very badly used and they are in great need, and our surgeon did not manage to escape from Venus."

"We have no physician, but our young Dr. Barry is a very capable surgeon." He nodded to Captain Hardy, who bowed in the air and ducked out the door.

The secretary arrived a very short time later, and even as he was readying his note-book and pen Nelson looked at Captain Singh with serious intent and said, "Please begin at the beginning, sir."

———

Hours passed. Tea was taken, and sandwiches as well, and Arabella's throat grew raw from talking. In addition to translating for Ulungugga—he did more than half the work himself, but between the two of them they did manage to get his point across— she was able to contribute a few motes of understanding, from her own experience with Aadim, regarding the science and navigation of ships raised by hydrogen balloon.

Nelson immediately comprehended the severity of the threat posed by *Victoire* and her armored sisters. "Our intent had been to engage Napoleon's main fleet above Mumnugwa," he said, pointing to a continent on the map of Venus spread out on the table, "but now it is clear that the capture or destruction of *Victoire*, preferably before she launches, must take precedence." He laid one long, pale finger on the location of the ship-yard.

"We lack the appropriate weaponry to destroy the ship-yard from the air," Captain Hardy said. "Nor have we sufficient Marines to take and hold it by land."

Nelson snatched his hand up from the map into a tight fist. "Then we will entice Napoleon into the air, and beat him there!"

"Indeed," said Captain Singh. "But how?"

The discussion now turned to *Victoire*'s specifics and capabilities. Lady Corey revealed that Fulton had bragged that the armored ship was equipped with a new type of propulsive sails which he had designed, intended to overcome her great weight. Captain Singh, surprised, noted that the refitted *Diana* had pulsers of an unusual design; these must also incorporate Fulton's improvements. He certainly had noticed that they seemed to draw more smoothly and offer more speed for less effort.

Fulton had also worried aloud in Lady Corey's presence about the dual pulsers at *Victoire*'s stern. The space between them, due to the air-flow requirements, had a complex shape which was difficult to plate with iron, creating a weak point in the ship's armor. Furthermore, Ulungugga knew that the ship's main hydrogen reserve was held at the ship's stern, very near the vulnerable point. "That, then, is where we must strike!" Captain Hardy declared.

"Easier said than done," said Nelson. "Her captain will surely be aware of this vulnerability and will take even more care than usual to protect his pulsers."

A knock at the door interrupted then, and a man Arabella had not seen before was admitted. "Our surgeon, Dr. Barry," Nelson introduced him.

Dr. Barry was a slim, soft-spoken young man of only about twenty, but he carried himself with assurance and navigated expertly in a state of free descent. His coat, Arabella noted, was flecked with blood. "Forgive the intrusion," he said, "but I thought Captain Singh would desire my report immediately."

Captain Singh looked to Nelson, who nodded his assent. "I do indeed, sir."

"I have examined *Diana*'s wounded," the surgeon said, "and treated those for whom treatment would be beneficial. Your chief mate Mr. Fox, I must say, has shown stoicism that would do credit to a Navy officer. The inner surface of the wound appeared sloughy, and the discharge was fetid and ichorous; the pain must be considerable. I have ordered the wound to be kept wet with the arsenical solution, followed by emollient poultices to promote the separation of the eschar. He should recover, but if he had gone even one day more without proper treatment he would certainly have lost the arm and most likely his life."

"I thank you greatly for your assistance," Captain Singh said, bowing in the air.

"As do I," Arabella said, forcing the words past a sudden lump in her throat. The news had struck her most gravely, most gravely indeed, and she felt herself quite taken aback.

The young surgeon replied with a modest nod. "Only doing my duty . . . ma'am. It is ma'am, is it not?" He gave her a small peculiar smile as he said this last, and suddenly she was reminded that she still wore her bloodstained "Cesario" breeches.

"It is," she replied with some embarrassment. "I gave up my dress for bandages."

Again that peculiar smile. "I imagine that female costume can be quite an impediment for certain activities."

Nelson interrupted then, saying, "I suggest that we adjourn for supper. You have given us much to think about, sir, and we thank you on behalf of the King for your efforts." This last was directed to Captain Singh, who bowed in acknowledgement of the compliment.

As the company gathered their things and prepared to depart

the cabin, Ulungugga touched Arabella's arm and asked whence they were bound. After she had answered that they were going to supper, he asked her if meat would be served—the question accompanied by a walking gesture of the fingers, clarifying that he meant "food that walks" as distinguished from the related word meaning "food that swims."

Arabella frowned at the question. Unlike the Gowanna, who gladly supped along with their English and French customers, the Wagala never ate meat—and avoiding meat at an English admiral's table would surely be an impossibility. "I am afraid so," she replied, as best she could manage in Wagala.

Ulungugga's throat-sac worked for a moment. Then he said that he was suddenly concerned as to the health and safety of his compatriots aboard *Diana,* and desired to return thence as soon as possible.

"I shall request transportation for you," she told him, relieved at his intelligence and concern for social niceties. He might resemble a frog, she reflected, but he was more polite than many a human man she had met.

Captain Singh and Lady Corey had already seated themselves at the admiral's table when Arabella joined them. She had been delayed by the necessity of changing her clothing—to dine with Viscount and Baron Nelson of the Nile in ragged, bloodstained breeches would simply never do. Somehow, she knew not from where, a perfectly lovely dress of Venusian silk had been obtained for her and quickly altered to fit by Nelson's steward, an aged and very proper man.

A parade of midshipmen soon arrived, bearing laden platters, and despite the difficulties of cooking in a state of free descent it was the finest food she had eaten in many, many months. A spit-roasted whole kid goat, done to a turn, was accompanied by Yorkshire pudding, spotted dog, and dried peas beaten into a paste and flavored with turmeric, and that was just one course. Admiral Nelson himself carved and served the roast, and shortly Arabella was fed beyond satiation.

Arabella was seated to Captain Singh's left, of course, but as the hero of the hour was naturally placed at the admiral's right this put her between them. "You set quite a generous table, sir," she said to the admiral.

"We are well aware of the privations you have suffered in His Majesty's service," he replied modestly. "Also, we know that you will not eat so well in the near future—none of us will, sadly. But we will share with you what provisions we can spare, as well as a detachment of Marines to supervise your prisoners."

"Prisoners?" Arabella asked, surprised. "We took no prisoners— every Frenchman who assaulted us as we launched was killed or went overboard."

Admiral Nelson spoke without looking up from his plate, where he was busily engaged with the peculiar utensil—a combination fork and knife—which he used for eating one-handed in free descent. "The Venusians," he said, as though it were obvious.

"They are not our prisoners, they are our *shipmates*! If it were not for their assistance we should never have managed to depart Venus at all!"

"You cannot trust them, my dear," Nelson said around a mouthful of roasted kid. "They understand nothing but force, and will serve willingly whoever holds the lash."

"You describe them as though they are mere animals!" Arabella replied with some heat. "But they are *people*! They have their nations and their tribes, as we do, each with its own character. These Venusians are of the Wagala people; they were slaves for years, first to the Gowanna and then to the French, and desire Napoleon's downfall as fervently as any of us."

"Your trusting nature does you credit," Nelson said with a pa-
tronizing air, "but—merely as a precaution—I will still send a squad
of Marines. I wish I could provide you with an escort to Xanthus,
but, as I am sure you are aware, we require every ship for the assault upon Napoleon's fleet."

Captain Singh interjected himself into the conversation then.
"We will not require an escort to Xanthus, *or* your Marines," he
said, as a flat statement of fact. "We will remain with the fleet."

"I am terribly sorry, Captain Singh, but we cannot defend your
ship in the midst of a battle. Xanthus is not a large asteroid, but it
is well-watered and defensible; you will be safe there until action
is concluded."

"We do not require defense." He took a sip from his wine-skin.
"We will participate in the attack."

Captain Hardy, at Nelson's left hand, sputtered, "With all due
respect, sir! Your *Diana* is a ship of commerce, not war; your crew
inexperienced and exhausted!"

"Although *Diana* was built for commerce, the French have
refitted her as a warship—indeed, a warship with unique capabilities. Not only is she now buoyed by hydrogen rather than hot
air, but she has been fitted with the very latest in French cannon
and Fulton's improved propulsive sails, making her equal to *Victoire*
in several important ways." He did not, Arabella noted, mention
Aadim and the automaton's own unique capabilities. "And as for my
crew, they are singularly motivated to take the fight to Napoleon,
and furthermore they are all accustomed to Venusian conditions—
especially, of course, the native Venusians themselves. Are your
Navy men doing well in the heat?"

This last comment was directed to Hardy, who glowered at the
implied insult to naval fortitude but said nothing.

"Given proper provisions and the opportunity for practice,"
Captain Singh continued, "I am certain that by the time we encounter Napoleon's fleet *Diana* will be every bit as proficient a

fighter as you could hope for." And with that, he buttered a bit of bread and popped it into his mouth.

A short while ago Arabella had despaired of Captain Singh's cool distance. But now, as he chewed calmly in the face of the assembled Royal Navy's glares, she loved him even more dearly for it.

"You yourself, sir," he said to Lord Nelson after swallowing and wiping his mouth, "have said you require every ship for the assault upon Napoleon. *Diana* and her twelve eight-pound guns are at your disposal, if you will but accept her. If nothing else, she will provide a distraction to the French."

Captain Hardy had been gradually turning red while Captain Singh spoke, and he opened his mouth to register what would certainly have been a withering rebuke regarding the capabilities of a mere Marsman as opposed to a naval vessel. But he was stymied in this, as Nelson touched Hardy's arm and said to Captain Singh, "Your bravery and commitment to the Crown do you credit, sir. I accept your offer, and wish you the very best of luck in the coming battle."

Lady Corey raised her wine-skin. "To Napoleon's downfall!" she called, loud and clear.

"To Napoleon's downfall!" chorused every one at the table, including Arabella, and drank.

In the following days they drilled and drilled and drilled again, while Venus once again expanded from a bright star to a globe, looming dark against the blue sky with the Sun nearly behind her. It seemed sometimes to Arabella that she was destined to go back and forth to Venus for the rest of her life . . . which she fervently hoped would not be the case.

Impressive though her martial capabilities might be by comparison with her previous configuration, *Diana* could not hope to participate in the coming battle as a ship of the line, so she was assigned to perform the role of a frigate.

Frigates, more maneuverable and less heavily armed than line-of-battle ships, were not expected to take on men-of-war, only ships of their own class. Indeed, it would be a violation of the etiquette of war—even for the French!—for a battleship to fire upon a frigate unless first fired upon. *Diana*'s role in the battle would be to stay out of the fight, keep the enemy under constant observation, repeat signals, assist disabled ships, and take possession of captured enemies.

This role of support and communication was quite suitable to the cautious Captain Singh, though grating on Captain Fox . . . but, as all acknowledged, *Diana* was Captain Singh's ship.

Fox, for his part, was recovering well under the treatments prescribed by Dr. Barry, assiduously applied by Lady Corey under Withers's direction. Though his forearm was now quite shockingly scarred, the skin twisted and bright red, the bleeding and suppuration had passed and he wore the scar as a badge of honor. "I will repay this injury to Napoleon a thousand-fold," he swore upon several occasions.

Nelson had generously provided *Diana* with food, water, gunpowder, cordage, and a few experienced crew—a surgeon, a signal officer, a master gunner, and a half-dozen Marine sharpshooters—to fill positions necessary for a fleet action. All other functions were performed by Dianas, Touchstones, and Venusians, and under Singh's and Fox's guidance they trained and trained until they were an effectual fighting force. The Venusians, to Arabella's surprise, proved surprisingly adept at gunnery, and soon eight of the twelve guns were entirely crewed by them. The Venusians in the waist also rose grandly to the occasion, and she and they soon worked out a lingua franca through which they could communicate effectively.

Finally came a day when Venus loomed as large as a dinner-plate held at arm's length, the swirling gray of her eternal clouds plainly visible even though the sun was behind her. Captain Singh, returning from one of his regular meetings with the admiral, called his officers, plus Ulungugga representing the Venusians and Mills and Arabella as translators, together in his great cabin.

Arabella was now attired as an ordinary airman, in clothing obtained from the English fleet. The fine dress loaned to her by Nelson she had returned, with thanks, saying that as she would be required to participate in any action as translator for the Venusians, she would be happier and safer—and, indeed, her modesty better protected—in trousers rather than a dress. Every one knew that she was a woman, of course, even as they had when she had been costumed as "Cesario," but there was a tacit agreement among all the men to disregard the shameful display of her lower limbs. Lady Corey had merely sighed and said, "I suppose I must simply refrain from regarding you below the neck."

"We expect to encounter the French fleet within the next day," Captain Singh reported. "Lord Nelson has devised a novel, and he hopes unexpected, strategy for the attack."

From his writing-desk drawer Captain Singh drew two sheets of letter paper and placed them in the air, parallel to each other and about one foot apart. "As you know, aerial fleets maintain this type of planar formation—the English in a square grid, the French in a hexagonal one—for ease of communication and coordination between the ships." The planar formation, Arabella explained to Ulungugga, allowed each fleet's ships to view flag signals from their allies up, down, and to either side while moving and firing forward at the enemy.

"In a typical large fleet action, the two fleets approach each other thus"—the captain pushed the two sheets together until they were about an inch apart, still parallel—"and they simply fire upon each other until one fleet or the other is vanquished." He then took one of the two sheets away, leaving the other hanging in the air, and tore it neatly in half. "Lord Nelson proposes to divide our fleet in two and approach the French fleet thus." He held the two half-sheets in his two hands and moved them toward the remaining whole sheet in a perpendicular fashion, torn edges first. The torn edges touched the whole sheet in two lines. "In this way we will cut the French fleet in three unequal parts, separating the smaller central section—we assume *Victoire* will be in the center—from the support of its flanks. Once the French fleet has been divided and disordered, our ships will engage theirs one to one; in individual ship-to-ship action Nelson is confident the English, with our superior ship-handling skills, will inevitably prevail."

"That's all well and good," said Stross, "but if we are all in two planes nose-to-tail, pedaling toward the French, only our lead ships can fire on the enemy, while the French can cut the whole fleet to ribbons with fire from the sides."

Captain Singh nodded. "Nelson is well aware of this. The plan is to drive hard at the French, putting every available hand at the pedals, and overwhelm them with speed. The French airmen are not nearly so well trained as the English and they will be unlikely to hit a fast-moving target. Then, as the English fleet approaches the French, we will shift crew from the pedals to the great guns and pivot left or right to fire upon the French ships' flanks. Again, superior English ship-handling skills will make the difference."

Fox appeared skeptical. "The Venusians are prodigious at the pedals, and their gunnery is improving, but I'd be lying if I said I thought *our* ship-handling skills were up to naval standard."

"Agreed. But we will be serving a supporting role—not in the thick of the battle."

"We hope."

Captain Singh inclined his head. "We do indeed."

Suddenly a voice interrupted from without. It was Watson's

high clear call: "Sail ho! Sail ho! Forty sail of ship! Hexagonal formation!"

Every one in the great cabin looked at each other, then to Captain Singh.

Captain Singh did not even blink. "We shall beat to quarters, Mr. Fox," he said with calm resolve.

"Beat to quarters!" Fox bellowed.

But before the drums could even begin to sound, Arabella had already sprung for the door—headed for her action station in the waist.

24

THE BATTLE OF VENUS

Arabella came out on deck to see the French fleet spread across the face of Venus, a hexagonal array of white flecks against the clouds, as tidily ordered as any honey-comb. There was no sign, from here, of French inferiority in ship-handling.

"Action stations!" she cried to the Venusians in the waist, though technically she should wait for Faunt to issue the command first. But Faunt, when he appeared, raised no objection to this usurpation, centering his attention instead upon chivvying his Venusians into proper order. Arabella did her part as well, shouting and pointing and occasionally physically propelling Venusians into position as they worked to maneuver *Diana* to her assigned station, just beyond the English fleet's eastern plane.

Meanwhile, above in the main-top, Mills and *his* Venusians leapt back and forth from mast to yard like spring *tokla*, setting sails, adjusting lines, and keeping the ship in trim. She envied him his physical as well as his linguistic skills, and strove to emulate him. Also in the main-top, like unexpected fruit, Arabella saw the red coats of the Marine sharpshooters, their long rifles ready to bring down French officers if the opportunity presented.

During the very occasional pauses in her efforts, Arabella looked out at the awe-inspiring sight of the English fleet re-forming itself from one great plane into two smaller ones. Never before had she seen so many ships maneuvering in space—pulsers whirling, sails flashing out, the sun glinting from their pristine copper bottoms—and all was done with such grace and precision that she was filled with English pride.

The whole operation was carried out in what seemed near silence, with only the occasional shout or the crack of a signal-gun being audible over the distance between herself and the fleet. Most of the communication between ships was carried out using colored signal-flags, a military code recently devised by a man called Popham, intended to be clear and unambiguous yet unintelligible to the enemy.

As no one aboard *Diana* understood this military code, she had been assigned a signal officer, a thin and spotty midshipman named Midgeley who, despite his youth, seemed entirely at ease with the complex system of colored flags. In addition to a small chest of flags and a fine telescope, he had brought with him a code-book, which he had orders to destroy in case the ship was captured. Midgeley took this last order very seriously; the code-book's cover was impregnated with pungent chemicals, and he carried at all times a small glass vial of sulfuric acid which would cause the cover to ignite. He had said, quite seriously, that he would sacrifice his own life if necessary to prevent the book from falling into enemy hands.

"Signal from the flagship, sir!" Midgeley reported to Captain Singh at one point while Arabella was taking a very brief respite near the quarterdeck. He handed the captain a slip of paper.

Captain Singh read the message, then nodded and handed it back. "Very good, Mr. Midgeley. Repeat the signal." The repeti-

tion of signals from the flagship was one of *Diana*'s most important duties during battle—flying outside the main fleet's formation
as she was, she would be visible to every warship in the plane.

"Aye aye, sir." At once Midgeley sprang to the mainmast, where
he raised signal flags in groups of two or three to the mast-head,
spelling out the message to the other ships.

As Midgeley was hoisting the signal, Captain Singh shot from
his station near the wheel to the forward rail of the quarterdeck,
stopped himself there with one hand on the rail, and called out in
his clear penetrating voice, "Attention all hands! I have a message
from Admiral Lord Nelson!"

At the name "Nelson," every man aboard instantly paused in
his labors and fixed his attention upon the captain.

"The message reads: *England expects that every man will do his
duty.*"

The whole ship seemed to catch its breath then. Arabella felt it
too—the great trust which Nelson was placing in all of them to
win through in the coming battle. It was a great responsibility,
and a humbling confidence, and it made her heart swell with
pride.

"Hip hip!" cried Fox.

"Huzzay!" responded every one in a full-throated roar, Arabella not least among them.

"Hip hip!"

"*Huzzay!*"

"Hip hip!"

"*HUZZAY!*"

As the echoes of the last "Huzzay" drifted away, Captain Singh
stood tall and proud at the forward rail, hands behind his back, as
firm and straight as though he stood in gravity. "I have every confidence in you. You have trained hard and well, and now you are
ready to put that training into effect. Now take your stations, and
make ready for action."

"Aye aye, sir!" chorused the entire crew.

Arabella smiled and turned away from her captain . . .

. . . and looked into the upturned, shining, and very much confused eyes of the Venusian waisters.

She tried to convey the captain's sentiments to them, but the best she could manage in their shipboard lingua franca—"we will now all raise the mast together"—was not only entirely inadequate but actually confusing, as there was no mast in sight to be raised. She turned to Ulungugga, whose understanding of English was the best of all of them—not that this was saying very much—and begged his assistance with words, gestures, and facial expressions.

Ulungugga, after a time, raised his chin in acknowledgement and turned to his people, delivering a gurgling peroration which raised a strong response of hand-clapping, slapping of feet upon the deck, and enthusiastic croaks. "What did you tell them?" she asked.

It took them a bit to work out a translation, but at last she understood him to have said something along the lines of "Tadpoles that swim together will survive and form a mated clutch."

Arabella swallowed, then said, "I could not have said it better myself."

Fox bellowed a command from the quarterdeck then, and Faunt called out "Let go the halyards and clew down!" Arabella translated this into Wagala, and the Venusians immediately leapt to comply.

———————

Swiftly Venus grew before them, and the French fleet with it. The whole ship thrummed with energy, three-quarters or more of the crew being vigorously engaged at the pedals, and the artificial wind of the pulsers was so strong that Arabella, even in the somewhat protected waist of the ship, was forced to hold her hat on with one hand. The *boom, boom, boom* of the drum that compelled the pedalers rang steady and fast beneath her feet, *Diana*'s great beating heart.

The English fleet drove forward along with them, two parallel planes of mighty ships in a precise square arrangement. Their great speed was made visible by the whirling blur of their pulsers and the way the pennants at their mast-heads streamed out behind. Unlike their previous formation, though, this time the ships were aligned with their keels and mainmasts in the plane, "nose to tail" as Stross had said, and Arabella realized how important *Diana*'s role in repeating signals would be, for the fleet's own sails and pulsers blocked their view to fore and aft.

Soon the French ships could be made out with the naked eye, six-masted first-rates most of them, each carrying eighteen great guns or more. Their hexagonal formation stretched across the sky now, too big for the eye to take in all at once. And there, in the very center . . . *Victoire.*

There was no mistaking the armored ship as any thing else. She gleamed all over, bright silver rather than copper and wood, and she loomed broader of beam and deeper of keel than any other ship in the fleet. During a break in the action Arabella borrowed a glass and saw with her own eyes the twenty-four gaping gun-ports arranged about her figurehead, which appeared to her to be a figure of Napoleon himself, costumed as a Roman emperor and holding aloft a scepter. The iron-clad prow beneath that figurehead, sharp and shining, cleaved the air like an axe-blade. And amidships, four round turrets like the towers of a castle housed her swivel-guns—each one larger than *Diana*'s original three cannon!

Suddenly a distant *bang* of cannon rang out from Arabella's left, and she scanned her glass in that direction to see smoke rolling from one of the French ships. This was followed by another and another, and she tensed, awaiting an incoming ball. But though long minutes passed, not even the whine of a ball sailing by reached Arabella's ears. "They're wasting their powder," Faunt muttered. "We're too far, moving too fast, for them to hit."

Signal-flags flashed out upon the flagship's mainmast then, and as Midgeley repeated the signal, Fox called, "Ease off pulsers two points!" The rest of the fleet, too, was slowing, as men moved from the pulsers to the gun decks in preparation for battle. Soon the ships began to pitch and yaw as well, each turning to the side, up, or down even as they retained their formation and continued to drive toward the enemy. Very soon, Arabella was certain, Nelson would give the signal to open fire and the French would begin to fall.

But *Victoire* was the first to speak.

Two dozen great lances of flame shot all at once from her gunports, followed by plumes of smoke. A moment later came the *boom*, loud even across this great distance, ringing low and deep like a giant banging on a huge iron box. And a moment after that . . . a splintering crash, and screaming, from closer by as the twenty-four ten-pound balls slammed into one of the English ships—*Tonnant*, she thought it was. The damaged ship's fast-whirling pulsers stuttered and slowed then, and two of her masts began to drift crazily askew. Soon she had fallen behind, tumbling out of control as the rest of the fleet continued to drive forward at nearly their maximum speed.

"Lucky shot," Faunt said through gritted teeth. Fox then called a command, causing Faunt to order "Slack halyard! Haul braces and sheets!"

Arabella was soon too busy with translating, and hauling on her own lines, to pay much attention to the battle. But every time she could spare a moment to look up, she saw death and destruction.

The English fleet was firing now, rapidly and in excellent unison, and the French ships were taking significant damage. One French ship exploded in an enormous sphere of flame—its pale color and the rapidity of its growth reminded her of the death of her own little balloon, and she knew the ship's hydrogen stores had gone up. But for every English ball that struck a French ship, two or three of *Victoire*'s found their targets in English wood and flesh. The sounds of shattering *khoresh*-wood and the hoarse screams of wounded airmen filled the air all around.

Plainly Napoleon had put his very best gunners aboard *Victoire*. Every single broadside seemed to do serious damage to the English fleet, and her powerful swivel-guns proved deadly, picking off English pulsers and mainmasts in every direction. She also moved far more nimbly than she had any right to; clearly Fulton's improved propulsive sails and other innovations more than made up for her great weight.

Victoire herself, though she was the target of many an English broadside, sailed placidly through the hail of cannon-balls; they glanced off her armored sides as harmlessly as a sand-storm off a *shtokara*'s thick shell. As near as Arabella could tell, the French flagship had taken no damage whatsoever, despite Nelson's concentration of fire upon her. And every English ship that tried to get behind her, to her vulnerable stern, was swiftly disabled by her rapacious swivel-guns.

Nelson's strategy had succeeded—it had separated the French flagship from the support of her flanks. But it had not accounted for the deadliness of *Victoire* herself.

"Signal from the flagship!" Midgeley called from the mainmast head. "*Engage the enemy more closely!*"

"Repeat that signal!" Captain Singh called back, then ordered Fox to comply.

Diana, of course, did not engage the enemy directly, nor was she attacked; she enjoyed a frigate's immunity, so long as she did not herself fire upon the French. But as the English ships moved in close, hammering the French with their great guns and being hammered in turn, *Diana* too found herself in the thick of the battle: repeating signals through the smoke, reporting her own observations to the flagship, and occasionally even towing a disabled ship, whose pulsers or masts had been shot away, out of immediate danger. Aadim's help, Arabella knew, was invaluable to Captain Singh in maneuvering through the chaos.

Smoke swirled everywhere, sometimes reducing visibility to just a few cables' length, and every thing stank of gunpowder and char and blood. The boom of great guns, shrieks of cannon-balls through the air, crash of shattered wood, and moans of injured men came from every direction, English and French mixed indistinguishably together. Two or three balls even struck *Diana*, sailing in without warning from out of the smoke, but these were plainly not deliberate and had come from some distance away; the blows were glancing and did little damage.

Suddenly Fox shouted out a series of unexpected commands, bringing *Diana* hard about and calling all available hands to the pedals. Arabella was immediately swamped with Faunt's orders, raising and lowering sails and canting yards to accomplish the course change with great haste. Clearly something significant had happened, but what?

A moment later the answer began to come clear, as a rapid series of cannon blasts sounded from the smoke in front of them, accompanied by flashes of flame. From the sound and what little she could see, it seemed to Arabella that two great ships must be pounding each other severely, shot after shot slamming in both directions, at close range, with relentless, disordered haste.

Then, as they drew nearer the melee, a gust of wind blew the smoke clear for a moment, and Arabella saw that the two combatants were very great ships indeed: *Victoire* to sunward, and *Bucephalus* to skyward. They stood very close, their figureheads practically touching, both ships' great guns and swivel-guns and stern-chasers flashing with fiendish rapidity, hammering each other with hot metal.

It was a horrific and amazing sight.

The noise alone seemed sufficient to kill, and the stench of powder and blood was inescapable.

And *Bucephalus* was losing. Losing very badly.

Her pulsers were a wreck, completely incapable of turning. Three of her six masts had been shot away completely, and two of the others were shattered. Her sails were in tatters, her deck torn to splinters, and so much blood hung in the air that in places it seemed a red fog. Yet, gamely, she fought on, firing every remaining gun again and again and again.

Victoire, for her part, seemed nearly undamaged, with both pulsers still intact and only one mast broken. Her sails were torn, and her armored hull was stained and dented, but by comparison with Nelson's flagship she was almost completely whole. All four of her mighty swivel-guns pounded *Bucephalus* relentlessly.

Bucephalus's return fire was diminishing, and appeared to have little effect despite the close range. The ships stood nose-to-nose, and the only part of *Victoire* that was at all vulnerable was the space between her dual pulsers. But the only way to attack that space would be to get behind her, and between the power of her guns and her surprising maneuverability no English ship seemed capable of that.

"Make way!" came a voice from behind Arabella. It was Gowse, gleaming with sweat and eyes red from the smoke—she supposed that she herself must look little better—swinging a weighted line over his head. He let it fly, and it sailed across the space between *Diana* and *Bucephalus*, where a man on the quarterdeck caught it and began hauling away. The light line soon pulled across a heavier line, which *Bucephalus* made fast to her capstan.

"Idlers and waisters to the pulsers!" shouted Fox. "Back pulsers! Smartly, now!"

Arabella, Faunt, and the Venusians immediately scrambled belowdecks, where they sorted themselves into the available seats in a mad rush. Lady Corey was there as well—as her action station was in the cockpit, assisting the Navy surgeon, she was considered an "idler"—but neither of them had any time or breath for conversation, engaged as they all were in pedaling with every ounce of strength to haul the disabled *Bucephalus* away from *Victoire*. *Diana*'s timbers groaned from the strain, but soon Arabella felt the joined ships begin to shift. Arabella grinned fiercely and pedaled still harder. The flagship could yet be saved!

And then there came a crash, and a jerk, and suddenly *Diana* was tumbling—tumbling backward, away from *Bucephalus*. Cries of dismay, and more distant cries of triumph, sounded from abovedecks.

"Waisters to action stations!" came Fox's voice through the scuttle. Arabella, Faunt, and the Venusians returned abovedecks to manage the sails . . . and saw a horrific sight. *Bucephalus* hung in the air above, torn quite in two, with men and barrels and coal spilling from both broken ends. The *crack* of small-arms fire sounded from *Victoire*'s tops; floating bodies jerked as the bullets struck them.

"Bear a hand, man!" Faunt shouted in her face, and Arabella realized that she had been hanging stupidly in the air, stunned and appalled by the carnage. She shook it off and forced herself to perform her duties.

"Vice-Admiral Collingwood signals from *Royal Sovereign*," Midgeley called down to the quarterdeck. "He is taking the flag and requests assistance!"

Arabella looked around. *Royal Sovereign* was not far away. She had already taken heavy damage; her pulsers still turned, but fitfully, and two masts hung broken. Coal drifted in a black cloud from a great rent in her hull.

Victoire, still appearing nearly undamaged, was turning swiftly to face the new flagship, plainly intending to do to her what she had just done to *Bucephalus*. But as she turned, Arabella saw that *Bucephalus* had not died in vain—before the end she had managed to destroy both of the swivel-guns on *Victoire*'s starboard side. The forward turret had blossomed outward like a huge, grotesque metal flower; the aft one was more intact, but smoke streamed from its ports and it stood silent and unmoving.

But, like Nelson himself, *Victoire* might have lost an arm or two but she was still fighting. Both pulsers still turned, and she was driving hard toward the *Royal Sovereign*. Surely she would have no trouble bringing down that already-crippled ship, and once she had done so—having taken both the admiral and the vice-admiral out of action—the battle would surely be lost.

Still, the loss of two gun-turrets might be significant. Begging Faunt's leave, Arabella rushed aft to report her observation.

"Don't worry about us, girl!" Faunt called after her. "I've picked up a few words of their jabber!"

When Arabella arrived at the base of the quarterdeck ladder she found a vociferous argument in progress between Captain Singh and Lieutenant Cotterell, the master gunner who had come over to *Diana* from Nelson's fleet.

"*Victoire* will be past us in minutes!" Cotterell was shouting. His face was beet-red. "If we wait until she passes, then strike without warning—all twelve guns, right between her pulsers!— we might destroy her with a single broadside! It is England's last hope!"

The expression on Captain Singh's face was thunderous, and Fox's mien was no less displeased. "We have been treated fairly by the French," Captain Singh said. "They have respected our frigate's immunity. For a frigate to strike a ship of the line from behind, without herself first having been fired upon, would be an act without honor. I would never bring discredit upon the Honorable Mars Company—indeed, upon England herself!—with such a despicable, cowardly attack."

"Perhaps we could open hostilities with a shot across her bow," Fox offered. "That would make it a fair fight."

"And a short one!" Cotterell countered. "Once we've fired at that monster she'll be free to shoot back—and she'll blow us right out of the sky without even pausing!"

"If you please, sirs!" Arabella called up from the waist. "I have some information that may be of use!"

Cotterell, Fox, and Captain Singh all looked down from the quarterdeck. "Of course, Ashby," Captain Singh said, momentarily forgetting to call her "Mrs. Singh."

Arabella pushed off of the deck, caught herself on the quarterdeck's forward rail, and saluted. She quickly reported what she had seen, that *Bucephalus* had destroyed the swivel-guns on *Victoire*'s starboard side.

"If we approach her from that side . . ." Fox said, his eyes brightening.

"She'll just turn and demolish us with her great guns!" Cotterell interrupted. "You've seen how quickly she turns! It's those d—d pulsers of Fulton's!"

"Pulsers which *Diana* shares," Captain Singh mused. "We may be able to move faster than *Victoire* expects."

"Fast enough to get behind her—to her one vulnerable spot—before she destroys us?"

"Perhaps not," the captain acknowledged after a moment's thought.

"To strike from behind, without warning, is our last chance!" Cotterell gestured dramatically at *Victoire*, driving hard toward the crippled *Royal Sovereign*. "It is now, or never at all!"

Captain Singh did not respond at once, merely tapping his chin in concentration. His face showed that he was weighing three distasteful options: utter defeat, a dishonorable attack, or an honorable attack certain to fail.

If only there were some way to guarantee the success of such an attack . . . some stratagem, some maneuver . . .

"If you please, sirs," Arabella said again, nearly surprising herself.

Cotterell glared at Arabella, plainly *not* pleased by the interruption, but Captain Singh nodded acquiescence.

"While aboard *Touchstone*, I built a navigational calculator—a simple clockwork—and with it I worked out a maneuver which I believe may greatly improve our chances in an honorable fight."

"Who is this *girl*?" Cotterell sputtered.

"My wife," Captain Singh said. That shut Cotterell up.

"I do not recall you mentioning any such maneuver before," Fox commented drily.

"I . . . I did not share it with you at the time," Arabella admitted, her gaze dropping to her feet. "I did not wish to be . . . complicit in privateering. In any case, it proved unnecessary."

"Describe it," said Captain Singh.

"It . . . it is complicated. It involves simultaneous yaw, roll, and back pulsers, but it permits reversing the ship in just a few lengths. If, having opened battle honorably with a shot across *Victoire*'s bow, we drive in at our best speed along her damaged starboard side, we may be able to use this maneuver to strike at her pulsers before she can strike at us. I have the written sailing orders in my reticule." Then she realized an important consideration, and her spirits fell. "But they were created for *Touchstone*, a four-masted ship." *Diana*, of course, had only three masts, and many aspects of the maneuver, such as setting two masts' sails hard a-larboard while simultaneously sheeting home the other two, could not be executed with three.

Fox glanced at *Victoire*, which had already drawn nearly abreast of their position. *Royal Sovereign* hung helpless directly in her path; no other English ships capable of moving under their own power were any where nearby. "Can you convert the orders to three masts in . . . five minutes?"

"No," Arabella admitted miserably. Without the help of the long-lost greenwood box, she doubted she could perform the conversion in five *hours*.

Captain Singh looked directly at her. "Can Aadim?"

Arabella looked back, feeling her jaw sag open. *Could* Aadim? "Perhaps."

The captain's gaze turned upward, to where *Victoire* gleamed nearly undamaged. "I will move *Diana* into position for an honorable battle. If you can perform the conversion before *Victoire* opens fire upon *Royal Sovereign*, we will use your maneuver. Otherwise we will proceed without it."

An action which would almost certainly result in *Diana*'s destruction and England's defeat. "I understand, sir."

"Five minutes," Fox repeated.

"Aye aye, sir," Arabella said. She saluted, reversed herself in the air, and dove toward the great cabin.

25

ARABELLA'S MANEUVER

The great cabin, when she reached it, was a shambles. One of the cabinets had come open during *Diana*'s recent violent maneuvers, and papers, pens, and inkwells drifted everywhere. She slammed the cabin door behind herself to prevent any of the objects from escaping and causing havoc in the rest of the ship, then batted her way through them to reach her duffel-bag, which was stuffed in one of the cabin's upper corners. Flinging the duffel's contents every which way, she quickly located her battered reticule, and from it extracted a torn, stained, and much-folded paper bearing the sailing-order she had worked out so many months ago aboard *Touchstone*.

"Aha!" she cried in triumph, then worked her way through the drifting papers to Aadim, who sat ticking quietly and staring straight ahead as always. Quickly she threw open the doors on the front of his cabinet, exposing the full array of levers, dials, and knobs through which he could be directed . . .

. . . and stared stupidly at them. There was simply no means to specify the problem in sufficient detail for Aadim to produce an equivalent solution for three masts. It had taken many, many hours of trial and error, going over the same basic idea time after time after time with very slight variations, to produce the maneuver she now clutched in her sweating hand. To expect even the marvelous Aadim to do the same in five minutes or less was clearly an impossibility.

Nonetheless she must attempt it.

Clutching the paper in her teeth, referring to it frequently, she set Aadim's dials and levers as best she could. But the maneuver was so unusual, indeed unprecedented, that even her best was inadequate—the controls simply could not represent the maneuver she required. She knew without a doubt that if she pressed Aadim's finger upon the chart right now, with the levers set as they were, Aadim would give her nothing but a very simple looping path which any competent French gunner could easily predict.

She hesitated, with her sweating finger resting upon Aadim's cool wooden one. What she asked of him was far beyond any automaton, even an astonishingly sophisticated one.

But then, Aadim was not just any automaton.

"We desperately need your help," she said aloud, looking directly into Aadim's unseeing green glass eyes. She swept away the chart of Venus's airlanes which was clipped to his desk—a space which lay in the view of at least three of Aadim's lenses, scattered about the cabin—and replaced it with her own written sailing-order. "We need a course that drives hard along *Victoire*'s starboard side, then yaws and rolls simultaneously while reversing pulsers. The goal is to turn the ship about in as small a space as possible, to put us in position to fire the great guns at the enemy's pulsers. We have less than five minutes." She paused, swallowed, then said in a small voice, "Please do your best."

Then she closed her eyes, held her breath, and pressed down upon Aadim's finger.

A click sounded from deep within his cabinet, followed by a high-pitched grinding whir she had never before heard from him. It sounded as though his gears were turning far faster than they ever had before—faster, indeed, than they had been designed to withstand. A smell of hot metal and whale-oil came to her nose, and Aadim's wooden torso and arms vibrated as though from an ague. But his face—his lovely face, carefully carved and delicately painted in a marvelous approximation of life—remained as impassive as ever.

After an endless time, which was probably less than two minutes, the bell sounded, and Arabella bent in the air to read the result from Aadim's instruments.

The sailing-order represented by the dials and number-wheels there seemed at first to be completely incoherent, and Arabella's heart sank. Nonetheless, she snatched a scrap of paper and a lead pencil from the drifting detritus and scrawled it down. As her pencil flew, she pictured each specified turn of sails and pulsers in her mind, feeling the flow of air along the imagined ship as though along her own body . . . and it began to make a certain kind of sense. Though each individual action seemed arbitrary and aimless, she could feel a sort of flow in the whole. This sailing-order was unprecedented, bizarre, and incomprehensible, but somehow she knew that it would work as requested.

She finished transcribing it and examined her work. Her rapid scrawls were horrifically slipshod, but legible enough, and as near as she could tell they accurately recorded the sailing-order Aadim had invented. That the two of them, she reflected, had invented together, with the help of the greenwood box.

Suddenly, impulsively, she grabbed Aadim's shoulders and kissed him upon his wooden lips. He did not react in the slightest. "Thank you," she said, and sprang to the door.

When Arabella came on deck she found that *Diana* had matched course and speed with *Victoire,* moving ahead of the French ship as both drew nearer *Royal Sovereign.* The crippled English flagship now lay dead ahead, nearly within cannon range, while *Victoire* hung above *Diana*'s stern like some huge, gleaming, malevolent moon. The thought of those twenty-four great guns trained on *Diana*'s pulsers, with only the etiquette of frigate's immunity as a shield, sent a chill down Arabella's spine. If the French captain chose to disregard what was, after all, little more than a gentleman's agreement, he could destroy *Diana* with impunity at any time, perhaps the moment she showed the slightest sign of turning to attack.

She shook off her presentiment of disaster and ascended to the quarterdeck, where she presented the sailing-order to Captain Singh. Fox, nearby, craned his neck for a better look at the paper but did not shift from his station.

For a long minute the captain studied the paper, and Arabella began to fear that he would reject it out of hand. "This is . . . extraordinary," he finally said. "What combination of settings—?"

"If we are going to attack," Fox interrupted, speaking low as though *Victoire*'s captain might hear him otherwise—which might indeed be the case, so close were the two ships to each other— "we had best begin our turn now."

Never had Arabella seen Captain Singh so uncertain.

"In answer to your question," she said, "I simply asked Aadim to do his best."

At that the captain's jaw firmed with decisiveness, while at the same time his eyes softened with warm sentiment—an extraordinary expression she had never before seen on any human face. "Put some distance between us and *Victoire,* Mr. Fox," he said, "but do not reveal our full capabilities as regards speed. Keep us on her starboard side. When we are in position to attack, turn and put one shot across her bow, then immediately employ this maneuver at maximum speed." He handed the paper over to Fox. "It should put us into position for a solid broadside on the vulnerable spot between her pulsers."

"Pulsers ahead! Cheerly, now!" Fox bellowed. Only then did he read what was written on the paper.

"You will remain here," Captain Singh said to Arabella as the ship surged ahead beneath them. "Your navigational services may be required."

"Aye aye, sir."

Fox's eyes widened as he read the paper. He kept reading. His eyes widened further. "Sir?" he inquired, looking up with raised eyebrows.

"You will follow the sailing-order exactly as written."

"Aye aye, sir." He did not seem persuaded, but he turned to Cotterell. "Ready one bow-chaser to fire a shot across the enemy's bow, and the great guns to fire a broadside targeted between the enemy's pulsers, each at my command."

"Aye aye, sir," Cotterell said to Fox, then shouted, "All gun crews, action stations!" As half the men on deck crowded down the forward ladder, he saluted Captain Singh. "It has been a privilege, sir."

"Make that broadside count," Captain Singh said, returning Cotterell's salute. "We will be unlikely to have an opportunity for a second shot."

"I will do my best, sir." Then he departed, following his crews to the gun deck.

Captain Singh straightened and placed his hands behind his back. "We are committed now," he said.

So quietly did he speak that Arabella was not certain whether he was addressing her, or only himself.

Diana pulled gradually ahead of *Victoire,* though Arabella could feel by the thrum of the deck beneath her feet that the men at the pulsers were not exerting themselves to their utmost. The deck seemed remarkably deserted, with almost every man at the pulsers, the guns, or aloft in the rigging; only a few waisters dashed here and there, keeping the lower sails on the mainmast in trim. The sounds of combat all around seemed to be dying away—were the other ship-to-ship battles playing themselves out, or was it merely Arabella's concentration upon the immediate action to come? She could not say.

Brindle brought up a harness for Arabella—a leather belt with stout straps, ending in hooks, which she used to fasten herself to the quarterdeck. Now she, like Fox and Singh, stood with her feet pressed to the deck as though by gravity, secure against even the most vigorous maneuvers. The maneuver upon the sheet, she knew, would be vigorous in the extreme.

In the tops, the Marines readied their rifles.

Arabella kept glancing between *Royal Sovereign* ahead and *Victoire* behind. *Diana* must get well ahead of the French ship, so as to build up speed for her final pass, but not so far ahead that *Victoire* would have time to fire upon her during her run; yet she must attack *Victoire* before *Victoire* could fire upon *Royal Sovereign.* It was a delicate balance, and Arabella could not tell what the proper distance might be.

Captain Singh, though, could. "You may begin your turn," he said quietly to Fox.

Arabella's mouth suddenly went dry.

"Strike the jib!" Fox cried. "Brace all up on a larboard tack! Ready the bow-chaser!"

Majestically *Diana* turned, looping around until she had completely reversed herself and faced *Victoire* nose-to-nose . . . close enough that Arabella could see airmen milling about on the French flagship's deck. What were they thinking of *Diana*'s actions? Would the French captain fire upon her before she could attack, or would honor stay his hand?

Captain Singh drew himself up straight.

He looked down the length of the deck, up into the mainmast rigging, down to the port and starboard masts. His eyes missed nothing.

He paused, considering.

Then he took a breath, turned to Fox, and spoke one single word: "Attack."

"Pulsers ahead! Smartly, now!" Fox bellowed. "Fire bow-chaser!"

Diana leapt forward with a great surge that pressed Arabella firmly against her harness. Simultaneously, with a ringing *bang*, the bow-chaser sent a single shot speeding across the air ahead of *Victoire*'s bow.

Victoire was far from unprepared for this eventuality; she reacted instantaneously, firing her great guns with an ear-shattering *boom*. The French ship vanished behind a cloud of fire and flame; a moment later a flight of cannon-balls shrieked through the air . . .

. . . and the shriek passed well abaft of *Diana*'s quarterdeck! The great effort of the men at the pedals, combined with the unexpected advantage of Fulton's improved propulsive sails, had given her a burst of speed that *Victoire*'s gunners had not anticipated.

They would not be so lucky again. And *Victoire* could fire a broadside every hundred seconds.

But in less than half a minute, still driving forward at the maximum speed of the Honorable Mars Company's very swiftest ship, they were alongside *Victoire*—too far aft for her great guns, and on the starboard side where her swivel-guns no longer functioned.

Victoire did her best to turn and follow, but though she was nimble for her size and weight, she was not *that* nimble.

Snipers in *Victoire*'s tops, and a few small bow- and stern-chasers, fired upon *Diana* as she passed, but the damage was minimal.

Diana kept pushing ahead at her best speed, and soon came abreast of *Victoire*'s churning dual pulsers. As soon as she did, Fox, who had been studying Arabella's paper for the last few minutes, began calling out the apparently irrational commands which Aadim had devised. "Back pulsers! Set the jib! Strike the spanker!" he cried, and "Sheet home main royals and courses!" and "Brace larboard-t'gallants up on a starboard tack!" and other such nonsense. Though the individual words made sense, they had likely never before ever been uttered in these combinations on any working ship, either in the air or at sea, in all of human history.

But though Fox's commands seemed pointless, *Diana*'s gallant airmen—including, Arabella was proud to note, the Venusian waisters she had helped to train—obeyed them with swift precision. And with the ship's rapid passage through the air, the peculiar shape of the sails soon sent her into a tumble—a wild, whirling tumble, corkscrewing through the air while simultaneously turning her bow to starboard.

It was a dizzying, disorienting maneuver, and seeing and feeling the sun and sky and smoke and wrecked ships spin about so crazily gave Arabella's stomach fits. It seemed to go on for ever—though it was really less than a minute—but it did eventually end, and at the end of it they were facing *Victoire*'s spinning pulsers at nearly point-blank range.

"Fire!" cried Captain Singh.

The command was immediately repeated down the length of the ship—Fox to Cotterell to Gowse and the other gun-captains—and in a moment a terrific *boom* erupted from her bow as all twelve great guns fired in perfect unison, sending the whole ship jolting backward beneath Arabella's feet.

Fastened to the deck as it was, her leather belt jerked hard at her stomach, driving the wind out of her with a *whuff.* Singh and Fox, having more experience in action, rolled with the blow and were not so discomfited.

But even they were not prepared for the second blow that followed, as *Victoire*'s hydrogen stores exploded, sending a gigantic blast of sound, flame, and scorching heat rushing across *Diana*'s deck. It passed in a moment, but left chaos in its wake—sails and rigging scorched and smoking, men crying out in surprise and pain, others calling pitifully from the open air where they had been blown overboard. Even worse was the wave of wreckage that followed, a deadly hail of wood and metal fragments that sent every one ducking for cover. Arabella shrieked and curled into a ball, feeling her back and arms pelted by sharp hot metal bits that left her shirt in smoking tatters.

When the rain of metal subsided and she looked up, she saw that *Victoire* had vanished completely, replaced by an expanding ball of smoke and flaming wreckage. Though most of the smallest, fastest-moving pieces had already passed *Diana*, many larger ones were still heading in her direction, and though they were slower their speed was still considerable. The smell of burnt wood, powder, and flesh was strong and nauseating, and her ears, still ringing from the explosion, were filled with screams and the crashes of pieces of wreckage colliding with each other.

Even in the midst of this chaos, a shriek from the mainmast head was so horrible that it drew Arabella's attention. It was Midgeley, the young signal officer: one of the larger metal fragments had struck him in the chest. The injury did not seem nearly bad enough to justify the intensity of his screams, until she realized that the spreading dark patch on his blue uniform jacket was not blood but sulfuric acid! The bit of wreckage must have broken the bottle of acid which he carried in case it should become necessary to destroy his code-book.

Midgeley tumbled in the air, clawing at the spreading stain, which smoked and blackened as though his body were burning from within—and screaming as though that were the case as well. No one nearby was able to help him, concerned as they were with their own injuries and safety.

Captain Singh, horrified at the gallant young midshipman's pain, unhooked himself from his harness and sprang directly to the mainmast head, sailing unconcerned past flying chunks of twisted metal. "Alert the surgeon!" he called down to Fox as he took the young man in his arms. "Tell him I am bringing an acid burn to him."

"Aye aye, sir!" Fox called, then shouted the captain's message down the scupper to the cockpit.

"The code-book!" Midgeley cried through his pain. "The code-book!"

"Ashby!" Captain Singh called to Arabella. "Find the code-book and secure it. I will take Mr. Midgeley to the surgeon. Mr. Fox, the ship is yours. Bring her out of danger as swiftly as you may."

"Aye aye!" Arabella and Fox replied in chorus.

Arabella, not so confident as her captain, made her way by short leaps to the base of the mainmast, then up its length. She found herself frequently compelled to pause, dodge, and backtrack in order to avoid the large smoldering hunks of wood and metal which were now crashing into the ship; they were less frequent and slower than the initial blast of small pieces, but those that did strike still struck with deadly force. She hoped that Fox would be able to bring the ship out of the area of wreckage soon.

Eventually she came to the mast-head, where she found Midgeley's code-book and telescope tucked safely into the gap between the trestle-tree and the mast. She had feared that the code-book's chemical-soaked cover might have ignited from the heat of *Victoire*'s explosion, but though it smoked slightly and stank still more than it had before it seemed intact. She did not open the book, but tucked it under her arm.

Before returning to the quarterdeck she thought to use Midgeley's telescope to look around, in case there might be some obstacle nearby which could be seen from this vantage and not from the deck. But even as she extended the glass and raised it to her eye, her attention was drawn by a most peculiar sound from the quarterdeck below. Quite unlike the sounds of pain and despair coming from the wounded men all around, this was a sound of *anger*—an animal growl like an enraged bear.

She shifted her glass to the source of the sound. It was Fox, who was holding his own glass to his eye with one hand, aimed forward; the other hand was clenched in a trembling fist. To her surprise he flung the telescope from himself, sending it tumbling away with the rest of the detritus, and called through the scuttle "Pulsers ahead! Smartly, you b—ds!" Then he leapt to the wheel and turned it hard to starboard.

What in all the worlds could he possibly have in mind? To drive *Diana* forward into the thick of the flying wreckage? Arabella turned her own glass forward, seeking whatever Fox had seen to prompt this behavior.

She did not find it at first. But suddenly a bit of deliberate movement, quite different from the drifting, colliding pieces of flotsam that otherwise filled her view, caught her eye.

It was a gig—a small, lightweight airship—moving swiftly away from the largest chunk of *Victoire*. Its destination seemed to be another French ship, not very far away and still fairly intact. Four French airmen labored at its pedals, directed by an officer in a torn and charred jacket; two midshipmen manned the sails. The gig also carried three passengers, who were not engaged in running the boat. One of them looked like . . .

No. It could not possibly be.

Arabella focused her telescope and peered hard through the detritus-strewn air. Could it be?

It was.

Napoleon!

He had been aboard *Victoire*, yet somehow had survived her destruction. And the two other passengers . . . yes, they were Fulton and Fouché!

Arabella hoped that the young empress Marie Louise was safe back on Venus rather than blown to bits with *Victoire*.

But she could spare no further attention for Marie Louise, as a bang and a crash sounded from below, together with a shudder that ran up the length of the mast and nearly flung Arabella away into the crowded air.

The bang had come from the quarterdeck, where Fox had moved to one of the two stern-chasers—small swivel-guns mounted to the taffrail—and fired it in the direction of the fleeing gig. The range was great, and there was much intervening wreckage, but still he fired, and fired again, and again.

The crash, meanwhile, was the sound of a large piece of wreckage slamming into *Diana*'s deck near the base of the mainmast. Other pieces, even larger and more dangerous, were approaching fast.

Arabella looked ahead. The ship was driving forward at full speed, ever deeper into the cloud of debris, and several more huge chunks of twisted metal were bearing down on her.

She shifted her gaze to Fox. He was still shooting at Napoleon, face twisted with rage, and had taken no notice of the danger into which the ship was heading.

"Ahoy the quarterdeck!" she called from the mast-head. "Flotsam ho!"

Fox did not acknowledge her hail. No one else was near him; the danger from flying debris had driven most of the other crew below for safety's sake.

"Captain Fox!" she shouted, at the top of her lungs. "Captain Fox!"

He did not respond, nor even look up. Either he had not heard, or did not choose to hear. He simply kept firing the stern-chaser, sending two-pound ball after two-pound ball sailing toward the fleeing Napoleon's tiny gig.

Arabella began making her way back to the deck, as quickly as she could. She was hampered by the code-book, heavy and awkward, and by the increasing number and size of fragments of *Victoire* that were filling the air. The men at the pedals belowdecks, unable to see the danger into which they were driving the ship, continued to pedal, following the last order Fox had given them. If the order were not countermanded, the ship would collide with the thickest part of the debris cloud and surely be wrecked.

"Captain Fox!" Arabella continued to cry as she descended the mainmast, dodging flying bits of wreckage, torn sails, and tangled lines. "Captain Fox!"

Then, just as she touched the deck, Captain Singh appeared from belowdecks. Leaping directly from the aft ladder to the quarterdeck and catching himself on the forward rail with one hand, he shouted some imprecation at Fox—Arabella could not make out exactly what he had said, but she had never before seen him so angry.

Fox, still enraged, became even more so at this interruption. He shouted back, something extremely rude, and continued firing at Napoleon.

Then a shadow passed across both men.

Arabella looked up. An enormous, twisted piece of metal was bearing down upon them at great speed. In mere moments it would strike the quarterdeck and smash both captains flat.

The two men had not noticed. They were still shouting at each other.

"Captains!" she cried, but neither of them took any notice.

Without thinking, she leapt—thrusting off the mainmast with the considerable might of legs strengthened by months of pedaling—and shot through the air, even as the wickedly edged chunk of wreckage drew rapidly nearer.

She collided with Captain Singh just before the debris fragment did, pushing him out from under the ragged metal even as it struck the *khoresh*-wood deck with a sickening, tearing crunch.

Sudden agony ripped through her leg.

Blackness.

26

VISITORS

Time passed. It was a dire time, full of fear and darkness and nausea; a sharp, bright pain and the dreadful sound of sawing; screams, moans, horrible smells—a nightmare from which she could not wake. But eventually the nightmare faded away, and she simply slept, without dreaming.

And then she awoke.

She lay in a hammock—a proper airman's hammock, clean and straight, laid out in the midshipmen's berth aboard *Diana*. Every thing about her told her that she was where she was meant to be, relaxed and calm, drifting comfortably in a state of free descent. She stretched luxuriantly and yawned.

"Welcome back, my dear."

Arabella turned her head to the voice—the familiar, warm voice of her captain—to see him smiling down at her. His cheeks seemed thin, but he was clean and tidy and attired in a fine civilian coat. "Thank you."

"Are you in any pain?"

She paused, attentive to her body. "No. Though my right boot is a bit too tight." She reached to loosen the laces, but his hand gently stopped and held hers before it reached her foot.

"It is not your boot."

"I . . . I am not sure what—" And then, suddenly, she knew perfectly well what, and the breath caught in her throat.

"Lie back and rest."

She ignored him, moving her feet beneath the hammock's light cover. The left toes were bare, and brushed lightly against the fabric. The right toes . . .

There were no right toes.

Her blood ran cold. "How much?" she asked, her teeth clenching and her hand squeezing her captain's hard as she stared into his face, willing him to honesty. "How much have I lost?"

"The right foot, just above the ankle. Nothing more. There is no infection, and the stump is healing very nicely. You have Dr. Barry to thank for this; he did what I am told is an excellent job. It certainly was very quick."

She went to throw back the covers and see what she had lost, but Captain Singh stopped her with a gentle touch, saying, "There will be time for that later."

She nodded, swallowing, but still she gently rubbed the truncated limb against the cover, feeling where it ended. The missing foot . . . the missing foot still felt as though it were there, somehow, yet she could see and feel that it was not. The stump moved disquietingly under the cloth like some small burrowing creature, not a part of her at all.

Arabella was not a vain girl, but the unexpected loss of a part of her body was still distressing. She and her brother would be like book-ends, she thought, clumping about on crutches together. Still, if Nelson could weather a missing arm, she supposed she could learn to cope with a missing foot.

"I have some sketches I would like to show you, when you are ready," the captain continued. "A prosthesis, with a clockwork mechanism to mimic the foot's natural spring. I am having some difficulty designing the trigger for action, and I hope you will have some ideas. In any case, it will not be needed until we make planetfall; the lack of one foot should not be much of an encumbrance in free descent."

"You are always so considerate," she said, and smiled. "Thank you."

"It is I who should be thanking you," he replied. He raised her hand and kissed it.

"For what?"

"For saving my life."

Arabella's throat tightened suddenly as she recalled descending ragged metal—smoke and wreckage everywhere—and a sudden desperate leap. "Fox!"

Captain Singh squeezed her hand again. "He survived." She relaxed the clenched grip which she had not even noticed herself applying to his hand. "Again, thanks to Dr. Barry. His injuries were more severe than yours, but Lady Corey has been diligent in his care and he is expected to recover nicely."

"Lady Corey?" Arabella raised one eyebrow and smiled.

"*Extremely* diligent." Captain Singh returned her smile. "And he has been *most* receptive to her care."

Lady Corey had been assiduous in her defense of Fox as a potential husband for Arabella; it should not be a surprise that she, a lonely widow after all, might seek him for herself. "I wish them both the very best."

"I am relieved at your reaction." He kissed her fingers again. "I had thought that there might be some . . . regret on your part."

"No." Now it was she who kissed his fingers. "There might have been some . . . uncertainty, at first." His eyes widened at that, and again she squeezed his hand. "But when the critical moment came . . . when you both were threatened and I was forced to choose without thinking . . . it was you to whom my heart went out, only you. And my body inevitably followed."

A little while later, a polite knock on a nearby stanchion caused them to break off their rather intimate embrace. It was Stross, whose expression was quite smug. Gowse, Faunt, and Mills were with him; they at least had the decency to look slightly embarrassed. "We heard you were awake," said Stross, "and wished to pay our respects and inquire as to your health. I see you are doing quite well."

"Quite well, sir," she said, straightening her chemise. "I am pleased to see that you all came through the battle in good health yourselves."

"Most all of us did," said Gowse. "Thanks to you, and that *amazing* maneuver ye worked out. That French monster would for sure have put an end to every mother's son of us elsewise. Though from all that spinning and tumbling, I nearly shot the cat . . ."

"Watch yer language," groused Faunt.

"And the Venusians?" Arabella asked Mills. "Did they all survive?"

"Yes," Mills replied, nodding slowly. "Every one. You should see them, ma'am. Swimming like guppies, in free descent. So happy to be free." He bent in the air so that his head was close to hers, and spoke quietly. "I am free too, now."

"How so?"

"I was slaver once. Then slave, then sailor, then airman . . . but never forgave myself. Now I have brought fifty slaves to freedom—paid back my debt." He placed a hand on his breast. "My heart rests."

"Mrs. Singh!" cried a happy voice. Arabella looked up to see Fox, heavily bandaged but with all his limbs intact, with his nightshirt floating about his feet. Lady Corey was with him, chiding him for leaving his bed without permission, but he hushed her with a gesture. His hand, Arabella noted, then rested briefly on her shoulder . . . and Lady Corey did not object to this intimacy.

"Mr. Fox," Arabella replied. "I am very pleased to see you."

"And I you!"

"It was a very close-run thing for all of us, to be sure." She allowed a degree of opprobrium to enter her voice, then, to show that she understood his actions had jeopardized all their lives.

"It is true that my pursuit of the tyrant Napoleon was rather . . . single-minded. But though I nearly died, and *Diana* was nearly wrecked, I regret nothing! For one of my little cannon-balls managed to disable the gig, and Napoleon and his men were captured. Oh, except Fouché; he was killed. And good riddance!" He rubbed his hands together.

"Has any one told you about Fulton yet?" Lady Corey asked.

"What about him?"

"He is meeting at this moment with the admiral." She gestured to the deck above, where the great cabin lay. "He has agreed to turn over all his designs to the Navy in exchange for leniency. The man is, to speak frankly, a filthy pig, but there is no doubt he is a mechanical genius, and his inventions will surely ensure that Britannia rules the airlanes for ever more!"

"Nelson is *here*?"

"Alas, no," said Captain Singh. "Lord Nelson survived the wreck of *Bucephalus*, but was shot by a French sniper afterward." Every one present bowed their heads in respect for the dead. "Dr. Barry deeply regrets that he was unable to save him. He did at least live long enough to know that we had won the battle."

"I am so sorry to hear this. If he had not destroyed those two swivel-gun turrets, we would never have been able to defeat *Victoire*. I wanted to thank him."

"Indeed. He is a great hero—possibly England's greatest hero ever—and he will be greatly missed."

"Aye," mumbled the assembled airmen, and Lady Corey as well.

"The admiral in question," Captain Singh continued after a respectful pause, "is Vice-Admiral Collingwood, now in charge of the fleet . . . or what is left of it. After the battle, *Diana* was the best and least damaged of the surviving ships and he transferred his flag here. *Diana* will be remaining in the vicinity of Venus, in the role of flagship, until our victory can be consolidated; a detachment of the European Fleet is already on its way to take control of the Venusian airlanes."

Dr. Barry entered then. "I hear that my favorite patient is awake?"

"Indeed, sir," Arabella said. "Thanks to you."

"Tut tut," the doctor replied modestly. "Only doing my duty." He shooed out her visitors—except Captain Singh, who refused to leave—examined her briefly, and proclaimed her to be making excellent progress. "Vice-Admiral Collingwood will be here shortly," he told her then. "He insisted upon being notified as soon as you woke. You are a hero, you know."

"I?" she replied with unfeigned surprise.

"You. Your navigation, not to mention your personal bravery and sacrifice during the battle"—he gestured to her missing foot—"were absolutely critical to its successful conclusion. Quite an impressive feat, for a mere girl." He winked then, a brief peculiar gesture which Arabella could not quite fathom.

She did not have a chance to ask him about it, though, as Collingwood himself arrived then. He had a high forehead and kindly eyes, and Dr. Barry bowed out to give them some privacy, closing the door behind himself. "I wish to congratulate you, sir," he said to Captain Singh, "upon your wife's recovery."

"It was entirely her own doing," the captain replied modestly. "As was our victory, and my own personal survival."

Arabella was pleased at Captain Singh's defense of her, but though the admiral's description of her as merely the captain's wife rankled, it also rang false . . . and now, she realized, she was in a position to do something about that. "Sir," she said to the admiral, "I have a confession to make."

"Surely the heroine of the hour has no need of confession!"

"I am afraid that I do, sir. I am sailing under false colors . . . Captain Singh and I are not, in fact, married."

"Oh dear!" the admiral said, quite charmingly scandalized.

"I assure you, sir, that we have not engaged in any . . . *untoward* behavior during the months of this deception." Captain Singh, she noted, actually blushed at this. "But we have long intended marriage, and every one believes we are married, and now at last we can change the reality to match the perception. Is it not true that the commanding officer of a ship in the air can perform marriages?"

"It is *not* true, I am afraid. It would go against the Navy's regulations."

"Oh!" Now it was Arabella's turn to be discomfited.

"However, *Royal Sovereign* carried a minister, who survived the battle and is now aboard *Diana*. I believe he will be happy to correct this, ah, small error of yours, and do so quietly, so that no one will know it was ever other than the case. Shall I ask him to do so?"

"Yes, please," said Arabella, and simultaneously Captain Singh said, "Immediately, if possible."

"Very well. I shall put matters in train at once." The admiral then took Arabella's hand in his right, and Captain Singh's in his left, and looked each of them in the eye. "Let me be the first to offer my congratulations to the both of you."

"Thank you, sir."

"I suppose I should leave you alone for a bit, then, to compose yourselves before the ceremony."

And so they did. Though not immediately.

ACKNOWLEDGMENTS

This book was written and edited under extremely difficult circumstances, as my beloved wife, Kate Yule, struggled with brain cancer and eventually lost that struggle. It is only through the support of my friends and family—chief among whom are Sue Yule, Janna Silverstein, Michelle Franz, Shannon Page, Teresa Enigma, and Jason Engstrom—that I was able to survive at all, never mind produce a novel. Thanks also to Mary Robinette Kowal, Allan Hurst, Brenda Cooper, Tom Whitmore, Karen Anderson, Mary Kay Kare, Dave Howell, Will Martin, Amanda Clark, Geri Sullivan, Cynthia Nalbach, Marc Wells, Paul Weiss, Ulrika O'Brien, and Catherine Crockett for helping take care of Kate and me, and to everyone else who came for a visit, provided assistance, or shared a meal. Special thanks to Clare Katner and Daniel MacLeod for service and friendship.

I'd also like to acknowledge the caring, professional doctors, nurses, and staff of Compass Oncology (especially Dr. Robert Lufkin, Jamie Newell, and Amber Case), the Oregon Clinic (Dr. Oisin O'Neill and Dr. Steven Seung), Providence Integrative Medicine (Dr. Kenneth Weizer), Providence Medical Group (Dr. James Kern), Sinai In-Home Care (Margie Amspacher, Brittany Berry-Hill, JJ Ahmed, Genesee Etter, Samantha Lambert, and Heidi Olson Jones), and Providence Hospice (Susan

Beam, Tina Abich, Stacy Morgan, and Ranetta Aaron) for their expertise, dedication, and compassion.

For the book itself, I must extend my sincerest gratitude to the team at Tor (editor Christopher Morgan, head of publicity Patty Garcia, art director Irene Gallo, publicist Desirae Friesen) and my agent, Paul Lucas of Janklow & Nesbit Associates. Thanks also to everyone who provided advice and feedback on various drafts (Sara Mueller, Walter Jon Williams, Janna Silverstein, Mary Robinette Kowal, Doug Faunt, Sherwood Smith, Dave Goldman, Jennifer Linnea, Felicity Shoulders, Mary Hobson, Kate Yule, Oz Drummond, Kelly Horn, Jen Volant, Lawrence M. Schoen, Diana Rowland, Michaela Roessner-Herman, Kim Zimring, Nina K. Hoffman, Rick Wilber, and Alex Jablokow) and to everyone who joined me for writing at Rainforest Writers Village and various coffee shops. Writing is a solitary business, but the fortunate writer is never alone.